SURFING

with

SNAKES & DRAGONS

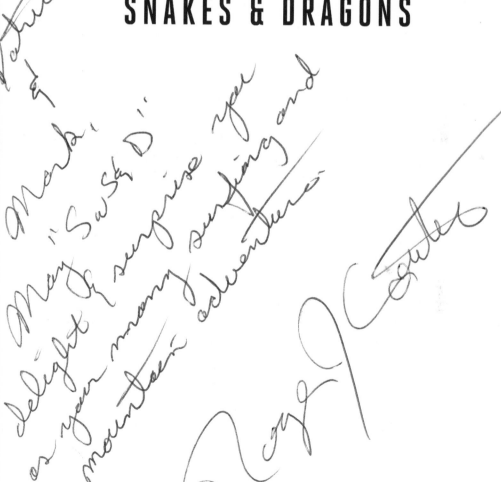

SURFING

with

SNAKES & DRAGONS

and Other
TALES of SUBURBIA

ROGER J. COUTURE

SOUL
ARCH
PRESS

This is a work of fiction. Names, characters, organizations, places, events, and incidents are either products of the author's imagination or are used fictitiously.

Published by Soul Arch Press, Thousand Oaks
www.RogerJCouture.com

Edited and Designed by Girl Friday Productions
www.girlfridayproductions.com
Editorial: Ryan Boudinot, Scott Calamar
Interior Design: Rachel Christenson
Cover Design: Connie Gabbert

ISBN-13 (hardcover): 9780998321202
ISBN-13 (paperback): 9780998321219
e-ISBN: 9780998321226

First Edition 2017

Printed in the United States of America

Mr. Ed Petty,

my eighth-grade remedial English teacher at

Cooper Middle School, McLean, Virginia.

A brave teacher who had the courage to read

with a passion that conveyed an assumed air

foreshadowing the future lives of his students

—a small class of half a dozen naïve thirteen-year-old boys—

those stories, and show those movies,

that delved into the veiled and enigmatic themes of the grown-up world,

to wit:

"A Perfect Day for Bananafish," J. D. Salinger;

"An Occurrence at Owl Creek Bridge," Ambrose Bierce;

"One of the Missing," Ambrose Bierce;

"The Tell-Tale Heart," and many others, by Edgar Allan Poe;

Shane;

To Kill a Mockingbird.

CONTENTS

SURFING
with
SNAKES & DRAGONS

Our brief time together
    abruptly came to an end.
I never had the opportunity
    to personally tell you
That knowing you
    made me a better, stronger person.
I hope, by some small measure,
    I was able to return the favor.

~~~

He stood alone, apart from the small gathering, a bit farther along the bluff, a silent, staring statue dressed in a thinly protective black suit that hugged his body as a second skin, from underneath his chin out to the small of his wrists and down to the ends of his toes, his arm casually wrapped around his tall, standing gun. From this precipice overlooking the cove, the colored lights of the Queen's Necklace shone brightly and draped elegantly along the distant shoreline, twinkling and dancing off the ocean's dark waters for a short while before all would soon silently wink out in the competing eastern skylight of a new day. He turned away from the sun's first blush to scan that vast well of depthless gray that was the melding of ocean and sky. He searched for those lumbering lines that pulsed over the horizon to wrap around the point and then rose with a ponderous momentum ever higher into the air until they threw themselves over in a grand avalanche of cascading water that rushed headlong towards shore in a luminescent froth.

Henri could not as of yet perceptively discern the specific details of those energy lines that advanced to become large-standing walls of water as the decreasing shoals began to push them out of the depths. Nor could he yet peer within those shadowed and even blacker vertical faces, where a waterman prefers to precariously perch, of winter's first Bering Sea storm waves; yet still, there were two important facets that he could deduce, for their intimidating size and formidable power were not in doubt.

Each mighty set-wave impact announced itself in a booming cannonade that rolled and rolled from around the point into the cove. The ground reverberated under his feet, and the detectable concussion he felt nearly matched that of his own wildly beating heart; all spoke of awaiting giants. For his heart thumped hard within his chest as much from his own anticipation of entering the surging ocean and awaiting predators as from something more. For today, in a coincidence with nature, he had decided to challenge himself to detach from that entanglement of what was once an emotional light of delight in the impassive dark and had then wormed and squirmed to become an irrational obsession. "God, let me return to this sand to be my own free man," he quietly intoned to himself.

As he waited for dawn to turn the canvas of sky blue and reveal nature's spectacular water show, he took note of the desert-warm Santa Ana winds that brushed across his cheeks and into those oncoming waves—an offshore breeze that he knew would suspend and stand tall the wave face for just a moment longer than gravity would naturally allow before all came crashing down in that giant avalanche of cascading water. Henri understood that this swell, which had begun its journey from an Arctic-cold storm in the Gulf of Alaska and whose long lines of pulsed energy would have passed unseen and unfelt across thousands of miles of depthless, open ocean, had just a little too much northwesterly direction for perfect surfing. Rather than wrapping gracefully from around the point and into the cove like the closing of a smooth zipper, these waves would break too fast in long, unmakeable sections to thus block a surfer's exit up and over the top and out the back into the safety of open water. He tossed around the thought of riding winter closeout sets, shuddered, then said aloud, "All is good."

Henri had earlier rolled his van into the parking lot with the Offspring headbanger music cranked up to a window-rattling volume. Loud, thumping music was a momentary escape from his raw emotions and a calm fog to obscure obsessively replaying scenes of his past with her. As other cars filled with sleepy surfers had begun to arrive in the cliff-side parking lot, he had slipped into his wetsuit and tugged his booties on with a laugh; he was such a wimp, always wearing booties, even on the hottest summer days. The embarrassment of wearing booties in even warm water was offset with the knowledge that this small bit of foot protection would save him from a multitude of minor irritations: rock and coral rash, needle-sharp and fire-red sea-urchin spines that would break off once inserted beneath the skin, or in tropical waters, the barbs of stingrays resting unseen under sand, which would curl around to hammer one's ankle if stepped upon. He could endure the pain but not the loss of surf time, as any such injury would take him out of the water and could cause him to miss a surf session, or an extra hour of surf, or even just one barreling wave. Henri had loved surfing his entire life and he could live with the pack's laughs and pointed commentaries about booties on hot days or in equatorial waters. Prior to zipping his wetsuit tight under the base of his head, Henri had slipped a baggie-enclosed cell phone between the inner and outer layers of the suit. Certainly not the ideal way to carry a phone out to surf, but once again he thought, *All is good.*

Against those first early ribbons of red that bled out to pink in long streaks against a black sky, the crew of surfers began their ritual gathering at the trail's end to check out the much-anticipated surf from atop the sea cliff's bluff. Hovering about, the young grommets were abuzz with nervous energy and animated in their speech and movements—a little bravado and swagger in the presence of something much louder and bigger than all of them. The watermen stood casually quiet and still, introspectively searching for a calm within themselves, attempting to sense through their ears and feet what they could not in specific detail distinguish with their eyes prior to the sun cracking the horizon. Each tried to dissipate anxious jitters in his own individual way, for an irrational excitement at an inopportune moment could in an instant turn into a mind-freezing fear and physical inaction that could leave you stranded in the midst of nature's power, which will then unconcernedly lash you with its wrath.

For this loose tribe, the gathering was rather more social in nature this morning so that they could take in a shared awe of the ocean's intensity and beauty. The forecasters had prognosticated—with the numbers gathered from the weather satellites and many arrayed ocean buoys, all crunched with their supercomputer-based models—that ideally one more day was required for perfect waves to grace this part of the coastline. In that one day, the Aleutian storm would shift just a tad farther east, altering the swell's angle of attack from a direct onward charge of wild energy that more often than not pitched over in long and unmakeable sections to a more glancing blow that would smoothly wrap around the point and be cleaner and more predictable for both paddling into and riding upon.

It was that soft light of an early morning's blue hue in which those still growing and whip-thin grommets stood strung out along the bluff's edge that brought a vision rushing back to Henri of that first glance upon Nicki's elegant face—so emotionless and thus to him so sad for one so young. Yet it was her eyes that would flash with a wild excitement followed by her infectious giggle that warmed him to the cockles of his soul. A radiance as when he would lie lizard-like content, wetsuit stripped down to the waist, upon sunbaked boulders in the protective lee of a seaside cliff after a physically spent, winter-chilled surf session of double-overhead waves. In those still-sleeping, quiet hours of a predawn morning, Henri had given himself a self-guided tour of the Central Valley Hospital. Along his inspection route prior to meeting with the hospital administrator and staff to present his credentials as an independent emergency-preparedness consultant, he encountered Nicki.

As he slipped past the locked doors and into the restricted psychiatric holding ward with the assistance of an exiting attendant overloaded with full arms, Nicki's shock of golden, sun-kissed hair in the room of subdued lighting caught his attention. She barely lifted her head from the chest-high nurse's station, revealing her small, melancholy face to give him a cursory look over of dismissal with quickly observant eyes and pursed lips, before turning back to her paperwork. He had been inexplicably drawn to that impish face, denuded of makeup, her high cheekbones accented with freckles that originated from the bridge of her nose to free range under almond-shaped, dazzling amber eyes, and a small mouth that did not part. Her sun-bleached blonde hair was bunned high in a hard knot to display a slender neck.

He knew well, as he advanced upon her, that there was no mistaking in that brief glance of nonaffect the apparent and inherent vice of beautiful California blondes who expected to be entertained and amused by men until those caring and giving souls were unceremoniously tossed and discarded for new, obsequious court jesters attentive to their every mercurial whim. But business is business.

With twenty years' experience working with hospital personnel had come a well-practiced affinity to approach and engage and question staff in oblique dialogue so as not to reveal his true objective, thus eliciting honest answers not tainted or colored with an expected or defensive response. And so he naturally eased into such a conversation with Nicki, who had succinctly and with judicious professionalism answered his few questions without taking her eyes off the paper that she continued to write on with a pen. He had gone to thank her for her time and assistance, his head cocked down low to the counter, whereupon she had put a hand over her name tag with: "If you give me your name for the ward log, per protocol, I'll give you my name."

He laughed. "Touché."

"You're really cool and all what with your fancy suit and tie and that lanyard around your neck, but you still don't have authorized hospital ID."

Bemused, he had waxed something Shakespearean, somewhat inelegantly, about a rose by any other name and then commingled it with a thorn on a rose or a thorn of a blonde still being a prick indeed that bleeds. And he could easily curse the day he heard that effusive little girl giggle of joy that clutched at his heart, for she had laughed with: "That's the corniest thing I've heard in the longest time. But let's say for conversation's sake"—and she had looked up with a restrained smile—"they call me by my middle name here: Nicki. That's because of family that works here and let's say other . . . complications."

"Well, quid pro quo then. Henri, from my French grandfather, you may call me. But tell me your real first name and I'll show you mine."

She had laughed again. "I don't think we're there yet."

"Oh? And I didn't actually know we were going anywhere?" And they had played and danced and he had taken advantage of what he would come to find out was her naturally adventurous disposition, challenging her to come along for some sushi and rice wine later, which, when he explained it was raw fish, elicited a derisive "Ewww!"

At the sushi bar later that evening, Nicki had revealed a captivating personality full of enthusiastic curiosity as she questioned each and every dish and how it was prepared. She also displayed a stubborn streak with her determination to master the chopsticks and yet was self-effacing, laughing each time she dropped a slice. And he'd had fun as he pushed and pulled her, teased and taunted her, as he explained to her scrunched-up nose that bright orange-and-red octopus suckers and raw, dime-size quail eggs were quite the delicacy. They discovered that they shared a kindred spirit of adventure as Nicki loved to ride motocross at high speeds in the vast open desert or along technically difficult, single-track trails high into the mountains, while Henri sought to pursue his passion by circling the globe to seek the perfect wave. There was an inescapable surge of energy between them each time they touched in the close intimacy of the sushi bar.

Relaxed from their open and friendly dinner conversation, and feeling a warm satisfied glow from hot sake, Henri commented reflectively on Nicki's melancholy expression earlier that morning and the incongruity with her now relaxed and bubbly personality. Nicki glanced down, scrunched her face, and played with her chopsticks while she spoke in a small voice of having witnessed her father's death at the racetrack when she was young and the recent dissolution of her marriage. Both these events caused her periods of great anxiety and depression whenever she was alone. Henri realized that Nicki used a melancholy mask to hide the true depth of her emotional loss and suffering from the outside world, but he had also learned in a very short time that beneath this façade was a woman excited about and interested in the world around her. He suspected that she only infrequently revealed that elation to a close few.

When she finished speaking, Nicki glanced up with a shy smile that invited him in, closer. Those golden-amber eyes reeled him in, closer. He could smell her freshly washed hair, closer. He felt her warm breath with its faint scent of spicy wasabi, closer still. Their warm lips, infused with a sweet dessert wine of unfiltered sake, touched, and Nicki pressed back, now hungry for something more than sushi.

~~~~~

It started with a silly little laugh; how dare he think it would last. Henri chided himself before dismissing the thought and coming back to the task at hand. He had concluded that the usual jump-off rock into the ocean with its short paddle to the take-off spot would be impossible to reach in the direct assault of the waves now climbing over the access trail itself. And more importantly, any miscalculation or mistiming of the set frequency would have sent him diving long and deep only to return embroiled in turbulence—to a surface of volatile air bubbles of froth with no traction for swimming or paddling for escape. Instead, Henri knew that he would have to walk around the cove to jump out at a spot sheltered from the swell and then paddle out and around about half a mile into the open ocean to avoid any set or rogue waves. Then, when sufficiently clear, he could turn north to the point for another half-mile paddle back to the calculated take-off spot and then pick off one of the set waves of his choice.

The few upon the bluff who actually took notice of Henri as he walked away in the morning light attempted to reconcile a rational action to that curious surfer. For his path did not seem to make logical sense since he was heading away from the usual jump-off rock and moving down the coast in the opposite direction. The surfboard he carried was an archaic single-fin, big-wave gun, a smaller, West Coast version of a Hawaiian rhino chaser that typically had not been used by surfers in twenty years. He was soon forgotten.

Henri attempted to clear his thoughts and concentrate on the task before him as he hiked down a well-worn cliff-face trail and then began his walk around the cove. Lately, though, his psyche had become a single track of past visions that constantly replayed in his mind. It was an obsession that was all consuming. He was without an elixir that would remedy his depressing predicament.

Along his beach walk, he became consciously aware of the warm Santa Ana breeze across his face, an Indian summer zephyr that sucked all moisture out of the air; the roll of his feet as coarse sand fell away under his booties; the slimy kelp newly washed ashore on which he slipped and slid; and the clamor of pounding surf that reverberated from the open ocean and then rushed and rushed towards shore to lap around his ankles before the returning water attempted to suck him out to sea. His thoughts kept coming back to Nicki.

~~~~~

Henri unexpectedly experienced an out-of-water free fall and emotional pounding with Nicki one morning as they entered her car. He laughed when he noticed her bra tied to and dangling from the center globe light. Nicki calmly admitted that she had attempted to take her own life the previous evening by hanging herself with the bra.

"Oh, *mon chéri*," Henri said as he put a hand to her cheek. "Talk to me."

Nicki looked away and her eyes welled with tears as she began to speak. Henri reached his hand behind the small of her head, laced his fingers through her fine hair, and pulled her to him. Her lips pressed gently against his ear as he attentively listened so as each and every whispered word would be heard.

Haltingly, in a quivering voice, Nicki sobbed that the previous evening had actually been her seventh such suicide attempt. She had been wrestling for her sanity with what she called the malice of her incessant "snakes in the brain." Phantom, psychic snakes that slithered with a will of their own through her mind to strike unexpectedly and plunge her into despair. Those snakes had imposed themselves upon her brain to slither around ever since that childhood day when she had witnessed her father's death at the racetrack. Each of those multiple serpents represented a traumatic experience in her life: her mother's drug and alcohol addiction ignited by her father's death, which had caused Nicki to be placed in foster care; her own drug addiction; and then her doomed marriage to her drug dealer. She felt as if her mind and sanity were assailed on every front by a pitiless enemy which sunk their fangs deep in an attempt to cloud her mind with venom and thus fill her with a melancholy that rendered her unable to rationally think or act.

That nonchalant demeanor that she displayed was a counterweight to all the emotions of malice in her heart that raged from the reptiles in her brain. Snakes that constantly wiggled and squirmed within her psyche, wrestling for control. Too many snakes for her to watch or control all at once. Not one giant, malevolent dragon that you could grab by the throat, stare into the void of empty, dark eyes, and never turn your back on, but dozens of snakes swimming in the brain. Each serpent attempting to slip around the back, sink its fangs, and release its mind-numbing poison of anger and hate. Dozens of poisonous vipers that slithered unbeckoned from out of their shadowy lairs to rattle and rock and roll her mind and throw her off balance as they then injected their venom of dissolution to suffocate her happiness.

Henri was stunned to silence once he realized the depths of Nicki's torment. He accepted, without judgment or comment, her every rational and irrational action. She trembled and sobbed as she spoke. Henri stroked her hair and let her cry to ease her pain.

~~~~~

He had made the walk around the sandy and rock-strewn cove to then jump into that relatively sheltered and quiet part of the ocean where the dissipated waves rolled by in deep water. He paddled out and around the cove's end to effortlessly move from lying on his custom-built surfboard to a sitting position for a short rest. Balanced on that hand-crafted board of fiberglass cloth thinly glassed around Styrofoam specifically designed for his body size and riding style, he shivered, then shook, and flapped his arms back and forth to stay warm and loose. He took note of the size and frequency of those distant breaking waves while intently searching for some consistency in their initial breaking points. The Santa Ana winds, warmed from the kinetic energy of having rushed up and then down mountains prior to arriving at the beach, had extricated all moisture from the air. With all the haze sucked out, Henri had crystal-clear visibility of the horizon and that small rock island solely under the purview of gulls and sea lions that jutted with vertical walls out of the ocean, a lone monolith watchtower at the intersection of water and sky. The ocean had an alluring calm of false complacency.

As Henri bobbed along with the ocean swells, he recalled the first time he had taken Nicki surfing on a weekend retreat to the beach. With her long blonde hair and richly tanned skin, Nicki may have given the impression of the typical beach bunny; yet as a Central Valley girl living far from the ocean, such excursions to the coast were a rare event. Having grown up at the beach himself, Henri understood the ocean could be used as an elixir to charm Nicki's intractable snakes, for he himself often used the sea to resolve issues and bring balance to his life, or just to forget and escape life's problems for the moment. For existence in the waters of open ocean becomes uncomplicated and simple—primal even, as all physical and mental focus is required to survive the churning surf with no room for any other thoughts or emotional crowding. One's attention is immediately grabbed and all other side thoughts lost with the initial shock of bodily emersion in the Pacific Ocean, as the cold water slowly rises up the body and the skin begins to tingle in a rush of blood. This physical discomfort is obligatory before one can even begin to grapple with paddling through the onrush of unrelenting surf pushing everything in its path back towards shore. And, in the back of every mind, from a grommet to a water-man, is the primal instinct of knowing, reinforced by that damned Hollywood movie, that there are fish much larger than a man in the sea, that he has entered the food chain, and that he himself has now become the hunted.

At the rental shop along the strand, a local woman surfer sized and fitted Nicki for a ladies' spring wetsuit and boogie board. Nicki casually broached the question of sharks in the water, which elicited a laugh from the clerk. "Of course, there are sharks in every ocean. The question one should ask is how big are the sharks and how hungry are they?" Henri also laughed.

When Nicki launched on her first breaking wave, Henri witnessed her melancholy mask fall quickly away to be replaced with a glow of childish joy. Her broad smile from ear to ear was accompanied by a loud primal squeal of excited fear as she experienced the speed and unstoppable power of the wave. Henri smiled as he saw the utter absence of any emotional pain upon her visage. Nicki's façade reflected an expression of happiness and an intense love of life. For the moment, for an hour, for the day, her constricting, dream-strangling serpents had slithered away back into their reclusive den.

~~~~~

Sitting atop his surfboard, lost as a speck of insignificance in that vast expanse of open ocean, Henri was determined to come out of the water free from that damned emotional grip of anguish that manifested itself as physical pain assailing him from all those indefinable points of his body. He wished to return to shore with some semblance of that previous, albeit somewhat detached and unconnected, life of lucid thoughts and actions. He postulated, however, that where he presently and purposely sat was neither rational nor sanely defensible.

He reached behind his back to find the dangling leash to unzip his wetsuit and to pull out the tucked-away sandwich bag. Carefully, with fingers numb from the cold seawater, Henri pulled the cell phone from its protective wrapper and exhaled. This was the fracturing of his character façade he had been dreading. An avalanche of welled-up emotions ripped right through him. His hands trembled. He dialed voice mail and put the phone to his ear. "You have one saved message." Henri pressed "1."

"Hey, Henri, it's Nicki. I was just going to call to say hey. Whenever you get this, give me a call back." He allowed her voice to permeate his senses and thus transport him back in time. From what seemed like ages ago, he could picture her face unmistakably aglow with contentment as they stared at each other, not a word spoken, just sharing a blissful moment of being together during their ritual morning latte.

~~~~~

Henri had come to realize that at some point during their beach retreat he had passed through that stage of a purely physical relationship with her to something very passionate and emotional, which placed him conflicted and torn between his selfish desire of possessing Nicki within his life and that inevitably painful separation of sending her off on her own. Survival instincts told him that the safe course of action would be for him to kick out now before their relationship jacked like a bad wave and dashed his heart upon rocky shores. But Henri did not kick out of a wave because he was surfing in shallow waters, and he had long passed the stage of living his life safely, afraid to get hurt. Henri was committed to Nicki. And there is in that conscious awareness of a September man having fallen heavily under the spell of a fragrant May woman a forlorn emotional abandon to melt with her, as the bloom shall soon enough be off the rose with an inescapable early frost. For experience and maturity told him that with the impetuous nature of a young woman there is no false illusion of control, and that she would quickly pass out of his life. Such foreknowledge would not mitigate the trauma of an emotional pounding. For such emotional loss is as painful as any bodysurfer experiences when from high above in the watery folds of a shore-pound surf, and he is then thrust onto exposed and unyielding sand.

"Nicki, I will support you any way possible to help you get your life back together," Henri had told her. "I ask a couple things in return. For my sanity, as we live so far apart and because of your soon to be ex-husband dealer and his druggie associates, I would like you to call me every day to let me know you are safe and okay. Also, that you let me know where we stand. If you are just using me, or if we are friends, or if we are very personal, it's all cool. Or, if I am nothing at all to you and you want me to walk out that door right now and never look back, I will."

"Goddamn you, what do you want from me?" Nicki cursed Henri as she wiped tears from under her new designer sunglasses that she had become so fond of, purchased from a beachside vendor. "Can't I just call us more than just friends for now?"

He yearned for something more, but as he sussed out Nicki's emotional state, he simply replied, "All is good," and squeezed her hand. "So, I don't promise you the moon, I don't promise you anything at all, but I will do everything I can to give you the possibility of becoming the person you want to be and the ability to live the life you choose. Do you understand the difference?"

Nicki had never before seen anyone splay themselves with such an openness and vulnerability in front of her and felt conflicted as to whether this was a weakness or a strength, an offering or a trap? "Go on."

"So, we need to get you registered at City College so when summer's over you're back in school."

"I told you I don't want to waste my time in some dumb-ass school with classes like math and psychology and I'm the old person sitting there. I want to get on with my life now, like you, with a house near the beach and with a family with PTA meetings and a career."

Patiently: "Be careful, *mon chéri*, what you wish for, for everything is not what it appears. Besides, school is living your life. I'll be going back myself to my JC for salsa or photography—I haven't decided yet. Everything you learn in school with your education will come back to you at some point or other in your life. What you learn today you carry with you forever. So if you miss it, not only would you be cheating yourself, but you would be cheating your children and your grandchildren." And so they had fought and fought, for the capriciousness of the young and intractably headstrong is legendary. And so he had pushed and pulled, and he had teased and cajoled, and he had bribed and taken away. And so she was soon enrolled in the three Rs plus one more.

That rogue wave of an unmakeable relationship had not as of yet risen up from idyllic, clear-blue skies to jack and dump Henri upon awaiting shoals; he had made it around this section delicately perched in the face of another long, vertical wall that stretched away before him.

~~~~~

A college semester is a relative time period, depending on one's perspective. A grueling seminal event for one experiencing for the first time the workload of an adult as one learns to balance the responsibilities of many tasks. A seasonal respite for a mature adult who, having once passed through that crucible of selfish study, now seamlessly juggles those simultaneous tasks of work and family and schooling, commingled with added social responsibility, and none of the authority, for the welfare of many others. But time and time continued to pass for both, and prior to the winter break Henri felt a crushing deluge rip heavily upon his bosom when Nicki shyly informed him that she "may have a new boyfriend." Nicki's excitement and happiness were clearly evident upon her face, just as they had been after her first day surfing. Henri was emotionally torn in fitful throes of despair, yet happy that the melancholy mask of Nicki's was fading. She assured him that nothing had changed between them. His anger and fears went unspoken.

And then, one day, after their morning lattes . . . Nicki was gone. He was soon certain that she had passed out of his life for she was not on the hospital floor later for the swing shift and she was not listed on the psych unit's monthly schedule. The real surprise—one Henri thought worthy of any self-absorbed, sadistic Hollywood screenwriter—came when his phone rang with her caller ID. And yet it was T-Man, her drug-dealing soon-to-be-ex-husband, who had spoken to him across the distance.

"This is T-Man. You must be Henri? I've heard about you."

Henri felt his gut float to his throat and croaked out some primal animal noise that could not be identified for the laugh it was meant to be.

"I see your cell number called a lot in Nicki's phone list."

T-Man's voice was too friendly and assuming for Henri's liking. "Yeah," was all he had managed to say for his brain had gone to mush.

"Yeah, well, you could say I was letting Nicki use one of my so-called business phones while we were still married. But I guess that's over," continued T-Man. "This morning Nicki dropped the phone off with court papers serving me with a restraining order. Because of the restraining order, I can't contact her. Maybe you can give her a message for me?"

Henri had not found it necessary to take a breath since T-Man had begun speaking, but he could hold his breathing longer than most. Inhaling: "T-Man, all I am going to tell you is that if you and I are having this conversation on her cell phone, I can assure you that Nicki and I will never be speaking again."

"Well, that's too bad because I thought you two were really close and you would want to help her out of a *jam* that she has gotten herself into," T-Man had said in a menacing tone.

"T-Man, you and I don't know each other," replied Henri as he thought to himself, *although, if my luck continues like this, I'll be T-Man's best new customer.* "But I'm going to do you a favor anyhow and hang up before you say something that you shouldn't and we may both come to regret. Don't call me back." Henri stabbed his phone off.

He stared at his phone with nauseous sickness and thought, *this is really going to hurt.* He had been pitched a thousand times or more from breaking waves and instinctively knew how to survive the free fall, the bone-crushing impact entering the water, and the long hold-downs. Suck in as much air as possible before going under, assume the fetal position to protect vital organs, then . . . relax . . . *relax*, for any and all struggling is an exercise in futility. Don't move a muscle, slow the beating heart, and wait for the violence of the wave to completely lose its embrace before making any attempt to reach the surface. The grip of a wave is inescapable and yet it will eventually relent.

Sick and lost, he wondered to himself how one steeled the tormented heart in free fall prior to impact? And how deep and for how long would he be held under? In her own way, Nicki had informed Henri that she was now safe. Henri would keep that in mind and use it as a surf leash to pull himself back to the surface and out of that vertigo-inducing abyss that held no sense of direction or purpose, which he was about to enter.

~~~~~

The hurt of a disappearance without a word. And as time had passed, that insidious thought that pervades, which is that perhaps she never really cared. And which would be better, an unrequited vanishing, or a love lost in the bowls of scorn and spite, verbal abuse and physical fights? And what remains when time passes and then nobody cares? For now, no one cares. Henri realized that he was blankly staring at the cell phone in his hand. He pressed "1."

"Hey, Henri, it's Nicki. I was just going to call to say hey. Whenever you get this, give me a call back."

Henri pressed "3." "Your message has been deleted, you have . . ." He squeezed the phone to smother any more sounds from that disdained device within his grasp. With all his physical power and emotional will, he reached back and hurled that useless object towards the horizon. Henri did not know or care where his tormenting dragon now lay. There was nothing but a detached calm. No anger, no hate, no love, no fear . . . and no tumultuous, reptilian psycho.

Behind his back, the sun-crested Earth. Ahead in the distance, rolling mounds began to rise out of what had been, only moments before, an apparently flat and unbroken ocean surface. Those lumbering lines in the water that pulsed towards Henri darkened and slowly began to take shape and definition as they rushed upon shallow shores and rose ever higher into that canvas of clear-blue morning sky. These rolling gray mountains already blocked his vision of the horizon and would soon consume his entire forward line of sight as their growing mass was now already his singularity of thought.

The casual observer may perceive no individuality in oncoming set waves. The discerning eye of a waterman will critique waves with a vision that can distinguish each as unique as a snowflake. He examines every wave to calculate the possibility of catching and sharing the energy and the permutations of shredding upon that face . . . and surviving unhurt. In that slight rise above the ocean surface paddling over a pre wave, Henri had discerned in the tips of humps that rushed towards him that this was most probably going to be a four-wave set.

The first wave that approached was broad and squat and passed harm-lessly underneath him.

The second wave, still with a nice shape, was larger but had shifted too far south for any chance of him reaching its peak. As Henri crested the second wave that was in the pre-throws of pitching over, salt water rained down upon him as if he had been caught in a sudden storm. It was the Santa Ana wind that had rushed up the vertical face to rip water off that thin, tapered edge and blow it into the sky only to return in a salty rain shower complete with a brightly lit rainbow of color from the golden rays of the morning sun refracting within its hovering mist.

Henri cleared the back of the second wave, looked over and past the third wave, and took in the looming fourth. In that horizontal line that reached into the sky higher than the previous three waves, he casually calculated that this was a daunting monster indeed that would close out the entire cove in a single swoop with anything caught in its path buried within its frothy folds and bodily thrown onto the awaiting rocky shore. Henri realized that even should he wish it, there would be no time to paddle out and climb over this last mountain. He had no choice but to commit to the third wave.

Pushing aside what could have been a mind- and body-freezing panic to another compartment of his mind, Henri simply ignored the fourth wave and its eventual destructive power, and concentrated on what would be his wave: the third giant. As he had predicted, this wave's initial breaking peak had shifted just a tad north, which, with the water of two previous waves filling in the low-tide shoals, offered a small possibility of cleanly wrapping around the point and into the relative safety of the deep water cove to thus provide a lucky individual with the ride of a lifetime, for what might be a very short life indeed. "But all is good."

~~~~~

In a surge of determined physical effort, Henri willed his eyes off his target and dropped his head to more efficiently align his body for strong and quick paddling. As he took note of the swiftly passing water that lapped at his board, his mind inexplicably flashed back to an earlier winter swell when he, with his brother and another friend, had risen for a dawn patrol of what they had expected to be some tasty big waves.

From where they had parked along the street, they'd looked out between the beach homes to witness perfect A-frame waves that slid both left and right with wave tips feathering delicately back from a steady offshore breeze. As they'd stood upon the sandy street, from that distant view, they had had no perspective with which to judge the size and power of those waves breaking in open ocean, and so each with childish excitement had anticipated a tasty ride for themselves on one of those pitching beauties. They had then seen with unbelieving eyes the glimmer of a surfer on one of those cascading giants. But this man had been just a speck on a vertical wall of water that was three or four times overhead. The pits of their stomachs had fallen away and the air had become heavy and difficult to breathe, and their excited anticipation had quickly turned to thoughts of their own insignificance and mortality. Only in an oblique manner had their friend been able to express their common fear by squeaking out, "Uh, hey man, this is like a totally gnarly beach break that's gonna snap our boards, and the locals here are totally agro territorial, man. I think we should go far-ther north." They had all laughed as the tension broke. Hey, what are true bros and friends for if you can't talk each other into the wilds of untamed nature complete with hostile, blood-lusting natives? And yes, it had been an epic day.

~~~~~

Henri pushed that long-ago winter day aside to concentrate on pad-dling for all he was worth into the awaiting peak. Speed was now of the essence to reach the ideal take-off point. A lifetime of surfing had made his body hard and strong. He glided his long board quickly and effort-lessly across the ocean surface, a study of coordination, efficiency, and determination. He had a momentary false thought of the awaiting and unmakeable closeout wave that followed, but Henri was too seasoned to be thrown off his game, and he compartmentalized that vision away to turn his focus back to the forming peak of what he anticipated would soon be his. This was going to be a very close thing indeed.

Yards from the base of the third wave, which was actually a shallow well deeper than the ocean surface, Henri faced his moment of truth as he looked up at that moving wall of water three stories high. In a single swift move he sat on the tail of his surfboard to point the nose vertically skyward and then, falling backwards, reversed the board to aim down the wave that was attempting to suck him up its face. He paddled as he paddled for every wave, as if it were to be his last. Henri's choice of a mini rhino chaser from his quiver of handcrafted Styrofoam-and-fiberglass sticks—covered with a thin resin shield that could easily snakel even with one's head bouncing off its deck—now began to prove its worth as the board's length and stability added speed to his downward thrust. He paddled for all he was worth, the wave continuing to draw him up the face, seeking to pitch him off the lip and over into the yawing cavern below. Henri experienced a long moment of weightlessness as the equilibrium of the wave's pull was finally matched by his downward thrust and, in a single motion, he lifted himself from lying on the board to a crouching surfer's stance, low and well-balanced on the balls of his feet. Caught up high in the wave's sheer vertical wall, his takeoff was late and critical, with the surfboard angled to the right and slanted straight down with only the right-rear edge trimmed into the watery face, thus preventing a disastrous free fall into oblivion. Feathering the airborne surfboard with his toes, Henri delicately floated the remainder of the right-hand length of the surfboard's edge into the wave's face, and for the moment, he was an insignificant rider within the throes of a rolling giant. "All is good."

Henri pumped the board once to accelerate into that shadowed canyon at the wave's bottom. Then, with maximum speed gained from his controlled falling, like a single swoop of an artist's brush across virgin canvas, he carved off the bottom and angled the surfboard up into a depthless open sky to then precariously reside just under the wave's pitching lip. That now-frothing lip with droplets torn away from its edges and flown sky-high was an impenetrable opaque ceiling with a power and thickness that prevented any punch-through escape out the back. The wave's lip was leaping out from top to bottom, creating a liquid-blue cavern within which Henri stood at its calm eye. He fell heavily under the spell of nature's forces that had conspired to sculpt this beautifully perfect vortex of moving water and that smooth-as-glass surface in which he caught his own reflective image flashing by. Casting his gaze down the line, he was conscious that the wave had walled up and was thus about to jack and spend its entire physical energy in one single, grand avalanche.

In surprisingly calm defiance, Henri sculpted himself into the classic surfer's soul arch: standing tall with back swayed, left arm high overhead with open palm to the watery ceiling, and his right hand skipping across the wave's mirrored face in which he could see his own reflection streaming past. He was not oblivious to the patiently awaiting abyss that was opening beneath his fragile surfboard. The rolling giant that pitched over shallow shoals and unrelentingly rushed to shore, with Henri speeding along high upon its vertical face, slowly began to gather him up and hide him from landward view, to instinctively envelop him back into the folds of nature's primal womb. *But all is good.*

~~~~~

Henri came to in a disoriented state lying facedown on a clean, white sandy beach that felt unusually soft and somehow as comforting as the smooth feel of freshly applied baby powder. From previous experiences of many violent and tumultuous thrashings, he made a quick mental check to distant digits to confirm that all his body parts were attached and functional. Henri had that rare sensation of his skin being lifted from his body and his mind separated from his head. This physical and mental illusion, he postulated, was the result of a combination of long submersion in cold, North Pacific-fed water; the impact and body shock of the crushing wave; vertigo from rolling and tumbling along the ocean bottom with eyes closed; and the lack of oxygen for which he could give no time estimate. He wondered which beach he had washed upon since he could not recall such a clean, white sandy beach anywhere as that upon which his face was now lying, and he was familiar with most of the beaches and rocky shores from border to border.

"Here, I think this might be an easier way to kill yourself."

Henri looked up to see the haloed outline of a woman holding a lacy bra by the shoulder strap. A cool fog of white mist had rolled in to obscure from view the high bluff at the edge of the beach. All that was visible through the hazy glare was the white sandy beach that stretched away and the angelic vision of some familiar woman standing over him, a bra dangling from her outstretched hand as a hangman's noose.

"Your way just seems like way too much work to off yourself. Why paddle out a mile into the middle of the freezing winter ocean when there is this perfectly good bra waiting here for you?"

"Nicki?" asked Henri as he tried to focus his eyes and overcome another shock to his battered being.

"What do you mean 'Nicki'? Who else do you know that would be offering you their bra to do yourself in? Silly."

Henri was dazed and confused but he asked the first simple question that came to mind. "What are you doing here?"

"Following you of course. The weather newscasters were all about the big Alaskan swell arriving this morning and I knew you would be leaving early so I sat in my car all night waiting to follow you. Dude, why do you play your music so loud?"

Henri knew why he played the stereo so loud. It was to forget Nicki and keep his dragon at bay, but that could wait for the moment. "No, I mean why are you following me at all?"

"I was thinking about what you said: 'Just enjoy the moments when you are happy and forget about the past and future pain.' I realized that when I was with you, I was content. So I just wanted to be with you today and be happy again. Then maybe we can chill together tomorrow as well . . . if you'll have me?"

Henri exploded: "You have to be insane to be with me!"

"Silly, you always said I was as sharp as a tack. I'm the sane one as I have nothing to lose and nothing and no one waiting for me. You're the insane one, to possibly give up and lose everything you have worked a lifetime for. I exposed my scarred life to you and you did not flinch or even look away. You took my past life and accepted it as it is, without judgment, without comment, just me. How long do you think we have together—and please lie?"

Henri realized the sanity, the insanity of what he had told Nicki earlier. What is the purpose of everything you do in life, if you are not happy, if you do not live it with a passion? "A lifetime," he replied.

"For sure?"

"Who really knows how long we have, how long anyone has? We have to enjoy our moments together and live them as if they are a lifetime," he honestly told her. "What about your snakes?"

"My snakes? From the things I have seen of your crazy surfing adventures this morning we have to worry more about your dragon than my snakes."

Henri knew it was too late to hold anything back; with nothing to fear from open honesty, he responded, "*Mon chéri*, you are my dragon; you are my only dragon, *mon chéri*."

Henri was warmed to see a flash of Nicki's smile as she extended her hand without the bra. He happily clasped her outstretched arm to pull himself up from the sand. He felt Nicki place a hand behind his head to lace fingers into his wet hair and pull him in close. He felt her gentle tug to walk with her along the beach. He affectionately draped an arm around her shoulders. And as the high surf will surge only to recede and thus erase all trace of footprints from the sand so, too, do those curling eddies of misty fog that roll in from the open sea soon shroud the rest of the world from the strolling couple.

~~~~~

"Eh, Scotty A, what'cha got lying there?" Dex Zimmer, the local sheriff station captain, asked with a hand over his brow to shield his eyes from the glare of a morning sun still low on the horizon.

As he kneeled in the coarse gray sand, Scott Anderson, assistant coroner for the county, ignored Dex and continued probing the body beneath him. Not so much to answer Dex as to work the problem before him, Scott spoke aloud: "We have a white male, apparently age forty to fifty, washed up and lying on the beach at the cove in a wetsuit with no apparent physical trauma to the body. No massive head wound, no major breaks or dislocations; just some minor wetsuit rips and epidermal abrasions, but nothing traumatic or serious. Nothing is readily visible on the body as to an apparent cause of death."

"What the hell, Scotty, my man, I could a told ya that. The guy drowned. You'd have to be nuts to go out in that ocean swell today. You see anyone else out in the lineup now?" Dex seriously questioned.

"Well, that's the strange thing," Scott replied. "I spoke with the life-guards that worked on him for a while after he washed ashore and they said he had no water coming out of his lungs."

"Yeah, the guy was nuts or on drugs—PCP or meth. Probably all those toxins shocked his ticker into stopping. Seen it before. I would've guessed that just from his lunatic actions this morning, attempting to surf this swell," retorted Dex. "All right, let's bag 'im so we can get this body out of the heat and open the beach. You can finish the examination at the medical center. God, I hate these surfer deaths: no IDs, no keys. Now someone has to wait until the parking lot closes tonight to see which car is left. Then we can trace the plates, get an ID, and notify the next of kin. What a bundle of joy that assignment will be, but that's what rookies are for."

Scott was not so sure about the drugs, a drowning, the trauma, or anything else pertaining to a cause of death for that matter. He had read the medical journals of a few surfer deaths in which toxicology results had definitely ruled out drugs and drowning and yet no defini-tive determination could be reached of why they expired.

From the edge of the crowd that had gathered, Dex spotted Heather as she observed their work and he motioned for her to come over. Dex knew Heather as a good local surfer who ran an in-town concession stand along the strand for the rental of bikes, boogie boards, and wet-suits. She managed to get her fair share of rides over the more aggres-sive male surfers in the lineup and used her quick wit and bright smile to smooth over any of those bruised male egos should she happen to drop in on them.

"Hey Heather, do you possibly know this surfer or did you see him out in the water this morning? Did he look like he was on drugs or something, or just a kook that couldn't surf and got in over his head?"

"No," Heather said, "he was not a kook." His vaguely familiar face gave her the disquieting feeling that there was a missing mischievous grin from something he knew that no one else did. Heather reflected back to the surfer's last chance of escape when he could have dropped down the wave face in front of the crashing lip and possibly belly boarded with the rolling whitewash through the rocks to shore. Her heart had leaped into her throat when, instead, the surfer had ridden higher upon the wave face to tuck, suspended, under the pitching lip and then casually leaned back in his glorious pose to be devoured by that advancing avalanche of water as he slowly slipped from view. Heather had felt an overwhelming sense of sadness accompanied with a sudden cold chill that permeated throughout her being as someone had finally pointed out the surfer washed up on the beach, not moving. "No, he was not a kook," Heather said once again. She looked up and gazed thoughtfully out to the open ocean and the last of that discon-nected stub of a Channel Island that stood as a lone watchtower above the horizon line of water before she continued. "He was a true water-man," she softly said with a smile that came to her lips as she eloquently waxed on for that which was not lost, "and the unforgettable sight of his slipping across the face of that powerful wave in his majestic soul arch will forever be etched upon my soul."

~~~~~~~

Dawn Patrol

Life would have been simpler,
    and I would have been happier
    had I never known you.
But I'd rather spend a day
    in paradise with you,
    a blissful radiance upon my face,
And then forevermore live
    a lifetime of hell
    that is your absence
Than exist
    in that oblivion
    of having never known you.

~~~

I am pulled most unwillingly from the depths of a most deeply satisfying slumber that comes all too easily to those who revel late into the evening and early morning hours. *For the sanctuary I seek.* I struggle from my nebulous dreamworld to kick-start my brain. *I will run and I will flee.*

    I reflexively search under my pillow for that insistent ringtone that so irritatingly nudges me to full consciousness. *I will fling myself into.* I crack a single, weary eye that is most unpleasantly and painfully greeted by a cell phone light—an illumination that is made ever more harsh in a darkened room of predawn. *My beckoning mistress the sea.* I struggle to swipe at the target LCD and cut the Surf Frats lyrics to silence. "Ugh," is all that spews from my lips into my cell's receiver. *Yuck, that's me and I'm alive?* The unexpected, unintelligible, guttural response I hear snaps me from that foggy state of *where, what?* to a semilucid state, for my physical and mental degeneration caused by a night of self-abuse and lack of sleep is a valid excuse, whereas my brother's voice should be fully pronounced with a TV newscaster's didactic elocution.

Brushing aside the cobwebs and grappling for control of that thick tongue, I am able to twist out: "Who the fuck are you?" I clear my throat, *gross*, before continuing with stretched vocal cords, "You're not backing out on me are you?" Phonetically, when compared to a thousand years of the modern English language, the response would have been an unintelligible Neanderthal communication of "Nnnn, gooo'ta ggoa." But, I could understand the pre–Homo sapiens answer to be: "No, good to go." Enunciating with modern English words understood even by the wireless generation, I bring this still-evolving Neanderthal at the other end back to the twenty-first century and put him on notice that we will meet at the Bagel Nosh in fifteen minutes. And in the event that he's unable to handle the mental gymnastics of simple addition, I check the clock. "Five thirty a.m. sharp." I question his affirmative answer for validity, and his second, positive response confirms to me that he will, in fact, be there as agreed.

"*Agh.*" I drop my head back into my waiting pillow. I analyze the paradox of a world where the paradise of lying alongside a warm, silky female in a soft, luxurious bed is somehow less alive, less fulfilling than the mental prodding of awakening from an alcohol-induced slumber and the masochistic pleasure incurred with the physical machinations of launching one's naked-ass body into a churning and freezing-ass ocean. *Too much, too early;* so I simply delay the inevitable and allow my mind to momentarily wander in a picture-and-sound replay of RA! Sushi, Hollywood's B-list restaurant and after-hours backroom karaoke club, where a star was never born. Yet many rally to the spotlight to perform, and a few gloriously shine in the dream of karaoke stardom, and those poor other souls who do not measure up endure the crowd's slings and arrows of abuse that may follow in cast looks and behind-the-back whispers. Whereas I, standing in a dimly lit back corner with definitely no talent and simply no guts, could only at best be called a lurker. *Too complicated, no thinking. Just roll the happy film.*

As an animal composed of weak, male desires, my eyes had of course feasted over a plethora of those gorgeously statuesque honey blondes and brunettes—*oh, that lovely redhead*—with short skirts and long legs made even longer with those now-fashionable four-inch stiletto heels upon which they so expertly balance. Low-cut tops were more than amply filled with exposed flesh pumped fully ripe with saline, completing the ludicrous variety of self-abuse. Honey-blonde Barbie with her Malibu friends were quite the candy eyeful in those barely ass-covering, skintight dresses that appeared to have been spray-painted on, or those push-up bras that pushed up significantly more than a handful. Thirty minutes in the adult gourmet candy store eyeing Barbie incarnate and one's eyes are sated, and yet never really bored, with seeing.

As I was musically entertained by a cast of unknown and unanticipated characters, one happy cocktail led to another. The evening flowed seamlessly into the early morning closing hour. A one-two combo that had thus contributed to my present state of a mind that was unable to motivate the body to perform that simplest of tasks—moving the feet. It is that first light of a new day that comes so early that may separate the wannabe amateurs, who party all the night and then sleep away the entire day, from the seasoned professionals, who may revel with the crowd through the evening and yet still rise with the sun to continue to rage in their own personal way.

With a reputation to maintain, and a pride to keep safe, my well-fabricated composure that displays a happy façade for all the outside world to view has the purity of a measured white picket fence enclosing an ever-expansive land of manicured, lush greens. Such a happy life, with a perfect wife, a *fabuloso* family, a . . . *stellar* . . . *dust* . . . *just f'n fabulous and fragmented stardust.* Hidden deep within, camouflaged from probing, prying eyes, there is some scary-to-me containment shell that pulsates with a manifestation of feral emotions. An incubating egg that radiates with illogical thoughts and feelings. Crack the shell—expose the fire-breathing entity within that would take control of me and run roughshod over my being with a self-destructive psychological meltdown that thus reduces my DNA to a glowing glob of bone morphogenetic protein. An impending psyche implosion is averted by only the thinnest margin of human rationale, critically held in check by an ever-so-thin mask of sanity on edge. And with any such inappropriate, self-delusionary binge that should result in complete self-destruction, those loved ones who bask to grow and thrive in a sheltered and nurturing warm glow would be emotionally burnt and forevermore disfigured should that fire-breath belch out: a *familia* conflagration too horrible to contemplate. Responsibility . . . pride . . . fear . . . guilt . . . whichever, whatever crutch it takes to maintain the dome's spherical integrity and shield me from the emotional clutches of an alluring paramour.

My destiny, I understand, now lies a mere two and a half feet of gravitational pull away—the distance my bare feet must actually travel from my warm, down-comforted memory-foam bed, to touch the cold hardwood floor. My drugged mind and lactic-acid-laced limbs are each cloaked in their own uniquely obscure den of hibernation and conspire as individual sentient beings to remain hidden and unmoving, thus abandoning me in place. Such primordial abandonment may suit my instinctive animal-being to flee for mental quietude and continued physical rest, but, assumingly at an advanced edge of human evolution, conspiring with my deeply seated emotional angst, a personal psyche rages like a fire-torch whip to keep those base usurpers at bay and under my nominal control.

Thus, with a contentious mania, I know that the pleasures of continuing to lie in the warm physical comfort of sleep nirvana is but a false temptress. The discontent of my core siren gives me no rest, provides no succor and, even with just a few hours of sleep, resistance is futile. So I will run, I will flee, I will fling myself into the beckoning sea.

~~~~~

Spawn of nature's She-Wolf fury, a rambunctious litter of wolf-pup waves surges forth from their violent whelping in the farthest reaches of the cold and isolated North Pacific. Her womb is that incubating eye of the hurricane-force winds that churn the ocean surface into a turbulent jumble of violent undulations. Chaotic and fragmentary wave energy of that thrashing storm radiates to all points of the compass.

Traversing great oceanic distances, these raw pulses coalesce over the days and nights from irregular, bathtub-type chop into regular sets of massive energy waves that begin to roll over Earth's curve as unified, sled-braced packs of three to six waves. The great ocean depth offers no resistance to the amplitude of each wave's long frequency as these packs travel unfettered across thousands of miles, as if in frictionless ether, their speed and intensity undiminished until landfall. In the open sea, energy waves pass underneath unseen and unnoticed. Viewed from a lookout point upon a bluff, this moving energy is first spotted as a dark shadow rolling in from across the horizon within the depths of an apparently flat ocean surface. Oblivious to their inevitable destruction, the now-synchronized packs appear to gain speed and momentum. They charge headlong towards shore until closing in upon land and a diminishing continental shelf; the frequency of the wave length becomes longer and deeper than that of the depth of ocean over which these waves glide and, thus with a push, the water begins to rise up into the sky. And with the simplicity of a mathematical equation—with just over one-half of the energy wave now above the ocean surface—the waves begin to pitch over from their own top-heavy mass. An offshore breeze will momentarily suspend each wave in an equilibrium of neither rising nor falling. Whipped by the opposing wind, the upper edges of the feathering lips are torn away, blown skyward, globular water droplets raining back to sea in an audible rip.

In echelon from north to south, the waves jack to then cascade in a surfer's curl. Waves crash to burst in effervescent billows that rebound high into the air; compressing forces vaporize water that then hovers to luminously befog the entire shoreline. Their thunderous cannonade rolls in, then warbles to fade away down coast. Their barking thunder is replaced with a continuous white noise of phosphorus sea foam wildly rushing shoreward. Their yelping "whoosh!" as they scamper to land is the last dissipating residue of that distant She-Wolf's lonely labor.

Silently, they linger a moment at the littoral edge before being gently pulled back with a "shhhh" whisper within her sea.

~~~~~

Below the earth's liquid brim, the still-rising sun has swept away the black onyx of a somber predawn and painted orange-glow streaks of light that radiate low across the horizon.

A new day of exciting possibilities greets us as we pull into the free public beach parking lot that is exclusively held in reserve for the first of those early birds lacking any sense or sensibility of two thousand years of modern social decorum—proper sleep, proper dress, and proper manners—yep, that be us. The parking lot is already abuzz with nervous excitement as surfers begin to take in the northern swell.

Into the light of a sun still below the horizon, the Pacific Ocean expansively spreads out before us, slowly changing color, like a rainforest chameleon that moves from the royal black of night to match and emulate the early morning sky of a soft blue hue.

Perpendicular to the new light, distant and bulky cargo freighters jut with vertical walls from the water upon the edge of the horizon as faux Channel Islands.

Closer still, sleek and slender warships of camouflage gray are ghostly images that blend within that depthless ocean surface of no direct light as they surreally glide like bathtub toys seemingly floating within a child's arm's reach.

A crisp autumn breeze that has cooled considerably, having passed over the brown coastal foothills, snaps at our exposed legs and sandaled feet. We shrink within our plush Patagonia Synchilla hoodies. The wind continues its gentle flow past our goose-bumped legs into the face of the oncoming sea swell.

"Can you turn that crap off now that we're here?" my brother asks in reference to Nirvana's Kurt Cobain crooning about a gun, throbbing through six speakers, a pair of tweeters, and a sixteen-inch subwoofer, all channelized and boosted by the power of a one-thousand-watt amplifier from within Shamu, the black-and-white family minivan converted to a surfmobile. "How can you drive—even think—with freak'n noise that loud?" His patience apparently has been worn thin by our short concert ride.

Well . . . actually . . . that is the point; noise was but a single brace to maintain a dome of sanity, overwhelming the senses so that there was no thought, no memory, no emotion, just the mindless singularity of that moment. "Sure." I lean in through the driver's window. "And, like, what do you care anyhow as I swear I don't have a gun?" I chide him as I punch the power knob with my knuckle.

"Shit, if I sang like that I would'a killed myself." He slips out.

"Yeah . . . what? What do you mean 'like that'? This is great shit . . . I like . . . well . . . actually he did . . . don't you know . . . ugh, WTF?" *Got me,* I think, turning to him with a wry smile, but his back is towards me as he peers out into a clear, horizonless expanse.

We cast our gaze to the many black dots of surfers already in the water seeking to tap the distant hurricane-force energy before—in a fickle fit of Mother Nature: with a wind direction change, a rising tide, diminishing wave strength, or any other varietal of Her excuses—the waves dissipate, or lose shape, and are forever lost. Along the shoreline we observe a low-hanging, misty microclimate of salty air created from the crashing surf.

We glance at each other as we share a knowing look, and our lips spread with self-congratulatory smiles of *Good call.* Surfers are optimistic gamblers, and we have correctly calculated the results of a raging storm from days before and an ocean's distance away. Not a word said, yet our unspoken tension rises as we begin unloading surfboards, checking leashes, waxing decks, and reversing our shiny, black neoprene wetsuits, pulled inside out from their last use and subsequent fresh-water rinsing. Peeling off a warm layer of clothing, our naked bodies flush pink with blood to keep exposed skin warm against a sharp crispness; we slip into our sealskin soft full-suits: legs poke in first, followed with a sharp tug and feminine butt wiggle as we pull the neoprene over our hips. Then our hands reach to the sky as we slide arms through the sleeves, then finally perform a short, sharp shoulder-and-head curtsy to whip the backside zipper-leash overhead. The leash is grabbed, then pulled straight up to close the wetsuit snugly around the neck—a nice, tight thermal barrier that captures a thin layer of water after submersion in the sea that is then body-heat warmed as an insulating blanket.

Mouths are closed. Nostrils flare. Our voices are silent. Our eyes carefully survey the double-overhead-plus swell lining up from beyond Indicators in the north and wrapping south all the way to the pier. North and south are relative directions only for the American continent relative to the north and south poles. Most of our classic surf spots are, in fact, warped from true north and south, with this particular coastline tracking almost due east to west on the compass.

Observation of swell height, speed, and power will dictate fin placement on our longboards: forward for maneuverability in carving the face of slow, mushy waves, and farther aft for down-the-line speed and blasting around sectioning walls. Sussing crowd vibe is now an essential part of pre-evaluation of any modern surf session. From our vantage point atop the parking lot wall, we can view six surf spots beginning in the south with the Pier, rolling north to Old Man's, Sewers, the Point, River Mouth, and finally Indicators, almost a mile away. It doesn't take a rocket scientist to see the Point is going off! Sets of three to six waves at four meters high each are stacking up on the horizon, pitching into huge bowls with solid curls still overhead high a hundred yards down as the waves continue to wrap with the beach's curve . . . epic. Even exposed white-skinned, Bermuda-shorts-clad tourists from Kansas, seeing the ocean for the first time in their lives, would immediately have their visions lured to the Point's classic lines: the groomed perfection, the power, the spectacle—what a rush!—of watching several scores of surfers jockeying for position to dance solo with a morphed offspring of nature's wild fury.

My brother casts sideways glances of anticipation at me while rapidly moving his arm back and forth across his surfboard as he lays a fresh coat of sticky Sex Wax on the deck. His peeks are an attempt to assess which take-off spot my vision is drawn to while putting subtle pressure on me to make the call. He will stand by my judgment to evaluate all the variables: swell height, tide, wind, crowd control, and our own physical capabilities. He also relies on my decision to determine both where we will jump off and where we will eventually sit atop our boards waiting for waves. "Pull your skag all the way back, we are going to River Mouth," I tell him, indicating that we would be charging . . . big, fast, and slightly out of control . . . just to his own personal and demented liking.

Swinging his head up from deck waxing, he squints slightly, focusing his vision with a long look to the River Mouth. In measured cadence, he responds, "A little walled and closed out. Not anybody else is out there right now." This is not a challenge to my expertise, but rather he's trying to understand my logic, which runs counter to the two hundred surfers already spread in clusters along the coastline.

"We have a low tide right now." I speak in a calm tone of secure confidence to mask my growing excitement and the insecurity of a mistaken decision. No need to spread that fear. "As the tide begins to fill in, the peak will stretch out from the Point to the River Mouth," I defend. "We should be able to jump on a few perfect waves solo before the crowd realizes the peak has shifted out."

His blank expression remains unchanged as his gaze shifts from the ocean to my face, but I know he is thinking: *Where do you get this shit from?*

"*Whaaaatt?*" I respond with Hollywood's best acting whine. "I don't make this stuff up, ya know; I've seen it happen before. Hey!" I turn on my brother to make sure he is in sync. "Ya wanna surf in the pack and get yourself all worked up with nothing but frustration? Or would you rather take the chance of a walled-up face turning into a super-tube ride?" I lean hard into my brother's self-charging nature, knowing that just on the edge of reckless and scary is much more to his liking than consistently safe and boringly predictable.

He says nothing. I pass the now-mandatory sunscreen for smearing on exposed face, neck, and hands. *Yeck! And women do this twice a day, every day? Gross.* Casually, with his laid-back attitude and with years of practice and care for a fragile object made of soft foam and finished with a thin glass veneer, he tucks his stick under his arm and we begin our walk from Sewers north past the Point to a beckoning River Mouth.

"How ya feelin'?" he asks.

"Feelin' fine, no pain. The doc was right about not noticing my braces too much that high up on my spine. Just don't have the endurance though, after a year of doing nothing," I reply as I hurry to catch up with him. "We should be back on short sticks soon. Kinda like Rat's, huh?" I remind him of younger days. Back then we would carry the boards down the cliff together as a paired set, nose to tail, so that our young, short arms could reach around the tapered ends of the old, heavy logs. We had thought secluded Rat Beach was a perfect spot to surf uncontested until, at the end of summer, we realized it was devoid of any other surfers because the breakers simply sucked.

We continue past photographers setting up their foot-long telephoto lenses to take advantage of the soft morning light and epic surf conditions, and my brother continues with his quizzical look. "Are you good?" he asks with a bit more intensity. He is not probing the capabilities of my diminished physical fitness for what awaits us, but rather he is fishing for the quality of personal character and emotional stability.

"I'm solid, good to go, never better," is my honest, self-delusional response, after a wild night of debauchery.

"You were out kinda late again last night?" His emphasis on "again" prods me to bite on his baited hook to see which way I jump.

Choosing to ignore his deeper inquisition into my soul, I cheerfully offer, "Oh yeah, just went with some friends to Hollywood for sushi while being entertained watching some karaoke. Just a good time."

"Close the place down?" His eyes narrow as he peers deeply through my faltering orbs, peeling back a layer of protective shell. He begins to sense I am concealing something.

"As usual, with a little help from Kirin beer and unfiltered sake, of course." I beam with a reassuring smile. I glance away from his gaze to idly observe the sand on my bootie-covered feet. An internal heat rises from my psyche, which is less covered than a moment ago. The inquisition somehow energizes me, as a cornered animal that seeks to escape.

"We are not going to have a repeat of our last session out, are we?" His monotone masterfully hides his intensity: *Do I really know you any more? Is there something you want to tell me?*—so apparent to a brother.

"Simply an aberration. Just some crowded conditions and bad luck," I respond, throwing out a false mask of normalcy. *So to whom do we lie? Ourselves, to make us believe what's not true? To others, to protect them? Protect them from what?* In silence we continue walking down the beach to the river estuary and our exit point. We stay on the hard, compact sand, above the exposed cobblestone beds and below the mean high-tide mark.

"So," I indifferently start, while silently screaming to myself, *hide it, disguise it, conceal it, avoid it, pretend it does not exist.* "Hypothetically speaking, is it fair to burden another with one's problems?" I continue to look at my feet, watching sand first cover my booties as they sink under the soft top layer, and then fling the dry sand off into the air with each step. Thinking . . . hiding . . . not revealing. *Things that another cannot really help with or assist with. A burden that they then must carry without sharing or speaking of with anyone, or else it would harm innocent others? A burden of knowledge now shared and exposed for which you are also responsible: a keeper of secrets?* Waiting . . . my whole world now focused down to moving feet pitching sand.

"What are brothers for . . ." comes the certain, unhesitant answer for which there is no doubt, no concern, no other from my brother. But is it a fair question? The question itself now becomes a weight to bear: . . . *if they can't carry each other's burdens?*

"We'll paddle!" I holler over the din of rushing water, focused now on flinging my surfboard out and underneath me with maximum forward momentum into the brown river filled with a flowing sludge of mud and rocks that we have reached and must now traverse. In our dry, Mediterranean climate, this barrier is considered a surging river. In most of our tropical travels we would simply consider it a fast-flowing stream as it is only hip deep and seven meters across—and yet no snakes, no crocs, no piranha. It's ours . . . we'll keep it. The river will continue to swell for another day with yesterday's first seasonal rainfall. The previous day's storm event has carried fine sand, coarse gravel, and large rocks along streams into this rushing water.

Many months of arid weather had left the hard-packed hillsides parched. Initially the heavy downpour rapidly soaked into the dry, rocky slopes of the mountains and foothills. As the rain continued to fall, the pummeled ground quickly became saturated.

Angular slopes freely gave up loose dirt and dust to the gentlest of rainfalls.

Flowing water patiently picked and cut and then carried away to erode the landscape.

Beading raindrops began to trickle along with fine silt to merge with others that formed rivulets flowing heavy with sand, which merged into swelling creeks that carried coarse gravel, with all eventually dumping into and forming the muddy, pugnacious river that pushes along large rocks.

Pressing folds of the imposing hills now constrict this runoff into narrow culverts through the undulating and imposing terrain that gives the rushing water a surge of power beyond its weighted mass.

Flowing thick with silt and debris, the creamy, chocolate-brown soup displays shades of petulant black in the river's crescent folds.

The silt and sand, cobbles and rocks are pushed along by the river flow until reaching the sea, whereupon the sediment is deposited to form both the sand and cobblestone beach and the extended fingers of underwater sandbars and shoals. It is these unseen underwater jetties that incoming surf wraps around and peels as fast-closing zippers to the delight of surfers and spectators.

Without these submerged reefs warping the energy frequency, the surging waves would crash flat in a single swoop against the exposed coast.

The shoreline is not a permanent fixture, for along the littoral edges of ocean tide and breaking waves the sand is continually brushed away eventually to be deposited down coast within the oblivion of submarine canyons. Upon strong storm wave surges, heavy sand flow exposes the smooth, gray cobblestone beds that rest below the mean high-tide mark.

Over the millennia, the continual sedimentary outflow, rich in nutrients and topsoil, forms at the river's terminus a wide coastal plain that grows lush with life. Silvery-gray coastal sage scrub tickled by the pelting rain laugh up their lavish musky scents. Fuzzy evergreen woolly blue curls are coaxed with each drop into releasing sweet lavender perfumes. Many more exotic fragrances are exuded, wafting through the hills and combining into a molting, gamy scent made richer and deeper by the freshness of the cleaned air. Dominating this flat riparian strip, clusters of dense centuries-old coast live oaks swoop out widespread and low-branched to form majestic sovereign crowns upon the land. Massively thick and gnarled trunks sprout serpentine scaly boughs that snake out until, with their untenable weight, they bend in graceful ballerina curtsies with outstretched branch tips delicately caressing the ground. Densely layered dark green leaves, spiny and saw-toothed, complete the thorny laurels. The oval, thumb-size leaves initially shield their proprietary turf from a pelting rain, as the same canopy of cool hoards moisture from summer's unblinking heat, until finally the water-laden leaves begin to release heavy drops that fall onto a dense and soft mulch layer of brown decay. Ascending the coastal mountains, the oak groves gradually thin and trees grow smaller until, high upon the stark coastal mountain divide, the last of a solitary dwarfed oak stands twisted and hunchbacked as an ever-vigilant sentinel to the fertile Central Valley that lies beyond.

Six quick strokes across the muddy outflow and we reach the sloping far shore. Legs off the boards, pointed downriver, our feet plant into the cobblestone-strewn river bottom. The rushing momentum of water, in a single swift motion, lifts our sidesaddle bodies up to stand with boards quickly tucked under our arms. In only knee-high water, we feel the river tug forcibly at us in a fruitless effort to pull us under. Four cautious and labored steps upon the rocky and uneven river bottom and we are out.

The flotsam-littered water continues its gravitational descent without us to shortly mix and stain, with an ugly and disfiguring café au lait, its larger, ocean-blue, salty sister.

Briskly I walk ahead of my brother to cross the last stretch of open beach and, at the perpendicular angle of ocean and river mouth, place my log in a dune's downward sway. Neither of us will violate the personal sanctuary of our ritualistic preparation for what awaits us: entry into a cold, deep, and churning ocean. Silently we begin to endure our individual struggle of discomforting preparations, contorting limbs to warm and stretch tired muscles, loosen abused joints, and test healed bones. Age and ancient battle wounds appear to be more of a factor in bringing my blood up to operating temperature rather than the evening before, or the morning of, hedonistic debauchery. Thin but efficient wetsuits insulate us from the cold ground while we sit to limber up. Self-consciously my eyes avert a brother's stare of inquisition by simply looking at loose sand falling off my wiggling big toes, isolated from their smaller siblings within protective black booties.

The physical rush of a cold-water plunge and the excited anticipation of duck-diving eardrum-bursting waves sharpens my senses to everything around me: my brother's protective Mother Hubbard compassion, the freshness of the salty air, the cool autumn breeze at my back, the blueness of the ocean, and the humanity of the beach culture of which we are a part. Consciously I focus on a brother's admonishment not to repeat the socially aberrant behavior I exhibited during our previous surf session, and thus avoid my thoughts floating over the coastal mountain divide to the abutting Central Valley where lies the paramour of my discontent.

~~~~~

Days earlier had found my brother and me expectantly sitting atop our surfboards outside the Point to catch some tasty waves as they rolled in. Surrounding us was a pack of hungry surfers attempting the same feat. Our tandem team, with my sharp eyes coupled with his naturally aggressive style, and a little luck, had combined to enable us to successfully pick off a few set waves each, rides that we usually shared with a fellow surfer. Tiring of the Point's congestive rat race and emotional intensity, we mutually agreed to attempt to connect our next ride through Sewers ending up at Old Man's, where the crowd would be thinner and the vibe less intense, albeit with smaller, mushier waves.

Stroking for a right wave, I spotted, over my left shoulder, a priority surfer dropping into the same clean face. His expression was clearly one of self-preservation as his wide eyes focused on the sucking bowl of the wave to make the bottom turn rather than looking down the line in anticipation of shredding. Selflessly—'cause that's just the kinda fella I am—I reasoned to myself that he was too late, too deep, too steep, and unable to connect the sections. Not wanting to let this beauty escape a virgin, I shoulder hopped into a pristine head-high breaker. Invitingly, the bowl sucked, the wall warped concave to line up nicely with infinite possibilities to carve my artistic freestyle across its pure unblemished canvas—*damn I'm good.* This budding Picasso was squelched in puberty, however, as my free-flow face carving became merely weaving my log safely around the thick crowd still milling about. Each turn was simply a defensive move to avoid colliding with paddlers still clearing the impact zone from the breaking set. After a short ride, the pack thinned and I lined the board up for the inside speed section with pent-up frustration about to be released in a burst of physical energy required for vertical maneuvers. My vision was all too quickly drawn away from the wall rising before me to a laggard slowly paddling out. Soon to intersect my path was a solo surfer struggling through the impact zone. As this laggard appeared to be the last obstacle to connecting with my destination, Old Man's, and my predetermined lazy-ass mind-set to avoid any more paddling, a simple smack off the lip floater reentry should have done the trick quite nicely to get around him.

Damn, missed it by that much, I thought to myself as the forward half of my surfboard cleared over the paddler while in a nauseous, crunching rip, my trailing fin plowed through his glass-and-Styrofoam surfboard, slicing his stick into two cleanly cleaved halves. Our boards shuddered with the impact. The instant deceleration of my board's fin lodging in a stationary object catapulted my body forward, Superman style.

Flying through the air, I brought my hands together overhead as if a cliff diver about to deeply penetrate the water. Entering the wave mid face resulted in my getting caught in its watery folds that instantly shot me skyward before pitching me over a two-meter waterfall. Instinctively, with many years of practice—and some spectacular failures—I tucked and trusted. Balled up tight into a protective embryonic fetal position, I pulled my legs up, knees to chest covering my soft belly with heels over ticklish loins, arms forward to protect my chest, wrists protecting my throat while my hands covered my pretty face, and if sucking my thumb would have helped, I would have done that as well. Any protruding limbs are subject to liquid hydraulic forces that can cause them to be immediately pulled and whipped into grotesque, anatomically incorrect contortions—most commonly, dislocated shoulders. With me inside, the head-high wave came crashing down.

Tons of exerted water pressure squirts the human body along the path of least resistance, like a watermelon seed spit out by a champion hacker. Unless one is careless or just plain unlucky, there is little danger of actually striking the ocean floor, as the bottom will be just as deep as the height of a breaking wave. There are exceptions, including protruding reef and coral heads that grow to the surface like mountain peaks, or those gnarly breaks where the sea floor rises up so suddenly that water is sucked out from the bottom as if with a giant straw, and a wave lip thicker than a bus dangerously pitches one into unforgiving shallow water. The abusive spin cycle is nevertheless endured in an absolute state of mental and physical relaxation: a Zen state of nothing—no moving, no struggling, no looking, no thinking, and, of course, no breathing—all to conserve the most precious resource of all, oxygen.

A concern for the laggard and his imminent mortal peril gnawed at my conscience. He would be pitched backwards, headfirst over the watery upsurge, unable to separate himself from three foreign objects that can eviscerate, disembowel, decapitate, or cripple. Tumbling together through the crashing whitewash with his now-two-piece board, plus my log, any one of which could mutilate him in as many varied ways as the imagination can conceive: razor sharp tail fins easily slicing through or slicing off body parts, the surfboard nose a deadly spear cracking ribs or collapsing a lung, or in tropical waters an ankle leash wrapping around a coral head for a hold-down that . . . Well, we all play the odds of living our own lives the way we want, in one way or another.

After an unexpected initial vertigo-inducing backflip on my part—my fave—I did two barrel rolls with a few horizontal spins just for shits and giggles, and the tumbling surf slowly dissipated its cocoon-enclosing grip, releasing my impressed limbs. Surfacing from the water with arms protectively overhead and a deep refreshing breath of lung-filling air, I quickly scanned for the other surfer. Drunkenly, he rose through the soupy froth, more a layer of white, soapy foam than water really; his ashen face drawn long and droopy; vacant pupils dilated larger than those of a deep-sea fish reeled in unexpectedly from the dark abyss to the surface; an unfocused, blank stare; head hanging listlessly, not moving. The laggard blinked, then blinked again harder.

Eyes moved; his head tried to catch up. Eyes passed over and then focused back to the tail section of his surfboard lying slightly behind and a few feet away, still attached to his ankle leash. Reaching for the tail, he began vainly searching outwards from the impact zone to shore for the nose section, which was now MIA.

"Oh no . . . what the . . . my board? Where?" came out of the laggard's mouth like a drunken low moan. His hands glided around the board's rails and came to rest at the ragged edge of his now-defunct surfboard. Surrounding previously virgin, white foam core, ragged shards of stringy fiberglass cloth mournfully reached out for their disconnected other half.

Worried for his welfare after our underwater ballet, I narrowed my gaze upon his face, searching intently for any observable grimace of pain, or red blood flowing, or his reaching for a damaged appendage, or some other sign indicating physical injury other than the mental discombobulation of a high-speed gyration and spin cycle. "Hey, you all right?" I asked as I reeled in my board with its leash before it could be whipped around as a limb-shearing scythe with the next oncoming whitewash.

He hesitated a moment as if not quite sure. In a dazed, sluggish fog, he turned his head slowly in my direction and looked at me with eyes that appeared to have some semblance of focus. "You cut my board in half!" The stirrings of sense and emotion with a warm glow of pink seeped back into his face.

Wow, that looks totally badass, I thought. More gently, though, I asked with genuine concern, "But are you all right?"

"What? My board is crap now."

"Screw the board. As long as you're okay, that's all that counts."

"No it's not."

"Trust me, it is." Never a truer statement, spoken from a lifetime of cracked ribs, banged heads, coral slashes, and enough other assorted injuries to keep me on a first-name basis with my orthopedist and physical therapist.

"I don't have a surfboard now," the laggard whined as he continued to survey the water's surface for the missing piece. His voice was tinsel high and wavering, but I attributed his emotion to having just survived and surfaced from a particularly intense wash-and-rinse cycle.

Well, he is all right, I thought to myself as I slipped my surfboard underneath and began to paddle out to Old Man's, the paddle that I had attempted to avoid.

Lackadaisically climbing over the first inside swell and out to deeper water, I noticed the unmistakable bright-red pinstripe of my brother's board just outside the break line as he propelled himself perpendicular to me on his way to Old Man's. He had been unable to connect his wave through to our next surf spot and his arms, after several hours in the water already, were clearly laboring as he paddled in slow motion. Most would have mistaken his pained face as an indication of the effort required to lift his arms and stroke them under the board to move forward in the water, but it was clear to me that he had already seen enough of the eviscerated surfboard to realize what had happened with my encounter on the last wave.

Instilled with the animal instincts of a killer shark, my brother could perceive from a hundred yards or more, by the focus of the prey's eyes or the angle of the hunted's head, their physical condition and their ability to attack, defend, or run—an important skill when sizing up a competitive surf pack. Yet, as our proximity came within conversation distance, he asked, "Everything cool?"

My consciousness swirled with the relativity of his question as to this time and place. Or was it rather a question plumbing to determine the disposition of my soul and emotional stability? I went for the easy answer, and giving an indifferent shoulder shrug, I spoke a half-truth: "He's all right," as to the physical state of the other surfer, and, "Everything's cool," for the relative heat of my core id.

We pulled up alongside and parallel while continuing our paddle in mutual silence to Old Man's. As wingmen on a mission, no other words were spoken, nor did we glance at each other as we glided in unison across the smooth ocean surface, drawing on each other for strength to continuously move our flagging arms. Over our right shoulders we gave an occasional glance at the horizon as we kept a constant vigilance against sleeper waves that might catch us off guard. Over the sound of controlled breathing in sync with arms paddling, the flat, sometimes hollow, noise of ocean riplets rhythmically slapped into our sticks to then lap overboard. More from having tired spaghetti-noodle arms than from conscious analysis of wave conditions and the ideal take-off spot, we sat on our logs on the outside of Old Man's waiting for the infrequent, larger sets, rather than continuing our paddle into the more consistent yet smaller lineup farther inside. Several other surfers casually lounged outside with us and seemed to share our desire for a short respite to recharge old muscles and creaking bones while warming our blood as we waited for Godot. Early morning glory had faded and the outside surf was now irregular and mushy. Even then a few head-high rides put our mind-set right again.

Paddling back out after a short ride that had started with such promise but quickly backed off with the rising tide, my brother was stranded in the middle of the take-off zone when I spotted an oncoming solo wave and turned to catch it. Not wanting a long drop-in in front of my brother to leave me caught behind a sectioning wave or a repeat aggressive off-the-lip spectacular failure, I angled my paddle hard right down the line to drop in on the shoulder rather than the center peak. The wave caught and lifted my surfboard's tail overhead. I lied to my wiener arms, telling them, *last wave, give me all ya got and you can rest, promise,* and dug in hard for one last, strong stroke before a short glide and then alighting for a weightless free-fall entry.

I was about to accelerate down the rising wave face, my right arm in the middle of a paddle, when up from the darkest depths of nowhere a crushing weight climbed up my right leg and slid over my hip and waist. Pinned between board and the oppressive weight, listing at thirty degrees and sinking deeper into the sea, I looked back to see what under the sun—or rather from the deep—was driving my limbs and board beneath the surface. An instinctive, reflexive head snap back saved my face from impacting a speeding lime-green surfboard and turning said face into the sloppy, gooey consistency of kelp. GDMF! The green board continued to slide over the length of my body, sinking my entire right side underwater with a weight that pinned my right arm uselessly between the two boards. Agh! The green stick streaked past my face, releasing my right side and righting my surfboard that then sprang upright to the surface again. If that had been a tri-fin rather than a single, the outside skag could have cut my fucking arm off! GDMFer!

A sharp rooster-tail spray slapped at my face as Asshole Surfer flashed by, pulling a left reverse under my nose. Grabbing my surfboard with both hands, he attempted to flick me up off the face and out the wave's back. A classic, childish move that I only playfully use on my brothers . . . well . . . and sometimes a few close buddies . . . and there was that guy in Cabo . . . but he was a real dick. The wave was vertical, about to pitch, and I was in a motionless stall about to be sent airborne without wings or parachute. Ignoring an instinct for survival, which would have had me rationally sitting on the tail of my board allowing the wave to safely pass by, with delusional optimism clouded by an animal's rage of revenge, I precariously shifted all my weight forward and thrust my surfboard into empty space. I hung motionless until gravitational forces took hold, and I dropped. Internal organs rose up in an attempt to escape through my throat in the accelerating free fall. Before the board plunged away from reach, my feet were loosely planted on the tail, and a thin rail edge was delicately laced in the watery wall.

Caught inside, my brother had an unobstructed ringside seat of the entire ambush and mugging and would later say, "You scared the holy bejeezus out of me. I thought I saw in your face the devil rise up, eyes fire red and spitting blood."

Lacking any speed from wave thrust, an agonizingly slow bottom turn ensued. Only just outracing the cascading avalanche, I had my sights set on pursuing and catching the quickly escaping asshole and satisfying a burning desire for revenge. A quick board pump, then a half step rearward while shifting weight to the inside rail edge on the ball of the right foot, created starboard drag. The resistance angled the board up the face. Just under the lip, my weight shifted to the heels and outside rail. The nose snapped from sky-high and flat to forty-five degrees downward as the tail cast a wide wake spray. Racing down the face, I did a quick board pump to accelerate around the base of a blocking section and . . . success! Target acquired! I aimed my crosshairs squarely at the back of a black gargoyle positioned just a few meters above me. Framed against a cloudless sky was the newly found object of my consuming hate . . . Asshole Surfer.

Asshole appeared to be lining up for a lip-smack reentry, which, I anticipated with cold, calm calculation, would briefly leave him motionless and squarely in my crosshairs to blast him away with a fiberglass-and-resin javelin. Oh sweet revenge, best served Arctic cold, with no recoil of the mind in the bloody horror. His mortal back, a human bull's-eye, was squarely at the tip of my high-speed javelin board . . . piercing and gutting him from backbone to sternum . . . fish food, blood bait, shark chum. *Well . . . hold on back there a moment, Killer . . . maybe just a tad bit too intense.* But his snap back would leave his board momentarily flat to my perpendicular missile, his stick's soft underbelly exposing a vulnerable center stringer to my penetrating nose, snapping his board in half like a thin, dry twig. My forward momentum would allow me a safe exit over the top while Asshole fell into a churning mass of foamy water with three scythes, his split board, and my log, banging together en masse. *Yeah . . . well . . . calm down there Buffy the Slayer . . . also maybe a tad slightly too harsh.* How 'bout if I just give him grandmother's feisty, *"A good boxin' in the ear I will"* as I swing up and over him with my own off-the-lip reentry? That should at least get his attention, and we could then begin a mature and intelligent adult conversation . . . *a tête-à-tête with tea and crumpets you say? How lovely, indeed.*

What!? Bursting my self-delusional fantasy of mortal combat mano a mano, for some unknown reason, Asshole forwent a lip-smack reentry off the fat, juicy, inviting lip by continuing over the wave and out to deeper water. *Why?* Oh well, sweet, precious lip . . . all mine . . . Asshole can wait. All righty then, a quick slash and tear with a weightless reentry and then I could satisfy my burning desire for revenge after finishing the wave with a sky-high flying kick out. Oh . . . take a gander at that *sweeet* inside section lining up.

The wave rushed the shallows inside and jacked to an overhead vertical wall of water as straight and smooth as rails for a bullet train to eternity. Speed so fast the board hovered over the surface as a skipping stone, barely creating a ripple.

Wow! Already at the pier? My limbs were emasculated . . . the distance too far to paddle back out to Old Man's, so I lay on my board to belly ride the whitewash to shore. As the beach approached, I slid my legs off the board and planted my feet into the sloping ocean floor. My thighs were burning from the constant g-forces while cranking repetitive bottom turns from Old Man's to the pier. With wobbly legs, I leaned on my surfboard for support to walk the last few meters out of hip-high water.

Once on hard-packed sand, I tilted my head forward and shook like a wet, shaggy Labrador retriever, seawater spraying from my long hair in a large arc. Replacing the cold, salty brine with a captured layer of air, the warmer thermal quickly acted as insulation for my scalp, keeping away the morning chill for one simple scientific reason: water cools the body ten times faster than air. Morning rays were absorbed by my glistening black wetsuit. Hot blood pumped to my extremities, numb from hours in the cold ocean. A warm, tingling rush pulsated through my body. Fingertips beat in rhythm with the heart. My face warmed with a glow to flush pink. The effects of long physical exertion in a cold environment combined to affect my body with a total loss of basic motor skills: no legs, no strength, no balance. Feet cold and numb and stumpy to the touch of the ground moved from simply trusting not to misstep and fall.

Turning to face the sun, I closed my eyes against the unfiltered light and took a deep lung-filling breath, then slowly exhaled. Calmly thinking without emotional attachment, I replaced the animal instinct for fight with the meditation of human rationale. With a relaxed, floating detachment, calm permeated my being.

From a distance, the tall, lanky frame of my brother was easily identifiable awkwardly wading through thigh-deep water. He trod slowly, feet searching for flat-surface traction on the rocky seabed. Soft-soled booties continually slipped and slid upon irregularly shaped stones and into odd angled crevices that uncomfortably twisted ankles. Slightly hunched over while resting an uncovered hand on a waxy surface, he supported a portion of his body weight to steer the surfboard shoreward. A small swell occasionally nudged him from behind, pushing him along at a quicker pace. The water level dropped to knee high, and he wrapped his stick snugly under his arm. The wash receded from shore, visibility cleared, and he looked for sandy spots between rocks in which to step. With a last burst of energy, he lifted his gangly legs gazelle-like above the surface and, before the next whitewash obscured his vision of the seabed, sprinted the remaining few meters to shore.

Approaching with dark hair glistening and matted to his head, he greeted me with piercing eyes narrowed to bunker slits. His face relaxed ever so slightly as he gave me a wicked reptilian smile of no exposed teeth, wrinkling the corners of his eyes. "The man gets run over, does a no-paddle, vertical takeoff behind a breaking section with a blocker in front, and he still surfs out of sight. You should have fuckin' TOAD! How'd you do it?"

Searching within that detached state of myself, an answer that I cannot identify as delusional self-confidence, true ignorance, or just the pure pleasure of physical drainage and being—for I am jelled—I replied with casual aplomb, "Lucky," truly believing what I said. For the moment I accepted and welcomed an emptiness of emotion; a fire was quelled. The gnawing of something hatching inside would return, but . . . I'd deal then. "You can buy me a chili-cheese omelet and maybe I'll tell you about it."

My brother laughed silently to flash pearly white teeth in his small-framed mouth. Showing approval to my response, he relaxed his intent stare to a happy sparkle in his eyes. "Yeah, sounds good. Keep the music down and let me check and see if I brought my wallet."

We laughed together at our inside joke.

~~~~~

Autumn is an impetuous three-year-old throwing capricious tantrums. Hot winds that occasionally blow in from the deserts will sap all moisture from air and land. Should a single spark ignite dried sage, it will kindle into a raging firestorm. These devil winds may then push the fire, which for miles and miles will consume everything in the inferno's path and will be extinguished only when reaching the sea. Bright orange-red clouds rise up from the blaze into the windswept sky; particles of soot fall as gentle snow along the coast, coating everything with a ghostly gray ash. Only tough ancient oaks survive the inferno, the ground-touching tips of their thorny crowns singed and withered as they hold back the licking flames. A fickle autumn may then whip ninety degrees, fetching Gulf of Alaska–incubated storms thick with thunderheads pouring buckets for days on end. Stripped of covering vegetation and ground-holding roots, denuded hillsides fall away in landslides smothering homes and highways alike. With luck, the rains fall first—as they have this season—and brown brush at the end of season will swell and plump with the water to bud green, preventing further firestorms from raging over hill and vale.

Shaking off the lethargy of a Mediterranean summer in expectation of winter's bone-chilling leviathan fury, surfers use autumn for preparation of mind and body. Sitting on the downward slope of a low, soft dune in the crook of river and ocean, my brother and I lean into our hurdler's stretch, pulling taut muscles tighter. Exhaling, my body compresses close, nose to knee, right hand pulling back the left foot, a dull tug at hamstring and lumbar, a discomfiture stretching and loosening muscles. Our breathing is deliberately controlled as we collect our thoughts. Our anxious tension dissipates, replaced with a growing sense of excitement.

My cheek flush against my knee, I face across the river to the shoreline of the jutting point and observe the ragged line of surf paparazzi taking advantage of the soft morning light and clean, epic waves. Tripod-mounted cameras with telephoto lenses line the shore as if they are stalking stars at a Hollywood bistro. These protruding lenses, some as large as rhino horns, will struggle to reduce the distance from dry land to open sea in an attempt to capture the water-launched aerial maneuvers framed against an infinite, blue screen lit with the soft light of morning's glory.

I realize that in a lifetime of surfing there is not one picture, a single negative, a translucent celluloid, or any digital photographic evidence of either of us actually surfing on a wave. A busy life? Missed opportunities? Laziness? No connections? No friends? All of the above?

We unfurl our tightly wrapped leashes and strap the Velcro securely to our right ankles. We lift our boards under our right arms as our left hands gather up the excess leash, which we then safely tuck between right hands and board so as not to embarrass ourselves tripping over the slack while walking to the water. In silence, we approach the ocean. From a vantage point atop the slight rise of the last wind-groomed dune, apexed in the crux of river and ocean, we survey the incoming swell. Chasing away the last wafer-thin ribbon of yellow that hugs the earth's curve, the sun inches above the horizon: a pure, white, incandescent bulb with only a beguiling promise of throwing a warmth sometime later. The ocean surface ripples with the offshore breeze; the refracted light from the horizontal sun shimmers as it dances from dimple to crest and bursts forth upon our eyes in blinding silver-star points.

The previous day's rain has washed from the sky all the airborne pollutants and driven them to ground, affording us a crystal-clear view for miles up and down the coast. Perfectly groomed waves peel and break in echelon from Indicators past River Mouth to eventually wrap around the Point whereupon they disappear from our view. In front of us, the thick lips feather with sea foam blown back to be suspended for a moment, hovering in space. The gnarly lip reaches out to the breaking wave's base and explodes in a white phosphorescent plume.

Slate-gray cobblestones lie bare below the high tidal zone. The covering of coarse sand has been swept away from the storm surge and constant littoral drift to be forever deposited in the dark depths of the patiently awaiting deep-sea canyons. And as the ebb and flow of the ocean's tide smoothes the sands at land's edge, so, too, the morning's light offshore breeze stands tall to polish the surface of those cresting waves. In ankle-deep water we stand on the cobbles observing the thunderous spectacle nature has laid before us. From this distance, the strength and violence of impact is muted. Previous experience has taught us that the power is sufficient to snap a board or burst an eardrum. Pickled, lazy asses, lack of proper sleep, weenie arms, and choice of longboards all conspire against us and dictate a shortcut approach to leap off the rocks straight into the teeth of the ocean . . . "damn the torpedoes, full speed ahead." Nothing new for us. Wait for a set to shatter, roll in, and expire on the beach, and then, with Indicators's calm and a clear view to the horizon . . . jump! In unison we leap into the backslide of the last set wave, and the riptide draws us irrevocably away from shore. Butterflies flee our stomachs as we hit the water and concentrate solely on paddling. There will be only precious moments to open ocean before an annoying re-formed shore pound rises up to catch us midway or a larger return set follows.

The calculated throw of gambler's dice, motivated by . . . our lazy asses lacking motivation . . . immediately pays dividends as we soon paddle over the last shore break and realize we have made it through the impact zone unmolested. With arms strong and hair dry—a minor victory in cold autumn surf—I give my brother a knowing smile that he reciprocates with a bright gleam in his eyes. We soon reach the take-off zone and sit atop our boards. We sit casually relaxed as we scan the horizon for incoming set waves.

To our right, at half a kilometer away, several dozen patiently waiting black-dot surfers are loosely strung out across Indicators. Their northern position relative to us will serve as an early warning system to alert us of any incoming sets.

The approaching northern swell will first break and barrel here, giving us an indication of all the affecting variables: approximate number of waves per set, breaking points, wave size, wind strength, and water depth that increases as each successive wave rides higher over the back of its predecessor prior to reaching us and closing out somewhere across a half-dozen interceding and shifting sandbars.

Separated by several paddle strokes from each other, each surfer has hedged his bet as to the optimal take-off spot per the shifting swell and tide.

Over our left shoulders, three hundred meters away, a tightly packed crew sits in a clearly agitated rat pack of several score. Today the Point is consistently breaking in perfect right peels on only one of two adjoining cobble and sandbars; the take-off zone is well defined, moving either in or out depending on the size of each individual wave. The consistent machinelike precision of the wave's breaking apex dictates a single ideal take-off location, and thus, the compactness of the crowd. As conspirators in crime pulling off a midnight heist of the Queen's jewels, we lie isolated and ignored between each well-known and easily identifiable surf spot, selfishly hoarding for ourselves a double-overhead wave that has shown no other consistency than to wall up, jack, and pitch over in a super fast, unmakeable, stand-up right-hand barrel.

Heads on swivels, we continually shift our gazes in an arc from Indicators across the vast ocean, over to the Point and back, searching for any indication of advancing set waves. This simple head motion will keep our minds alert so as not to become falsely lulled by the deceptively calm tranquility of the ocean this far from shore. Small swells pass underneath us unnoticed, the ocean floor too deep to cause the water to rise up.

With some consternation and a growing tingling sensation, I interrupt our single-minded focus and weakly call over, "Hey, hey?" Scrunching my lips to one side, eyes looking absently out to the vacant open distance, I add, "I have a problem."

A scan of the horizon and my brother turns to catch my faltering eyes. His intense scrutiny a question, I again cast my eyes down, all of a sudden mesmerized by the abstract pattern of layered Sex Wax on my deck. "Uh, I don't know how to say this," I mumble, as it seems it is now my turn to become an unintelligible Neanderthal.

He sits up and rocks back, shifting his weight to the board's tail. The nose lifts skyward with the tail driven into the water. He rolls forward and the board, as if without cause, slings effortlessly towards me. He cocks his head to one side, a sudden look of curious consideration in his eyes telepathically conveys the thought: *Bro, you can tell me anything?*

"Uh," I utter, delaying, having been unexpectedly caught short. "I have to pee," I hastily blurt out.

His whole face scrunches in a superfluous question. "What?" he asks, silently gliding closer.

"I have to pee . . . like really bad," I reply, scanning the horizon while trying to ignore his penetrating look.

"*What?*"—leaving "the fuck" off his now-repetitive response. Silence. "Then piss!" His voice is a reprimand of wasting his time. His face changes from one of real interest and concern to a baffled look of wonderment at my statement's stupidity.

"No. I really have to pee. Bad," I continue. Then, defending against his facial cross-examination, I add, "And, I'm dry," as I try to convey an urgent immediacy of the moment rather than addressing his questioning look of expecting the dilemma of a lifetime.

My consternation regarding bladder control now dawns on him as his face imperceptibly relaxes, softens, and maybe, just maybe, displays a slight twitch of lips. I am dry, therefore I am warm and would like to remain so for as long as possible.

After an hour or two of sitting in the cold sea, a warm urine flood will be a scarce commodity and therefore much more valuable. The risk taken and the advantage gained by our entering the ocean directly into the body-smacking set waves to thus remain dry and warm, and physically strong, will be nullified should I now intentionally let in a layer of cold water to dilute the pee, prematurely chilling my body. My puppy-dog excitement of viewing this morning's perfect surf has set my kidneys hyperactive in processing last night's indulgent consumption of beer and sake. *Damn*, I curse myself, *why can't I hold it until after my first ride? I'm sure to get wet either falling off the wave or paddling back out and duck diving under a set wave. Shit.*

I can see my brother's face wrinkle into that of disgust as he purses his lips tight. He sits up and looks away; his eyes open larger to a wider field of vision as they quickly scan the horizon. Satisfying himself that no wave set is imminent, he again lies on his board, cups his hand, and slaps ocean water at me—the ultimate insult. Without a word or glance, he silently strokes away north and leaves me to suffer within my own personal bladder hell.

I silently berate myself as the dull inconvenience now becomes an intense prostate issue that must be addressed immediately. I relax to let a stream of liquid gold jet down my legs. Aware that my brother will be my coal miner's canary alerting me of approaching danger, I close my eyes and wallow in my self-induced pleasure. The heat quickly dissipates and the warmth fades to be replaced by a cold . . . *yuck*. With a shudder of anticipation, I open my eyes, take two shallow breaths, a single deep one, then roll limply off my surfboard. Before disappearing from the rest of the world, I tightly shut my eyes and mouth to the raw, unfiltered crap dumped by the mass of humanity into my playground. Feet flutter kick as I dive below the warm upper thermal layer and into the cold darkness. Forcing myself, I slip a finger under the skintight collar and pull it away from the flesh to allow entry of an icy blast of silted, chemically contaminated, petroleum-laced, bacteria-infested, feces-laden, *clear, clean,* ocean-*blue* water.

Sliding back on my stick, I shake my hair like a wet puppy and resign myself to a colder existence with a breeze that nips at my exposed flesh and chilly seawater in my suit.

Indicators shows signs of life! Surfers crisscross each other as they scramble for the horizon to gain priority positioning. One by one, the strong, the smart, the lucky, begin to turn and drop in on double-overhead waves. Observing their actions, we become more alive—our muscles receive a surge of subconsciously driven adrenaline, our senses sharpen. Shadowy gray masses slowly rise above a flat surface, obscuring the horizon line. The first wave is a blocker that allows only the tips of two following waves to be seen. Silent since my bladder evacuation, we now begin a verbal jabber dissecting the merits, advantages, and drawbacks of what lies before our eyes as we vigorously paddle towards our destiny.

"You want the first wave?"—a gambit offered—I ask, without looking over to him as he is ahead and off to my right. His location relative to me puts him in the priority position of picking off a right-breaking wave of his choice. Of course, he knows it, and I know it, and he knows I know it. My disingenuous offering is just an opening move to sucker my brother into taking the first wave, clearing him out for an uncontested option of picking the best of the rest. I know it, he knows it, and I know he knows it.

"Naw. You can have it if you want. It looks a little small." Gambit refused.

"It looked like there's a big A-frame peak on the second I think we can pull under," I continue.

"Yea, saw it just off to our right. Looks nice. Third one's bigger, though."

"But do you know where it's shifting to?"

"Too far south? Or walled up maybe?"

"Can't tell. What's coming after?"

"One more. Bigger for sure. Possibly two."

Half the sky is obscured from our view as we come under the base of the first wave.

We can feel its power as we are drawn up its three-meter face. Crashing over the crest, our speed and momentum lifts the front half of our surfboards into the air and we land with a *plop*. We gather in our first unobstructed view of the second wave and a teasing glimpse of the tips of at least three larger waves that follow. The second is a clean, double-overhead wall with a slight peak just within reach to our right. From this apex, the wave will pitch and barrel for an excellent short ride for whomever drops in.

We slide into the backside trough and are now concealed from the view of anyone observing from land. We paddle smoothly and easily across the early morning calm sea. I holler over, "I'll take this one," thinking, *a bird in hand*.

"No. I got it." Bro pulls trump.

"All right," I acquiesce to da big dog. "I'll pass over and get a view of what's following."

"Ten four." He affirms my decision. With that, we diverge and he angles north to get under the visible A-frame of the second wave, while I continue paddling straight out to the much larger, yet unknown, set waves following.

Excellent choice, I think. His wave will break farther out to our right than anticipated and depending on his skill, nerve, and *machismo*, my brother will choose how deep onto the wave's shoulder he wants to paddle before turning around and dropping in. The farther into the peak he paddles before takeoff, the deeper the barrel ride; yet he also runs a far greater risk that he will be too late and TOAD . . . *take off and die*. But . . . it's neither my wave, nor my decision . . . so I concentrate on containing my galloping emotions at the thought of what lies beyond as I continue with a strong, fluid paddle.

Scaling the towering wall of that second wave, I steal a glance over my right shoulder to witness my brother hunched low in a well-balanced surfer's stance, fearlessly charging down the face. Turned in my direction, his emotionless squinting eyes focus down the line; he does not see me, so intently is his mind focused. His tall, lanky body is framed from behind by a cascading wave that reaches out to its base, with crashing white water shooting back into the air overhead. At the center of this swirling commotion is a dark void, an empty cavern that will soon gather him up and devour him. He is as certain of this as I am, yet his fixed expression of determination does not change. *Right on,* I think, *that'll be fun,* as I continue over the top of the wave's elevated crest and lose sight of him.

I discharge the pressing anxiety of the unknown and replace it with the exciting potential of possibilities as, dropping down the gentle backside slope, an even more imposing wave looms. Stretching out from my target-fixated peripheral vision, a thick daunting wall lumbers. Lady Luck still rides with me as directly ahead an ever-so-slight peak bulges above the rest of the wave. From this bump, the wave will first pitch and grind before the rest of the tumultuous avalanche follows. The wave is looking good . . . I'm feeling good . . . let's go deep . . . as deep as possible.

Reaching the wave's base under the feathering peak, I sit on the tail of my surfboard and, in a single well-rehearsed movement, lift its nose skyward, pirouette the log over my left shoulder, and point the nose down the rising escalator face.

I have somehow miscalculated the spin of the galaxy a bit and haven't compensated for the third wave riding higher over the water mass and volume of the previous waves. This has resulted in my stroking too far into the face for what I thought would be an easy turn and drop, for I must now make up for my error by paddling harder than expected while trimming my surfboard perfectly to gain maximum speed. Irrevocably drawn up the face, I feel the power of the wave rise up while lifting me higher into the air. The heaving swell continues to build under my thin Styrofoam-and-glass stick. The underwater shoal drags and slows the wave's bottom, sucking water from its base, shaping it into a looming bowl. The high peak is not slowed by the seabed's resistance and continues forward unimpeded.

In the instant before my board's now-almost-vertical tail is pitched somersaulting ass over head, I quickly transition from paddling to gripping the rails to half rising with feet softly planted on the deck. There is a brief moment of suspended animation when the board hangs motionless, neither rising nor falling upon a sheer face. My heart in my throat, I lean forward a tad into the awaiting well.

Squatting low and balanced on the surfboard, I free-fall down a vertical wall of water with only the right tail edge planted securely in the face. Like my brother, I ignore the swirling mass of energy that expends itself behind me and set my vision down the line.

Without warning, all is a visual confusion of the world. From the rising wall of water inches from my face, and out to the horizon, across an ocean of water, a polished surface sparkles in refracted and bouncing light from the rising sun dead ahead.

My eyes squint to adjust. Any view of what lies directly in my path is obscured . . . I can only see down into the well . . . or up to a mass that looms high overhead.

As if with a will of its own, my surfboard completes a bottom turn in the depths of the wave's sucking bowl and angles up to lodge directly under a thick, watery ceiling. Inches of the board's right rail delicately bite into the vertical face to be perilously perched high on the sheer wall. The overhead canopy unfurls. A leading edge of white froth blows away, arching back out to sea. For speed . . . for fun . . . for survival, I carefully trim the glass rail at the wave's critical upper edge, the point just past vertical where the surfboard itself should be grabbed by the wave and pitched up and over. Borne upon the wave, the curl completes the encasing cocoon. My vision of the world is slowly reduced to a single periscope view of white light at the end of a watery, green tunnel. As if in a slow-motion dream of futility, the tube's opening teasingly stretches away out of reach.

Having entered a temporary sanctuary—a gravity-defying temple composed of liquid columns that rise up, bend, and then wrap around—I lose all spatial awareness and become mesmerized by the opening oscillation . . . out . . . then back . . . smaller . . . then larger. There is no passage of time, no motion of speed, no sound of the thunderclap underfoot. Looking into the rising sun through the seawater shroud, a kaleidoscope of aquamarine sparkles flashes by.

Clear translucent pillars become muddy. The tube darkens noticeably as when the sun fades behind a thundercloud. Receding into a deepening and darkening danger, the foreboding brown announces that the wave is entering shallow water. Reaching deep into its bowels, the sea vomits up its bile of loose silt and sand unattached to the patina floor lining. Turning burnt-coffee brown, the ephemeral temple walls become mausoleum menacing and begin to close in. The tube end, and my escape, permanently snaps shut.

In self-preservation mode, I take two quick shuffle steps rearward, thrusting my stick forward as I fly off backwards to create precious space between myself and the surfboard prior to entering the wash-and-spin cycle. I skip and bounce across the water's surface. In preparation for being sucked up and over the falls and entering an underwater ballet, I quickly exhale, followed with a large, lung-expanding intake of air, cross arms over the chest, draw up legs to the belly, close eyes . . . then splash, sink, pitch up, and free-fall . . . relax . . . patience . . . no fighting . . . no oxygen-depleting fear . . . enjoy the ride . . . crush . . . ugh!

"Dude! Fully throaty and stand up!" I beam to my brother's inquisitive smile while paddling back to our take-off spot.

"You make it out?"

"Shit, not a chance. And you?"

"Same. Didn't make it as far as you, though, and got worked."

"Yeah, I got hammered!"

Mutual smiles convey an intimate feeling of surfing in the tube that can only be shared with brother surfers; no amount of money can buy the e-ticket barrel ride. Twenty million dollars may get one a rocket ride into space as a Russian cosmonaut; a few thousand may get one into a passenger seat for a high-speed NASCAR banking on the oval; but pay one's way to be pushed into Hawaii's Pipeline and all one will end up with is a torn and shattered body, if one is lucky. A one-dollar bar of Sex Wax and a full tank of gas is all it takes for adventures that money cannot buy.

Surfing can become a consuming lifestyle. Ocean sirens beckon with sweet whispers of euphoria more attractive than any chemically addictive dope—an endorphin addiction, altering both body and mind. We run to the sea with long, sun-bleached blond hair flowing behind, to enter the enchantress's embrace. All physical aches taper. Emotional scars forgotten. Pressing problems ignored. In this moment upon the wave, all else washes away. This motivating force gets you up before the sun rises, and isolates you in the middle of the ocean with hungry sharks or, in the extreme, water so cold ice could float by. It's an addiction that takes you around the world to unknown destinations where no one else, you hope, ventures. Soon you're compelled to miss class or to arrive late to work. Eventually, you take a full surf day off. Extended flat spells seem to be physically painful, a form of withdrawal. Driving for hours looking for surf you know won't be there, you continue to drive on. After graduation, shoulder-length hair is cut to conform to society's norms. Society constantly reprimands, "What, you still surf? At your age?" And somehow there is always the eternal dilemma of surf now, or savor the pleasure of Delilah's flesh now? The distant thumping of surf calls the strongest, for the precision barrels will, with nature's fickle 'tude, be gone in a moment with the shifting wind, or a changing tide, and will definitely fade by tomorrow. But Delilah? She will be there when you get back . . . won't she?

~~~

The morning continues to unfold in a repetitive cycle of peering upcoast to Indicators for incoming sets, setting off madly scrambling surfers, and then shifting our gaze to the horizon in anticipation of spotting camel humps that swell up high against the skyline. Our primal animal inheritance has subliminally taken measure of the ocean's cadence as we become in sync with the ocean's pulsing rhythm. Selective taste made even more discriminating with our isolation from the pack, we pick out the juiciest wave of each set for ourselves. We turn to paddle down the smooth face and the wave lifts us skyward. Standing, we drop weightlessly into long, thick, image-reflecting walls that jack into cavernous, unmakeable barrels that end in crushing wash-and-rinse cycles. Never escaping from the swirling vortex that catches and engulfs us, we return again and again to our take-off spot to greet each other with shit-eating grins on our faces.

Still low in a late autumn sky, the rising sun is a stark white sphere levitating against an expansive, pale blue space. We attempt never to look directly into the white light so as to avoid an inconvenient moment of blindness. Belying the sun's glaring blaze, it sheds little heat to cut through the breezy, crisp air and leaves our bodies shivering for more thermal intensity as we sit gently rocking atop our boards waiting for the next ride. A rising tide continues to fill the shallow shoals, slowing each wave's onward rush to shore and its eventual self-destruction while simultaneously shifting the take-off peak, as we find ourselves drifting farther down coast and closer to the crowded Point.

With all of the excited anticipation of a discreet rendezvous with an illicit lover, an uncontainable smile sweeps across my face as I again arc a line at the wave's bottom while my mind projects the path I will carve across the vertical wall of water to hide safely in the enveloping folds of the tube's swirling vortex. The sight fills me with an overwhelming sense of being, as if in my presence is the exposed nude body of the most beautiful woman in the world, coyly smiling a charming invitation. Even behind the privacy of bedroom doors, I ignore her sensuous female form and flesh, and am solely captivated by the alluring fire in her eyes, beckoning me closer . . . breathe out . . . breathe her in.

Pulling under a thick, pouty lip, I am slowly concealed from the outside world by the perfection of what would appear to be another machine-created tube ride, a cylinder seemingly much too symmetrical and consistent to be a natural phenomenon. With a sense of déjà vu, I see the narrow-framed exit flirt away, an accordion escape tantalizing, stretching out of reach . . . smaller . . . smaller. Trapped and looking to flee, I feel a huge adrenaline-laced injection course through my body, awakening fatigued muscles and pushing aside the mental resignation of the door inevitably snapping shut and the resulting helpless spin cycle. The claustrophobic perspective of water light fantastic skirting past my peripheral vision ends abruptly, and, in the blink of an eye, it is replaced by the incandescent, blinding spotlight of full sun . . . I have exited the emerald-laced cavern! Unexpectedly transitioned out of the shaded, tubular confines from which I have been struggling to seek deliverance all morning without success, I am momentarily stunned and lamely stand there, gliding across the face with no thought of what to do next.

Fully stoked, I flee high up the face, turn to drop down the wave, and rapidly gain speed. Upon reaching the valley floor, I crank a huge bottom turn and angle my stick back up vertically. In triumphant celebration, just as the nose passes over the lip, I lean back and, with the full strength of my legs, thrust the surfboard skyward like a Nike missile blasted from a Vandenberg silo. The board rotates slowly clockwise on its axis as it reaches for the stars. The wet, glassy surfboard glistens, trailing water droplets as rocket vapor trails that are shattered crystals sparkling in a rainbow mist of bouncing sunlight. At an apex of thirty feet, the surfboard is a sun-reflecting lighthouse beacon that can be seen dazzling for miles up and down the coast. Launched over the crest, I perform an airborne pirouette that would certainly persuade the Olympic diving judges to award me four points of ten. *Damn, I'm good.* I gently splash down in the waiting sea. There is a moment of self-congratulatory satisfaction as I float on my backside, admiring the results of my handiwork until the realization . . .

Uh, this is Houston control, you have a problem. Having recalculated the rocket's reentry zone based upon projectile trajectory, velocity, weight, wind speed, air density, Earth's rotational mass, and the stars' alignment, we have concluded that the impact point will be . . . your fucking head . . . dumb ass!'

DIVE! DIVE! DIVE!

Like the USS *Thresher* chased by an enemy destroyer, I madly scramble underwater in an effort to put as much cushion between my body and the incoming weapon of individual self-destruction that will puncture a sizable hole in my thin-skinned cranium, thus leaving me a heap of neoprene flotsam. The thickness of a surfboard rail is just the difference between disaster and success.

Hearing the board luckily impact flat and thus harmlessly on the water without penetrating the surface or nicking my body, I gleefully relax to float underwater for a moment. Surfacing with hands held protectively over my head, I sheepishly grab my now-inanimate surfboard, slide my body over the rail onto the deck, and begin my paddle back out to the lineup and my brother's awaiting look.

Chagrined that I may have been spotted for the fake I am, I nevertheless put a Cheshire cat smile upon my face in an attempt to project an artificial impression of confidence and pleasure. Closing with a brother with whom I feel guilty for boasting about my fortunate ride, but humanly unable to contain my nerves still on edge from the narrow escapes—one from nature and the other from self-imposed stupidity—I burst out, "Dude, that was *completely* clean."

"No way!" he responds, eyes widening perceptibly with interest and wonder at the news of my success.

"Way!"

"You made it?"

"Fully throaty and deep stand-up barrel." I use two fingers of one hand to demonstrate the surfboard, and the other hand, thumb and forefinger touching in a circle, indicates the tube exit stretching out and then back again. "No way I thought I was going to make it!" I slip my fingers through the artificial wave.

"Dude. Did it spit?"

"Huge blowback, *Dude.*"

"Fuck'n A."

"Fuck'n aye."

A little known, yet undeniable reality is that there is nothing more scintillating, nothing that makes you feel more alive, than to slip through what appear to be the inevitable fingers of nature closing around you in destruction, and then to escape whole and unharmed, a ride with little possibility of success and a significant personal price to be paid for failure; this indelibly burns into one's memory and emotions as epic.

Natural opiates still lace my bloodstream, keeping my extremities warm and the mind alert, but I feel an inevitable fabric of weariness descending. It will soon be time to leave this stage. A closing curtain of dullness lazily drifts down on my brain, making it both critical of every wave my eyes see and also unwilling to send the required message of urgency to stimulate my muscles to action. For two waves now I have lied to my weenie arms and beseeched them for maximum effort with the assurance that *this will be the last wave and no more; you will get a rest.* Limp spaghetti-noodle arms now hang from my trunk like appendages not to be trusted to perform even a final encore.

"So, do you want to take the next wave in and walk back to Shamu, or should we try to surf past the crowd at the Point?" I bluntly pose our quandary to my brother, knowing that the answer will be the same as every other time that he has been asked that question. But he has to be teased onboard, to be in agreement with his wingman while we attempt a complicated operation together. In our own perverted male world of machismo, our folly is not facing the slings and javelins, both figuratively and literally, of carefully maneuvering through a hundred other surfers, but rather of getting stuck outside with no "last ride." After a morning of luscious perfection shared only among ourselves, it would be a bitter pill indeed to have to suffer belly boarding the white-wash to shore with a long walk to the van.

"I think with your eagle eye and my blocking, we should be able to tag team our way through," he says with optimism belying the difficult task before us. "One connector wave to the Point, one set wave, and we're in," he says with a false bravado that neither of us believes.

But, "I'm in," I find myself saying. Lying on my board, I begin to paddle with renewed vigor out and south to the Point as another set rolls in.

"Shit! You ass wipe," my brother mutters, realizing I have sucker punched him. He quickly lies on his board and feverishly starts pad-dling after me. His back had been turned to the ocean while speaking to me, as I was facing the horizon scanning for our next catch. I laugh at him for falling for such an old trick as we are both reminded once again of rule number one: never turn your back on the ocean.

Our good fortune for the day continues as I again pass up the sec-ond wave to my brother in exchange for the third wave, which is, in turn, passed over for an even larger fourth set wave. The decision pays off handsomely: a strong, clean, double-overhead, A-frame peak even-tually tapering off into multiple head-high speed sections. The pre-ceding three waves, combined with a rising tide, have grown a layer of water over the beach shoal and pushed the ride through the inside section close to shore, under and past the Point. Ignoring my burning thighs, which scream for a rest after only sixty seconds and four hun-dred meters, I continue to work the inside, shoulder-high, mushy slop until it dribbles out in the tranquility of Sewers's cove.

Dropping to my log, spent and content, I relax in the deeper draft of the calm cove, which offers relative immunity from breaking waves and rolling whitewash. With shoulders slumped forward, head hang-ing, thighs spread wide across the surfboard in a V, and legs dan-gling underwater, I mindlessly stare at my royal-blue, racing-striped surfboard as my fingernails numbly pick at the dirty, gray layer of knotty Sex Wax covering the deck.

Without the top film of sticky wax, a wet surfboard would be useless—in fact dangerous—to the surfer, as but a single drop of water will turn the highly polished resin deck into a traction-less surface slicker than the best quarried Grecian marble. Grab the rails of an unwaxed surfboard in water and it simply squirts away like a slippery banana underfoot. Inversely, the underbelly is kept as clean and smooth as possible, a frictionless surface that at speed appears to levitate across sheer walls. Bottom dings and divots are quickly sealed with a new coat of clear resin, thus offering no pockets of resistance while hydroplaning across the surface, and preventing the board from absorbing water and becoming waterlogged and heavy.

As I listlessly rock on the swell, the current carries me slowly down coast. With indifference, I lift my eyes from a stubby montage of pixelated wax, and gather in my surroundings and whereabouts. The shore is close, a few stones' throws away. Surfers can be seen entering the water singly and in groups. Turning my gaze out to the Point, "You've got to be kidding me," erupts out loud to myself.

"Ha." A deep baritone laugh surrounds me. Looking over my shoulder, I see a young, square-jawed surfer with sun-bleached, sandy hair, two days' stubble growth, and amused eyes sizing me up as he paddles out to Sewers. "And you were expecting?" he asks with a laid-back surfer's nature.

"Jesus. I've been looking at the Point all morning long from the backside and didn't realize it was this freakin' crazy crowded," I lament. A quick count of surfers around the Point combined with a little elementary math results in my determining that even if there is a wave every sixty seconds, and I queue up for my turn, it will be at least an hour and a half before my number is called. I should just turn around now, paddle to shore, dry off, and change into some warm clothes. "Shit, my brother's sitting out at the Point somewhere and there's no way he's getting a ride or coming in unless I go out and help. Shit."

"What'ya gonna do?" he asks, sliding past me.

"Shit, I'm going out, of course," a self-delusional voice filled with irony responds. Belly down on my stick, back arched high for a more responsive board trim, I begin to paddle.

He laughs again, a contagious sound from deep within his chest. He infects me, removing my pinched scowl of honest reflection and replacing it with an optimistic hint of a smile.

"What's your name?" I ask as my board draws parallel and to the left of his.

"Jonny, Jonny Paul."

"John Paul Jones?" I ask, unable to hold back, my contained smile broadening into an outright laughing face.

"No, just Jonny Paul," he deadpans back.

"Okay, just Jonny Paul. I'll see you again soon on my ride back from the Point." The prophetic understatement lands with the inevitability of worlds colliding. Dropping my right arm in the water and locking it into place, the drag slows and simultaneously swings my surfboard right so I can cross behind Jonny's stern and proceed out to the Point, while he continues stroking straight out to Sewers.

Like a swarm of black neoprene ants all scurrying for position on a liquid hill, the Point is alive with an animated mass of surfers. An inside section of worker ants sits patiently waiting to pick off leftover crumbs and drop in on the shoulder of waves should outside priority surfers outreach their capabilities and splash in spectacular fashion back into the sea. A midsection pack is randomly clustered across a football-field-size area; those outside await rare set peaks that shift south and bypass the Point, while insiders look to pick off smaller waves that roll in unnoticed and unexpectedly rise and break on the inside sandbar. The largest crowd sits outside at the Point above the underwater reef where big sets consistently stand and jack into long clean right peels, eventually petering out in the deep water of inside Sewers. From this distance there are too many identical, shiny black clones crossing and weaving for me to identify my brother's thin frame. I must pick my way through the ant farm and close the gap.

While I snake my way through the midsection, still looking to sort a brother out of the pack, a small blocking wave interrupts my view of the horizon. I use the activity of those surfers sitting outside for any hint of approaching sets. As a collective hive, the Point crew begins to stir noticeably and then swarms outside. Rather than give any indication to the midsection pack of a potential approaching set, I bluff the crowd by continuing across their beam at a forty-five degree angle while gaining a full head of steam before passing out of sight over the blocking wave. The feinting maneuver works to perfection as the local cluster still sits idly on their boards while I paddle over the wave with full momentum. Into view comes a lovely swell that will pitch into a nicely shaped, just-overhead breaker. More than a dozen surfers in various stages and at multiple angles of catching the wave make any attempt by me worthless . . . so I will let it pass.

Even without a view or hint of what is to follow, experience has taught me to assume that there is a next wave and that it is larger—and as such, to place myself in a position of priority. But with every stroke I feel as if a pound of weight is being added to my arms as they resist with a burning sensation. Only the repetitive muscle memory of many years of practice keeps them in motion. Waiting on the other side is . . . *Oh Lordy, Lordy, what do we have here, my little precious?* A rush of excitement pushes back the lethargy.

Lumbering in, two hundred meters away, a large mound of water rises with its peak taking shape just off to the right. Several surfers are already paddling down the mound, but they will slide out the back as the morning's rising tide brings the wave closer to shore before it breaks. Other surfers attempt to cheat over from the main Point take-off; however, I can see that they will be caught behind the A-frame peak that continues to shift south. Three grommets cross my bow from right to left to escape what they think will be the crashing impact zone. No need to turn around and observe what will surely be the mass confusion of a collective hive abandoned.

My immediate concern is for the four surfers in parallel with me on the right. Each is a strong paddler with good trim. With them on my starboard beam, I must yield to their right-of-way should any one of them catch the wave. Attentively eyeing the competition, I notice that these four appear to have a similar chink in their armor that may be used to my advantage, for all are target-fixated upon the onrushing peak as none of their eyes shift to take into account their situational awareness in relationship to the crowded conditions. I angle my stick just a tad to the right in violation of their personal space . . . and sure enough! Like dominoes in sequence, each surfer nudges the next just perceptively north, and in my estimation, this has pushed the outside two onto the other side of what will be the pitching A-frame. Two down, two to go. Dealing myself one last bluff card and with a burst of will, I pull lead on my competitors. Not to lose out, they aggressively follow and I lure them farther than ideal into the face whereupon I sit on the tail of my board for a quick snap turn under the peak. With two grunting strokes—*honestly arms, I won't ask anything else of you today . . . well, maybe*—I use the cresting lip as a catapult and I have the wave. A priority check over my left shoulder is required to see if any competitors have dropped in behind. This glimpse serves as an important safety check as I don't want to be speared from behind with the nose of a surfboard as notification that I should yield to their right-of-way. As planned with the right nudge, the outside pair are now behind the peak and must pull back or TOAD. And as planned, the near pair of surfers has been induced too far up the face. They are too slow to turn around and, with the help of a stiffening morning wind catching them like sails, they both slide out the back.

My backside clear, I now turn my attention down the line. Three surfers in various stages of shoulder hopping are in my path. They look at me to discern any sign of physical weakness or mental indecision so that each may pounce this wave for himself. An intense mood change alters my face; my narrowed eyes of confidence express a commanding, *Yo Bro, I've got this wave. It's all mine, and don't let your head get in the way.* With their eyes now locked on me, there is a slightly humorous curl of the mouth that indicates to them, *I'm gonna rip it, and it's gonna be fun.*

With a huge sense of relief in neither having to share the wave nor to play hydrofoil bumper cars, I watch as all three sit on their tails and are drawn up and out the wave's back side. Standing, I slip weightlessly down the face, legs flex upon reaching the wave's trough, and I crank out a long drawn-out 2G bottom turn. Posing with an indifference to the power unfurling overhead, I nonchalantly stand tall and cross to hold hands low behind a soldier-straight back, *so cool.*

Ascending in the near vertical, I swiftly bring hands forward, as I lean my body back with full weight on the right rear foot to snap turn the board horizontally just under a lip. The rising tide and diminishing surf wrap around the Point to create a light and feathery wave lip, like a wispy soufflé quickly rising to fluffy perfection.

Smaller than River Mouth's early morning grinders, this wave's breaking reach is only down to its midsection. The offshore wind continues to tear at the thin, foamy edge, creating airborne water crystals. Imitating the cylinder's watery form, I duck small and tight, and fit snugly into the wave's enveloping cocoon. Adeptly adjusting my balance on the balls of my feet, I unconsciously lean forward to trim the rail for more speed, and tuck my body lower to avoid my head being bitch slapped and upended off the board into an uncontrolled free fall. The tube exit stretches out and away.

Bogey! Bogey! Bogey!

Shit, pops into my mind as through the restricted view I become aware of three slow-paddling surfers crossing the line directly ahead, attempting to avoid getting smacked by the wave. *Gremmies,* I think, as they have had almost a full minute to paddle out of harm's way—and my way—of the oncoming wave. An optimistic analysis has me believing that the first surfer will cross behind, to be drilled by the waterfall, unless his duck-diving skills are up to par. The second surfer will, with a bit of luck, punch through the lip just ahead of me to clear a path, although I remind myself to tuck even tighter and to avoid hitting my head on his momentarily exposed tail section.

And the third lagging surfer . . . well . . . *shit.* Locked into a moving cylinder just over a meter in diameter, I have no room to maneuver, nowhere to go, and no time to bail without looking like an intentional spearing. *Shit, shit, shit!* repeating the catch phrase of the day! In the moment before impact, I step forward on my log to perl the nose and drive it underwater, instantly stopping the surfboard. Momentum launches me airborne and I again fly fully prone, Superman-style, over the gremmie. The audacious maneuver has prevented the surfboard from spearing the gremmie's unprotected right flank but his luck may change as he is about to be pitched backwards and headfirst into a cement mixer from two meters high with intertwined surfboards.

The petite beauty that I have been riding is relatively small at a little overhead, and thus causes me to underestimate its ferocity when it breaks in shallow water and I am unexpectedly worked like a rag doll in a pit bull's clenched jaws. The energy of the whitewash flood to shore eventually dissipates. With hands overhead for protection from flying surfboards, I rise up and hear an artificially forced laugh. So familiar? Senses orienting to the laugh, I turn to see a recognizable face looking at two pieces of a stark white Styrofoam board. What the fuck? It's Jonny examining the serrated edges of his surfboard snapped in half! "Jonny, you all right?"

There is confusion and disorientation in his unfocused eyes and his ashen face.

He stares at his severed board as if at an incongruent lump of limp and decaying seaweed. He gives a haunting, disconnected laugh. He pulls guppy-glazed eyes away from the floating junk before him to follow the sound of my voice. He looks at me with an unrecognizable, blank stare.

"Jonny," I repeat. "Are you okay?" I ask as I probe into his eyes for signs of pain or lucidity, neither of which are apparent.

Jonny blinks his unfocused eyes slow and hard, taking a few shallow breaths—"Yeah, I'm fine"—and begins to contemplate the unique design of his new, two-piece, custom wave rider. His surfboard is sliced across at a forty-five degree angle with ragged edges tapering out to a sharp point.

He speaks in a disconnected whisper. "How the hell am I going to explain to my friends that I snapped my board in three-foot surf?"

Oh, Jonny, you kindred spirit, you are back. Fuck the piece of refined petroleum jelly, clear hard resin, and stringy fiberglass junk. You're all right. I'm okay. Buy another stick. The humiliation of losing face in front of friends in fun surf, now therein lies the real tragedy. Five-meter waves with ten-meter faces, an adventure that gets your gonads tight even if you never actually catch a wave; now that is a story to tell. Head-high shit like this, you're just gonna look stupid.

"Jonny, just tell 'em there was some old, out of control kook that ran you over and snapped your stick," I suggest, gladly playing the fall guy.

Something instinctive raises the small hairs at the base of my neck. Into my periphery glides a spring-suit covered surfer, arms and legs bare to the chill elements, who diverts my attention from Jonny's endeavor to marry the two-piece puzzle laid out before him. I curiously glance at the the chiseled surfer as he throws out "Idiot" just loud enough to reach across the ten meters separating us. Our eyes lock and he attempts to stare me down with *the look.*

My face goes blank with retrospective thought. Is he saying I am an idiot because by some flaw of observation I dropped in on what was actually his priority wave? Or, was he sitting inside and saw the unfortunate, destructive collision between Jonny and me? Or, more threatening to my physiological being, does he really know who I am and that I am truly just an *idiot*? Or, as I begin to lose it, is he a messenger from a demonic demigod sent to expose my façade of fake, rational normalcy? The thin, containing shell within me cracks, and something worms out. "Keep paddling and mind your own shit," spits out of my mouth with a fire-breathing burst.

He hesitates for a moment, not quite sure, as if not quite able to comprehend. "You!" His jaw sets hard, his back flares, arching higher off the board. "You're outta the water, Bro."

In an uncontainable instant, I am a complete psychotic Chernobyl meltdown with radioactive poison spewing. "Fuck ya kook, Brah," are the corrosive words of sarcastic brine I spew as I then sign my death warrant with a handful of seawater splashed at him. I have acknowledged him as "da brah" of watermen, yet I have insulted him with the lowest level of surfer: "kook." I have told him I am going to kick his fucking little weenie ass. I have slapped water at him. I am about to be murdered.

The incredulous look on the face of someone who believes the whole world bends to his physically intimidating presence is almost worth my impending mutilation and resulting total physical paralysis.

He freezes midpaddle as his pea brain overheats in an attempt to digest the shock of my Euclidian repartee. Slowly his eyes illuminate in understanding and a hardened mask of determination is cast upon his chiseled face. He slips off his board—the quicker to reach me—and swims barracuda fast towards me.

"Brah" easily outweighs me by fifty pounds of hardened, sculpted muscle. A lifetime of surfing without a protective wetsuit has made his sun-bronzed skin as thick as rhino hide and impervious to our hostile environment as he is apparently indifferent to my challenging stare. Curiously, an interesting little ditty loops around my thoughts with the funny possibility that, given some time and space, it may be a comical dirge sung by all gathered round me one last time: *Forearms bigger than my thighs and I'm gonna die. Forearms bigger than my thighs and I'm gonna die.*

There is not an intensity of hate or anger in my assailant's eyes but rather a blank, empty stare, a void seen in attacking sharks, which sends a shiver through my soul. It will be a long while before I will physically be able to surf again, after, of course, many years of psychological counseling so that I can even enter the water—perhaps a first reentry somewhere high up in the High Sierras fly-fishing for rainbow trout in a secluded and tranquil lake.

But it's too late. A reactionary, ancestral reptilian being hatches from my cracked and now-shattered core, and I reciprocate his charge by sliding off my surfboard to swim in a collision course towards my jousting opponent. Some primordial instinct for survival awakens as I hit the chilled water and realize my only chance to see another sunrise is to use those two pounds—apparently shorted well below the three-pound average—of gray matter between my ears. Human survival and ascendency have never been about our physical prowess; we are relatively slow, have weak muscles, and are thin-skinned. It is rather our intellectual ingenuity and our intrinsic adaptiveness that make us the dominant species on Earth.

I have a quickly diminishing minute to live . . . think . . . adapt . . . before being devoured by . . . nothing.

I vaguely take in the thought that at least my corpse will be found with the ankle leash preventing a still and lifeless body from sinking to flesh-feeding bottom fish and recycling back into the sushi food chain. Wait . . . the leash can be used as a garrote to strangle Brah around his neck . . . except I don't know how to make a garrote . . . nor do I know how to use a garrote . . . never mind that I don't have the arm length to actually reach *around* his stump neck.

Moving between Jonny and his cleaved surfboard, my hand unconsciously reaches out to clasp the severed nose section. Perhaps today is
not the day I shall so easily be dispatched? Flipping the wreck around, I
point the shattered half, sliced to a jagged and sharpened end, directly
into the face of one who is about to assault me. My arm reaches back,
muscles flexing taut as a catapult, ready to sling the newly created javelin into the surface-level eyes of my attacker. The impromptu weapon
will not kill him or knock him out, and it may not even blind or hurt
him, but the pointed stick with razor-sharp shards of broken fiberglass
and resin will cut him badly and make him bleed like a stuck pig . . .
perfect shark bait.

Just inches from the weapon's release point, Brah looks up from
his charge. He pauses. He treads water with his chin at surface level.
He cocks his head at an angle, attempting to understand the strange
configuration aimed at him. A coiled sea serpent, I coldly, emotion-
lessly, wait. There is no worldly awareness other than that of our eyes
trading heat half a board length apart. He feels the desperate, cornered
animal within me. He suddenly realizes his impending mauling. He
says, in a slow, measured tone, nothing moving on his face other than
lips, "You'll both be outta the water before the next set." A lifeline that
should be wholeheartedly embraced without pause, and yet unable to
contain myself, with salt-crusted sarcasm I reply, "We're done for the
day anyhow with a snapped stick, duh." *Really! And have I lived so long,
how?*

Brah coolly swims to his surfboard and without a look back slips
over the rail and begins stroking out to the Point. My blanched-white
fingers relax their grip on my impromptu pike. The constricting
band around the chest loosens and allows for a deep, relaxed breath.
Quivering bowels come back under control.

"Jonny." His distant gaze staring after Brah. "Jonny!" He turns to me,
silent and sullen and withdrawn. "Here, get on the board and we'll belly
board in. Now!" Muscle memory has him reflexively grab the offered
nose piece, trimming the partial board with his weight evenly distrib-
uted over its surface. With the board leash still attached to his ankle,
the tail piece is tossed to our opposite side, reducing the possibility

of the flotsam hitting Jonny in the back of the head as it follows us to shore with the next wave.

Reaching the water's cobblestone edge, we hustle out before the next wave unceremoniously sweeps our feet from underneath us. With surprising serendipity, my brother awaits above us on the slight incline of beach. Beyond the high-tide line, standing in sunbaked, ocean-smelling seaweed with the scent of death and decay, he is still dripping and shakes his head with water flying off in a minishower.

"Hey." I try to sell him on a life of normalcy with a harmonious tenor voice and a single word.

"What's that?" he demands, flicking his eyes to Jonny and the unique two-piece wave rider, one half held under each arm.

A quick sideways glance at the figure above us causes Jonny to ask me, with life coming back into voice, "Hey, is that your brother?" Our natural resemblance is unmistakable, despite my obviously superior good looks.

With some deep-seated need not to disappoint, I engage Jonny to distract my brother and respond, "Yes, Jonny, this is my brother." And for show, "And this is my new friend, Jonny. We just met in the water." No truer words ever were spoken.

Jonny's eyes instantly flare up with the intensity of a zealot. Lips stumbling to keep up with his brain's thoughts, Jonny fires off, "Your brother is a fucking maniac who almost got us fucking killed . . . twice!" *Nice and subtle Jonny, thanks.* "Jesus!" *Did I say zealot or what?* "Jesus! First your brother tried to kill me by taking my head off . . ." Jonny is off and running, an unstoppable burst of steam from a leaking boiler, recounting from our first accidental meeting to Brah swimming away, all laced with expletives, arm gestures, and body puppeteering.

Jonny's excited tenor voice soars upon the sky to orchestrate with that chaotic chorus of seagull screeches as they swoop overhead. In the morning's vacant blue sky, stark white gulls—orange webbed feet, streamlined underbelly, outstretched white wings with tips of gray charcoal, and an unnaturally rose-red teardrop on the underside of each of their bright yellow beaks—glide along the stiff breeze back and forth, to and fro. "Awwwk! Eeew. Awwwk! Awwwk, awwk, eeew." The repetitive shrill cries are at an attention-grabbing octave and volume that rattle and become like the annoying cackle of an old woman with nothing more interesting to say than, "Look at me, poor me, look at me."

In the hours since our early morning arrival in that gray cast of dawn, the shoreline has become alive with activity. The sun has risen sufficiently to provide an inviting heat to those with an ordinary sense and sensibility who arise from their down-comforted beds to enjoy a revitalization of their being in the crispness of a spectacular autumn morning. The salty sea air is wonderful to breathe, as the large breakers that continually shoot heavy salt water sky-high leave a low, foggy mist blanketing the coastal margin to ionize the air and drive all pollutants to ground. Beach-cruising bikers slide along the path in their lowriders, many with dogs—some with recalcitrant dogs in tow, some with happy dogs leaning in to tow, and some with small and seemingly nervous dogs in baskets. Happy couples walk together, hand in hand.

Bleary-eyed beachcombers with puffy faces and mussed hair that may be making a fashion statement move in a staccato gait upon the sand above the cobblestone edge, as a late-morning stiffness still grips their joints. Bundled against the moist, penetrating air, they plow the sandy strip hunting for unique, weatherworn wood that has washed up from distant shores, or those with metal detectors dig sifters into the sand hoping to pull up golden treasures that have slipped from inattentive bathers.

Arriving along with the others are those noon-gooners, surfers who arise only after they are fully sated with sleep and who are unwilling to discomfort themselves in pursuit of a lifestyle. Noon-gooners who, under fairer and temperate weather, arrive much later in the morning with a hot café mocha in hand, or, worse yet, in the early afternoon with girlfriends in tow.

Noon, when the sun glows warmer to thus raise the Earth's temperature and kick up thermals that twist the wind onshore to blemish and crumble the waves' youthful and clear faces of early morning. We, who so adamantly deride those noon-gooners, fear that we ourselves may one day become one of them. For with a certainty the body slowly ages and eventually falters, unable to endure nature's forces, unable to compete against the pack. We, who often with a guilty conscience shirk and avoid and resist the pressures of societal responsibilities that may keep us away. The fire inside quells, unwilling to rise, unable to perform, and then we are no longer unique as adults still living out a childish pursuit.

Gazing up at that annoying colony of squawking seagulls, I fantasize about being one of them. For sensing an approaching weather disturbance, they simply escape by spreading their wings to catch the uplifting thermals that effortlessly carry them over the coastal mountains to the calm serenity of a lush and green valley that waits beyond.

I deceive myself knowingly for there would be no tranquility in my escape. I purposely look for the aligned ripples of nature's distant fury; I fling myself into my other mistress of the breaking sea. I expel all irrational thoughts, with nothing left to feed the entity that silently incubates within, with that physical exertion and mental focus . . . and there is then a short emotional respite. Eventually, as a human, as a man, as the responsible one, at some point, I will have to turn and face that which torments me so.

Jonny's excited narrative is coming to the end of his story, our story, with the paddling away of our mutual antagonist, "Brah." His continuous run-on sentences have increased in pitch and speed as he seeks to complete his words before his lungs run out of air.

Framed from behind by the rolling brown foothills, my brother continues to stand above us, seemingly indifferent to Jonny's excited pantomime. Listening, observing, glancing now and then between us, his face shows nothing.

Eventually my brother fixates a stare upon me. He bores in, mining me for some quartz vein that leads to the mother lode of my explanation for my recently aberrant behavior. Sunk deep and buried into the sand would be a good place to be, covered and hidden from his unspoken inquisition. "Who are you now? Do I know you anymore? What the fuck do you want to tell me?" There is something within— still unidentifiable—attempting to worm its way up from a deep and dark place to protrude an ugly reptilian head from which one should recoil in horror. Enigmatic thoughts and crazy notions are still too slippery to grasp, never mind an ability to articulate and share them with comprehension. And what of the turmoil and pressure of that other's inherent, binding obligation never to share, never to speak of or even acknowledge the existence of such nebulous thoughts of the one sharing? Then there is an overriding apprehension that unburdening such a poisoned psyche may in fact spread a contagion to those close to us and within our realm of responsibility.

The wind is off Jonny's sail as he luffs in the pause of his completed tale. My brother and I continue to size each other up. Everything we have has been left in the sea, nothing to spare. We are wrung out and jelled.

"All is good, Brutha. No worries," I concede, while adding to myself, *Just you being here with me is enough, more than enough.* "Hey! You owe me a chili-cheese omelet, and Jonny can come along as well." By wrapping a free arm over his shoulder, I pull Jonny along, a human shield deflecting from my brother, should it be necessary. My submissive, conciliatory offering can only elicit from me a weak and self-effacing smile. We silently size up a lifetime of each other—many things understood, others taken for granted—silent but together.

"Let me check and see if I brought my wallet; I may have left it at home." My brother chuckles. Smiles broaden reassuringly. We laugh together at our inside joke. We walk across the beach to stack our logs in the van. We peel off our wetsuits with jerks and tugs, twists and pulls, before we crawl into dry clothes that will soon warm us. Exposed for the moment naked to the elements, I gaze up and follow those meandering contours of the brown coastal mountains and allow my thoughts to drift beyond to my sanctuary of a still-slumbering seductress.

The Pacific Ocean is a brilliant expanse of shimmering silver white as sunlight bounces and dances along from furrow to crest of each little windswept ripple.

The spawned litter of a distant She-Wolf's fury intermittently scampers up the beach as if to shake off a perpetual wetness and impetuously suckle while firmly planted upon terra firma. Fluffy sea-foam paws scurry shoreward with abandon in a sudden yelping of rushing excitement, "*Whooshhhh!*" soon followed with a subdued whimpering warble of retreat, "*shyyyyyyy . . .*"

Earth accompanies water's brash chorale in second chair as rolling cobblestones noisily coerced up the beach with the swiftly rushing white water bang along to resonate in hauntingly hollow and sullen bass tones. The slate-gray cobbles, intersected with intricately woven spiderwebbed white veins, have been worn slippery smooth over the millennia of their attempts to escape a perpetual drowning before inevitably rolling back into the salty sea's eternally wet and cold clutches.

~~~~~~~

PRANCING
RED STALLION

You and me
    are not meant to be;
      that is easy enough
        for both of us to see.

Yet that which will never be
      conspires to unbind and set us free,
    free for thee to melt with me
with me forlorn and lost in thee.

For married and not,
    or no matter,
  May and September,
    We've simply had enough,
    and we disregard
the glancing barbs
    of polite society.

"We tolerate the prying eyes
                        ("We bare our souls)
that calls out our masquerade,
                            (as we dance
                               in privacy,)
beneath our lover's courage,
                        (not in marriage,
                        sanctimoniously,)
as we must live in fear of sin,
                        (that love unfurls
                   naked and unmasked,)
pretending to tame the demons
                         (undeniably,)
    hiding in our heads,
                    (as upon our demeanor
               the truth plainly displays)
               and tomorrow upon life's stage
                        (for all to see)
we'll play out the tangled blues
    of our paltry bit parts,
                    (and thus we confess
              the tempest of our hearts)
come what may, or be,
    and all in between."
                  (that no mythical Greek Muse
                         can foresee.")

Indubitably,
  upon our final parting way,
    proper manners dictate
    tacit courtesies;
Inevitably,
  as one exits beyond
    the shine of stage lights,
      and reach of lover's embrace;

Pensively
  lower your shy eyes
    prior to our polite, last bodies entwined
      and long kiss good-bye;
Justifiably,
  no bargaining,
    no looking back,
      nor awkward, false friendships.

For you and me
  are without regrets,
    —having lived and loved freely—
That we never told each other
  of those parts that we dearly
    love of one another,
      "Forever of me will be
      your tall, gangly femininity."
No regrets that we never spoke,
  spoke of those parts that we love,
    —unafraid of what will not be—
Love of one another,
  of you, of you . . . and of me.

~~~

An enshrouding foul mood has Sheri's right foot firmly pressing the throttle while racing her little rice rocket as fast as it can pedal towards town. Ignoring the frenzy of wind-tossed hair in her face from the car's open windows, she traverses miles of straight and narrow roadways bisecting farms of well-groomed crop fields, her mind a swirl of introspective thought at her mother's morning betrayal. Perfectly measured and machine-dug furrows rapidly flash by Sheri's peripheral vision in a stuttering blur. As the muddy, black grooves flick, flick, flick along, her racing mind goes, *clickity-clickity-clickity, clickity-clickity-clickity,* and she is reminded of the rhythmic slapping of a wooden stick against a white picket fence while riding a bicycle as a young girl. *Clickity-clickty-clickity, clickity-clickity-clickity*—her thoughts run wild.

Those long, water-trickling rows of soil are the open slots of her envisioned picket fence. Alternating with each long furrow that stretches away into the distance are rolling mounds of plowed dirt breached with the growth of morning-glistening green crops, the white posts of Sheri's childhood fantasy—*clickity-clickity-clickity, clickity-clickity-clickity*—that keep her mind bouncing. Protruding from the earthen mounds are short, floppy headdress greens that hide a rainbow of colorful vegetables under cool, moist soil: hip-high shrubs with broad and sun-mopey leaves shield plump, ripening fruit from view; stately, pole-straight green stalks bolt upright overhead, capped with plumes of sun-yellow silk threads that are the proud crowns encasing vaults of golden, sweet kernels.

The blended shades of green crops form the weft and warp of an expansive, ripening tapestry that has been embroidered with images of lush life undulating out in all directions. Only the occasional farmhouse, surrounded by the requisite shade trees and driveways connected to the byways, interrupts the regimented green carpet of a plant world with signs of human overseers. Naturally embracing this grand expanse of man's intricately woven tapestry of produce in a gently sloping swaddle are two congruent mountain ranges that run the north-to-south length of the Central Valley. The flowing evergreen valley itself is eventually dammed at its southern terminus by a third, perpendicular range of mountains that rises up from the unbroken farm lands as a confining fortress wall.

Driving into the morning sun, Sheri faces those distant, rolling brown-grass foothills, which are the sputtering end of the grand Sierra Nevada. As they stretch northward, these gentle slopes will soon begin to rise and meld to become those pointy, castle-keep spires of glacial-chiseled granite and quartz-veined mountains that display the most fascinating shades of gray. North-facing granite walls with deep and angular crevices hidden from the sun are slashed with white snow year-round. With an occasional glance in the rearview mirror, Sheri can see the southern terminus of the California Coast Ranges that separates the San Joaquin Valley from the blue Pacific Ocean. The northernmost end of this range extends beyond San Francisco before the mountains themselves drop off and disappear into the sea.

To Sheri's right and closer still are the east-west running Tehachapi Mountains that suddenly rise up from the tabletop-flat valley floor to a height of eight thousand feet, acting as a bridge that connects the terminus of the Sierra Nevada foothills with the coastal ranges. So steep is this rise of the Tehachapis that no tracks can be laid for a locomotive to climb that face and connect the rural fruit and vegetable and nut basket that feeds the world to its distribution points at the outskirt land of imagination and fantasy, the dream capital of celluloid illusion. Thus the world's busiest single-track railroad must escape the grand valley by heading east through a crease of the Sierra Nevada foothills and ascend this sloping grade through eighteen tunnels along rails that uniquely spiral once in a loop over themselves before descending onto the high Mojave Desert and then off past Hollywood to awaiting trucks and ships.

Whipping along the raised asphalt roadway, Sheri ignores her loose, shoulder-blade length two-tone hair—sun-bleached blonde on top with a vivid auburn tint underneath—that flies around her head in a chaotic golden halo as she absentmindedly views the rapidly passing crop fields, *clickity-clickity-clickity, clickity-clickity-clickity*. The buffeting wind from open windows is her poor man's cooler, keeping her from baking under a late summer sun in the metal oven of a car sorely lacking air-conditioning while traveling upon a shadscale scrub desert plain made fertile green only by man's ingenuity—or theft, depending on which side of the state one resides. Sheri imagines retreating to curl up like some small furry animal into the cool darkness of those shaded and reclusive furrows that flick, flick by, to, for a moment, escape the valley's oppressive heat and rest her weary mind.

Her small, freckled nose begins to twitch like a little rabbit alone and exposed in an open field of alfalfa, scenting for the best of budding greens to eat. Her breathing is a sharp sniffing, allowing the sinus cavities high in the nasal passages to sort through a sampling of both strong and subtle smells that the high-speed wind tunnel offers up from the fields. Folded within the mixed bouquet, childhood memories guide her through a plethora of fondly remembered fragrances. Suddenly she snorts, most unladylike, exhaling a dose of putrid, petroleum-based pesticides recently laid over a nearby tomato field. She holds her breath, waiting. Tentatively whiffing again, she relaxes, drawing in a deep breath and wallowing in the unmistakable—and her favorite— smell of sweet Spanish onions.

She welcomes the pungent essence of bolting onions on her daily commute as the morning's refreshing awakening to the mental exhaustion of her seemingly continuously contentious life. Her foot eases slightly off the accelerator as her hands release their stranglehold on the steering wheel, and her shoulders slump forward to relax. Sheri focuses her thoughts on those events from earlier this morning that have her so agitated. Only on those rare occasions when she is alone does she delve deep into her complicated and conflicted emotions, for she is soon frustratingly swept up in an internal emotional tempest.

She recalls the two unanticipated admissions from the emergency room up to her unit just after midnight that had both delayed, and lengthened, staff reports at the end of her swing shift. Anxiously rushing, Sheri had been relieved to arrive home and find Robby up and dressed, sitting at the dinette table, and watching the Comedy Channel. Opening the refrigerator door to prepare a sandwich for him to pack off to school, Sheri was more than a little bit dismayed to find only a can of Cheez Whiz and a box of crackers inside. Knowing what would be found elsewhere around the house, Sheri's heart sank and her jaw clenched with feelings of anger and betrayal.

The previous day Sheri had been late for class. Prior to dashing off to school, and knowing that afterwards she would study in the campus library before heading off to her twelve-hour swing shift at the hospital, she had fumbled through her purse to find what little cash was lying at the bottom and handed it to her mother for groceries. At the time, Sheri had thought that putting the cash in her hand was a safe bet as her mother had been sober and lucid for several weeks running. Now, standing motionless before the open refrigerator and feeling the cold air envelop her, Sheri knew with certainty that she would only have to look under the front porch to find empty liquor bottles and in the bedroom to find her mother passed out in a drunken stupor on the bed, if her mom had even made it that far. Her disbelieving gaze was returned by the refrigerator's cold and vacant hold. Suppressing a fiery, quick temper that had her wanting to burst into her mother's room, throw cold water in her face to wake her, and confront her, was the immediate, pragmatic reality that it was late and the school bus would be arriving shortly for Robby.

Hiding frustration that had her wanting at first to cry and then to strangle someone, Sheri asked with restrained control, "Hey Robby?" Not wanting to be interrupted from watching the TV show, his only acknowledgement of her existence was a quick glance in her direction before his eyes refocused on the flat-screen Claymation. Robby smirked as a head exploded.

"Uh, there's gonna be some Cheez Whiz and crackers in your lunch today. See if one of your friends maybe'll share a sandwich or have something that they don't want that you can have. Okay?"

"Yeah, sure, Sis, like no problemo," all said while not taking his eyes off the television.

Continuing her drive along the empty and isolated roadways, Sheri reflects on Robby's unconcern with going to school with nothing other than a few saltines and some emulsified cheese. She knows Robby was correct, and that it would be no problem for him to find a friend with whom to share a lunch. Robby is a resilient kid—maybe like all kids? she wonders. He has an affable and unassuming nature that endears him to those he meets. He is calm and polite, always listening, rarely doing the talking himself. But when he does speak, he knows what he is saying, conveying that he had been not only listening but also comprehending what had been said in the greater context of everything else that was going on.

At the most random times, Robby would wistfully question Sheri about their adventures with their father, a time farther back than he could remember: weekend trips river rafting in the mountains, morning rides over the coastal ranges to the beach for fast and seemingly dangerous dune-buggy rides over the sand, or especially the late summer-night excursions to the noisy drag strip. The only images from "before" that were on the fringe of his remembrance were those of the helmeted racers in colorful jumpsuits and his primordial fright of the loud, nitrous-fuel explosions and the shooting exhaust flames of burnt orange.

Sheri has a different set of questions, though they were never broached and they are for her mother. She often wonders at the disparity of siblings with such contrasting dispositions as that of his laid-back "whatever" personality versus her own quick and confrontational in-your-face temper. As Robby matured, Sheri began to notice and understand the physical differences between brother and sister. He, with his Black Irish dark locks, wide-open dark eyes, and pale, freckled skin that never tans but only burns to turn a painful pink, has traits not known on either side of their family lineage. She has, on the other hand, with her naturally blonde hair, Eastern European almond eyes, high cheekbones, and golden skin that tans to reveal an inherited hint of Indian ink, all recognizable, traceable family traits. Only in the freckles across the bridge of their noses and out under their eyes do brother and sister seem to share the same characteristics.

Sheri wonders if Robby is the fortunate one to never have ever really known their father and thus never to feel the inconsolable loss and helplessness one feels with the passing of a loved one. Or whether she is the lucky one for having glowed in his love, if only for a short time. Sheri had not yet come to realize that this loss had instilled in her a fear of being alone, of not being with a man, even if it was only a boy, and that driving was the only time in her life that she actually allowed herself to be alone.

Slipping two fingers into her jeans pocket, she rubs the old, classic Camaro key that no longer has an ignition to turn over. Touching the cold steel, she once again feels the pang of an empty space in her heart that has been there since her father's passing.

The road endlessly, mindlessly stretches away before her. Tired from the demanding hours of work, mentally worn down by challenging class assignments, and emotionally drained from enabling her mother's dependency, which resulted in that morning's events, Sheri ponders one slippery noodle of thought she had not previously cared to grasp, like many thoughts squirming through the recesses of her mind she did not dare to confront, that demanded a look over.

In the unfolding clarity that had come to her since going back to school, Sheri has concluded that the time constraints of being a good student requires the same focused selfishness as any professional athlete; there will be only one chance to prove herself and there are only so many hours in the day. She has pondered an offered opportunity to move out on her own, closer to school and the hospital, to allow more time to concentrate on her studies.

Yet she is conflicted that doing so will result in having to once again farm out Robby to another family member or neighbor and to leave her mother behind, and alone. Before Sheri moved back in, when her mother was drinking heavily and unable to even take care of herself, a neighbor family had opened their home to Robby. With his eventual return to Mother, the temporarily adoptive family had called to notify Sheri, their only comments being: "What a pleasure it is to have him around, and he is so polite." This is her Robby? They did not lecture, and they did not pry, other than to ask, "How are things going, Sheri? Anything we can do to help?"

Within her weary mind she is torn between blood loyalty to family—taking care of her mother and younger sibling—and what others might have viewed as a youthful, self-centered selfishness, to move out on her own. A gnawing, guilty sense of responsibility for abandoning them, again, weighs heavily on her conscience.

She had left them behind once before, at the time happily so, to run off and marry Fish Face—Travis Mannship—the day after she graduated high school.

Two wasted years of snorting and toking, stoned and high. In that time there had been little contact with her mother and little brother, for which she was now very sorry. It had taken another two full years to climb out of her addictive hole and to sober up, but Sheri was clean now, and Travis would soon be sloughed off, and inked over—physically, legally, financially, and emotionally. Her previous abandonment of family is a thin black veil that lies heavily over her heart. To stay, she only foresees an empty, unfulfilling future where they all sink together. To stay, she only hears the torments of sweet calling sirens that charm her snakes back to their addictive ways.

Beginning in the near distance and stretching out to the horizon, the surveyor-straight road shimmers under a thin layer of mirage water. The mind-bending optical illusion merges the simmering-hot black asphalt with the vacant blue-gray sky. The reflective mirror so blends road and sky that the two are indistinguishable, and the roadway drops off into an empty gray chasm of infinity. Sheri wishes she could drive fast enough to catch that void and disappear from everyone and everything . . . forever.

A sudden glint of sparkling light interrupts her sullen, self-destructive musings. Glancing at the side mirror, from which the reflective sunlight flashes, Sheri spots a large white object swiftly catching her from the left rear quarter. A quick surge of adrenaline lifts her from her inner funk and her heart begins to race. With a quick left foot clutch-in, she drops the stick shift from fifth to fourth gear, her right foot presses the accelerator pedal to the floor, and the car leaps forward. The engine loudly whines up to a high pitch as it climbs towards maximum revs. Sheri turns her head with a happy smile as a small and low-winged crop-dusting plane pulls parallel with her. She honks the car horn twice even as she knows the toots quickly will be gathered up and lost in the wind.

The crop duster has been flying since sunrise, laying a fine, light film of pesticide before the earth warms and the winds blow and the fine mist then misses its intended targets. The gull-white plane is spotted and splattered at its leading edges with the black-dot guts of impacting bug kill. The single-engine plane zooms at car-top level over the croplands. Sheri observes the pilot's helmeted head through a large, clear bubble canopy. At the forehead of his white helmet is the half arch of a rising sun with blood-red rays streaking back overhead. Bug-eyed, large mirrored aviator glasses reflectively stare blankly back at her.

Sheri has often wondered if the crop-dusting pilots ever attempt to escape the pressing summer heat of the lower valley and fly the short distance over the Santa Ynez Mountains behind them to reach the cool breezes of an awaiting Pacific Ocean. If she had the chance, she knew she would.

She waves and the pilot responds with a thumbs-up salute and a dip of the right wing, seemingly as a challenge. In the thrill of a race, she excitedly leans forward in that self-delusional effort to squeeze out the last bit of speed from her small and now very vocal four-banger. The road's painted white center dashes flash by ever more quickly, blurring into one seemingly continuous solid stripe.

Upon reaching the overhead power lines with the state-dividing aqueduct running underneath, the small plane, with its broad, strong wings, deftly swoops up and over to smoothly descend again once safely clear of the entangling cables. The road ahead of Sheri rises in a slight ramp, traversing the gently flowing aqueduct, and in an unconscious moment of the wildly young, she keeps her throttle foot to the floor, takes her hands off the steering wheel, and places her palms flat against the car's headliner. Upon reaching the road's crest, the car launches airborne to weightlessly sail over the clear blue, life-nourishing water. The road, the fields, the horizon all disappear from Sheri's vision; only the cloudless, dispassionate sky opening to the vault of heaven fills the windshield's view. Sheri's stomach feels tickled by the wingtips of fluttering butterflies attempting to take flight and escape through her constricted throat before an impending annihilation. To set her butterflies free, Sheri screams!

The car impacts the unforgiving blacktop, bottoming out the old springs and spongy shocks. The seat belt tensioners do their job of keeping her from being speared in the chest by the steering column, holding Sheri's upper torso erect against the bucket seat, but are destroyed in this mission from ever being used again. Her unsupported head snaps forward. Heavy from the g-force-laden, descent-arresting crash, her roof-planted hands instinctively fall to grasp the steering wheel. The car bounces . . . airborne again.

She slowly lifts the leaded weight of her head. She blinks hard to focus her vision and clear her mind. A still-confused Sheri observes the passing road lined straight and true, trailing out to . . . the end of Earth.

Unleashed from her primitive being, Sheri emits an ear-curdling, primal yell . . . loud . . . and long . . . warbling into shrill laughter with a broad, open-mouthed smile, indistinguishable from animal crying. Slapping her palms on the steering wheel and stamping her feet into the floorboard, tears soon begin rolling down her high cheeks to drip off her chin. Breathing in short hiccup gasps with sniffles of sputum and with her entire body shaking from her self-induced scare, Sheri wipes tears from her face with the back of her hands and then, with her fingers, catches the moisture pocketed in the corners of her welling, still-sultry eyes. She goes limp. Her mind is a blank screen with no more thought than that of drugged intoxication and the simple pleasure of existence. For the moment . . . she is jelled. Her remaining drive to town is a quiet, misty blur, nothing more than the pack animal's mindless repetition of following a well-worn track day after day. Nothing is seen . . . or felt . . . or remembered of the remaining journey—only the awareness that one has somehow finally arrived at her destination.

~~~~~

"Make it stop! It hurts!"

"Oh stop yourself, you whiny little girl."

"I'm not a little girl! It's burning."

"It doesn't hurt that much."

"*Please*, I don't want any more."

"Oh please. Ya knew it was gonna hurt."

"Yeah, lika, I knowa. But not this much. *Please?* Maybe later?"

"Like, don't be a prissy little shit and get all girly soft on me now."

"I'm not prissy. It's like that part of my skin is really sensitive, ya know?"

"You are a prissy beeatch, fer sura. You're getting what you wanted, so suffer."

"No, you're just a self-centered bitch, that's what it is."

"No, you're a—"

"*Ladies!*" Sean says with a sharpness in his tone that reaches the girls to still them. The compact room is momentarily silent as he takes his foot off the pedal. "I need Marissa to stay still, or I'm gonna fuck it up, got it?" Said with a look to Sheri. Sean takes a deep breath and, after a moment's pause, is once again composed. Eyes refocus down to Marissa's exposed milky-white ass. The girls turn to look at each other, and locking eyes, they both simultaneously contort faces while silently sticking out their tongues. Slowly exhaling, Sean cautiously increases the pressure of his left hand to firmly press down for control of Marissa's right cheek. Stretching her soft, compliant skin into a flat, workable palette on which to finish his artistic design, Sean presses the tube tip to her flesh and steps on the pedal. A low, humming vibration resonates around the small room as Sean works smoothly to color a section of her milky skin with jungle green. Small beads of perspiration form on his brow as the overworked air conditioner is unable to adequately dissipate either the heat of three tightly confined bodies or Sean's wandering and lusting mind.

The seductive exposure of Marissa's female form lying facedown on the masseuse table with her shirt pulled up under ribs and her jeans and panties pulled down to her cheek-thigh crease is a consternation to the animal-man within Sean. He reasons to himself that the requested exposure of so much of Marissa's smooth, soft skin was not because he is such a leching perv—no—but rather that he is the consummate professional with the vision of creating a work of art on a virgin canvas of flesh. Any two-bit hack with a tattoo machine can place ink on the spot that a customer points to; however, a true artisan will share a client's dream to display their desire as a work of art on their skin. His experience and his talent enable him to place lines that flow harmoniously with the individual's human form and are designed in relation to other existing tattoos, not just as blobs of colorful ink floating out there in space. Once Marissa was comfortable enough to peel her clothes away for Sean to survey her canvas of skin, he simply left her lying there to calm her flighty nature from fleeing with a partial redress. Contributing to Sean's carnal agitation, he has to admit, is the recognition that Marissa has a really fine, tight, white ass. And there lies the rub—in his left hand.

"It's looking really good, Marissa," he calmly reassures her, and himself, with a soothing tone that he hopes will still the twitchy little bird. "This location on your cheek gives some nice, fleshy, animated lines. Here the color and depth is awesome, making it look beautifully alive." Beautiful may not be in Sean's daily, parlor-grunge vocabulary, but he knows his audience and so plays the commercial artist well.

"Beautiful? Really? For sure?"

"Yeah, it looks like some green snot hangin' on your ass," Sheri chimes in.

"Nuh-uh. Does not! It looks really tight."

"It's not a tree frog clinging to your ass. It's some green thingee crawlin' outta your butt hole."

"No, it's totally badass is what it is."

"Yeah, badass like *your* droopy ass."

"Liar!"

"Now you finally got your own little tramp stamp of approval."

"Better than your huge USDA certified whore whomp of used and abused!"

"You sure you wanna be going there?"

"Like you're a virgin."

"Says Miss Saint Bernard."

"Fuck you!"

"Sheri!" Sean snaps. Calmly, with a display of control and a change of tone, he continues, "I need you to go see Peewee and get me another set of inks. Also, bring me a Diet Pepsi." His unusually short temper is assumed by the girls to be the result of his weariness from hours of concentrating on his meticulous work in the warm room while simultaneously listening to their constant barrage of girlish bickering. If he were questioned, he would simply reaffirm this misconception that is, in fact, a fallacy he at times hides behind. Nothing so mundane as smelly bodies in summer heat nor the sound of nails scratching across a chalkboard conducts that electric current along the cold film of his body perspiration and snaps his skin to shrink drum tight and frazzles his brain with a warning of something more insidious lurking within. Years of experience battling a conquered addiction have taught him to play for time and to make it to day's end . . . "For this, too, shall pass," would be Grandmother's well-worn refrain. The voltage intensifies like a leech sickly sucking at every pore of his skin, with a fear arising that he is losing and wants to, and will, fall prey within the hour. He tells himself to stay busy. "Sheri, could you do me that favor now, please?"

"I kinda wanted to stay and watch your handiwork, but sure thing," Sheri answers as she uncrosses her skinny legs on the adjacent table and stands up while giving Marissa a look. Facedown with her cheeks nestled in the open face cradle of the tattoo table, Marissa's jet-black hair splays out in an arc to cover her upper back. Sheri feels a burning irritation that can only be scratched if she is able to give that exposed, sweet, white round mound of Marissa's, perched waist high and oh so very vulnerable, a sharp backhanded smack. It takes all of Sheri's self-control, a commodity of restraint that she has always shown to be a limited resource, not to reach over and slap that naked butt. But she will not do so with Sean still needle-etching Marissa's skin. Sheri opens the door and walks out of the tattooing room.

To distract himself from his inner cravings, Sean contemplates the unseen dark-matter gravitational force that binds these two disparate personages together as friends. Marissa's teenage-thin, pretty little nymphet girl body, with silky, flowing hair that frames a flawless porcelain-doll face of fairest complexion and thin lips, is an irresistible lure to attending men. Good looks she may have, yet with an underlying personality as easily shattered as her porcelain-thin skin of no natural colors, for this effervescent fairy that floats among the men of the tattoo shop seems to seek some boost of confidence and self-approbation within by glancing upon herself in every reflective surface she passes. In personal conversations, Marissa reflexively nods her head in agreement as if in understanding; yet her dark eyes become twitchy—like little furry prey looking for predators upon open plain, about to bounce and flee to another place—whenever the topic shifts from either complimenting her fine physical attributes, discussing upcoming social raves, or imparting especially scintillating gossip about any other woman who she appears to be in constant competition with. Marissa's flighty nature, of the much-sought-after and yet still-immature high school drama queen, continually sets the parlor *social drama club* abuzz.

They are a curious mix of personalities, reflects Sean, knowing that Sheri has recently taken Marissa under her wing while introducing her to the parlor crew and guiding her through the social intricacies of the maturing pack—offering something of a maternal protection, as a mother goose to her gosling. A few years older, with a wisdom gained from life's experiences, Sheri is a no-nonsense girl who generally speaks only when spoken to, but when pushed, offers up refreshing, penetrating honesty of herself and others. Stoic, revealing nothing, her tan face is a blank slate. Only exposed tattoos of floating fairies, blood-dripping daggers, and bleached-skull faces outwardly reveal an unspoken bitterness within. Half-hidden under lazy, low lids, golden eyes peer out motionless, until tickled with a little girl excitement; then they ripple as alive as a gentle breeze swaying plains of tall, ripe wheat fields. A personality with a pinch of tomboy matched with a daredevil predilection for speed, she is a favorite tagalong with the boys on their late-night Ninja motorbike rides and weekend lifted-truck off-road adventures, and, as "one of the boys," she engages in and holds a man's conversation on cars, racing, and . . . other women. Most endearing to the parlor boys is that quality that so very few women seem to understand to keep a man; Sheri knows when to just be silent for the moment. Sean knows, but does not understand, why most women are afraid to leave their man alone with another more beautiful woman, but with Sheri, even more beautiful women are wary. Other women soon learned never to leave this little beach blonde alone with their man for fear of being compared to, or losing him to, Sheri, and a few had been lost to this skinny girl whose endearing personality, when set free, could charm any man.

Easing back into his soothing voice as he works the buzzing tattoo machine, Sean comments, "Marissa, you have great skin," as his hand rapidly and easily moves back and forth with color shading. "Really easy to work with." Sean can feel the reassuring words relaxing her, as did Sheri's exiting the room.

"Thanks, Sean." Marissa lifts her head to turn in his direction. "Do you really think I have good skin?"

"Yes, Marissa. Your skin down here has not seen the sun; it's baby soft and unblemished. Your white flesh makes the ink colors really alive, vibrant, and . . . gorgeous," to again finish with a word he knew she would understand and appreciate. "The tree frog looks dimensional and alive." *Almost as if a real tropical amphibian were surprisingly caught in a camera's flash,* thinks Sean, admiring his own work. The jungle frog perched above the apex of Marissa's derrière looks out with bulbous blood-orange eyes—relatively large for its head size and contrasting nicely with black vertical pupil slits and a glistening, green body. A slash of tropical-fish fluorescent blue streaks down each inner thigh to four thin feet, which in turn balloon with three glossy orange sucker toes.

"You really think *soo*? How does my skin compare to Sheri's?" asks Marissa with what Sean perceives as an artificially sweet voice, even for her.

Warily, Sean pauses, knowing any attempt to answer Marissa's question will be walking into a trap of her setting that will, at any instant of her youthful melodrama, spring shut. Not knowing what the trap is, or where it is, or how it will be set off, he has no desire to hazard an answer, only to be ensnared. Therefore, Sean throws down his fail-safe response in any awkward situation while working. "Give me a moment Marissa. Let me concentrate through this section first."

"Okeydokey." And with that Marissa again buries her face into the table as Sean keeps his head down to bring life to his creature. Marissa's hidden face grimaces with the pain.

Without a word, Sheri quietly returns to place the color tray on Sean's crowded rolling workbench, and then sets the cold Diet Pepsi can on the table between Marissa's slightly parted legs. Sitting opposite Marissa, Sheri reaches into her purse to pull out a rhinestone-glittered cell phone and slides it open to begin typing out a message. In the moments of silence between Sean stepping on the foot pedal and the tattoo machine's noisy hum, the only audible sound consists of Sheri's French-manicured nails tapping a staccato rhythm on the keyboard.

Marissa lifts her face from its cradle and turns to Sheri, asking, "What'cha doin'?" Marissa wants not only to forget about the pain on her ass, but also, more importantly, to present an assured calm and relaxed demureness to both Sheri and Sean.

"Nuttin." Sheri's fingers continue to move rapidly across the keyboard in her palm without even a glance up to Marissa.

Laying her face sideways, Marissa peers with a lone eye over her head-cradling arm and between curtain folds of loose hair, and surreptitiously looks Sheri over—from her black-and-white-Keds-covered feet to her form-clinging skinny jeans and brightly colored designer T-shirt, from her updo blonde-with-auburn under-layered, highlighted hair that they had spent hours together that morning coiffing high atop her head, to her new, large silver hoop earrings dangling low on each side. Marissa thinks back on the few short months that they have been friends and perceptively realizes that along with Sheri's evolving fashion sense, she appears at times to display a more assured personal confidence, the slight alterations of appearance and demeanor passing unnoticed by the rest of the parlor crew. Sheri's attitude of calm, detached aloofness belies a hidden strength and power for which Marissa cannot ascertain the source, but about which she is curious as she continually plumbs for its wellspring. Wanting desperately to fit in herself, yet knowing that she lacks a level of social maturity and self-confidence and is easily bewildered by the intricacies of their group dynamics, Marissa compensates for this handicap by staying close to Sheri and emulating her fashion style while attempting to imitate her mature mannerisms.

"Oh I'm so excited about my new tattoo, Sheri," Marissa says, pulling her arm away from her face to look fully at her friend. Sheri pulls her eyes up from her phone display to settle on Marissa. "This tats gonna be hot and I wanna get some skinny jeans like yours to go with it, an' that'll make it badass and I'll feel so much better about myself, ya know what I mean? I told Ariel I was gonna get some jeans and she asked 'What size?' an' I said 'Two,' and she goes, 'Like no way you're a two.' She can be such a little catty bitch sometimes, don't ya think? Like my size really is a two in skinny jeans and that will be fine; they're not tight and they're tapered. Okay, but listen, so I also told Taylor I wanted to get some skinnies and he goes, 'Awesome, are you sure you're ready for the experience?' Funny, huh? What do you think he meant by that? Do you think he likes me? I think he has a big old crush on me 'cause he's said other things like that before an' he's been askin' me where I been hanging lately. So will ya go with me to the mall Sher? Huh? The thing is like you been shopping for skinnies before and you know the good stores and all, and the styles and the prices, and my body type, an' it will be fun together, you and me. Like will ya?" she asks as she brings a shy hand up to cover her mouth.

Sheri's blank expression is unmoved as she replies, "Yeah, sure, whatever."

As he pulls the tattoo machine away, Sean interjects, "Marissa. We're going to take a short break now. I'll be back after a bit"—*I hope*— "and you can let me know if you want to continue or come back later. You've been good but we have a ways to go for the final touches, and I've gotta check on a few things." Sean tosses the used needles, meticulously wipes down the tattoo machine, and then carefully places it in its tool-cart cradle. From the bottom of the cart he grabs a plastic baggie to pull out a cool, wet, soft cloth. As he wipes down the freshly tattooed skin, an unexpected, intoxicating chill of relief shoots up Marissa's spine and she lets out a pleasurable moan.

"I was pretty brave, huh?" Marissa mumbles, hoping for Sean to continue his rubbing.

"Yes, Marissa," he replies, containing a chuckle.

"Didn't really hurt that much did it 'cause I didn't move much, huh?"

"No, you were good."

"Are most of your customers as good as me?"

"No, Marissa, you were great."

"Sean says my skin makes the colors come alive. Right, Sean?"

"Yes, beautiful."

"Ya hear that Sheri?"

"Fer sure," from Sheri.

"What do you think Sheri, you like it? You have any green or orange, Sher? Does Sheri have any jungle green so we can compare? Who has better skin, Sean?"

And there lies the trap.

Ignoring Marissa, Sean pulls out a dry white workout towel from under the table. "I'm just gonna lay this towel over you an' you can rest awhile. You guys relax an' chill for a bit." Sean then grabs another towel to wipe his brow and face before he walks out the door, pushing his rolling workbench.

Marissa turns to Sheri with the look of an obedient puppy to its master, not knowing whether there is a treat or stick in hand.

Sheri remains poker-faced until Sean leaves the room, then, "Son of a bitch!" she explodes, throwing her cell back into her purse.

"What's that, Sher?" Marissa submissively asks with eyes cast down, not knowing why or which way or, more importantly, at whom Sheri's anger is directed.

"That goddamn little shit is not answering his phone or returning his goddamn text messages! I think he has a little girlfriend on the side." Sheri's voice is shrill and on the edge of a cry as she pulls her chin up, tightens her neck and jaw muscles, and begins to circle her thumb and middle finger together in thought.

"*Brad?* Really?"

"Yes, Brad, *really*. Who did you think I'm talking about?" She gives a hard look that makes Marissa wince and shy away. "You are so dense sometimes!"

"Oh, yeah, sure, Brad, of course. That's what I meant." But Marissa is thoroughly confused as her thoughts bounce wildly, attempting to find some logical connection between Sheri's outburst and this morning's events. Sheri arrived at Marissa's place earlier in the day shortly after the latter's parents had departed for work. With only a "Hey, I haven't slept all night," Sheri had gone straight up to Marissa's bed and crashed until noon. When she finally awoke, they both showered and dressed for going out. It seemed like hours of helping to brush, flat iron, pick, and pin Sheri's bangs and temple locks high on her head in a princess updo hairstyle, while leaving long, shiny blonde strands to flow freely over her shoulders and down her back. Helping Sheri to complete her look with large hoop earrings, Marissa knew that this was Sheri's intricately spun web for snaring an unsuspecting man. Boys would not consciously notice these subtle female adornments, but that was the point. Yet with Brad away on the Channel rig for at least another week before leave, Marissa had no idea who the fly was. Her thoughts swirled at the circle of possibilities, but her limited processing of causal effect came up empty—and still mystified.

"Shit." Sheri gives a hard, blank stare into empty space.

As growing tentacles of nefarious excitement worm through her body, Marissa buries her face so as not to reveal her mind in thought as she begins to formulate a simple plan. "Huf," she groans. Casually she stretches her body out from underneath the towel and places her right arm under her head as a pillow as she allows her left arm to dangle off the edge into space. "Hey, why don't you come with me to Kay's party tomorrow night? Her parents are away and she's having a big bonfire party and barbeque."

"KK? Brad's Kay?"

"Yeah, Brad's little sister. I was shopping at Vintage yesterday with Tif and we ran into Kay, and she knows Kay an' all from school so she introduced me and they started talking an' all, and Kay mentioned she was having a bonfire party and invited Tif, and since I was standing there she said I could come along if I like, like no problem. It's like about ten or so tomorrow, and I don't think it would be a problem if you tagged along, and we could just say I didn't have a ride and you gave me a lift. That would be cool an' all, huh? And then maybe Brad will get an unexpected leave from the derrick and be there, right?"

"Yeah, sure. But why didn't you tell me before about bumping into Kay and the party?"

"It was like just yesterday and you've been in school and I haven't seen you in a while and all, is all. And there will be tons of people there and you haven't met Kay yet so that'll be cool and we'll have a good time."

"Yeah." Sheri looks away from Marissa and now rapidly rubs her thumb and middle finger together. Turning back to face Marissa, Sheri, with a determined air, dictates rather than asks, "Yeah that's a good idea Marissa. You could just say that you needed a ride and that's why I came along, right?"

"Yeah, fer sure, no problem." Marissa keeps her face buried as her left hand flails rapidly in empty space. Uncontrollably agitated, she pulls out her pillow arm, places it over her head, and presses down with considerable force to physically hold herself still. "Hey, why don't we go shopping for my skinnies tomorrow before the party and we can just say we was shopping and hanging together anyhow and it was late and I needed a ride and we were together and that'll be perfect and all."

Yeah. This is just too perfect.

Sheri's Machiavellian machinations had already begun to infiltrate Marissa's own thoughts and actions.

As Marissa had wandered off to continue shopping for a new blouse the previous day, she had overheard Kay mention to Tiffany that Brad's

new girlfriend, Samantha, would be at the party as well. And . . . that
Sammie was pregnant! . . . and that Sammie was keeping the baby . . .
no matter what! *Fuckin' A!*

Marissa excitably grabs the table with her free left arm to calm
herself as she contemplates her plausible deniability of having heard
this part of Kay and Tiffany's conversation unobserved from just on the
other side of the clothes rack. "It'll be fun an' all, shopping and partying
and *everybody* will be there. *Partay!*" *Yeah, no fucking shit! Partay!* The
heady anticipation of Sheri's explosive wrath at the discovery of Brad's
pregnant girlfriend is too much for Marissa as she suddenly blurts out,
"OMG, I have to pee, now!" and she slides off the table while her left
hand holds her half-dropped jeans and her right hand modestly shields
herself with the towel.

"What ya telling me that for? Just go pee."

"Uh, in my purse is a test box. Could ya grab it for me?"

"*What?*"

"Yeah . . . I'm a little late."

"Who?"

Silence.

"Got it," claims Sheri as she chases after Marissa with the purse.

Marissa awkwardly stutter steps to the rear restroom while holding the towel hip high with one hand and her tripping jeans pulled
down below her buttocks with the other. "OMG, let's do it together.
There's two sticks in each package. It'll be fun."

"*What?*" Sheri's face screws up as she questions Marissa's back.
"What makes you think I need to take a test?"

"Uh . . . didn't you tell me you were a few days late yesterday? Right?"

"*Nooo.* Remember you just said you didn't talk to me all day yesterday? Talk to me now girl," demands Sheri with a sharp thrust.

Marissa's stomach involuntarily wrenches with the challenge
of thinking faster and farther ahead than Sheri's nimble mind as the
enclosing walls of a self-made trap begin to squeeze tightly around
her. Marissa was just smart enough to know her cognitive processes
were no match for keeping up with Sheri's penetrating mind, and in
any verbal jousting, Marissa inevitably came out the loser, unhorsed
and prostrate for Sheri's silencing coup de grace. Earlier that morning,

while Sheri lay sleeping in her bed, Marissa had opened and perused Sheri's purse and curiously thumbed through the pages of her personal day calendar. With a shared knowledge of Sheri's secret nomenclature Marissa came to understand that Sheri was a few days late as well.

Typically, Marissa's frozen, blank face would expose a secret she did not wish to reveal, but Mother Nature's continuing urgent call is pressing as she quickly half steps to the restroom with her entangling jeans still at midthigh.

"Well, somebody did." Marissa turns around in front of the toilet and drops her jeans. "Oh, that's it, it was Barbara. I must'a forgot to tell you, I went there yesterday 'cause when I got there the door and the gate was open and the dogs were all out running around the neighborhood and we had to chase them and leash them and bring 'em back. With all the commotion and all the dogs and all the kids, I was just confused and all and I forgot who told me, that's all. That's why I was thinking it was you, for some reason." She sits on the toilet, "Hurry, I don't want to finish."

Fumbling through the purse, Sheri finds the box as she continues to question Marissa. "So, Barb's preggers?"

"Well, late. Hurry," Marissa squeals as she reaches up with her left hand.

Fumbling between holding the purse and tearing open the plastic wrapper, Sheri finally rips the cardboard apart. "Here ya go," she says, and she passes to Marissa a thin white stick with its bulbous black X bull's-eye at one end.

Grasping the rabbit rod, Marissa quickly puts it between her legs and then, with both eyes still tightly closed, lets out an audible sigh of relief. With a return of breath: "Thanks Sher." After a short pause: "Come on, let's do it together. It'll be fun." Now afraid to open her eyes. "Even if you're not late, come on. Do it with me. I don't want to do it alone. *Please?*"

"Well, I might be just a few days late. Okay, since you already have a second stick."

Marissa begins to breathe normally again, more so from Sheri's agreeing to take the pregnancy test than from the welcome relief of her formerly pressing bladder. *"If boys are toys; if girls are tools; where shines the joy; if all play the fool?"* Karizma's rich, melodic voice floats up to fill the room.

"Oh, shit, Sher! Grab my phone for me, please?"

"Fer sura," Sheri responds as she reaches into Marissa's purse and pulls out the ringing cell. *"Helloo . . .* What? . . . Who the fuck are you? . . . Ya know who this is? . . . No, nice try . . . This is Sher . . . Yeah, I'm listenin' . . . No. You tell me now. I wanna know what fertilizer shit you're spreading 'round cause your mouth is sure full of it . . . You got no cause to talk to me like that an' I wanna hear why." Sheri speaks into the phone as if it were a real person. She pulls it away from her ear and then looks into the cell as she answers, as if she is expecting the screen to physically morph in response to her words. Her whole body animates into her speech; her head ducks low, directly into the phone as her shoulders hunch forward and eyes squint narrowly as if peering through the phone's small LCD display to see the person at the other end. Her pointed index finger is a lethal weapon jabbing free space in rhythm to her speech, as if plunging violently into the listener's exposed chest.

"I just wanna know where you get off talk'n smack to me like that, ya little tramp? . . . Don't play innocent with me, everyone knows you're just one big ho . . . It ain't my problem ya can't keep a man, or your man can't keep it in his pants . . . Yeah well, I ain't the one that has grandma and grandpa raising my kid. I at least take care of my own . . . Are you serious? That'll be the day . . . Well then bring your suck-up ass face on over if ya really think ya can!" Sheri pulls her gaze from the phone to turn a piercing stare through Marissa, whose pallor turns soap white.

Marissa shudders and wilts inside and avoids Sheri by looking into the bowl to remove the stick from between her legs. She then raises her arm to pass it along to Sheri. Marissa continues to pee and looks at Sheri with a question of "What" on her face, and a fear of the unknown in her chest.

"Ya know who that was?"

Marissa shakes her head no, too afraid to speak into Sheri's penetrating eyes.

"That was Kylee. She said that you climbed with Cory into his brother's backseat at Rooster's party last weekend!?"

"I swear to god Sher, nothing—and I mean nothing—happened! We just had a few shots and he goes, 'Hey, you want to check out my brother's pimped-out, old Cadillac lowrider?' And like he showed me how big it was and the new leather seats inside an' said we could have our drinks in the backseat and it was like as big as a couch. It was totally rad. The new leather seat was really soft an' all and I really love the smell of that new leather. We was just talkin' and drinkin' and laughin'. Lika he put his hand on me once or twice an' I just pushed him off and said 'now Cory,' and we just laughed and kept drinkin', and he said, 'Wouldn't it be funny if somebody thought we was doin' something in the backseat?' and we laughed. Holy crap, I swear nothing happened. What Kylee does isn't even really fair. The thing is, like, Kylee doesn't even really give a fuck about him. She's just totally using him. And we was just talking and laughin'. That's all. I just wanted to check out the pimped-out car and I thought Cory'd be cool an all, ya know? Is she serious? Really? Oh my god, I can't believe this. Sher!?" Marissa averts her eyes as she half looks up to Sheri, like a submissive puppy.

"What were you thinking?"

"I don't know, I don't know. We've seen each other around since middle school and I've seen the car driving round town before and it's totally cool, ya know, and I just wanted to check it out an' all. I thought the car would be bitchin' to sit in and Cory'd be cool an' all. Ya know?"

"Well now ya know that lowlife ain't cool."

"Is she mad? Do you think she's serious?"

"Ha, she's at least mad enough and serious enough to say she is going to come over and bitch slap you for trying to take her man, and me for just having a big mouth."

"God no. You ain't serious? Is she really coming over?"

"Well, that's just what she said. We'll see. Fuck. Now I need to pee, bad. Ya done?"

"What? Yeah," Marissa says, as she wipes herself and stands to pull up her jeans.

Sheri lays the first stick on the tray from the box that now sits on the counter, unzips her jeans, and switches places with Marissa. She drops her pants as she sits on the toilet while stretching her right hand out to Marissa. From the torn cardboard box, Marissa pulls out the second stick and hands it to Sheri. Sheri begins to let out a warm stream and slips the thin stick between her legs.

"If boys are toys; if girls are tools; where shines the joy; if all play the fool?"

A quizzical, expectant look passes between the girls. Marissa reaches into her purse, pulls out her cell phone, and gives a cautious look at the caller ID display. "Oh my holy hell, I think it's Kylee again," she says as her face blanches. "Take it Sher, I can't talk to her! You know me, I'll just get all jelly an' all and start blabbering or just go silent. I'm shakin' already. Please?" Marissa forces the phone into Sheri's face, and Sheri grabs it, more so not to be slapped than to answer it. Marissa lets go and backs away with both hands held up to her tightly pulled mouth as she stoops low, physically shrinking.

"Helloo," Sheri seductively drawls as she rapidly waves the pregnancy stick in the air with her hand. Marissa pulls her hands away from her face to reverently grab the white object from Sheri as if she were the bearer of a sacred religious idol. "What? . . . No, Cory, not even close . . . What makes you think like that's what was said? . . . No, Cory, I didn't say that . . . Well, Kylee's a liar, or deaf, or stupid, and from what I know about Kylee, probably all three, 'cause that's not what I said . . . Ya know like I don't really care. We all know Kylee's the queen-bee liar, always stirring up the stuff. The thing is like she needs to get her shit together before she pretends ta know what others are doing an' she's got a lot a shit so it's gonna be a while . . . I would like to see Kylee come over and try something like that . . . Ya got noah cause ta be talkin' ta me like that 'cause I wasn't even there. Furthermore, you're like the pot callin' the kettle black. Don't think like I don't know 'bout you and Talia, an' I ain't said nothing 'bout that to no one, so don't you go startin.'" Sheri's right index finger is a raging serial killer's switchblade furiously stabbing the air, again, and again, and again.

"You!? Lika I heard people sometimes mistake you for a girl an' all and if I thought you weren't such a punk ass I might be worried!" Sheri yells into the phone as her forehead knots hard, and wrinkles stretch across her hairline and the freckled bridge of her nose. "If ya think ya can, come on over as well! But 'til then, you can't talk to me or Marissa again until you're a real man!" she shouts, pressing the "Off" key with a verbal "fuck!" The air is now finally safe from a continuous mauling by Sheri's index finger as she grabs some tissue to wipe herself.

"Cory says he is going to come over and personally bitch slap both of us and then he's going to watch while Kylee beats the shit outta both of us. Like all Kylee can do is any more than just sit on us an' squish us, huh?"

"Cory said that? Oh my god. He can't be serious? Is he serious? Really? Fer sure?" asks Marissa, standing in front of Sheri with both hands waist high as she flails her wrists while pacing in a tight circle. Eyes flick to Sheri, then the ground, then back to Sheri . . . flick, flick, flick. "We have ta do something. What can we do?"

"Well, that's just what he said. He said he would be over in a bit and wanted everyone to see," replies Sheri as she stands to pull her jeans up. "Whatever . . . *Robby!* Ya little shit!" she yells with a quick twist, putting her back to Robby standing across the tattoo room in the doorway. She reaches to zip and then snap the pant button closed. "Like, howa long have ya been standing there ya obnoxious little twerp? I'm gonna tell Mom yer not in school." Sheri does a pirouette to then quickly advance on Robby.

"Teacher's conference, half day. Wes an' I grabbed the bus over, and if you don't say nothing to Mom about me being here, I won't tell her yer working on your tats and doing shots," he says with the obstinate doomsday dare of parental chicken that a young teenager, who only risks being grounded for a few days from video games, can say to a much older, independent sibling, who just does not want someone else being up her butt, knowing her shit, and then playing mind games in an attempt at artificial control.

Sheri pauses in her charge, worrying over the snooping, the incriminations, the yelling, and the inevitable battle. Truth is not important; previous history and approximate availability are more than enough for a conviction. "What'cha doing in the tat room?" she asks, standing erect with arms folded across her chest in an imitated parental-power pose.

A huge grin sweeps across his face. "Man down in the game room. Bring yer kits, quick!" pronounces Robby, who opens wide the private tattoo room door and steps out of the way for the girls to exit.

Without a word spoken, an understanding passes between the girls as they shrug their shoulders with the realization that all discreet conversations will be compromised with the presence of Robby in the room—and the stubborn, pubescent Robby will not leave until they leave. Reaching into their purses, each pulls out a small, nondescript makeup clutch. The girls' demeanors noticeably shift as they walk out and step towards the excitement of tending to a passed-out patient—the man down. Left behind is their apprehension of fighting a looming duel.

Following the girls, Robby hesitates, and then, upon reflection, stops. Paused motionless in the open doorway, his eyes follow the girls as they walk to the back of the parlor. When Sheri and Marissa disappear into the gaming room, Robby closes the door to leave himself inside the tattoo room. All alone, he stealthily creeps over to the massage table where the girls' handbags have been left behind. With a glance over his shoulder to confirm a still-closed door, Robby cautiously reaches into Sheri's purse.

~~~

Although they have made this walk numerous times before, neither Sheri nor Marissa are predisposed to accept the transition from the comfortable room temperature of the air-conditioned parlor to the pressing summer heat of the outside vented gaming warehouse. Sheri can only compare the high temperature of still air that presses at their bodies to a closed gold mine deep within the earth that she and her father had toured in the mountains long ago. The girls momentarily halt at the threshold and allow their bodies a moment to acclimate to their new environment. They cringe as they feel their meticulously coiffed and silky hair immediately begin to fall limp and flat. Their skin soon glistens, and sticky sweat begins to pull at, and then cling, to their clothing.

Their mouths part slightly, taking in only shallow breaths to block the odor-laden air containing a cutting mixture of human sweat, stale alcohol, wet and burnt hay, and something dead-like that is preferably left unknown. Opposite the girls' entrance, one of three ceiling-high metal bay doors is rolled open and empties out into a long and lonely alley, causing them to squint narrowly as they adjust to the glare of reflective backlight that pours into the darkened garage. In the corner, some unseen fan quietly wafts the air, providing a modicum of relief from the late afternoon heat that nearly tips triple digits outside.

Occupying the center of the long-ago utility-truck garage is an elongated Ping-Pong table with half a dozen shiny red plastic cups lined up in ten-pin formation at each end. Moisture pools around the cups, the excess liquid continually dripping over the sides to stain the bare concrete floor. To the girls' left and along the opposite wall of the bay doors sits an old, waist-high workbench converted into a social bar, complete with raggedy and unbalanced bar stools. Behind this wooden counter resides a similarly aged and overworked refrigerator that continuously drones a metallic buzz even in the coolest winters. Several rows of fluorescent lighting run the length of the warehouse ceiling. They are all turned off to maintain some false illusion of coolness. Against one closed metallic garage door are three segregated bins overflowing with glass bottles, aluminum cans, or trash. Around the walls are randomly positioned plastic patio chairs that add creature comforts for spectator viewing of the center-court action.

With the entrance of Sheri and Marissa, the lounging crew turns to linger their attention and appreciate the beauty of the two girls. Bull Dog stops his throw with arm paused in midair, a stained Ping-Pong ball clasped between thumb and two fingers, to give a warm and friendly smile to the ladies. Unless one were to know him, the radiant warmth of his flashing smile would appear to be incongruent with this short and powerful young man who has always looked a decade older than he is. His physical features—a thick no-neck; a round, folding face that rolls over to hide his recessed dark eyes; and strong, defined arms that seem to stick out from his rotund and wide body—all combine as if to complete a caricature of Mr. Potato Head.

Towering next to Bull Dog, Peewee casts the girls a look over before quickly averting his eyes. A mountain of a man-boy at six foot six, and older than BD, Peewee has a gangly boy body that will one day mature into that of a strong, powerful man; nevertheless, with a permanent layer of baby fat, he will forever retain his youthful appearance. These two physical and personality opposites are inseparable friends.

BD freely offers up his happy, outgoing disposition to be shared with and imbibed by anyone and everyone; it serves as a loose bridle to keep Peewee's shy, recalcitrant nature, and inability to articulate his thoughts and feelings, in check from ever physically venting these personal frustrations in a confrontation.

Sheri and Marissa identify the usual crew milling about as they play, drink, smoke, or simply sit there idly gazing. Across the table from BD and Peewee stand their opponents: Bat Boy, with his Dodgers cap tilted and twisted at just the correct angle of feigned, uncaring insolence, and Kill, so named because he's the only one who won't pull the trigger on the crew's annual fall hunting trips. Clinging to the walls or standing at the bar are Doogie, Cruz, TomTom, Lic, and other young cubs of the parlor pack. From across the room, Robyn and Ariel coolly eye Sheri and Marissa through a lazy haze of spiraling smoke. Their bored mouths hang open with no movement other than to press cigarettes occasionally to their lips while their eyes follow the curling eddies of smoke that blend to a room-fog obscure. Squatting and propped against a rolled-down metal garage door, Bud and Allen do not lift their eyes from the glass pipe that they pass between themselves as they take long, deep inhalations. Time has passed any longing within Sheri for the ganja. Marissa feels an excited curiosity.

The fashion *de parlour* is jeans, appropriately ripped at thigh-ass crease and atop knees for the girls, while waistbands hang low on the boys to expose vertical cracks, the unbeknownst-to-them prison sign of availability, or boxer briefs that ride high and billow out, and white wifebeaters for the girls and black tees for the men. Emblazoned graphic designs of hollow skulls, dripping blood, or naked women with cowboy hats are the most preferable vogues upon their shirts. Their bared skin resembles a similar panorama and lifelong exposé of past pain, escapism, or just a filling of an emptiness of nowhere else to go and nothing else to do.

A passed-out sleeper is draped over and instinctively clings to his patio chair as his rolled-back head is supported against the wall. From corner-mounted speakers and a hidden stereo, Kid Rock's "Rock n Roll Jesus" completes the den's ambiance of the young, bolting cubs.

With the room's attention now focused upon the pair of femmes, Sheri stands with cool indifference as her predator eyes survey the room with a hard look that separates the pride into some who are friends, some who are not, some who were past hookups, and some who are constant . . . haters, but that's okay. In a well-rehearsed move of practiced nonaffect, Marissa casually swings her head low and right, tossing her hair around to flow as a dark, cascading waterfall far down her back. Her head tilts down to the perfect angle of locks just hovering above her dark eyes, from which she now seemingly shyly peers out. Her peacock pose attempts to imitate Sheri's air of nonchalance but her edgy demeanor and porcelain skin framing twitchy eyes express a childish fright while wishing to take flight for another place to safely alight.

"Shots!" yells BD in his gravelly voice as he crosses the beer-stained concrete floor to greet Sheri and wrap his arms around her in a gentle bear hug that lifts her off the ground. "Hey," he says, putting her down and then pulling away to give Marissa a pleasant look. Her queer and awkward stance projects a fragile field of resistance that prevents him from touching her.

"Hey."

"Hey."

The girls' mercy mission to attend to a man down for which they have been summoned is postponed as BD wrestles Sheri around the waist and shepherds her over to the center table with Marissa following closely behind. Exiting from behind the bar, Cruz places a bottle of tequila and some plastic cups on the table. As the crew gathers, a squirt of clear agave juice is poured into each cup. Bud's and Allen's gazes have not shifted from the stained-glass pipe with which they are still occupied in the corner. Robyn and Ariel have not moved from chair lounging as they eye the goings-on around the center pong table. Cigarettes lazily hang from the corners of their mouths from which they draw occasional puffs.

Peewee steps through, placing two clear shot glasses down. "Hey, these are for the girls." He then pours from the tequila bottle until alcohol brims over the edges. Thanking Peewee, the girls exchange their makeup kits for the shot glasses and lift them to their mouths. In one smooth, continuous motion, they nod their heads back to finish the tequila in a single swallow. The fiery liquid burns their throats. They both shudder and cough with pitched laughs of discomfort, "Agh, ha," but neither spews.

Slamming his plastic cup on the table and crushing it, BD picks up a Ping-Pong ball and tosses it across the table into an awaiting ten-pin cup. He quickly shoots a second ball that also scores—with a hollow-rimmed "ping" and a splash of golden liquid. "Ggggoooooaaalllll!" he shouts victoriously, raising his arms overhead. Bat Boy and Kill each grab a scored-upon cup and pick out a Ping-Pong ball to drink the beer in single chugs.

"Let's take care of business now and get to Burrow," Sheri says to Marissa as they pick up their kit bags from the table and move to the man down. Burrow is slumped back unconscious with lanky limbs splayed around his chair. With his head propped against the wall his mouth hangs open. Fumbling through their makeup kits as they kneel before the lanky Burrow, Sheri pulls out red-flush rouge and Marissa withdraws her purple-glitter eye-shadow compact. Sheri pauses, tucks the compact in her belt line, reaches up to take off her silver ear hoops, and then wraps the tendrils of hanging blonde hair on top of her head, pinning them up with a clip taken from her bag. Her head cocked at an angle, Sheri then begins to delicately brush Burrow's cheeks with rouge powder.

The girls focus on their makeover task as they work together in silence. A mascara wand is slipped from its tube as Marissa crouches over Burrow to thicken his eyelashes. With a tequila warmth radiating and relaxing her, Marissa feels a devilish delight at having an uncom-plaining innocent under her to cross gender for her own use and gratifi-cation. Clumpy, street-whore thick now lies the mascara lash, *Ha!* Lost in thought while primping and preening, Marissa suddenly becomes aware of how unusually quiet Sheri is. *Huh?* It's strange that Sheri is not dissecting Burrow with her usual soliloquy about their lounge-chair victim's many physical and social shortcomings. Her many scathing commentaries, coupled with the passing on of scurrilous rumors that Sheri treats as fact, always leave Marissa nodding in silent awe as she attempts to determine what is true and what is fantasy, and what, more curiously, is the source of Sheri's extensive knowledge. Stranger still is that Sheri has not broached the subject of Burrow's recent breakup with his girlfriend, or, in particular, the well-known rumor persistently floating among the crew that his ex had contracted the clap as he, all the while, vehemently proclaimed *his* innocence. Such inside information Sheri would be well aware of long before Marissa. Sordid gossip such as venereal disease would normally be Sheri's opening salvo of character assassination.

Marissa switches to a brow pencil to extend eyebrows out past his temples. Usually by this time in the makeover process, and with a few more healthy shots of tequila, Sheri would move from the serious verbal scathing to entertaining Marissa by expounding on artificial accusations of the boy's perverted persuasion during the crew's most recent hunting expeditions, with various scenarios of hypothetical homosexual escapades based upon their camping accommodations and who slept in whose tent. Her detailed stories carried out to hellacious, illogical scenarios in her excitable, laughing voice would set Marissa giggling in delight. Those first titters would continue to grow until eventually belly laughs would bring tears to Marissa's eyes, and she would lean on Sheri for drunken support as everyone else in the room would look at them as *the lesbians*. A sideways glance catches Sheri delicately running her fingers through Burrow's dark, curly hair, rather than her usual briskness of palming gel hard onto the forehead and then energetically smearing it all the way behind the head. *What of that?* Marissa pulls out a small jar of nail polish and brushes a crayon layer of hot-pink enamel on each finger as Sheri applies passion-red lipstick that bleeds well over his lip line. Looking up from the nail appliqué, Marissa surveys Sheri to only just then note the unweaving of Sheri's man-web: the absence of the hoop earrings and the long hair, so carefully preened earlier but now spooled, knotted, and spoiled on top of her head. And with that soft look on Sheri's face . . . *No shit?* wonders Marissa.

There is neither a contemplative thought analysis, applying deductive reasoning, to her puzzlement, nor a review of historical action and reaction to reach a logical conclusion, but rather a woman's intuitive leap that results in Marissa correctly realizing Sheri's intent.

Continuing Burrow's makeover for Cinderella's comic ball, Marissa begins to appraise him anew with a competitive eye. Finishing now with the nail polish, which she has applied only to the left hand for just the correct *special effect,* Marissa pulls out a pair of clip-on swinging earring balls. Giving Burrow a better look over, she observes a nice, tall guy, close to her own age, who dresses in the parlor norm of low-riding jeans with a cowgirl-printed tee, and maybe considered just a kid when compared to Sheri's street-smart maturity. *Hmm? Maybe? Yes, possibly. I think I see it now.* All of Sheri's intricately woven spider's web— the French-tip nails, hoop earrings, and the updo—falls into place . . . *Shit, all for Burrow?*

And for the pièce de résistance, Sheri prints with the red lipstick across Burrow's high forehead: "SUCKS COCK."

"Ms. Charlotte Nicolette Olevsky . . ." Sheri and Marissa instantly snap their knees, bolting upright, as the contents of their makeup totes spill across the concrete floor in a high-tinsel clatter. They stand at attention, ramrod erect, with their eyes fixated, ". . . and Marissa St. Ber . . . *Miss* Marissa Bernadine Gustav. And how are God's children doing today, if I may ask?"

No sound emanates from either Sheri or Marissa as their unblinking saucer-wide eyes rivet downward towards Burrow's mother! who stands before them. Sheri's throat tenses with dismay at the interruption by the unexpected and unwanted guest. Marissa's cheeks burn brightly, filling with a soft rose color over the white porcelain skin as she seethes with humiliation at Barbara's inadvertent slip of her nickname, "St. Bernard."

The origin of Marissa's slanderous *nom d'amour* is clouded in history and controversy. Some say it derives from her Scandinavian heritage and the furry animals that live in a snowy environment with a lack of any sun that reminds people of long, chill winters and Marissa's milky-white complexion. A few snicker that it is Marissa's favorite coupling position. Among themselves, the boys joke that Marissa slobbers like a large-jowled dog when . . . well, we'll just leave that one alone for now.

The silence weighs heavily in the sweltering room as perspiration trickles from the girls' armpits. A barely audible "fine" tardily squeaks from the smallness of Sheri's constricted throat.

"That's sweet, my little ones. I see idle hands have been busy today."

"A . . . we was just a fixin' to . . . a . . . well, we just wanted to make sure Burrow was okay. We heard he was passed out in the game room an' all. Ya know?"

"I know the devil finds work for idle hands, and you ladies have been the instrument of his work."

"We don't mean nothing by it. We was just hangin', an' we wasn't even in here. We were just called over an' all, and we was just fixin' to make sure he was okay and all . . . and then they all wanted us to . . . an' we had our makeup kits . . . so we was jus' havin' a little fun and all . . . and nobody's hurt, and like it is fun and all, ya know? He looks kinda cute . . . don't ya think?"

"My dear child, beauty comes from within, not from golden ornaments or bodily decorations," Barbara curtly replies as her eyes follow Sheri's midriff tattoo of fairy dust cascading down from her pierced belly button as it eventually slips from view beneath the top of her low-slung jeans. Barbara's curious, lingering gaze clearly wonders where the colorful sprinkles may end, or if they do . . . which in fact . . . they do not.

"OMG, Barbara, we are *sooo* sorry. We were just having a little fun. It's happened to all the boys once or twice, and nothing's meant by it. I know you must be mad an' all, but we are sorry."

"We are all in this together, Sheri," says Barbara as her eyes rise up from Sheri's bejeweled belly button. "Tell me. How are you doing? I haven't seen you at church lately. What have you been up to?"

"Nothing much. Just been busy an' all with school and work. I'm just a little stressed lately and worried about my job 'cause the State has just changed the rules and now requires a personal background check of all health-care workers that attend patients even if you don't have a degree or a certificate to give orders or prescriptions, an' I just don't know what they will find, or what it will mean, if they do find some of my stuff, ya know?"

"Well, it is what it is. There ain't nothing that you can do about it now. You can't go back and change it. You'll just have to wait and see."

"I know that, I ain't complainin'. They're just cutting back my hours in the unit until everything clears with the State, to cover their asses and all, just in case, and with all the BS it'll probably take a few months and all to clear. What'cha doin' here an' all anyhow, Barbara? I ain't known ya to come down to the tat shop before?"

Barbara's face softens as a knowing smile parts her lips, and she replies, "I have my gang as well, Sheri, and I'm fed the info when I need it. No matter how old they are, you will always worry about your children, about one thing or another, and Burrow is still trying to figure himself out and it helps to have family there to pick you up when you slip sometimes, you know? Come to services Sunday. There're a lot a friendly folks there. They're not your family an' all, but we are close and we help each other when we can."

Sheri searches Barbara's furrowed face and sees a tired, honest woman, aged before her time from a hard life. "Yeah, fer sure. It's all good, right?"

"It can all be good. I know ya talk to your dad sometimes when you're hurtin' an' all. It may just be easier to hear what he has to say to you when you have the peace of mind to be receptive. Think about it, Sheri. I'd like to see you there."

"I'd like ta. I been meaning to. I just been busy and all on the weekends, work and studying, you know. This Sunday, fer sure, though."

Barbara tosses a glance to Marissa. "And you too, Marissa. We have open arms for everyone. Our Lord Jesus himself said, 'Come to Me, all you who are weary and burdened, and I will give you rest'—Matthew eleven twenty-eight. So"—Barbara turns from Marissa—"it looks like you're starting your own flock of followers, Sheri."

"Yeah, well, I was just thinking that it would'a meant a lot to me if when I was Marissa's age if I had someone a little older to show me the ropes before I got hurt, an' all."

"And as the apostle Paul told us, 'Each of you should look not only to your own interests, but also to the interests of others'—Philippians two four. I see something special inside of you, Sheri. You just need a little help and a dash of luck to learn what that is and how to use it. That's why we need you at church."

"Yeah . . . I been told that before."

"Well, opportunity comes at the strangest times, and God enters the heart when you least expect it," Barbara offers with a small smile and warm eyes. "Okay, I got a six-pack of hungry kids waitin' for me at home and Amber can only keep them penned up for so long before they scatter like sheep across the hills. I'll leave Burrow in the carport 'til dark and the young'uns are playing in their rooms. It should be cool enough in the shade 'til then, when Amber and Carol can help me bring him in. You girls pick up your makeup now, and I'll go and get some wet paper towels to wipe his forehead and face. I don't want to have to do any more explaining than I have to."

Movement comes slowly to the girls after standing rigidly in place at soldiers' attention before Barbara. Bending to pick up their cosmetics scattered across the floor, Marissa glances over her shoulder at a retreating Barbara. Reaching into her pocket, Marissa quickly pulls out her cell, snaps a picture of Burrow, and then quickly slips the slim phone back into her jeans.

Barbara returns accompanied with BD, Peewee, and Cruz to size up Burrow and the logistics of transporting him to the awaiting minivan. Barbara wipes the letters from Burrow's high forehead, leaving behind an illegible red lipstick smear that stretches from one temple to the other. Observing Barbara fawning over Burrow, Marissa smiles inwardly as she admires their handiwork and makes a mental note to observe Burrow more closely in the future for weaknesses that may be leveraged at some opportune time to her advantage.

With BD and Cruz each standing behind one of Burrow's shoulders, and Peewee between Burrow's legs, the boys grab the chair he is slouched on and, in a show of youth and strength, lift it shoulder high. Burrow's lanky frame remains draped over in place like a sleeping rag doll. Peewee reverses his hold to stand with his back to the chair and drapes Burrow's legs over his shoulders. Silently, all eyes turn to watch Burrow transported high up on the shoulders of obeisant servants. Their exit takes on a comical, surreal atmosphere with Burrow's face as colorfully made up as a Broadway stage whore and the somber presence of a silent Barbara formally trailing the entourage as it moves through the smoky haze and past the minions, Bud and Allen, still tripping with shit-eating grins on their faces. Through the open garage door and into the harsh light, the parade proceeds down the deserted alley as with an emperor of ancient times, before the advent of wheel and axle, held high overhead.

Sheri closes her eyes, trying to shut her thoughts to the presence of everyone and everything in the gaming room while seeking a safe place of refuge within her mind to hide. "Fuck, I need some air and a cigarette, bad," she says to no one in particular as she opens her eyes to glimpse the last of the parade as it disappears in a march down the sunlit alley.

~~~

Pensively sucking a deep drag on a fag, Sheri casts her gaze to follow the movements of the occasional dancing dust devils that whirl around the loose grit of the vacant dirt lot and whip about the scattered Sahara mustard plants into frenzied swirls that match her tempestuous emotions. These ubiquitous California-invasive plants have a ground-hugging leaf base with several nearly leafless straight stems that can reach thigh high. At the plant's crown sits a marble-size bulb of sun-golden flower that lacks any fragrance and has the annoying habit of leaving bright stains of mustard-yellow pollen on pants when one brushes against the bloom. Sheri wishes these insidious mini-twisters would Oz-like rip out all of the jean-staining plants by their roots and secretly deposit them upon the pillows of all her unsuspecting haters.

Back propped against a rough stucco wall coated with a film of dirty brown talc, Sheri squats, shaded in the lee of the sun's late-afternoon slanted rays as she occasionally winces from the sporadic dust swirls around her face. Ignoring Marissa, who similarly squats next to her, Sheri attempts to focus her thoughts on unraveling those emotions tightly wound around her mind. She ponders the complications of life that always seem to lie so heavily upon her. She slips two fingers into her jeans pocket and rubs the reassuring form of the forged-steel Camaro key. There was a time, which did not seem that long ago, when she could easily unwind the ball of her intertwined thoughts and lay each of the strands out as soft, wet noodles to be inspected and addressed individually at the occasion of her choosing. Each personal relationship, each social complication, each minicrisis would simply be laid out in her mind: wet, limp, and idly waiting there until she returns to analyze them at her leisure. No longer do they silently wait. Now when she unravels her conflicts and attempts to grab even one, she finds there are too many. They are too slippery. Her emotional issues squirm away. It is as if each is alive with an agenda of its own. They worm in and around her head to poke and nip at the most unexpected moments, tormenting her psyche until the constant mental wrestling is exhausting to the point she sometimes welcomes an early exit to her existence. Inhaling a deep, consoling puff, Sheri reflects with frustration at the autonomy of her irrational snakes that now seemingly overwhelm her life.

Marissa presses her head against the roughly textured wall while furtively studying Sheri's face in profile as she attempts to read her emotions about Barbara's unexpected appearance and Burrow's premature, ceremonial departure. Marissa shoots her smoke to intermingle with Sheri's lofting white curls that vanish into the sky. As usual, Sheri's stoic face is a mask of indifference, leaving her seemingly unfazed by the turmoil that unfolds around her. Marissa has long studied and often imitated Sheri's air of nonchalance. Frustrated at her lack of ability to ever read Sheri's emotional state, contrasting markedly with Sheri's uncanny ability to read her like an open book, Marissa irritably inhales long and deep, catching just the slightest whiff of the morose, vomit-inducing smell of death emanating from a distant slaughterhouse in summer heat. Her nostrils flinch as she thinks that it should be against the law for a place to call itself a city when the noxious country vapors of adjacent farmlands and nearby cattle pens can permeate the air with just a change of the breeze. She fantasizes that it is time for a change of fashion . . . it is time for a change of scenery . . . and it is definitely time for the elimination of the same hating personalities who she always seems to be surrounded by, and who themselves are going nowhere.

"Yo, Bitches! Whas'sup? Wha'choo ladies doing hiding out here?"

Fuck! Just fucking perfect, thinks Sheri, looking away from Efi and out towards the empty street as she sucks another long drag.

"Efi!" Marissa squeals, tossing aside her cigarette and freeing both hands to press against the wall and thereby stand up to greet him with a hug. With his strong arms embracing her willow-lithe body, Marissa feels a tingly sensation inside. She reluctantly disengages their warm hug to step back and return his lingering gaze with an inspection of her own that takes in Efi's swarthy, masculine good looks. A head taller than Marissa, he is broad chested with a mane of dark hair and inviting dark eyes that she readily falls into. His straight white teeth shine bright against his brown Mediterranean skin.

"Girl, you're lookin' good"—his voice turns low and musky—"and *feelin'* even better"—added with an admiring stare at her bare midriff. "You've got the tightest bod' in town." The luring song of his sweet tongue is a long, lingering enticement to Marissa. "How many boyfriends ya got now? An' why ain't you never gone on a ride with me? What's up with that? I got a helmet for ya, an' all, and you know it'll scare the pants off of you, an' ya *know* we'll have a good time." Efi plays upon the insecure, beautiful woman that constantly craves adulation with his casual compliments about her fine physical attributes with, in Sheri's listening ears, just enough artificial sweetness on which to choke and gag. Under his admiring gaze, Marissa feels all squiggly inside. The teenager playing as the grown woman bursts forth in the girly-girl giggle that soon follows.

Not waiting for Marissa's response, he turns. "What? No hug Sher?" he tosses with a tone of familiarity.

"Hey Efi, what's up?" Flicking her cigarette away, Sheri stands with her back against the wall to face Efi.

"I heard you girls were hiding out here after Burrow's mom came to collect him, and I thought you could use some company."

"We ain't hiding, and we don't need no company."

A bit impatiently: "Why you pulling a 'tude on an old friend? What's up with that?"

Under sultry, hooded lids, her eyes unwavering as golden wheat across the plains on a still summer's day, Sheri sizes up Efi's smile and his open arms awaiting her embrace. "What'cha want, Efi?"

Efi's mouth curls in amusement as he drops his arms. Marissa cautiously steps back from their line of vision. Efi moves closer to Sheri and says in a low tone, "Hey, I was wondering if you could set me up with a little bump for KK's party tomorrow? You know . . . like ya used to."

"What ya coming ta me for?"

"Come on sweetie, I heard you could take care of an old friend."

Her brow furrows and worry lines connect the freckles across the bridge of her nose. "Well, ya heard wrong," she replies, anxiously pulling her jaw tight and turning her small mouth into an unflattering frown as her finger and thumb begin to rub.

"That ain't what I heard. I heard you're still connected and still have a cell from your ex."

"I ain't done that in a long while, an' I'm not talking to him right now anyhow," Sheri sternly rebuffs Efi as her eyes flick away to the empty street.

"Don't give me that innocent good-girl crap. I've known ya too long, and I know you too well. You may fool everyone else in the shop as the new college girl an' all working in the psycho ward, but you ain't foolin' me." In falsetto, his left hand delicately raised to his brow, *"Code blue, code blue, I'm getting sober, I need a tequila shot . . . stat!"*

A smirk escapes from Marissa. She covers her mouth with both hands to stop herself from laughing, afraid of being pulled into their bout, or becoming the target of either's verbal jabs. Marissa is quite aware that Efi's humorous, accurate observations of others often come at the expense of exposing their idiosyncrasies and foibles to public display and ridicule. Efi usually culls the weak from the pack with his whimsical, biting rhetoric. Directed at the emotionally less secure who fear such encounters, these verbal barbs, or even the potential unleashing of such a tongue-lashing, are weapons enough that bend to his bidding without expending any real effort, and oh, how he hates to do any actual real work on his own. Marissa is quite aware that beneath the surface of Efi's natural good looks and camouflaged by his persona of seemingly debonair charm, he really is an indolent, self-possessed asshole. Yet she cannot help herself . . . and hates that part of herself that swoons to his whims in his presence.

Sheri feels her blood rush and her temperature rise. "You sure you want to go there now?"

"Come on college girl, give us some educated words from your psycho class—*schizophrenic, Freudian, narcissusisist.*"

Only a quick tightening of her jawline and the circling of her thumb and middle finger in thought give away the internal wave of rage building under her impassive surface. "Psychology, and it's *narcissist.*"

"What?"

"Psychology class, and simply *narcissist,* not *narcissusisit.*"

"*Whatever,* Ms. Smarty-Pants. *Looky you.* Where's the torn jeans and wifebeaters with skulls an' blood? What is up with that, girl? You think you're *special* or something just 'cause you're wearing skinny designer jeans and Juicy Couture? What, you're too good for us now an' all? Is that it?" He steps in.

In a well-practiced rebuff to stay and dominate a domestic male threat, Sheri puts a flat hand up to his chest and fixates an intimidating stare on Efi, but his glassy eyes are unable to focus and thus do not register her unspoken response. A doubt arises as to whether she still has the ability to bend and thus lead him? Or is he just his drunk old self . . . again? Or does he no longer care? In an unusual thought of maturity, she realizes a new approach to handling Efi is needed. "Now Efi," she entices as she leans in with a disarming smile and circles her hand lightly across his chest, "ya know we all appreciate the good boy crossing under the freeway over to our old town side to play the rich, bad boy. That's fun an' all, and we've had some exciting times." Inching closer, she can smell the stale alcohol on his breath and the musky ganja aroma permeating his clothes. "But we ain't all got a mommy and daddy to take care of us like you do. And some of us even have to take care of our parents. A girl's gotta do what a girl's gotta do to take care of herself and her family. You can understand that, can't you Efi?" She finishes her placating by placing her fingers lightly on his wrist. Sheri is not prepared for his base lust rising, and when his hand unexpectedly touches her cheek, she reflexively flinches.

"What?" His facial features morph to an expression of confusion.

Sheri's face hardens as she turns back. "We ain't like that no more, Efi."

From his tongue, he keeps in check the anger apparent in narrowed eyes and pinched face. "Come on, sweetie. Like old times, it'll be fun."

"I'm not some old country fiddle you can pick up and pluck any old time ya want. I'm a Stradivarius."

"A Strada what? Jesus, where does this shit come from lately? What are you talking about, girl?"

"That means you can talk to me again when you know how to treat a lady."

"Oh, yeah, well sure, like when I see a lady, I'll treat her like one."

"When you grow up you'll know one when you see one standing in front of you."

"What? For you? A lady? Who are you kidding? From someone who we don't need no invitation from 'cause when you see the dust cloud coming down the dirt driveway, ya still got plenty of time to clean up the trailer before the guests arrive."

"When you become a *real* man you'll know what I mean." The incriminating, sarcastic jab scores surprisingly much better than Sheri had anticipated.

"Who the fuck died and elevated you to *my lady faire*? You're more like my *bitch de jour*. I've heard there ain't no man that ain't had you."

"An' I hear when your drunk ass was hauled into the county holding tank, there ain't no man that didn't have you either. Everybody knows you was Bubba's little bitch boy."

Nothing. Sheri sees nothing . . . the broad figure of Efi standing before her has vanished. All sound muted . . . Marissa's giggling absent . . . Sheri is isolated in a solitude of silence. The burning rage has vaporized, leaving her a hollow shell. What is this strange transition from raging emotions charging headlong to confront Efi to this incomprehensible feeling of . . . nothing? Has she actually time-warped and fallen into that just-out-of-reach mirage fissure in the road she had so feverishly raced towards this morning? A distant childhood memory of Grandmother's old picture tube, a dot of white light at the center of her vision, expands to the full glare of a snowy, black-and-white screen. Sheri's unfocused eyes blankly stare to the middle distance of the buildings across the dirt lot reflecting the sun's glaring rays. Blinking back the sun's penetrating energy, she lifts a hand to her stinging face and numbly rubs feeling back into her left cheek. As she drunkenly awakens to full consciousness, it dawns on Sheri that Efi has just bitch slapped her . . . silly. Turning to face and attack her tormentor with French-manicured nails, she is surprised and confused to see Efi squirming and squealing with his face pressed and contorted into the stucco wall and his arm pulled painfully up high behind his back.

"You're outta here, fucker," Sean growls into Efi's ear. From the nape of his neck and a twist of his arm, Sean twirls Efi from the wall and towards the street and then quickly follows with a swift kick to his ass. Regaining his balance and with an air of self-affectation, Efi walks casually away with nary a look back.

Following Efi's swaggering exit, Marissa can only think to herself: *How totally badass is that?* But for all his charming good looks and worldly air, she knows that Efi had not been anywhere, while simultaneously realizing he is going nowhere.

"Ya okay, Sher?"

Sheri dully looks to Sean with her hand a flat compress against her cheek. "Yeah, sure, fine."

"You sure?"

"Yeah, it's over. It ain't nothing. I think he was just drunk an' all."

"Holy shit, it was like totally crazy, Sean. He slapped Sher an' then stepped back to like literally hit her again and then you grabbed his arm to stop him, and it was like *sooo* crazy, man. I still can't believe it." Marissa's heart is racing with excitement.

"Hmf, half drunk don't make you something you're not. It just brings out the real jerk from within, and pretty boy Efi can be a genuine piece o' ass wipe sometimes."

"He ain't that bad," answers Sheri, previous entanglements tempering her response.

"Sher, the shop kids are all good an' all, and I do what I can to give them a place to hang without being hassled and stay outta trouble, but most of 'em aren't half as smart as you are. Their thinking is only about girls, or just waitin' for Friday to come around to party and get all drunk ass. Their minds are stretched thin just thinking about the imaginary four-by-four they want to get and lift and trick it out with big rims so they can fill it with wood for tomorrow's bonfire."

"How come *everybody* knows 'bout the party except me?"

Sean smiles. "But you seem to be smarter, and I see it in the way you play with the boys' minds. You're way ahead of them. And anyone that thinks different, anyone that talks different, or just dresses different, can scare them, so they turn on you sometimes. And 'cause of their family situations and all, there ain't much chance of them getting out of here, so it's not all them. But worst of 'em all is Efi. He's got brains and he's got a helping family. He has the chance to do whatever he wants, but he just hangs here smokin' an' tokin' all day, doing nothing and going nowhere." Sean moves closer. "Anyhow, let's take a look-see, girl," he says as he pulls Sheri's hand away from her cheek and she turns profile to him. "Pretty, Sher. Nice an' red. You'll have a black an' blue shiner later, fer sure. I'll getcha some ice."

"Fuck, Sean, I don't need no ice. I just need ya to work on my tat, bad. I ain't got any money now, but I can pay you later."

"Yeah," Sean laughs, "I get that a lot."

~~~

"Ya little shit! Give it here!" Sheri's naturally melodious voice turns harsh and masculine to assume an air of command as she rushes Robby with outstretched arms and tackles him from behind.

Without lifting his gaze from the LCD screen, or even pausing his thumping thumbs from rapidly striking the keyboard, Robby deftly turns his much younger yet larger body to block Sheri from reaching the cell phone in his hand and casually replies, "If you let me keep playing Block Breaker, I won't say anything about the two pregnancy tests on the bathroom sink." Robby's repartee counters and thus neutralizes his older sister's determined physical charge.

Sheri freezes. She stands motionless over Robby, her right arm resting on his back, her left arm reaching around his side for the phone. Marissa pauses in midstride at the open tattoo room door. Afraid to cause any attention-getting sound or even to disturb the air, Marissa slowly closes the door behind them. Their eyes turn to the back wall and the open door of the adjacent restroom, and the test results that await within.

"Wellllaa?" asks Sheri, with a bitter inflection of unripe citrus on her lips as their eyes rivet upon the colored tips of two small sticks— one pink, one blue.

"Oh my god Sher, I don't know, I don't remember." The sudden relevance of the magnitude of her confusion over two different-colored sticks dawns on Marissa. "I just didn't think about it. You was yelling on the phone at Cory, an' it was Robby that came in the room, an' you handed me your test, an' like I laid it down next to the other, and then ya handed me the phone, and then Burrow was down, an' we got our kits, and then Barbara, an' Efi, an' Sean, and goddamn Robby again, shit!?" Her hands shake waist high while she tap-dances on two feet, all the while on the edge of releasing a well of tears—not from the single positive pink test result, but rather afraid of the wrath of Sheri that is gathering unseen and about to rise up as a giant wall and then descend on her, rendering her a worthless jelly blob. "And like I put your test down next to mine, and like I don't remember." Marissa, unsure of where to look other than to avoid Sheri, continues to tap-dance and flick her hands as she fixates on the two swizzle-stick-thin plastic rods lying on a paper towel. "I'm sorry, Sher; I'm really sorry, Sher; I don't know; I just don't know. It's an accident, Sher, with all the goings on an' all. Whatta we do? Whatta we do? Sher, please, *please*?"

"Just perfect, just *fuckin'* perfect," Sheri says in a cringing whisper as her eyes flicker from pink to blue, back and forth. "Do you have any money for another test?" Though she already knows the depressing answer to her rhetorical question.

"Huh? Ah, no. I can get some though; I swear I can. Okay, listen, maybe my parents, no, my brother, yeah he's cool. And what about Brad? Maybe just a little from him just to help a little an' I'll get the rest. I can get it if I have ta, like I swear Sher. Yeah fer sure, I will, no problem." Marissa ends her response more as a lingering question than as a statement of fact.

"Yeah sure." Sheri furiously rubs her thumb and middle finger together in thought. "What else? What fucking else?" She ponders random bad luck descending again into her chaotic life without the self-awareness of her own culpability.

"Hey, Sis?" Robby yells across the room. "I was just wondering if I happen to get some Dodgers tickets, could you give me an' Wes a ride to the game?" His eyes still concentrating on the cell phone display: ". . . Charlotte!?"

". . . *What!?*" Sheri hisses back through clenched teeth. "What'cha getting on about, Robby? Can't you see we're busy? You ain't getting no tickets. We're busy here. Leave us alone."

"Well, I have to know. If I got tickets for all of us to a game, could you give us all a ride?"

"Yeah, sure," answers Sheri with monotonic placebo words to placate and silence Robby, her thoughts firmly captivated by the diagnostic implications of two simple colors: *pink or blue, plus or minus, positive or negative, boy or girl, fuck or fuck?* Her stomach flutters in free fall as her mind flashes back to this morning's airborne flight and aircraft-carrier-deck landing. Sheri realizes with another weight of sick disappointment that her car is now incapable of even climbing Chavez Ravine to the stadium, never mind the steep grapevine pass out of the valley. Another, "Fuck, aah, no. No can do, Robby. My car needs work. If you do get tickets, Bat Boy'll figure a way to get ya all there. Ask him. I'll talk Mom into letting you go, fer sure. Now leave us alone." Sheri's attention returns to her transfixion with the power of two small, virgin-white sticks with different-colored tips. A bad rap riff begins to formulate and circle round in her mind: *Whose is it, whose is it? Who is it, who is it? Pink or blue, plus or minus, boy or girl? Fuck, fuck, fuck and more fucking fuck. I think I wanna cry, I think I wanna die. Oh please, please tell me, why, why, why!?*

The girls suddenly squeal a high-pitched alarm, *"Ahg!"* and clutch each other in frightened surprise as Sean opens the door to wheel his artist's workstation into the room. "Hey girls, ready?"

Sheri grabs the two sticks from the counter and tosses them into the toilet. As coconspirators, the girls are mesmerized by the pink and blue dots swirling around the bowl in an ever-tightening spiral before momentarily pausing at the narrowing pipe, causing an additional rush of fright as they envision the sticks not sinking; only then do the sticks continue their downward spin and disappear with sighs of relief from the girls. Sheri reaches into the pockets of her skinny jeans to pull out a shiny metal object, and, from years of practice, deftly hides it in the palm of her hand. She unsnaps her jeans and pulls them down below her hip bones and saddles up on the massage table. The hidden key, wedged firmly between her middle fingers, begins to probe into the base of her palm.

"You ready, Sher?"

"Yeah, let's get this started."

Sean carefully looks over the colorful artwork spread across Sheri's small hipline while he firmly rubs a disinfecting tissue back and forth across her inked skin before the piercing needles to come. Sean eyes the tramp stamp's intricate rigging of the pirate ship's sails artfully spun into a married surname. The process has already begun to shred the weave of billowy sails, thick masts, and tangled ropes, and transform them into a spider's lacy lair. Greco-Roman letters are artistically spun into silky cocoons, or splayed as caught prey, forever rendering them invisible as the former surname. Prior to permanently marking a client's skin, Sean will attempt to dissuade the client from tattooing the name of a girlfriend, a boyfriend, a lover, or a spouse. If he is unsuccessful in polite conversation from changing their desire of etching momentary love to be exposed on their skin for a lifetime, he will simply come out and bluntly say, "If you didn't birth them, or they're not dead, then don't fucking do the name." If the customer continues to insist on the value of this undying union—which most do—Sean had long ago learned to let go of his frustration and is down to fulfill the client's desire and take their money. He knows that most of them will be back as repeat clients to camouflage that once-cherished name. The tattoo stylus comes alive under Sean's hand as he skillfully blends the sailing mast and rigging into an intricate spider's web.

Despite the discomfort of the tattoo machine's sting clawing a continuous line of silvery spun lace across the base of Sheri's bony spine, her face remains a placid, reflective sea, the depths and heights of her underwater canyons of spirit and sorrow unseen . . . and therefore unpredictable. Sheri's mask of serenity neither reveals her pain nor displays traces of her anguish: the former, a strong will accustomed to many hours under the ink machine, as well as walking away from many a motocross spill; the latter, trained in hiding from the perceived slights of those weaved into her webs of intrigue along with an adolescent psyche still secretly mourning from the violent loss of a father. Her stoic face of detached, fatalistic temper only on the rarest occasions yields to either childish displays of innocent enthusiasm or to a woman's unbridled passion. Sheri's alternating medley of a tomboy attitude towards physical action—not afraid to play with the boys and get dirty—and a deceptive serenity broken only by an occasional little girl's giggle leads others to initially misinterpret her actions and responses as acquiescence to their will, presenting irresistible lures that inadvertently invite men to wade into her apparently calm, appealing waters of attention. In play, her lost child's joyful innocence hesitantly peeks out from the recessed safety of shallow emotional tidal pools, only to scurry quickly back as a shy crab when spotted. These seemingly gentle, lapping shores lull men into a false sense of security as they become fixated with catching another glimpse of this mysterious creature and then casting their finely woven nets to seduce the lovely female peeking out from superficial edges. In so doing, men fail to chart and fully comprehend the true history-creating abyss of events that taint her soul with a bitter resignation—this has left her emotionally arrested and brittle, and set to strike. Undulating in her deep, emotional canyons, her womanly passions of irresolvable anguish and misplaced persecution are carefully concealed from her family, never seen by her boyfriends, misunderstood by her erstwhile husband, only glimpsed by her lover as a shadow in the quiver of her voice and a silent, tearless cry, and is only fully known to her one true friend.

Behind that rarely perturbed face, Sheri masked well the irreparable disillusionment of the untroubled child, covering it with girlish squeals of delight at riding a bicycle that is then unexpectedly and prematurely kicked to the sidewalk to land in the problem-plagued world of responsible adults. She fantasizes that a man will return her to living those secure and carefree days of lushly watered green lawns behind white picket fences . . . *clickity, clickity, clickity.* The figure of the man in her mind never seems to measure up, and she's disappointed when she opens her eyes—for what lover, or spouse, or friend can ever replace a bitter parental loss? Behind that placid face, the seismic shift of her emotional loss has released giant amplitudes of repressed anger that pass unnoticed beneath her hidden depths. Any perceived affront, or a betrayal from someone close, sends her into a she-wolf's fury of frustration that manifests itself in tidal waves of rage that speed to shore, whereupon reaching shallow shelf, they unexpectedly rise up. Those casually wading in her warm, sheltered pools of calm are caught unaware and are ill-prepared for the stormy waves of anger that cascade over her littoral edges, washing out to sea the unsuspecting, the inexperienced, and the immature, whereupon she leaves them adrift as isolated castaways to search about for another. They fail to perceive her angry outpourings to be adventurously harnessed and ridden until dissipated and spent, and she once again morphs into a lapping lake of tranquil calm in which one may again bask in a woman's warm glow. Only her one best friend has stood by Sheri, having witnessed both her demonstrations of destruction and her emotional riding of the highs and lows of love and sex with the understanding that inexplicably each are of her unbridled passions of life that lie within.

Within the tattoo machine's buzzing, like an annoyed wasp, Sheri can hear her mother's recriminating voice with her liquor-loosened tongue sticking between her teeth: "Heeeth's not worthhh the salt in the Earthhh," *spit!* Sheri had come to the belated realization that if one's parents say, "Don't marry him," and one's siblings say, "Don't marry him," and one's friends say, "Don't marry him," then don't fucking marry him! Sheri had felt like a tooled fool, ashamed for a time to show her face to prescient family and friends. With each burning stroke across her back, a once-desperate longing for him continues to subside, as tightly wound threads of a lover's binding repression, excused as silky laces of love, fall away, and the last of him sinks under a sea of obliterating ink. A pointed steel ignition key to a big-block Chevy long gone is pressed deeper into her palm, cutting layers of skin. Sheri's relaxed facial façade fractures momentarily as her teeth pull at the corner of her lower lip.

"If boys are toys; if girls are tools; where shines the joy; if all play the fool?"

"Give it here," commands Sheri without lifting her head from the table as she reaches for Marissa's cell. Sheri answers the phone with, "Yeess?" to be followed with, "Huh, huh. Yeah, right . . . Whatever. I ain't stopping ya . . . It's a free country an' all, ya know . . . The more the merrier . . . Looking forward to it," all spoken into the phone in a monotone of calm with eyes closed.

"Cory says he's coming over here with Kylee an' his crew in an hour or so, so they can all watch Kylee kick the shit outta ya fer trying to steal her man, and then he says he's gonna personally bitch slap me for mouthing off an' spreading lies," Sheri says with detached resolution. Unseen, the ignition key digs deeper.

An eerie lack of emotion from Sheri rings with an inevitability that sets Marissa panicked with fright and nowhere to run. As the prosecuted and found guilty awaiting the presiding judge's verdict, Marissa looks at Sheri hopelessly and can only meekly ask, "Are they all really coming over, fer sure?"

"Yeah, they'll be here for sure. I could hear his drunk little-girl bitch posse in the background name calling an' laughing, and there's no backing outta it now." Her eyes closed, Sheri continues to lie there unflinching with all the outward demureness expected of a young princess napping.

"What can we do, Sher? We don't want them coming over, do we?"

"Like I don't seriously care anymore. I am so pissed off now . . . you like have no idea."

"Sis, I'm gonna go grab a Pepsi and see what Wes is up to."

"Yeah, sure, no problem, no problem at all. Marissa, put the tat song on."

"You sure, Sher?"

"Yeah, I just wanna sing like we do on summer nights cruising about town in the convertible with the stereo jamming."

Happy to have something to take her frightened mind off facing Kylee and her crew, Marissa busies her hands by digging into her purse. Finding her iPod, she reaches across the table and pushes the pink computer into the wall-mounted dock. From high in each corner of the four walls, the speakers pulse a simple, heavy booming rap beat. Sheri only taps her free hand while her body remains a stable canvas for Sean's artistic precision. The Penny Favors lyrics with voices of the young girls in chorus fill the small room: *"Cars and scars, tar and feathers. Your mark across my back once filled me with a thrill. Now the colorful art of our undying love, I chock and vomit as with a stuck, bitter pill."*

"I'm gonna whip Kylee's ass when she gets here," Marissa shouts above the music as her head bobs in rhythm, her loose hair a psychedelic blur of black obscure.

"Cars and scars, tar and feathers, where once there was no doubt, a heart with your name, in colorful art, I could never live without."

"And I'll make Cory squeal like a little girl!" as they giggle, escaping together in a childish conspiracy of fantasy.

"Tear my flesh till it bleeds, burn my skin till it smokes."

"How ya doing, Sheri?" asks Sean.

"For without a tear I grin with clenched teeth bare."

"I ain't complaining."

"As forever will be covered the name I can no longer stand to bear. Cars and scars, tar and feathers."

The rap cadence echoes the loss of love in Sheri's resigned heart. She secretly relishes her tormented pain with inked displays of skulls, daggers, and blood. She had long ago come to realize that she enjoys the pain of tattooing, or rather, she admits to herself, the addiction of turning pain into pleasure. Pain is the new endorphin drug of conscious choice to pull the self-imposed emotions of despair and loss out of her. The piercing burn of the machine tip etching her flesh soon dims as nerve endings are pummeled into submission with overstimulation. Blood rushes to heal the wound, replacing the sharp cut of cat claws with the tingly satisfaction of scratching an itch. Sheri flexes her hand with heady anticipation as she knows the radiant heat will soon simmer to the pleasure of a warm glow pulsating between her legs, and a banal lust for more.

"If boys are toys; if girls are tools; where shines the joy; if all play the fool?"

Sheri pulls her mind out of idle drift to lift her arm dreamily up, and the cell phone of reality is placed in her palm by Marissa. "Yeah . . . yeah . . . Jus' hold your horses, we'll be out soon . . . Don't get your punk-ass knickers all knotted up while you're waiting. It's not like you're gonna melt in the heat . . . Bye-bye."

"What, you playing all buddy-buddy now?" Marissa's humor perceives the inescapable grasp of the executioner while standing on the gallows.

"Yeah, that's too bad for him 'cause I think I might actually care that I really pissed him off."

"Oh my god, Sher, should you have really said that just before us going out?" The unwanted reality sets in.

"Don't be a suck-up, ass face. That's too bad for him, but yeah, his drunk ass is royally pissed off and whipped into a lather now, fer sure." Sheri laughs.

"All right, Sheri, we're good for now." Sean places the machine on the tray. "We'll still need a couple more hours later. Let me wrap this up. I'd tell you to take care of it for a few hours, but I know you're gonna do what you're gonna do."

"Okay, right on."

Sean pulls out a disposable wipe to gently clean Sheri's back. He draws a length of cellophane and places it over the angry, red worked area as a thin layer of protection from dirt, germs, and possible infection. Sheri subtly slips the metal key from her palm into her pocket and brings her hand up to her mouth to discreetly suckle blood while nimbly rolling off the table. Wiggling jeans over hips, she snaps the button shut and brings her eyes up to meet Sean's gaze.

"This is all bullshit, Sheri. You know you girls don't have to do this."

"Yeah, it's all bullshit anyhow. Let's see what these punk asses have ta say, an' get it over with." With that, she steps out the door, her future a colorfully woven tapestry of unknown possibilities and potential.

Sean follows closely behind . . . less than two years away from a hammer finding a ballistic firing cap.

~~~

Shielded from the beaming heat of a late afternoon sun by the building's lengthening shadow of cool, and separated by a few dusty brown yards of neutral ground, two opposing crescent lines of young men, sprinkled with a few women, are arrayed facing each other. Pinched faces of fallacious bravado stare at the others across the distance as their bodies attempt to posture a wolfish prowess of physical superiority. Those few who have previously passed through similar face-offs stand lazily with expressions of nonchalance, seemingly ignoring the center-court proceedings. In a dry summer's heat upon a vacant dirt lot, chalky dirt silently swirls around and then clings to the young wolves' shuffling feet. All attention is focused on, yet none dare to intrude upon, the arguing couple at the center of the domestic whirlwind. Leaning into Marissa with an overbearing presence, Cory intonates to her in a sharp hush, a few insulting words spilling over to the ears of the two confronting crews.

Cory had initially been intimidated by the group's face off, and it had taken Kylee's finger pointedly jabbing him below his ribs and her harsh chiding into his ear—"Don't just stand there like an idiot, go and tell her, or do you want me to go and do it?"—for Cory to act. In an apparent attempt at reconciliation, Cory had simply volleyed across the distance: "Hey, Marissa, we need to talk." With a push from Sheri, Marissa was separated from her crew and, with a combination of momentum and peer pressure, continued her now-obligatory walk to engage with Cory. Cory initially spoke calmly as Marissa stood there looking hopelessly confused, silently nodding her head. As a few bold declarations of accusation—"dumb ass, big mouth, slap you"—inadvertently reached his crew, they supported each denunciation with a cheer or with a louder echo of his own words. With his vocal pack at his back and Marissa's unresponsiveness, he grew more emboldened with a marked rise in the tenacity and pitch of his voice as he leaned over her.

Marissa now cowers under Cory's verbal abuse. Her head bows to avoid his eyes. Her face lacks her conciliatory smile of appeasement. She absorbs his diatribe. And yet, she does not flinch from his physical gyrations inches from her face. She idly ponders with third-person detachment and a girly-girl excitement of anticipation whether or not Cory is actually going to take a step back and slap her, as Efi had done to Sheri. Marissa's feet do not back up in retreat.

With the crowd focusing upon the quarrelling couple, Peewee slips away from his crew to slide unobserved along the building's wall to within a few feet of Cory and Marissa. Spying movement from the corner of his eye, Cory turns to confront Peewee and defiantly draws himself up to his full height. Even then, he still finds himself almost two heads shorter than the large man-boy. "Hey!" Cory barks out, "this is a private conversation . . . *Shrek.*" Smirks and giggles and the word "ogre" reach Cory's ears from his back-covering gang.

Embarrassed and confused under the sudden focus of so many eyes, Peewee hopes to disappear by sulking back against the wall. He bows his head and shrinks within himself to diminish his size and avoid the inadvertent transfer of everyone's attention. While looking down at his feet, he mumbles into the ground, "My momma taught me ta be nice to ladies and ya don't hit girls."

Emboldened by the amused laughter at his back, Cory continues, "Well, maybe you ought to run back to your momma then," as he squares up to Peewee while stepping between him and Marissa. "Meanwhile, Marissa an' I are having a few private words . . . if ya don't mind?"

Peewee hesitates a moment, as if not quite sure. Then he shuffles a half step backwards while lifting his eyes from the ground to meet Cory's bull-terrier glare. Turning his shoulders as he retreats to his side, Peewee's vision sweeps past Marissa, then stops as his eyes lock on her. "Marissa's with me," Peewee shyly offers up as an apology.

Cory's eyes open wide with astonishment. "What!?" With an incredulous look, Cory regards Peewee anew. "Marissa's your *girlfriend*?" The sarcastic, accusatory slur draws appreciative laughter from his pack.

Peewee quickly reddens. "No, no." Like a cornered, stomping bull demanding attention and respect, he kicks dirt up into a dust cloud. "I don't mean like that. Just friends . . . with us," he retorts as he glances over to his tattoo shop crew.

With the consummate stage actor's control of pace and timing in front of a live audience, Cory turns to face his gang with an unanticipated silence, a calculated, pregnant pause of effect. Dangling a grin of self-satisfaction before cinching the net of applause, Cory toys with them, allowing the tension to build to an inner crescendo of his choosing. When both groups are hushed to a murmur of anticipation, and with a grand sweep, he turns back to Peewee, and, with a mocking voice, asks, "Friends? What, like *with benefits*?" A scurrilous smirk drips over the edges of his face. Both sides respond with a spontaneous uproar of humorous approval.

"No! Jus' friends." Peewee's face blazes scarlet and his response is lost in the impertinent hoots and hollers of amusement at the oaf's expense.

At the center of appreciative attention, Cory finds that the cheering, entertained crowd fills him with a sense of bravado, which encourages him to play the role of the spotlighted ringmaster taming a great caged lion. "Well, seeing as you an' Marissa ain't an item, and we spent the last party drinking in the backseat of my brother's lowrider, I suggest ya mosey on back to your boys' and girls' club. And, if I wanna slap Marissa's ass while ridin' her, I will, and she's gonna like it." He turns in an exaggerated, choreographed move towards his group, his arm moving in a high overhead arc that ends with a snap of his wrist and with him barking the crack of a slashing whip: "*Snaap a!*"

Another boisterous cheer of spontaneous approval continues to inflate his self-importance as Cory completes his showman's pirouette, only to be surprised to find his lion-taming whip suddenly snatched from his masterful hand. He slowly cranes his neck to look up to the full height of Peewee leaning over him. Cory stands motionless like inert prey while Pewee twists his head in a curious, full inspection of a cornered rodent about to be consumed. All emotions out of his voice, all meaning strictly defined by the words themselves, Peewee whispers with the social etiquette of a ladies' intimate afternoon tea party of three, "If you touch her, I'll break ya."

Taken aback by the threatening whispered words spoken from the commanding presence of the man-boy above him, Cory can only remain motionless. Realizing that Peewee's words did not reach either crew, Cory quickly improvises by assuming a late-nineteenth-century boxing stance. "If you weren't so big, I'd kick your ass,"—fists circling in front of his chin, feet jitterbugging in the dirt. The whip-less lion tamer now the juggling clown.

"Yeah, I get that a lot."

"That's okay, Peewee, we're done," says Marissa with both arms tenderly hugging Peewee's arm like a fondly remembered childhood teddy bear of security and possessively tugging the now-pliant gentle giant towards their sideline. Cory continues circling in mock sparring. Young adult psyches braced for physical confrontation to validate their prowess now artificially laugh as tensions deescalate with Cory's comedic entertainment, none more relieved than Marissa.

Reaching her shop crew: "We did good, huh, Sher?" asks Marissa, in anticipation of a reward as her arms still snugly hook around Peewee's comforting biceps.

"Huh, yeah, ya did good."

The tat-shop group parts for the clutching couple to pass and, with a last glare across no-man's land, begins to disperse as they turn to follow Marissa, with Peewee in tow, towards the parlor's rear-alley entrance. Everyone except Sheri.

"Peewee's a better man than Cory ever'll be," boasts Sheri loud enough to bridge the empty space of neutrality, causing her crew to hesitate in retreat with a look back over their shoulders.

"Yeah sure, an' you know a little about a whole lot of men." Kylee turns to return the volley, drawing attention away from her youthful crew's congratulatory backslapping of Cory at standing up to, and walking unhurt away from, a much larger adversary.

"What'cha mean by that?"

"At least I ain't defined by the men I'm with."

"Yeah, and you should thank god every day that you ain't defined by your shoe size either 'cause that'd be kinda hard to see over your dress size, an all." In the slow, exaggerated walk of duelists appraising their opponents, these two mismatched girls are drawn towards each other by an unseen gravitational force. Sheri's heart begins to race, her throat dries, and her hands become clammy. Her stomach falls away to an empty hollow pit that sickens her with the realization that there will be no backing down from this confrontation with Kylee.

"Yeah, an' these shoes are just a fixin' ta kick some of your scrawny white ass, just like half the men you've been with."

"Fuck ya bitch. I ain't the one leaving my kid and lettin' them grow up with Grandma and Grandpa. I'd fer sure be a real mom and would take care of my own," Sheri says, exposing a deepening anger as they draw within arm's reach of each other, each with no idea of what to expect or what to do next.

"Yeah, well the way I hear it, you take care of everyone," Kylee counters with an arrogant laugh of assumed knowledge.

"Ya sure you wanna go there now? 'Cause I bet you don't even know who the father of your kid is."

Kylee pauses. The scowl across her face surprisingly relaxes into a knowing half smirk. With a touch of reflective contemplation, Kylee looks over Sheri's head and then glances behind to take the measure of each other's cliques. She then leans her face into Sheri's with the intimacy of a fast friend who is about to reveal an appalling secret. The self-satisfaction upon Kylee's leering face sends a scary shiver of premonition through Sheri. "Oh, I know who the father is all right . . . my dear, and when the moment is right, and I'm good an' ready, I'll let you know that you've slept with him as well . . . my little pretty."

The cold chill of a preferably left unknown and hated truth permeates Sheri's being. In that rarity of her guise, her usual stoicism melts as her whole face opens up in shocked surprise. Sheri's breath catches in her throat, her eyes glaze over with a blank stare, and the world recedes into the background, leaving her separated from everyone and everything. And then . . . nothing. Sheri sees nothing . . . the figure of Kylee standing before her vanishes to blackness. Sheri hears nothing . . . the cheering audience absent . . . sound muted as she is isolated within a solitude of silence. She feels nothing . . . her emotional chill dissipates to leave her a hollow shell of emptiness. Only her mind seems to function as she attempts to comprehend this strange transition from being gripped by the anger of Kylee's unanticipated elucidation to being enshrouded within this incomprehensible feeling of . . . nothing? Has she actually time-warped and fallen into that just-out-of-reach mirage where heaven and earth meld at the horizon that she had been so feverishly racing towards this morning?

A white dot of light at the center of her vision slowly expands and Sheri begins to comprehend, from very recent experience, that Kylee has just bitch smacked her. Flexing her hands in preparation for attacking her tormentor with French-manicured nails, Sheri struggles to focus her blurred vision as she simultaneously turns away from the reflecting glare of the sun.

As though suddenly awakening in the dark of night in a bed shuddering from the unexpected crash of the pounding surf of an approaching storm against the house-supporting pylons driven deep into a sandy beach, Sheri hears the roar of the entertained crowd's overlapping cheers that suddenly detonates in her ears: "Hit her!" "Hit her again!" "Slap that bitch!" "Woo hoo, Kylee!" "Come on Sheri!" "Look out! Look out!" Confused, Sheri shakes her head and looks up to see Kylee's back. Kylee is happily waving to her approving audience. Still dazed, and with an anger rising within, Sheri leaps at Kylee with a feline cry as she jumps on her back and reaches for her hair to pull her head back.

Marissa flinches against the wall as she watches Sheri and Kylee fall to the ground in a tangled mass of flailing limbs and rising dust. Shrill shrieks rake her ears like fingernails across a chalkboard. The grunting sounds of animal-rooting interspersed with cries of exertion from the wrestling women fill Marissa with a child's fear of being trampled by escaping circus elephants, and she attempts to find safety by pressing herself flat into the stucco wall.

Marissa is thoroughly befuddled by the social complexity of this afternoon's whirlwind of escalating drama that has culminated in their catfight, which she has only narrowly escaped. She emotionally disassociates herself from any complicity in the unfolding events behind a projection of hate towards Sheri. Marissa's gossamer fidelity enables her to justify her overwhelming relief that it is Sheri who is now the one rolling in the dirt with Kylee, rather than herself. With the cheering crowd's attention entirely captivated by the center-ring spectacle, and fearful of being sucked back into the swirling fray so scarily avoided, Marissa retreats from the imagined accusatory eyes of the others on her own cowardice with backwards half shuffles along the wall until she is suddenly stopped as she bumps into an unexpected body. Marissa sighs with relief to find only Robby squatting on his haunches against the wall, alternately glancing back and forth from the rhinestone phone in his hand to his sister wrestling in the dirt, Wes leaning upon his shoulder doing the same. Neither boy bothers to look at Marissa.

Movement across the vacant, sunlit lot catches Marissa's attention. Curious, she squints her eyes against the reflective light bouncing off the windshields of parked automobiles and distant buildings to study the lone figure that walks with purposeful strides directly towards her. Tall and lean, he is most inappropriately dressed in thick, grease-stained blue overalls pulled off the shoulders with sleeves tied around the waist to expose a black T-shirt with large, blotchy sweat stains at the pits and center chest. His eyes are hidden behind a pair of black mirrored Oakleys that are neatly tucked under longer-than-fashion-able dark hair, and wrapped around a most peculiarly misshapen head that is somehow oddly familiar. As this stranger strides closer and into the shade, Marissa observes an imperturbable face of determination: a small, expressionless mouth, his forehead smooth without a wrinkle or worry line, one of those lucky few who will remain forever ageless. Marissa suddenly giggles with a pinky loosely hanging from the corner of her mouth as she notices the most delicate, foot-conforming red booties on his feet. She thinks they are the sweetest, most adorable little things ever . . . for a little girl. What is this brightly colored pretty-man misfit doing walking out of the light of the sun into this shadowed den of tattoos, skirmishing cliques, and black anger? Marissa wonders.

Remaining curiously paralyzed against the wall, she finds her heart beginning to race as he draws nearer. Without a look at her, he stops beside her to stand fully erect and motionless over Robby. Robby looks up to see himself reflected in the mirrored glasses, and the stranger bends at the waist to exchange fist bumps, knuckles colliding and fingers exploding. Robby closes his eyes as his hair is playfully tossed and ruffled, and when they open again there are four blue tickets held up to his face, evenly fanned like playing cards. With an appreciative smile, Robby respectfully grasps the tickets, mumbling a shy, "Oh yeah. Cool, dude. Thanks!" The now-empty hand continues to hang open in midair, waiting in silence. "Oh, yeah, sure," says Robby with apologetic embarrassment as he swipes at the rhinestone-covered cell phone and places it in the hollow of the expectant palm. Closing his hand around the phone, the interloper again stands erect to his full height, momentarily gathering himself.

Marissa looks up at him and muses to herself that his misshapen head, sticky-flat in some spots with bushy peaks in others, is most certainly due to sweaty helmet hair.

Turning to approach the cheering crowd from behind, he casually says in a warm, mature voice without looking at her, "Hey, Marissa," and walks on past.

Marissa catches her breath as she falls back against the wall for support and lays a hand flat upon her bosom.

Her eyes following, she peers past him, and between the milling scrum's shuffling legs, to catch glimpses of two angry wrestlers on the bare dirt obscured within a dusty halo. With an impartial, detached air of curiosity, Marissa idly observes the rolling bodies now sporting unrecognizable, dirt-streaked faces contorted into grotesque masks of exertion and pain. Mesmerized by the entwined couple grappling, clawing, and squealing, Marissa suddenly realizes with a frightening dismay that a recognizable clump of matted blonde grabbed by one opponent is, in fact, Sheri's hair that together they had so carefully flat ironed, smoothed, and fastidiously coiffed high up on her head just a few short hours earlier. The irony of the meticulously spun web now ensnaring the spider fills Marissa with a perverse sense of delight as Kylee clutches a handful of once silky-golden locks and thrashes Sheri's head back and forth, to and fro, into the ground. A dull, pasty film of brown coats Sheri's brightly colored designer top and skinny jeans with angry mud stains collecting at the collar and armpits. Their grunts and piercing cries reach beyond the cheering crowd's rancor to Marissa's ears.

Averting her gaze from the tangled spectacle of her once-fashionable friend reduced to a feral animal rooting in the dirt, Marissa shifts her vision to BD and Peewee leaning attentively into the newly arrived stranger, their eyes fixated on the greenbacks hovering in their faces. Grabbing the money, with Peewee trailing, BD wades through the cheering audience into the center circle.

"Okay, boys an' girls, end of round one," officiates BD as Peewee snatches Kylee off Sheri.

With an audible protest from both camps, Peewee escorts Kylee back to her side while BD reaches down and grabs Sheri, still flailing with eyes closed, under the armpits to lift her to a standing position in a single motion.

Sheri finds herself being turned around by BD, and, with an arm around her waist, he simply lifts her to be carried as easily as a football underarm through the huddle.

"What the heck man, I had her, put me down," Marissa hears Sheri say as the crowd parts for BD. He swings Sheri head up to plant her in front of the expectant stranger, catty-corner and within earshot of a breathless and enthralled Marissa.

"What the fuck, man?" says Sheri as she first looks up at the stranger with apparent recognition and then quickly sidesteps to walk around him. With a dancer's fluid agility he shuffles with her, as his superior size effortlessly blocks her path when they collide.

Frustrated, Sheri steps back to command: "Shit, I don't need you here, and I don't want you here now." Looking up at him, Sheri twists her mouth to blow back a strand of long, loose hair that covers one eye, only to have the hair promptly fall back over her face again. She licks her thumb and forefinger and her face screws up in surprise as both digits stick to her tongue, which is thick with dirt turned to a pasty mud. She spits the dirt from her mouth while flipping her hair back over her head, which, on cue, falls back into her face again. She then conducts a surprise quick sidestep the other way, and again, with smooth reflexes, the stranger two-steps a blocking move.

Sheri's mouth purses, huffing a harsh whispered, *"What!?"*

Marissa leans her body forward with a cock of her head to eavesdrop. Although the replying individual words are unintelligible, she can hear a confident tenor voice speaking in a soothing, measured cadence of calm. Words evenly paced in a friendly manner, the tenor inflection of a question completing a sentence, to be continued without waiting for a response. Sheri folds her arms tightly across her chest and stares out into middle distance, impatiently awaiting the end-of-period bell and the teacher's lecture to finish.

"Lika hell'a no. There's-a no way I'm *ever* doing that." Sheri's voice rises as she brings her eyes back to defiantly meet his.

A happy smile of white teeth appears as he leans over, lightly placing both hands upon her shoulders. His rebuttal is a calming voice of quietude in the hurricane's eye. His continued chat is in a casual manner of reason with an emotionless focus of meaningful words to cut through and smother the anger pulsating from her pores. The words rise, the words fall, a momentary pause, a hard statement, an unanswered question. In unison, both heads turn and look out across the vacant dirt lot to the cars parked beyond. Marissa follows their gaze but notices nothing.

Their talking stops. Sheri's jaw clenches as she turns her head away and pulls tight her muscles across her cheek and down her neck. Thumb and middle finger rub together in thought.

"Where's that little chicken shit? Intermission's over." Kylee's acrimonious voice is once again an annoying irritant that floats over to the deeply engaged couple. "Bring that scrawny bitch back to me, I wanna finish kicking her ass," she continues to taunt, supported by an approving grumble of agreement from her pack.

Sheri gazes up to the man leaning over her. Her pensive look softens into an unreadable, blank stare as her jaw muscles relax and her hands flex. Without a word, he steps aside and Sheri steps through with a left-side pass. As she walks through her ringed tribe with head bowed, they lightly pat one of their own on the back with reassurance as they chant in unison, "Sheri, Sheri, Sheri!"

"Why, hello there again, my little pretty. Miss Manicure needed a powder break to take the shine off her nose?"

"Kylee, I just want to apologize for saying some inappropriate things about you. They were middle-school immature and way hurtful." Sheri eyes the ground while toeing dirt. "It was wrong of me to be so malicious and I should not have said such spiteful things." She lifts her eyes to confront Kylee. "I'm not going to fight you anymore. I hope this victory is enough for you. Sooo . . . peace out, Cub Scout." Raising her hand before Kylee's face, her fingers flash the *rock-on* sign. Finished, Sheri turns on her heels to thread her way back through her stunned, and now-silent, crew.

"That's right you little chicken; I kicked your scrawny ass, now run away," Kylee blurts as she laughs and her friends join in. Unsure of what else to say, Kylee, for once muted, stands there until swept up in her crew's boisterous celebration of victory.

"Hey, Bat Boy, I've got Dodgers tickets. Can you take me an' Wes?"

"What? What are you talking about?" Bat Boy replies, peering into Robby's hand. "Can't you see we're busy now . . . but . . . lemme see. What'cha got there?"

"Hey, hey," BD pipes up, flashing up the greenbacks. "Peewee and I have *mucho moolah* to *partay* downtown tonight. We're buying drinks for everyone." The tattoo parlor crew has clustered into two groups, one around Robby with a flush of blue tickets, the other around BD and Peewee, each with a layered green fan of Jacksons.

Only Marissa's eyes follow the couple's retreat across the vacant dirt lot to the parked cars. An arm is tenderly draped over Sheri's shoulder, not in that carnal touch of desire, but rather as a shield of flesh and bone protecting her from cast stones and flung barbs. She abruptly steps away to let his arm fall off into empty space.

The door to a red convertible with a black stallion on a yellow badge is opened and Sheri hops into the driver's seat. In a flash of deductive perception, Marissa understands the unseen presence, the unstated power behind Sheri's recent metamorphoses. With a jaded attitude of rage at having nothing other than the dirt hole she's standing in, and a gambler's willingness to risk all of that nothing, she has a self-deluding vision that she will either have it for herself or destroy them both in the process. Marissa knows, as that part of herself they share as a common trait, that Sheri's pretty-girl impatience of wanting things now—and in her own way—will soon bring her to grow tired of, and casually cast away, this novelty, as she did with all her boy toys. She can well then imagine herself being there to pick up the discarded piece. Yet Marissa can only wonder what clutch Sheri could possibly have over him as her mind begins to formulate an ill-conceived plan that will be poorly implemented and, in a very short time, result in a lifetime of penance, a hell on earth, in her own private eight-by-ten space. As a voyeur's vision magnetically drawn to a lighted window requiring closer observation, Marissa pulls away from the cool wall of shade into full sun for a better view.

Lifted from the floorboard and ceremoniously passed to Sheri is a baseball cap of sparkling rhinestones intricately inlayed in a human skull and a red rose that elicits an appreciative little-girl squeal of delight, quickly followed by a peck of thanks on his cheek. Flipping the rearview mirror, Sheri gives herself an inspective look over while she smooths stringy, matted hair from her face to behind her ears.

The stranger reflectively looks out the passenger window. With an elbow resting on the doorsill, his pointer finger pensively flips his lower lip, and his thumb hooks under his chin. His lips begin to move in a slow and deliberate speech, unheard by Marissa's ears. Sheri alternately glances from grooming herself in the car's mirror to the full, dark hair on the back of his head as his face is turned away.

Marissa observes in distant profile his passionate face of sustained control and his eyes averting Sheri's.

Finger fiddling with disheveled strands of blonde, curling and poking, and finally resigned to being out of control, Sheri twists her small frame to a sideways kneeling position on the car seat and leans over him, an arm lazily draped over the back of the passenger seat. Feeling the shift in her presence, he turns to meet her gaze with an expressionless face. Gently leaning in, Sheri nuzzles her nose across his unmoving face to linger her lips, tantalizing, over his, then firmly presses in. Slowly pulling away, their faces remain calm, blank slates registering a mutual understanding.

Flashing a wicked smile, Sheri tugs her new rhinestone skullcap lower, spins back into the bucket seat, and snugly tugs her safety belt over her shoulder. The car fires up a deep muscular rumbling of restrained power ready to leap. When slipped into gear, the car moves forward to turn around and then momentarily disappears behind the corner shack before entering the street.

The two young packs have separated into their respective social groups, each aware of their dissing by purposefully ignoring the others as they slowly migrate back to their marked territories.

A big-block Italian engine revs up a throaty opera-baritone roar that reverberates off nearby buildings, drawing the packs' attention to the onrushing convertible that quickens their hearts as it rips down the street towards them. Adorned with her new rhinestone cap, Sheri smiles as she waves to the crowd from the open cockpit and toots the car horn twice.

"Yeah, there goes that little chickenshit running away scared! I bet we ain't never gonna see that little piece a garbage around about here again," Kylee barks out her parting shot above the noise of the racing car.

"Huh, that would be nice and one can only hope, but I doubt it." Sean offers his thoughts of consolation to no one in particular. His soft-spoken words are either lost in the increasing din of the passing *bella machina*'s revving engine, or the well-intentioned meaning of the statement itself is misconstrued by the few of his own tattoo-parlor shop crew.

Neither side bothers to dwell on Kylee's or Sean's words as all eyes are captivated by the elegantly sculptured red prancing stallion galloping away down the street with an increasingly joyful neighing of raw power. Only a few in the crowd can actually put a name to the deep-chested, bellowing steed that Sheri is now attempting to tame after setting it free from its dirt lot to canter and then gallop unrestrained upon open roadway: a Ferrari F355 convertible with 389 wild horses.

~~~~~~~

SPIN . . . COCK . . . PULL!

Goth-girl lark
 who fears not
 the stigmata mark,
 take thy covers off!
Expose all of thee,
 inked of love lost,
 pierced of pain present,
 of flesh and of art.

Adorned by grace
 with fairest
 luminous skin,
Thy sun-shy face
 concealing a fragile
 porcelain soul within.

Paranoid, twitchy
 and ever lost,
 caught in a witchy
 watchtower of white,
 vaporous haze,

Elixir enslaved
     and unreachable,
     floating aloft
     from crystal shards
     of meth's blaze.

Addiction affliction, worse
     than mere mortals'
     slings and barbs
     upon this world,
     these sins you're
     childhood born:
Sins of father,
     sins of mother,
     no morals of cross,
     no innocent child
     should be conceived
     to bear and borne.

No Jesus, no savior,
     no haloed
     archangel's
     guiding light
     in your life,
Cloistered alone,
     drapes drawn
     in a den of night,
     a less-than-nothing
     satanic wife.

And yet . . . I pray . . .

As silky laces of love
     tie me up,
     tie me down,

bound as glove
to thee I lay,
Press me hot,
    press me hard,
    let me help restrain
    thy flighty,
    witchy way.

~~~

Seductively beckoning apparitions of the flesh-burning artist's long-forsaken past wax forth in his hallucinatory dreamscape from the cryptic recesses of his subliminal conscious. Lovely women that are the incarnate spirits of the artist's previously debauched life effortlessly float in his mind's eye to lay an unshakable dread of earthly misery upon his mortal soul. These half-clad female specters appeal to his latent desires they so well know for him to once again accompany them unto that mystic dementia of hanging aloft in euphoric clouds of no time or cares. Their carnal entreatments implore upon his wanton lusting to heedlessly embrace their lecherous cravings. Cravings that result in a barren and most immoral affliction that he so well knows to begin in lazily lounging among wafting, luminescent vapors of their coven of no cross. A confliction of desires and confusion of character reigns within.

This spectral vision, with all known physical laws thereupon abandoned, transfixes him, as all nightmares do, with eyes wide open, staring into their fathomless abyss that contains no future for a chaste and mortal soul. Mesmerized by these delinquent and petulant spirits hellbent upon ingratiating themselves once again into his life, he can only remain frozen in place, stationary in time. His fright is of not trusting a decision of mind or a move of his discombobulated limbs for which either an incorrect selection, or false misstep, results in his tripping into the dark-angels' embrace and thus his eternal doom.

Senses swooning, he is utterly disheartened at how these lacy wisps have arisen from beneath the patina of his lightly buried, dreary gray ash of his opiate-laden and ignoble past. He knows not what emotional shock has occurred to rip asunder the weave of his life and fracture forth this visceral tempest of his bad witches, all of whom he has accompanied prior.

Having given no fair forewarning of slipping past those rusty gates of hell before spontaneously appearing before his eyes where they weave the enchantments of their desires, these swirling, ghostly apparitions now lustily tease *for his essence*—thus seeking *their* material form upon Earth. He wilts, he profusely sweats before these, his intractable, beseeching demons that have escaped from behind the unmoral bars of perdition to now abruptly appear within his mind's eye and flip the switches of his previous addiction that awaken his banal predilections. For as he well knows, taking that one wee step forward, seeking succor within those offered womanly folds, would be the beginning of one decadent descent into their deviant den of damnation.

Oh a vile curse upon the abomination that is his long-banished desire to partake with these lovely she-devils of Satan's own sweet elixir, so innocuously disguised as insipidly wafting white vapors caught trapped and swirling within an artisan-crafted, colorful stained glass that once again knocks, knocks, knocks on the portal of his consciousness to play, play, play with his fallible cravings. Oh yes, to throw oneself prostrate before these lovelies and once more experience the instant orgasmic rush! To suck the nectar of that lung-expanding breath of the Devil's own special recipe of chemically altered compounds that allow mind and body to detach together from commonplace cares and imaginatively flirt as lightly as a hummingbird in deep shadows of fragrant spring wildflowers seeking sweet pollen of pistil and stem. Alas, the comforting swaddle of white clouds does not last, followed by the gradual and inescapable descent of self-destruction into an emotionally and physically detached existence: afraid of everyone, afraid to step out, afraid of the shining sun's simple daylight, eventually cloistered alone in a room with drawn drapes seeking the dark of night.

Suddenly a sharp cry! of the hopeless and lost parts from the tormented artist's lips, as he abruptly plunges over the ledge headlong with a vertigo-inducing free fall into that foreboding pit of his imaginative hallucination! Terrified by the vivid force of launching into weightless flight, he convulses awake in a full-body spasm to feel himself physically planted and safely alighted upon terra firma. Still in complete dark and isolated seclusion in his sudden awakening, there is yet some confusion within as to his time and space. To escape this enveloping disorientation he . . . with a gasp . . . hastily pulls away the sweat-damp hand towel that has covered his face and blinded him. A stirring awakening from the weightless free fall of his horrific and unsettling nightmare has brought neither the clarity of sanity nor escape from melancholy desperation as every moral fiber of the artist shudders, staring upon the corporeal appearance of his dreaming dementia that now lies before him as reality incarnate!

With wary trepidation he peers, between propped-up feet and crossed ankles resting on an aged and stained wooden desk, into a scary score of haunting faces with returning gazes from unblinking eyes of empty spaces. Weary and bleary-eyed from a week's lack of proper sleep, he attempts to focus and discern a clue of realism within the shimmering and floating gray lines of apparent mortal matter separated from him by a thin human-vision-reflecting two-way mirror upon the dimly lit far parlor wall. He observes within the quiet tattoo parlor, with lights turned off, those spectral illusive images of his own artistic creation that, illuminated by the summer's heat-wavering sunlight filtered through the multicolored hue of storefront stained glass, elusively shimmer and eerily dance—now apparently unbound and alive!

Seeing the exquisitely detailed portraits of his illustrious past thus hauntingly illuminated, he feels an inconsolable despair seep into his mortal core. For he stares upon the opposite wall into the vapid glare of a lascivious harem of scantily clad witches—coddling cold, scaly, reptilian pets—that seductively lounge amid their wantonly malicious and misogynist warlock with his leashed dragon-dogs, and a pair of red, bleeding eyes from a bleating goat's head centered in the middle of a magical, inverted pentagram. Their vacant eyes plumb to the depths of their creator's restless soul as he reclines in his office chair.

Unblinking eyes stare back to fathom his hidden character, for he knows their ceaseless efforts are ravenously bent upon wrenching away the spirit of their creator to then release themselves from their confining prison wall and thus roam the earth freely as incorrigible apparitions desiring only to quench their own thirst for life.

Vicariously, all have tasted the ecstasy of human flesh, and they all desire more. And so they offer the irresistible lure of that intoxicating elixir that he has tasted before—a rational remembrance that sends a cold shiver of fear through him.

"Only a delicate breath of us . . . please?" he can hear the love-lies' innocuous taunting of the coven's cauldron brew. A calamitous stew that he knows spins an entwining and caustic web, which insipidly reaches out to dissolve every moral and Christian fiber within, and thereby sets them—witches and warlock—wantonly free to promiscuously play.

How is it that these two-dimensional ghostly temptresses from the world below, devoid themselves of souls—with their thick and black-as-deepest-night painted eyeliner surrounding wide-open unblinking, colorless, luminescent eyes devoid of pupils—see to fathom the depths of his soul and sing their seductive sonnet to the world above that only he on Earth can hear? Thus seductively spellbound, he thinks in his quiet, cornered desperation: *Oh God, how have they once again ascended from immortal darkness and coalesced to appear before me in this corporeal flashback?*

"Hush," he hears the wall-bound witches whisper from across the parlor floor as they continue to shimmer and shake on their far canvas ashen wall.

In the dim cloak of dreary light, his blurry eyes and weary mind attempt to focus on and discern the reality of the mélange of eclectic art wavering upon the far wall as dimensional, mercurial lines. A violent pulse now pounds in his head as, in discourse with himself, he questions his sanity: *How is it that these foul, ethereal remains buried long ago, these emotionally and physically binding old bones, continue to soil me with an oppressively suffocating film that can never be shaken clean from?* The walls beat and the walls vibrate in sync with the pulse that pounds in his head to loosen and shake alive the black-and-gray lines of his painted wanderlusting beings.

When will the misery of my chemical affliction ever end? His body begins to tremble and shake anew with the long-ago physical effects from his chemical addiction withdrawals. *Do I need more sleep, or should I seek a shrink?* With a deep breath he blinks hard as he places two hands over his face to clear his aching head, focus his vague vision, and calm his racing heart as he thinks in his artificial darkness: *Or . . . do I require just one more hit?* Opening his eyes, his lips curl a wry smile as he looks directly across to the Gothic, now-mocking figures of a previously sinful life adorning the whole of the far wall. He thinks back to a time when ironically those dark lines of a black-and-gray charcoal-relief mural had served to be the exorcism of his addiction demons. With a sardonic twist, the skin artist of flesh-burning ink fatalistically accepts the realization that during that time of his translucent, paranormal, chemical haze, these wantonly malignant, prescient spirits had materialized within his artistic hands, dancing across the smooth, ashen wall of his tattoo parlor hall—now covered from floor to ceiling with portraits of naked women, Satan's possessed children, and people hiding their pain—and had then forsakenly conspired those same sublime lines to be the future, hieroglyphic *curriculum vitae* of his now-to-be self-made sarcophagus entombment.

"Ha!" he blurts as he questions: Are the results of this picturesque pictographic herein presented thus a story befitting a great pharaoh and his kingdom through the ages? Are they an honest reflection of my precision as a skilled craftsman? Are they a worthy testament to the poor, sublime tortured souls of those I render in portraits? Or are they just the squiggly penciled lines of a wannabe artist struggling to master his craft from behind opaque shrouds of a mind-altering, designer drug? Is this mural the story and the quality of my life by which I choose to be remembered?

Malignant musings, deep and foreboding, cloud his mind while he idly stares, then blankly gazes, though no longer seeing, really, at the Gothic mural's charcoal lines with ashen-wall reliefs of the Devil's friends—black and gray shades absent of color as their underworld lacks soul—all fiends who now insufferably find a place to rest upon *his* soul. Suddenly this dark and melancholy introspection, now a self-loathing and resonating fear if truth be told, ruptures at the unexpected entrance of a young teenager eagerly walking—puppy-dog loping with growing, lanky limbs too long—across his field of vision of the otherworld through the two-way mirror.

With a barely containable boyish eagerness and exuberance, the youngster pauses in the center of the pentagram-dissected door. On the door, a large goat's head with staring, glaring red eyes painted by the artist's quill dipped in devil's blood peers and leers on either side of the boy's head, penetrating the full-wall office-side windowpane and captivating the artist's idle, mindless gaze. The artist reflexively shudders within from *thine* cold chill. Atop the header of the triangularly dissected and bleeding-goat-eyes-painted doorway, cursive Gothic script reads: *"Only the pain of burning flesh awaits all ye who enter here. Welcome!"*

With a hasty reach by a boy young and brash, the doorknob is grabbed and the door is flung wide open with an impetuous rash. The goat's soul-captivating stare swings inward into the ink room of flesh and pain and thus releases its spellbinding clutch on the momentarily mesmerized artist. In the blink of an eye, the boy's awkward friskiness fades as he stops, frozen and lost in a social maze. His carefree, animated demeanor instantly evolves into that of an experienced, hunting wolf—motionless, crouching, silently observing—his body tensed, alertly awaiting an opportune moment to pounce. The artist curiously studies the stealthy standing pose of the lanky teenager imprinted by nature with wolfen limbs, long and strong, and his immature human mind that is curious to the world around, interested in all the goings-on that are behind a closed, and sometimes locked, door.

Reflectively, the artist recalls his own time past, and what seems to have been another life, now another person, with only more questionable observations that arise within: *It's hard to believe that I, too, was once so young and carefree. How happy those days were with eyes wide open and curious to a world full of wonder, beholden to no one with no constraints on my time for my free spirit to roam wherever and whenever I wanted to be. So very long ago, those simple times cloaked and comforted in the all-embracing love of the deity Jesus.* Pressing back his reawakened, self-consuming, devilish craving for the witch's white brew, and seeking within the tightly wound moral fiber of his being to save himself and restore some semblance of a righteous soul worthy of salvation, the artist recedes to a simpler, happier time to whisper-hum:

Jesus loves me! This I know,
For the Bible tells me so.
Little ones to Him belong;
They are weak, but He is strong.

Jesus loves me! This I know,
As He loved so long ago,
Taking children on His knee,
Saying, "Let them come to Me.

Time slows and idly drifts for the artist and boy in their heightened state of alertness in the refractive sunlit parlor-den weirdly colored opaque from the stained storefront windows: one stealthily stalking, still and quiet, tensely poised to ambush as an agile predator on unsuspecting prey, while the other attentively observes as he reclines in a reflective repose and quietly hums to keep himself from leaping with his escaping witches over the infernal ledge.

Suddenly fractured from his half-crouched pouncing stance, the boy bolts alive in excited animation, waves his hands in cadence to some unseen conversation, and finishes with an exaggerated flair of his right arm pointing in the air to the parlor's rear social den—once an idle warehouse, now a converted, interactive space for gaming. Angled with his view from behind, the artist sees only a single cherubic cheek of the teenage boy swell high with the muscle contractions of the disarming contrite smile of an innocent to combat the full-body blitz of two annoyed women who hastily approach him from the rear of the tattoo room. The two women abruptly pause in their charge to confront him. Creviced wrinkles across their foreheads relax and then disappear, and their worried, old-women looks morph—one with a shocked face of panicked confusion and the other with an unreadable countenance both hard and penetrating—to softer expressions of the pretty, young women they are. The female pair silently passes knowing glances of relief and then exchanges casual shrugs of resignation. With nary a word, the girls gather their womanly clutches in hand to exit the private inking room and excitably pass by the artist's office and other tattoo stations on their way to the seemingly safe haven of the unseen gaming crib. The loyal young pup turns to follow suit, then hesitates to momentarily pause in the open doorway with only his eyes narrowly following the ladies' carefree gait. The change in the boy's demeanor as he clandestinely and inexplicably closes himself alone back into the tattooing room does not go unnoticed by the ink artist who watches unseen from across the parlor floor behind his two-way office mirror.

Upon the closure of the tattooing room's swinging door and the return of the pentagram-framed, staring goat's head with eyes of blood red—one of only two actual colors upon the far wall—the artist again becomes aware of the deviant den of unblinking eyes from the warlock's harem of black-and-gray-wash witches who effortlessly hover and vacantly stare out from that far, flat wall of skin-tone ashen to visually hypnotize him in an agonizing suspension of a self-consuming dread. *And, how is it that their vision penetrates my protective, light-reflective mirror with their lurid gaze hauntingly piercing a consumptive blackness concealed within my heart?*

Sinking still deeper in despair at his loss of free will into that intimate void of their hollow, wide eyes that continue to bore down upon him, the artist can feel within his slightly unstrung head a faint wind that carries a seductive whispering song with melodious finger-hole flute voices: *"Cometh . . . hitherto us . . . our love . . ."*

Flat witches with two-dimensional lips unmoving though they may be, he can nevertheless hear their thinly forked tongues terrifyingly begin to flicker with their sweet, lulling cadence of intoxicating invocations. Their subversive cauldron brew that first confuses and then exhausts, all to instill—no!—to expose that which already exists within: salacious urges that would soon overwhelm even the Trappist moralist to be tempest-tossed prostrate before them.

> *Sssurrender thyself*
> *within our comforting folds . . .*
> *and once again be bold!*

Feel thee transition
> *above thine physical confines*
> *of a body's old bones*
> *and of humans'*
> *oh-so-very limited, linear minds.*

The erotic RUSH!
> *of hanging fore'er aloft*
> *above the earth with US!*

How long, how high
> *can we together fly,*
> *in our mind-expanding*
> *billowy cloud?*
> *with us beside thee manly proud.*

How far can thee sssee
> *floating unbound and free?*

How discerning are one's thoughts
> *to the vision of our Satan's truths?*

How much the pleasure
> *of our together, intense, orgasmic pulse!?*

Together again with us!
> *Ever again with us!*

"No, no! Not!" he rails a sharp protest to stop the witches' black mass circling within his throbbing head, "will I go there again. With or without you incestuous bitch tweakers! Be gone ye of the cursed . . . be gone now, I say!"

"*Ohh? And how ssso?*"—a simple, momentary pause to formulate a haughty riposte from these two-dimensional, ephemeral apparitions that attempt to suck the life out of an unsuspecting other so they may escape their confining prison wall and live vicariously within another.

We ssshalt! have thine eyes, and
> *thine eyes shall open*
> *to Himith within'th!*

Lie again, play again
    with us our favorite one,
    and we shall expose,
    then expand thy deviant mind
    whilst giving thee the courage to act
on those craven desires of thine.

Thou wants her,
    thou arts lusting them both, yesss!
Thee knowest,
    we ssspeaketh, this truth.
Again, when thou art with us,
    we shall make it happen,
    with us, thine shalt have only us to blame
    —nay, thank us—
whence they all cry again.

Within the four-wall confines of a very still and isolated room, womanly whispers of an incantation for *their* manifestation are a hypnotic lilt that picks and plucks to court his emotional strings in their search to resonate his basest chords. Their chorale fades with a carnal climax of an enticing street whore's chaste promise of safe satisfaction.

Yes! The anguish of insidious truths! convoluted with appetizing lies! With self-loathing revulsion, the enlightened artist understands what only the acceptance of a hated reality of one's own can bring. There is no logical reasoning with thine own self's impetuous beast wantonly teased through the constraining bars of pious morality; only the continuous sting of a human's righteous whip of physical restraint can overcome the loss of emotional control. The coven's bewitching invocations cast a long shadow of demoralizing gloom across his foreseeable future and a prevailing sadness for all that would be lost. He does not desire to join these black witches again in their unholy alliance, devoid of the cross now manifested before him, and with it the loss of family and this safe haven of momentary shelter for all others—his successful business built upon an impressive artist's reputation—that he had worked so long and hard establishing. Within these walls of adobe and stucco is a place of business to ply his craft and support his family. Yet this structure serves as even something more for him and others: it is a safe refuge for those who have been overwhelmed to refresh their sanity; a social den for misfits to mingle and fit in; a pad in which to crash a few hours for the chemically addicted; a temporary respite for some to escape from the craziness of dysfunctional family life; and for still others with nowhere else to go and nothing else to do, simply a socially comfortable place to casually hang out. In helping others, the artist feels himself gain some meaningful redemption for his previous juvenile delinquent life of crime.

As the subliminal echoes of the female ritual chanting slowly fade, a fearful realization is upon him that no matter the length of time, and no matter the distance of space, the sirens' sweet, lulling cadence of intoxicating singsong voices will always resonate within; they will never go away and they will never let go.

"*Tina* is not my soul mate. *Tina* is not my lover. *Tina* is not even my friend. You witches are just the beguiling, street-whoring bitch tweakers of my being!" The artist volleys to bolster his faltering, demoralized will and to hold back the light-absorbing black mass beginning again to swirl.

A deathly silence bears down upon him and a bitter sadness—for all that will be lost should he fail to act and fall once again under their spell—seeps into his soul. With sudden resolve, he shakes off his trepidation to swivel in his chair and reach for another everlasting temptation that awaits but an arm's length away, hidden from prying eyes and sticky fingers at the bottom of a lower desk drawer. With a fixed gaze, he reaches for that special box tucked away below a sheaf of miscellaneous papers, to banish them all, once and for all. The artist asks aloud, "Oh my devilish pretties, what say ye now?"

A momentary pause of silence . . . within the room . . . within his throbbing head.

Lifting the weighted mass of a square tin container from the bottom drawer, the artist asks himself, *So, is this suicidal device that silently awaits within this box the ludicrous indictment of my degenerate youth and continued, consumptive moral rot?*

His fingers lightly caress the old cookie tin, decorated with faint and fading pictures of a faraway place from a time long ago, that now sits on his desk. In his dark and morose musing, exhausted from a week without real sleep, a vestige silhouette of a long-ago dream from the recesses of his mind, the celestial apparition of his grandmother, appears as a nebulous outline upon the reflective glass to interpose herself between him and the swirling far-wall witches to ask disconcertedly, *"Is this really what you want to be doing now, young man?"*

~~~~~

"Is this really what you want to be doing now, young man?" Gran asks as she leans over his shoulder to observe him working at his desk. "Is this what makes you happy?"

"Huh? Yeah, fer sure, I like it. Pretty cool stuff, huh, Gran?" The young artist beams unabashedly as the red marker in his hand completes the finishing flourishes of burning flames emanating from a spiraling Mitsubishi Zero with a bright red rising sun meatball only moments after it was strafed by a Messerschmitt Bf 109 with its black tail-painted swastika.

"You do know the Imperial Japanese and the Nazis never actually fought each other, don't you?"

"Huh? What? We fought them both in World War Two. I saw it on TV?"

"Yes, but they did not fight each other. What grade are you in now? Haven't you had any history classes yet?"

With a questioning glance, the grandson looks up at his stately grandmother with her still-jet-black hair pulled back in a nurse's bun, not sure of what answer she is seeking. "Why fourth grade, and, of course, we have history lessons, we learned about Columbus and the Pilgrims and George Washington and the Revolution War and all that stuff."

"Hmm . . . your drawings are very good, young man."

"Thanks! They're really fun to do. An' I really like the different lines of these planes. Look how the Messerschmitt has a coffin-top canopy with those straight edges and flat glass, and the wings are cut square. And the Zero is so opposite with that bubble canopy and rounded wing edges." The budding artist excitedly outlines the forms with pen in hand. "And I have tons of extra time in class to do this while the teacher is talking."

His grandmother winces. She cannot quite fathom how he has the time to draw during class, or why, if he likes the planes so much, half a dozen of the fighters with the Japanese rising suns and Nazi swastikas in his drawing are in various stages of disintegrating in midair from their enemy's withering tracer fire.

~~~~~

"Huh! Is this really what you want to be doing now, young man? Don't you have homework or studying or something to do?"

"No, don't have any, and I'm done."

"Uh-huh, you don't have any homework, and you're done? Well, young man, you do realize you're going to be in high school next year and your grades are going to start counting. So if you plan on getting a good job or going to college you should probably start doing well in school now."

"Yeah, yeah, yeah. I'm doing good in school, Grandma, and we just don't have any homework anyhow."

"Well. Doing *well*."

"Huh? What?"

"It will come to you later. For now, what are *those* things that you are drawing?"

"Oh, this? Nothing really, it's just kinda a mishmash sketching, ya know? Just a mix of *Star Wars* and *Aliens* and *Star Trek* spacecraft and others in different planes of perspectives, that's all."

"Huh, 'planes of perspective,' how very articulate, young man. And what's that large one there on the side?"

"Oh! That's a Klingon battle cruiser! That's my favorite. It kinda reminds me of one of those bitchin' praying mantises, ya know, when they're stalking an' all. You know with their big ass . . . ahh . . . oops . . . ahh . . . heads, an' bulgin' eyes and those long, slim bodies and how they pose motionless before striking. I just love the lines and form, don't you, Gran?"

~~~~~

"So! And, what *are* you doing there, young master, if I may ask?"

"Gran! Where'd you come from?" the young student asks, throwing his shoulder across his paper-strewn desk to cover the workings. "I didn't hear you come in."

"So, do you know these girls?" Gran asks, eyeing his various drawings of scantily clad, curvaceous women juxtaposed with their half-fleshy faces slashed with monster stitches and half-hollow human skulls.

"Agh, *nooo*. Well, kinda. Some girls. It's like some parts from some girls in my classes, ya know, that I like, maybe their eyes, or their lips, or something else that . . . ah . . . I like, and I just freehand the rest to complete their faces of my imagination and maybe with a partial skull . . . or not."

"And do you complete their bodies from imagination as well?"

The artist's face flushes red as he wilts under Gran's oblique probing.

"So are these the girls you like in your classes?" Gran asks, as much to herself as to her grandson. Her real puzzlement is not quite understanding why a young man would draw a beautiful young woman that he knows and likes with a half face and half skull.

"Agh, weelll, aghhh . . ." the teenager self-consciously stammers in his breaking adolescent voice, which slowly dribbles out to an embarrassing silence. He turns away to blankly stare at his drawing board with pen in hand, idly doodling in empty space over paper, fearful of providing a false answer that Gran would instantly recognize as a lie, or at least an incomplete truth, and more fearful of exposing those still-maturing feelings and emotions that he cannot yet fully comprehend and which he wishes to keep private.

Gran patiently awaits an answer to her question, which was asked more as a test of her grandson's self-awareness, not to be critical or judgmental, or even shocked by any answer he gives, as would be expected from a caring, wise one who has lived a full life, and has seen many a young man, not much older than him, sent off to war, and often feels a heartfelt remembrance of the few who did not return. "Well, I really like your contrasting lines of the soft, fleshy faces with the sharp, hollow white skulls. Beautiful form."

~~~~~

"Huh? Is this really what you want to be doing, young man? Is this what makes you happy? I may never understand it, but . . ."

"Yes, Gran, this is what I like," he replies, standing beside her at the back of the vacant parlor room as they together review the freehand drawing that spans from floor to ceiling—faint gray pencil lines that are the beginning sketches of an extravagant warlock and his harem of thirteen witches, which run the length of the blank parlor wall. "And others like my work as well."

"Yes, so I've heard," replies Gran in a not-all-too-convinced voice. "As you know, I've changed my will. I'm taking a leap of faith, but I think you're worth the risk. For now, Brian runs the store and you're an employee—Brian is the master and you are his apprentice—and I receive a percentage of the total proceeds. After me, the trust has been set up where you will still be an employee working for Brian and a gross percentage of the store business is split between you and the other heirs: your aunts and uncles. The building and the business will be yours to run, when, and if, you get clean and sober. If you don't get sober, or the business fails, the trustees can either rent to someone else or they can sell the property and split the proceeds. So, it's all up to you and how you want to live your life. I'd start by at least listening to what Brian has to say, though."

"Yes, Gran," the apprentice responds in his earthly detachment from way up above, logically understanding the significance of her words through his mental haze while wondering if his grandmother notices his flighty nature floating sky-high in the clouds with his good friend *Tina*. Physically craving yet another awakening tweak, he attempts to loosen the embracing web of threads woven through his muddled mind by the foggy chemical brew and to focus his thoughts and actions by telling himself with conviction: *But as of now, I'll do anything to continue drawing these naked girls, and bloody daggers, and human skulls.*

Alas, but sadly, as an imperfect human enslaved by chemically binding chains that wind tightly around limbs and weave an ensnaring web through one's mind, he needs something more than a momentary thought—something to shake him to the core—and thus forever break these addictive bonds. And so the love of his girlfriend, *Tina*, continues to hazily float him until the terrible fright—the stark, reality-awakening events—of that one fateful night.

The late-night—early morning, in fact—call, and the skittish nature of the accented voice on the other end should have set the street-smart artist's senses on edge with wariness. But it was his greed and the need for a double dip—the hefty profit of delivering a magic eight ball as well as working a full memorial portrait: *mucho moola* on both sides—that superseded his basic survival instincts. All was well upon his arrival, or so he thought, when a slight-of-frame young woman with a lethargic demeanor and a detached smile greeted him at the door. Several more girls casually lounged behind her in the cluttered living room as they partied in a smoky haze. Following the young woman through the house, he stepped into the back room to complete the deal and begin the tattooing when, without warning, all went empty and black. He awoke bloody and naked at the bottom of a stained porcelain bathtub, wrapped tightly in a clear plastic shower curtain with a revolver pressed to his face.

"*Buenos días* . . . dumb shit." A dark-complexioned, Mexican-looking thug, deftly holding a handgun, slowly leaned over the now-nipped-in-the-bud tattooist and greeted him as he struggled to focus and regain full consciousness from the dizzying daze of a blinding headache. The jilted artist immediately found that not only was he unable to move in his restrictive bindings, but with duct tape firmly stuck across his mouth, neither could he speak. His eyes opened saucer-wide in surrendered acknowledgement of his defenseless predicament.

Observing and listening, he quickly came to the lucid realization that he was about to experience fully and with finality the dire consequences of his chemical dependency and the material greed to appease the compulsion of his seductive witches; he was about to be disposed of simply so that all of the valueless little objects that he carried on his person could be taken.

Looking past the thug and his gun through the open double bath-room doors, he observed that the model-thin girl who had greeted him earlier at the front door, along with the lithe, pale beauties who had been partying heartily in the living room behind her, were now seated before a vanity piled high in disarray with compacts, brushes, and curling irons, as they preened in the mirror for what in his expe-rience he knew was an all-nighter of getting ready and dressed up to go out to nowhere. In an illusionary angle of the glaring vanity lights, their black-as-night lined eye rims appeared eerily void of natural life just as their uncaring demeanors appeared devoid of caring souls. His sense of hopeless self-pity was complete when, one after the other, they turned to see him raise his bloody head over the rim of the tub without any change of expressions on their bored, self-absorbed faces.

An overwhelming sense of unworldly detachment pervaded his being, as if he were an independent third party observing the action from above, and then, an incomprehensible unreality of him suffering such a pitiful demise alone and unbeknownst to anyone who cared—and left to wonder if anyone would care even if they knew.

"Sorry dude, nothing personal, ya know," the Mexican continued, the threatening gun circling around the artist's head.

"Hollywood!" one of the girls suddenly yelled with surprising excit-ability from one so seemingly dull. "You're gonna mess us all up with his blood an' shit! Take it outside, or wait 'til we're done. Think . . . dickhead!"

"Shut da fuck up . . . *puta!*"

Without even a glance from those empty shells of living eyes at the naked and prone victim in the bathtub, one of the girls nonchalantly rose from preening herself before the vanity to quietly shut him and Hollywood behind the bathroom doors.

"Now my friend," whispered Hollywood in his cigarette-raspy voice, as though hushed for an intimate conversation among bar friends as he leaned his sweaty, pockmarked face into the awaiting victim's, just as his cell phone started to ring. "Fuck . . ."

"*¡Habla! . . . Sí, sí. Él esta aquí . . .* No man, *yo lo tengo ahora, aquí . . .* What the fuck? . . . It's like no problem. I said I got him right here, just give me a minute, damn it . . . *Sí, sí,* all right already!"

Hollywood finished his brief conversation and stuffed the disposable flip phone back into his front jeans pocket. "Well, my friend, it looks like one of Jesus's little angels is looking over you, or you have some very powerful business partners, no? 'Cause I'm supposed to let you go." His accented voice was filled with not-so-subtle disappointment. "But . . . I think we have some fun first, yeah!?" he said as he reached for a milky, opaque glass pipe on the counter. Lips caressing the end of the hollow glass tube, Hollywood carefully torched the bulb and curiously inspected his dry dupe in the tub while expertly spinning the glass pipe before inhaling a deep lungful of trapped, swirling vapors. "You want some?" Hollywood asked in a harsh whisper, reaching over and sticking the pipe in his prisoner's face.

The tattoo artist hastily, and for the first time in his life, shook his head no to an offer of smoking crystal shards.

"Oh man . . . *really*? That's some really nasty shit man," he purred, blowing dragon's fire breath from his flaring nostrils with his dark skin glistening and his glassy eyes glowing.

"Now, *mi amigo*," Hollywood continued, casually replacing the smoky pipe in his hand with the pistol, "we're gonna play a little game." A wicked smile of delight creased his face. "You like games? I like games. This is my favorite," he said as he emptied the brass shells from the breached cylinder into his palm. "I'm gonna take just one of these bullets," he said, holding it up for the man in the bathtub to inspect, "and I'm gonna put it back into the gun."

The dry bather knew that he was really, really *not* going to like Hollywood's little game.

"And then I'm gonna spin, spin, spin, and the cylinder goes round, round, round, and where the little bullet stops . . . *donde estás, mi pequeño amigo*?" all said in that childlike rhythm and fun of a bedtime nursery rhyme.

Lying supine and vulnerable at the bottom of a dirty tub and facing his impending demise, the artist focused on all the little things that in a moment become everything—the mechanical whirring of finely married machined parts, and the silent hope that the cylinder spinning would never, ever stop.

"And now my friend . . . you pray," Hollywood casually said as he pointed the gun at the center of the artist's forehead. Looking directly down the revolver's barrel, the prone bather could observe three empty chambers and the next one, in clockwise rotation, loaded! Awaiting a cocked hammer!

The sharp *crack!* of the hammer pulling back puckered his sphincter tight and set him squirming in his plastic cocoon, rocking and rolling from side to side. With a short, sharp breath, he stole a cursory look through squinting eyes to see Hollywood's finger tighten on the trigger, and then he closed them again with a muffled animal squeal.

Click!

"*Dios mío!* Lucky bastard!" Hollywood laughed. "You win! Maybe next time?" He grabbed the plastic shower curtain and violently yanked the naked man out of the dirt-ringed bathtub in a single swoop, throwing him facedown onto the bathroom tile.

Confusion reigned in the artist's mind as to his continued existence—hadn't he seen the next chamber in rotation loaded!?—but that contemplative thought was soon interrupted as Hollywood slashed a razor-sharp knife through the plastic wrap from shoulder to opposite hip and down his leg, simultaneously cutting into his flesh. A searing pain all along the way caused him to squeal into his muffling duct tape. Rolling the artist out of the tarp, Hollywood briskly grabbed the man by a tuft of his hair to lift him, and then violently kicked him through the double bathroom doors.

Naked, he was shoved past the petulant young girls still seated before the vanity admiring themselves in the mirror—their only admission of his trivial existence was simply to lean forward so as not to be hit by any flying blood droplets. The artist with a creative soul was afflicted with an ungodly fear as his mind comprehended their beautiful, expressionless faces with black-as-night eyeliner around the inky void of blankly staring shark eyes—nefarious proof of animal life within—as angelic creatures of God on Earth utterly devoid of a human spirit.

Frighteningly, a coldness of *his* utter and ugly moral abyss passed through the tattooist as from some virtuous origin previously unbeknownst to him; a moment of self-actualized clarity came to pass for him to consciously ask, *And I live a life different from them? How?*

Hollywood ran the naked artist straight out the front door to send him flying headlong over the two entry steps, landing with a painfully hard belly flop onto the sidewalk path, and chillingly whispered out a harsh warning, "If I see you, I kill you," just before he slammed the door shut.

Staggering in a state of drunken confusion along the desolate, tree-lined street, the artist, with slashed skin searing his backside, momentarily leaned his naked body against a metallic corner post to hold himself up and gather his senses. The cold steel provided a welcome, refreshing slap against his flesh. In the quiet predawn stillness, the stripped artist could eerily hear heckling coyotes laughing in their high-pitched voices to each other across the scrub-brush lands of distant foothills. "Ark, ark, ark, ark, ark, arrrooooooguhhhh! Ark, ark, arrrooooooguhhha!" And in a moment of deductive clarity he realized that earlier, as he'd stared down the barrel of the revolver, opposite from any perspective that he had ever previously witnessed, the actual spin of the loaded round had been anti-clockwise!

He laughed, and with two arms tightly wrapped around the steel post, hugged his naked body to experience a tingly thrill of pure pleasure shooting up his spine; and suddenly he felt . . . unchained . . . wildly free . . . and his own man. Loosening his arms from embracing the morning-frigid light post, he stood tall on his toes to lean and fully arch backwards as he answered the pack animal calls with his own throaty, wolfen howl directed at the glowing streetlamp above as early morning mist idly drifted past in endless eddies of luminescent curls.

~~~~~

"So, is this really what you want to be doing now, young man?" the heavenly spirit of Grandmother probingly questions him once again while he sits isolated within his claustrophobic tattoo office of his soon-to-be catacumbal walls. Those other womanly figures of free-floating spirits that effortlessly continue to swirl about upon the far canvas are cautiously silent and watchful for the moment as they wisely defer to a celestial light in their presence.

Looking up from his fingers circling a cookie tin of long ago, the tattooist, from the corner of his eye, catches his grandmother's image fleetingly recede and pass back into the shadowy recesses of his mind. Only a pale, ghastly visage of himself remains, reflected in the office windowpane. Alone to contemplate Grandmother's lingering question, he stares back at his faint, unrecognizable self and shudders in shock to comprehend that behind the creased worry lines he can see the deep sadness of someone who is just oh so tired of breath. Anxiously blinking to tear away from the frighteningly painful self-portrait of *his* soon to be ether-world imagery, he focuses beyond to the casually lounging, expectantly awaiting tweaking witches of his past who, hauntingly framed in the large office window, return his gaze. Flat and with their oh-so-innocent faces, these sorceresses with eye rims painted heavy black, encircling large stark-white eyes void of color, empty of life, all stare back . . . except for the lone, sultry siren with unnaturally bright blue, full-eye irises hiding in the corner. A sweat droplet rolls off his brow along the side of his nose into the corner of his eye. He rubs his irritated orb to press away the salty sting and clear his blurred vision.

The hue of stained-glass-filtered sunlight entering the parlor casts surreal images that shimmer across the length of the shop floor and walls. In his fevered and emotionally tormented solitude, he witnesses the mural of haughty, Gothic witches dimensionally shift to cast themselves adrift from their flat, confining prison wall. These now-free mercurial witches desperately reach out in an attempt to physically stay his hands that lift at the rounded lip of the tin. To catch his attention to bide time in order to change his shifty mind, the coven screech in most acrimonious tones as they approach, *"No, no, not!"*

Where only moments earlier these wall-lifted witch tweakers sang with suggestive whispering of a lover's passion for private pleasures, there is now the shrill insistence of the strung-out begging for any loose coin on the street with veiled threats behind their rancorous voices, should one's back be turned without having donated a worthy amount. The rise in pitch and the frenetic tenacity of his sirens' song is unmistakable in its attention-grabbing, discordant-chorus attempt to return the focus of his fragmented mind to them and to cause him to drop that which he holds so lightly in his hands. While their intolerable rancor resonates with the dread of screeching felines and puts his nerves on edge, the artist stubbornly fools himself into believing that he has no reason to fear them. His fingers again begin to caress the circumference of the thin tin box, wishing to coerce from within an overdose of a final temptation to those now-swirling, dimensional demons that he no longer can neither readily discern from bodily dancing within the tight office confines nor from the witches' chorale within his crowded and throbbing head.

Not willing to play the penultimate game that might result in their ultimate demise, the nervously surreal witches now impersonate their alternate, manic personas and coyly whisper in his ear . . . for only him, alone, on Earth to hear,

Sssweetest love,
>   *we flutter upon thine heart*
>   *as free-flying white doves,*
> *from which we can never part,*

For upon thine soul we art the lover's ssseal
>   *as we drape across thine manly arms so strong*
>   *and adorn thinen cavern walls so tall and long*
>   *and from which no other soul may ever steal,*

Forever young and lovely, we're the envy
>   *for all on Earth who doth have eyes to perceive,*
>   *as we art evidence of thy artistic brilliance,*
>   *and the embodiment of thy stately masculinity!*

Thee that is enchanted within
>   *our clouds as soft as silk and lace,*
>   *and appreciates our ssswoon*
>   *within thine passssionate lover's embrace*
> *whence we together float, flutter, and ssspoon.*

"Oh, my sweet whores," he addresses, not believing his perception of the visceral womanly shapes that actually begin amassing. "I have tasted of your addictive witches' concocted brew all too often, and I verily shall not willingly partake of you once more," he responds, with the vertigo light-headedness of one looking over a bottomless ledge, and a vision of his body weightlessly free-falling again into that black void of their netherworld.

Under intense logical duress, he misconstrues to believe that simply all he needs to do to foil their tempting entreaties is to once again feel the reality of a balanced, weighted mass of cold blue steel in hand, to hear the metallic clicking of closely machined parts that freely spin about, to experience the intense mental shock as the hammer is cocked! Ah, and yet the heavenly curse and the satanic damnation of choosing the lesser of two unforgivable blasphemies. *"And so I find this law at work: Although I want to do good, evil is right there with me." Romans 7:21.* To deny this truth is to deny that piece of the Devil that resides within each of us, with whom we fragile mortals are tasked with wrestling for self-mastery of our earthly actions, thus perhaps saving our eternal souls.

From a long-forsaken floating dream from which he cannot seem to be shaken awake, the artisan indulgently feels the past pleasurable effects of his witches' alternative solution not easily forgotten. Blood rushes to his head in heady anticipation of the Devil's own elixir once again pulsing through his veins, extending with its addictive grip throughout body and mind. *"Yes our dear, come to us, hither here."* Twirl it about, torch it up, and let blaze the demonic stimulant that rapidly releases the brain's dopamine to let rave the mind in a self-contained euphoric high. Let float mind and body together in detached amusement high above earthly cares in a pure state of physical and mental ecstasy. Days and days without sleep floating upon that boundless high . . . nothing else to do . . . no place to go . . . keep unsheathed demons close . . . as one gradually slips into a sleep-deprived, alternative state of confusion where one views with glassy and opaque eyes that never clearly comprehend a shuddering and stuttering zoetrope world of unreality.

With repetitive inhalation of the fiery calamitous stew, gray matter shrivels as brain cells starve and brain cells wither to eventually die, and, with just half a mind firing, the tweaker shies away from the light of day and withdraws from polite society to huddle in a cloistered, darkened den. Tripping in a room of drawn drapes, denying all natural light while sharing a common glass pipe among "new friends," invited in for a day of party and play, the infernal, internal shrews of jealous paranoia wail their warnings as these other *parta and play guests* either overcooketh the brew or partaketh of far more than their goddamn fair share! The addictive warlock's glassy and wary eyes suspiciously flick away from every little idle glance, for all others are assumed to be either an undercover narc to take you in, or a snitch attempting to save himself by setting you up and taking you down. Dubious safety is sought and found when one secretly—*shh!*—tucks the magic eight ball low below the shoe line in one's sweaty socks, out of sight and therefore out of reach?

Deprived of food from inhaling the appetite suppressant, the body first becomes sexy model-thin—"hey hey'a there baby!"—then, with continued necrotic consumption, the body slowly withers from within as it searches in vain for the sustenance of missing nutrients. The caustic poison pulsing within eventually percolates to the surface as necrotic rot to eventually lay waste to all outward appearances of physical beauty.

The body slowly decays, as visibly evidenced with symptoms of sallow, patchy skin that prematurely wrinkles; hair that falls out in clumps; and the agony of badly stained, achy-breaky teeth. The feeling of the Devil's own little buggers crawling *underneath* the skin becomes incarnate with the appearance of bright red, cankerous crank-bug bites that blemish the skin's surface to be torn at with dirty fingernails. Oh, but the sexual cravings of a raging hard-on, a massive overdose far beyond anything that an over-the-counter little blue pill can induce, and that cannot be satisfied for days on end—even with the perfect partner—and thus leads to an ever-expanding, debauched repertoire experimenting in an ever more ludicrous variety of acts of sexual behavior in an endless search for ultimate satisfaction.

There was that brief, blissful time, another lifetime ago, but now over the mortal ledge and permanently lost to his earthly embrace—oh, how he still mourns! He still secretly pines for the intimacy of lacing his fingers through the dark weave of *his witch's* thick hair as he pulls her face to his to lock lips tightly and breathe in from her lungs the residue of Satan's chemically altered drug, intermingled with the lovely nectar taste of her sweet feminine essence.

Painted true to her lenses-enhanced, exceptionally royal-blue, anime eyes . . . the only human form with living color mixed into the swirling charcoal lines of the warlock and his harem upon the far wall . . . *her eyes*—time immortal—longingly stare out. He allows himself yet once again to be captivated by his enchantress of a witch as he wistfully resurrects those freehand-drawn lines of womanly form that lie splayed out for all to see upon a quiet, upper corner of the Gothic mural. Silently looking out while shyly hiding up high, her seductively nude body is demurely lounging, as she once warmly lay under him, wearing only her favorite shiny steel-toe-tipped Frankenstein boots laced up knee high.

Confession of the irrepressible soul—as not a spoken word would be said for now to another he be wed—his memory of her is undiminished with the passage of almost another life. *Wench! What could we have been?* Tucked deep within and never admitted, for fear of any excuse to forever dance at the witches' black mass and never leave, is his shame of not stopping her, the cowardice of not being there with her, and the guilt of still being here without her. Once, when he was for the moment sober and clean, he had attempted to reach the vain woman within by grabbing her thin shoulders to firmly hold her in place as he told her with harsh concern: "Girl! That shit's not gonna kill ya, it's just going to make you old and ugly before your time."

Rationally unreachable from way up high within the haze of *Tina's* blaze, those extraordinarily blue anime eyes had coyly looked up to him from beneath her unkempt, forest-dark hair, angrily cut short and mopped upon her head, and with childish unconcern she had replied with a frightening conviction, "Don't be goin' an' trippin' on me now, for fret not my dear, as I swear! prior to anyone's witness to the pox of my premature and unsightly decay, I shall have an untimely and solo demise." Within those darkly lined eye rims of a twenty-first century Goth, and from beneath that despairing persona born of the chemically addicted child, there still remained her sweet disposition of the good witch Gwendolyn, for tenderly she had consoled him from her dire prognostication with a sensual nuzzling of her sun-adverse, por-celain face across his manly stubble. A most beautiful rosebud blush of a cherubic Irish child in winter's-morning frost speckled upon her creamy cheek from their brush. And once upon a time, on a dark and moonless night, upon the eve of her thirtieth, as she had for so long promised, and years after he had married another, *his witch* had driven alone!—not cruising the highway together hand in hand—out to the desolation of the high desert, and had sat in the driver's seat to send half her remaining brain matter to the backseat. Thus, true to the words of her spoken desire, she would remain . . . forever young . . . forever beautiful . . . forever an unlocatable ache of sorrow that sweeps throughout his body.

Wistfully he sinks into those alluring portrait eyes and begins, in his off-key, cigarette-graveled voice, to whisper-sing a dirge to match his heavy soul, her favorite Kurt Cobain folk song:

> *My girl, Goth girl,*
> *Tell me where did you sleep last night?*
>
> *In the pines, in the pines*
> *where the cold wind blows*
> *and shivered the whole night through.*
>
> *My girl, Goth girl,*
> *where will you go?*
>
> *To the pines, to the pines,*
> *where the sun never shines,*
> *to shiver when the cold wind blows.*

Locked onto those anime-blue eyes of the only strung-out witch he knew to retain a thread of concern for another, he smiles for the still-remembered reality of her essence and wishes they could have spurned their mutual affair with *Tina*, which resulted in constant and dramatic conniptions of jealous rage and made hopeless their life together as an exclusive couple. Loath to let go, and wishing to hold back longer still the emergence of these newly impetuous images that shimmer about, he draws himself up with a breath and closes his eyes to keep sentimental feelings from running rampant. With that deep breath comes a change of emotions and a mental reset. He partially reopens his eyes with a squint of challenging sarcasm to push those delusional witches firmly against their flat prison wall. Bleary eyes unbelievingly observe the tripping harem continue to dimensionally shift and swirl. A sardonic smile slowly curdles at his mouth's tight corners as a tart warning to them of their soon-to-be-determined, random fate waiting within his hands.

Confined by the walls of his dimmed den of somber gray shades and defining black lines, and with the oblique consent of the witches' lingering, mutual solitude of silence, an oppressive pall of gloom descends upon him, as tightly wound and as suffocating as a young child trapped within an inescapable box in a juvenile's prank gone horribly wrong. The sour smile slips from his lips, for a bitter realization is upon the artist that he will never be completely free and unbeholden to the coven of craven compulsions that silently hibernate within and now manifest before him as these beguiling witches. No matter how long it is buried and briefly forgotten, he will never be absolved of his meth-head-omania and forever in him will reside a dormant desire that awaits any excuse to dance within the circle of his witches' black mass.

How false pride had mistakenly set him up to believe that through his busy artistic and family life he would be free to shun the Devil's temptation of sin. With a mind and emotions occupied with providing for family and maintaining this safe haven of misfits, and with hands constantly dancing across compliant skin and tall wall murals, he had envisioned to keep the charms of these fallen angels sleeping comfortably deep within. Alas, spurious hope is the last laugh of the Devil's little minions, for once one inhales the satanic elixir and the vaporized brew rushes to mix with pulsing blood, the intoxicating lure of falling into bed with witches' craven ways always exists and patiently awaits, quietly lurking below conscious awareness.

The profession of tattooing is a purposeful life sharing in another's artistic vision of enhancing the human form through flowing art; when blended with the poetry of their personalities, it can convey an allegorical story etched onto a bodily canvas. An artist's life is a traipse across a tightrope of the rational—observing below an unbalancing dimension of illusions seeking for that inspirational spark with which to alight a blank canvas with a fire of life—while the thin rope of sanity, and the artist, remains uncharred, connected, and whole.

That small measure of restored self-worth obtained from cultivating and maintaining this placid haven of respite, which others admired him for and with the long-sought professional respect of his family and peers—previously self-denied while lost in a haze and heretofore unattainable from a civilized society that demands a higher standard of reciprocity than that obtainable from the dim sphere of a skulking, crystal-blazing, deviant's den—agonizingly appears to be slipping away by the overwhelming desire of his for one more hit . . . one more rush . . . and then to float softly away within the affections of otherwordly witches.

What quake had occurred in his life to let slip through his emotional cracks this craven madness? Yea verily, what dormant evil had awakened and set in motion the long-forsaken and buried compulsion of his past addiction with the phantasmagoric appearance of his witches before him and their sweet enticements, luring him to fling away his current happiness, for which he had worked so long and hard, and to once again walk with them down their dark and twisted path? A lingering bead of sweat breaks free to trickle slowly down his face while he continues to stare back these beguiling, seductive shrews—their vacant eyes heavy with liner and mascara, peering out at him.

Where once he had a great desire to join in their black mass of earthly detached and emotionally apathetic dancing, there now resides an irrevocable horror at the thought of consuming their cauldron's crystallized brew. For his abhorrent dismay is not the wicked blasphemy of chasing ghostly vapors to become *their* vicarious, subjective zombie and eventual flesh-shedding, rotting corpse, but rather it is the continually awakening kernel that is the essence of the human core at the most elevated level rising above the quiescent, instinctively reactive animal: irrational sacrifice of oneself over logical self-serving survival. That awakened humanity within the artist that is his acknowledged burden of responsibility, knowing that there is now far more for him to lose than just his solo, pathetic existence . . . for as he once again willingly steps over the ledge unto that sinning netherworld that sets the warlock's wicked spirit free, many chaste innocents will thus be emotionally ripped and torn from within while watching his morally corrupt, decadent descent. The enlightened artist cannot permit the possibility of God's children witnessing his heretofore unseen black spirit that cast an insufferable pall over all.

For conversing in any social setting from way on up high in *Tina's* blaze, the clouded addict's head will lazily nod, then bob, and then snap awake to keep from falling asleep—even in the middle of speaking a sentence! The chemically stimulated brain sends electric shocks to idle nerve endings that twitch limbs to randomly kick and flap as they fly out of control in the air. Publicly exposed with his erratic behavior of the street-living, paranoid schizophrenic, he becomes the object of wild, unending amusement to staring little children, and the dread of the skulking, creepy unknown to wary guardian adults who wisely recoil in revulsion with their charges safely wrapped in embracing arms.

Eventually with the chemically impaired warlock's mind continuously lost and confused in a time-and-space-distorted, euphoric state of floating with no cares, the real world slowly fades to desultory gray shadows of no color, no depth, and no substance. The stuporous warlock loses track of time, of the day, of self, and continually flakes on family and social obligations to eventually disappear for days on end, leaving family and friends worried and confused. His sole existence is the appeasement of the addictive mistresses' debauched chasing of ghostly vapors. His only thoughts are the excited nihilism of the next *parta and play* tweak. Eventually, with his continued emotional detachment and physical absence, he himself becomes simply an elusive spectral illusion, only as noticeable and alive as the colorless shades of flat black-and-gray-wash tattoo parlor figures on a lifeless ashen wall.

With the artist's understanding and acceptance of the impulsive weakness of the human mortal's ardor for those billowy folds that irresistibly beckon to him from the other side of the spectral window divide, and which would mean his falling back into that mystic lifestyle of an all-consuming addiction for the blazing of a little harmless chemical haze, an utter desolation and despair of spirit overcomes the lonely and now-full-of-self-pity artisan. His own tiredness from this continuously gnawing consternation shows in the deepening lines in his worn and haggard face as he asks himself, "So, here I am all alone, and is this really what I want to be doing now?"

Faced with the devastating reality of his depraved desire, all his doubts vanish and the die is cast. With a conviction that startles even himself, the artist commits to walking the narrowest path of living unchained and free, with no possibility of a semilucid existence of the meek mortal above beholden to the capricious, maniacal machinations of the Devil's own elixir from their hell below. He contemplates a cylinder's random spin and the possibility of the cocked hammer's finality with a simple trigger pull. 'Tis far more noble to suffer the condemnation of a blasphemous demise than to risk an addictive life tweaking out of control as he takes his precious family and friends in a great fall of heartbreak and despair at his ruination. *And once departed over the ledge of infinity into that purgatory below, what is left behind, and how shall I be remembered?* The artist contemplates the unhappily ever after to his permanent demise. *Is there any way for the nonaddicted to comprehend such a calmative choice? And what of forgiveness? What of forgiveness?*

Absentmindedly staring at his fingers that lightly encircle the container's rounded tin lips, he reflectively contemplates the childhood significance of a long-ago learned scripture of dread that has now incomprehensibly come to be a binding weave of his life, *"When you were slaves to sin, you were free from the obligation to do right. And what was the result? You are now ashamed of the things you used to do, things that end in eternal doom." Romans 6:20–21.* As a child studying this biblical passage in Sunday school, the remoteness of a man to stray so far from the angelic spirit and then to be forever damned had been such an inconceivable phenomenon of his small-town upbringing that he could only imagine such sinning behavior to have been done by powerfully wicked men in ancient times and in remote lands far, far away. The innocent child's sheltered life is not aware that the righteous path is narrow and a continuous burden of moral choices that demand temperance on a daily basis and judicious self-sacrifice, which lies heavily on every imperfect human.

Ha! I once stepped away from His light to live a life of sin. And now I pray, and I shall play, so that I never do so again. Emotionally detached fingers dig into the smooth, cold lip that once hid a child's sweet buttery treats of delight. *Pop!* snaps the top. A whispered sigh issues forth from the opened container. "Oh my devilish pretties, our destiny together awaits the results of a cylinder's random spin. What say thee now . . . *puta?*"

Sssssss! The chilling, unmistakable warning hiss of deadly forked tongues about to strike causes the artist to flinch and momentarily pause in his perilous pursuit. *Sssssssssss!* continues the hissy-fit tantrum of the insecure and petulant little witch beauties that vie for his immediate, undivided attention. He shudders off their reptilian chill and ignores them as he would a concealed, venomous snake in tall brush whose whereabouts is now known with its spine-curdling rattle shaking and is thus no longer an imminent threat. With an outward appearance of calm, his nerves continue to resonate on edge from the dire warning of the she-devil's innately understood vile hissing—and he continues to weigh appreciatively the infinite significance of an effortlessly lifted, flimsy lid that is about to expose that tempting panacea that lies within.

"*Look at us!*" The witches' acrimonious demand for action eerily bounces and echoes from four walls. "*Please love . . .*" keenly and softly follows in womanly overtones laced with sugary sweetness to teasingly invoke within him a hint of the empathetic sadness of his young, lost love. The tattooist does not remove his gaze from the camouflaging cookie tin.

"*Coward.*" The highly agitated witches' once-harmonious tonal agreement is suddenly morphed into the shrill staccato pitches of savage pack animals' fighting rage.

"*Thou art not a man!*" the vociferous attack bursts upon his eardrums with an unworldly shriek. He impulsively winces.

"*Not a man! . . . Not a man! . . . and we shall fain! . . . sexual favors upon ye no more!*" they taunt as the ashen walls shimmer with the frenzied coven of black-line witches unbound from the confining bonds of their flat prison to reach out and grasp for his hand!

"We shall find another more worthy! . . . and tis thy loss, thy loss!" the vile chanting of their wicked vindictiveness continues in their attempt to ensnare him under their spell, to twist his mind, compel his heart, and stay his hands.

Slowly, deliberately, the tattooist looks up from the foreign landscape–decorated container controlled within *his* grasp and, with utter, frustrated exhaustion, stares back at his circling shrews to forthrightly answer with *his* barbed riposte, "Oh, how by thee foul breath you wretched bag whores have me crave the heretofore unknown misogynist me . . . ergo . . . fuck! you." And with that positioning retort of unconditional finality comes the instant silencing of all witches' wicked tongues and their incessant, shrill pitch of an apparently vain attempt to sway his mind that would stay his hand.

And yet! All heads simultaneously cock askew and all shudder upon hearing the first ominous rumbling of the world's core ruptured asunder. For this startling turbulence foretells the frightening warning of a cataractous deluge about to render forth a hideous incarnation of absolute terror upon mortal's earthly surface above from the vaporous crypts of the infernal underworld below. Smote with a foreboding chill of a painful whipping from the expectant emergence of their malevolent master, macabre spectral witch wisps—bad bitches—eerily slither noiselessly as dissipating, low-lying morning mist to cower motionless back upon the corner cracks of flat ashen wall with hollow, luminescent eyes meekly peering out.

"Ye!" a bellowing voice of corrosive evil echoes from somewhere out of the depths of those foul and unvisited catacombs buried deep within the earth, *"had better watch thy back!"* The scary shock effect of this constant witch-harem-watching warlock's nefarious pitch is not lost upon the artist even knowingly that this voice must have surely traveled from far out of physical reach within the depths of isolated darkness below rock and dirt.

"Ye shall have na friends whereth thou goest!" continues the sinister sorcerer, his wrathful voice and deep-felt intonations resounding from four confining plaster walls as if echoing from within the damp and foul confines of unvisited marble crypts.

Startled as though the impetuous beast had actually reached above ground from his hollow dominion to complete his intimated act of physical violence, the artist abruptly turns to see . . . nothing.

"I horny!"

Madly searching in a confused state to locate the precise whereabouts of the elusive, bellicose voice that now appears to emanate straight from unseen lips to his ears, and ready to strike, the artist turns the other way to see again . . . nothing.

"What's your son's cell number?" The unholy warlock's sneering question momentarily lingers as an unstated warning of his septic vileness about to smother all. *"I wanna molest him when ye be gone!"* The walls resonate from the malicious power of his base curse to shake loose a fine talcum dust. *"And then I'll give your wife AIDS."* His voice drips with the utter vitriol of a sulfurous and decrepit rogue having no known moral bounds. Diabolic words all said to set alight a wrathful fire of vengeance upon the benevolent heart and cast him along a soulless path of premeditated murder!

Legions of the Damned released, howling hell's terrifying cackle of delight! Charmed witches dimensionally lifted join in hell's crescendo with their own hellacious gales of giggling laughter. Elusive lines of wispy witches wildly gesticulate as they circle round and round their victim with incantations of unintelligible devil words. All with spitefully wicked tongues that are whipped into an unearthly, shrill crowing that boldly declares the withering artist's cowardice before evil resurrected. Perhaps such wicked winds reeking of wet ash might have wilted the spirit of a less resolute man and sent him with hands supplicant to lie quivering prostrate on the ground before the noxious presence of those threatening demons, and to plead mercy for him and his family in mortal fear of the entities' terrible wrath. However, the long-suffering artist simply ignores their mocking, metaphysical menace as background white noise as he fatalistically steels his heart and continues to concentrate on performing—and completing—the solo and solemn ritual held so lightly within his grasp.

Fully over a year has passed since the tattooist had last fitfully sought to remove from Grandmother's cookie tin his addiction-mitigating, chambered roulette wheel of life to quench his cravings and to dispel this spectral demon and its attending harem back to their Master, who eternally awaits in hell. Hidden from sight . . . silently waiting . . . never far from his thoughts, his special tin box is kept tucked away . . . buried under a pile of loose papers . . . at the bottom of a lower unlocked desk drawer. With a life-draining weariness, the artist resigns himself to the freewheeling spin of the revolver's cylinder and the awaiting, random fate of the five empty and one loaded roulette chambers.

As he feels a faintness of heart, his vision blurs and his hands slightly tremble. Carefully . . . he removes the thin lid of no monetary worth and that which is within is at last revealed. In that moment of enlightened clarity comprehending the significance of the exposed handheld mechanical device and the implications of some spirited, mischievous imp's thievery, a welcome, all-pervading silence descends within the confining room upon his ears and within his head. The howling, soul-ravenous, self-consuming pack of hell's masters, monsters, and minions suddenly clamors no more . . . and time stands still.

The artist is certainly not known among his circle of family, friends, associates, and clients as an emotional or overly expressive man, more often than not communicating his feelings of either pleasure or distaste with nothing more than a quiet, lingering look of curiosity, possibly a narrowing of eyes, or just a hint of sarcasm in a rhetorical question for the other to interpret at his will. This innate social reticence makes his impromptu vocal outburst that much more surprising, as from deep within his chest, a contemptuous laugh of scornful derision rises up to pause the circling demon minions in midflight and thereby all his fears subside.

Crack! snaps the ionized air in a violent, hair-raising electric shock, casting the room in an eerie, unearthly, dried-blood-red hue that illuminates spectral, sucking fissures unto that voidless vault of purgatory. Upon their Master's humanly unheard summons, the ethereal lines of evil incarnate in earthly airs, the ugly ash of agitated spirits that lie so heavily upon his soul, silently begin to scurry around in a moon-shadow swirl of fleeting black crows. Unto the oblivion of that infinitely empty cavern of their corrupted Hades of twisted and forever tortured souls, they begin to disappear.

The last residing witches circle as murderous crows flying round and round the impassive tattoo artist caught within the whirlwind of their retreat into that black chasm of their mystic realm. Haughty, playfully lusting witches teasingly caress his cheeks to blow their wicked wind-breath laced of wet ash his way. Scaly lips seductively whisper with forked, flicking tongues, as the competing coven of an unintelligible language unify as one nerve-retching voice:

Foolish Lover,
false guardian of mortals'
moral watchtower,
pobrecita chica,
lesssst! thee soon forget
from whence
and what we beget...

When misty fog of evil blight
is trapped stealthily lingering,
ssssteathily lingering,
under evening's pale moonlight,
in confining folds of valley's pleats,
thus blinding thine heart,
thus binding our hearts,
to truer and nobler feats...

Wandering, coven witches we,
scourge of every earthly mortal's
chaste yet wanton soul,
wanton sssoul,
shall appear mirthfully circling,
assuredly not heavenly sent,
en masse unholy before thee,
decidedly too late to repent,
and thus set thine raging
and craven passionsss free...

Salacious witches we, for you,
*   shall mix our cauldron brew*
*   and thus play our part*
*   that as one akin*
*   shall bind our sentimental hearts*
*   and satiate thy lusting skin.*

Verily thee
*   doth knowest*
*   this reality.*
Do not attempt to shiver,
*   ssshiver away.*
For, once found,
*   thus thee are bound*
*   always with us!*
Us coven witches we
*   appeasing thy wonton,*
*   wicked spirit*
*   of thy blacken heart*
*   that we be.*

And in assumed fait accompli of their spun lyric incarnate, they lustily retreat in one last lingering pass of his being.

The slow-motion flocking, mocking withdrawal of these wingless specters unto those sucking fissures of their godforsaken catacombs sets not a single sheet of paper upon the antique desk aflutter. Under the sheen of an ominous dried-blood hue, in the empty silence of isolation complete, a cold shiver of gloom permeates the artist from the clammy surface of his sweat-damp skin to the marrow of his old bones as he feels the infinite desolation of those lifeless, passing souls—*akin to his own?*—and is left in a prevailing black cloud of apprehension and exhaustion.

Now that he is left all alone in desperation after his sordid travels upon the path of attempted redemption, a fallacious belief arises within his fatigued mind that some, any, real physical action is self-evident proof of an independent free will and self-determination. He therefore resolutely reaches into that open cookie tin to touch the metal bar-rel. He lifts the finely milled steel device from the plastic-molded, felt-lined, form-factor cradle of a coddled revolver. Gripping the smooth, cold steel, he feels an electric shock of living pulsates to every nerve ending, stimulating his weary body and crystallizing his thoughts in a manner unlike the bump of any chemically altered drug he has ever used and abused.

I am and shall remain my own man. Lifting the cold machine over-head so as to be silhouetted against the faint ambient light reflected off the low ceiling, the tattooist mentally checks for five empty chambers and the one loaded round, and then . . . with fingers randomly flick-ing to spin, spin round the coils . . . he simultaneously pantomimes a thumb hooked on the hammer and, with only one step of his previ-ously performed ritual to complete, he steels his heart to accept the result should it be one exhilarating free fall to meet those guardian hounds awaiting before hell's rusty gates . . . and points the steel barrel at his head! Spin . . . cock . . . pull!

Under the hot sun of an arid land's late summer afternoon, within the private office of a quiet tattoo parlor saloon with all lights turned off, the monotonous ambient drone of distant electric motors and the sporadic metal creaking of overhead hollow vents passing refreshingly cool air are the only sounds to be heard, and, from the window side of a wall-size two-way mirror, the faintly reflected vision of a tattoo artist's motionless, ghastly pale countenance lying head down on his desk is the only sentient being to be seen.

Then a deep, joyful laugh of life bursts forth to fill the air and pull back that veil of pervading gloom that shrouds his suffering soul. Once more, those insufferable apparitions that have waxed within his mind to corporeal form and tormented him so are sent fleeing behind those morally confining gates of their self-inflicted purgatory. Rusty hinges will no longer swing wide those gates and cause him to cringe in mor-tal fear at the release of his recurring nightmare of old bones and burnt remains that casts an oppressive pall about him. He has barred those swinging iron doors with a corroded skeleton key snapped off at its shaft within the gate's now-not-so-hollow lock. Flat upon the oppos-ing wall, those hand-drawn charcoal lines of previously dark and degenerate temptations peer back from the void of their insipidly hollow eye sockets—unmoving, unfeeling, uncaring.

Thus does the imperfect human mortal, continuously led astray by the temporal witches' cauldron of corruption, choose to plot a perilous and not so pious path, and once more pass through a crucible of blasphemous temptation for a life of temperance and good works by the elimination of one addictive sin with the fright of an adrenaline-driven, life-ending shock. For not the first time, he has been shaken to the core, and his addiction demons lie quiet. He questions how those fallen angels, now in the company of the Devil, ever fathomed that hidden dark spot of his heart—of every living soul—to discover and tempt him with his destitute predilections. Quietly chuckling to himself, the artist is confused and amused as to how and when the mirrored switch was made. With two cold-sober hands, he replaces the benign tattoo gun, of skin-piercing needles with colored ink, and which oddly fits into the velvet-lined case molded for the cold blue steel of a deadly Magnum handgun. He reflects on how he will miss his grandfather's polished, old Colt that had, not for the first time in fact, saved the tattoo artist's life.

On their very first wild-pig hunting excursion together deep in the folds of an overgrown wash of the valley's foothills, the flush of unseen quail on their left had momentarily drawn their attention. Thus distracted, their vision was unexpectedly drawn back to a charging boar breaking unseen from the underbrush on their right. The young child froze in place, mesmerized by the sharp white tusks that were aimed at him, throat high. Grandfather, with years of experience in keeping his composure in critical situations, simply back hooked a leg around his grandson, dropped to one knee, and skillfully sighted the onrushing boar. With the student looking down the handgun's sight from behind his grandfather, the boy saw the faint puff of smoke and the barrel rise, but he never heard the shot. The man-size boar lay dead at their feet, a single dark spot between its eyes.

"Son, that was poor hunting saved by lucky marksmanship. It's best you not tell any of the lady folks, as it'll just get them mightily upset." Grandfather knelt before the wild pig and, with a timbre of sadness in his quiet voice, intoned, "And so once again, we have ascendency of the weak but are blessed over the strong and powerful."

Returning the cookie tin container to the bottom desk drawer, the tattooist bears a forlorn, fatal resignation, feeling the oppressive wrath of the intractable, impatiently waiting dark angels that taunt and tempt as they grapple for ascendancy to bend his will and force his hand, and a perceptive foreknowledge that Grandfather's missing, shiny silver revolver will soon be replaced. *Huh, it's best you not tell anyone, as it'll just get them mightily upset.*

Tenderly rising from the desk, his body feeling the weight of ages upon stiff, achy joints, yet his soul lightened with repentance and a new faith, the tattooist slowly walks from his private office towards the rear gaming room and the awaiting adult adolescents who should not be left alone for more than thirty minutes, any more than three-year-old toddlers can be safely left alone for thirty seconds. The artist has always had an affinity for these social misfits who for some odd reason look up to him much as young pups begging his petting hand of approval. He reflected on how, as time and time passed, he took more and more pleasure and pride in providing this temporary haven of refuge for this pack of still-maturing cubs.

Grasping the warehouse doorknob, the artist, with electric needles in hand pressing upon a human canvas of compliant skin, gives a nervous glance over his shoulder to briefly peruse those haughty, charcoal-shaded, Gothic portraits that are an intimate reminder of a previous life and which somehow, at the most inopportune times, attempt to reach within his most intrinsic and base morals to etch their lurid airs upon his soul. He ponders their supernatural manifestations upon his reality—and his delusional hearing and conversing with these incarnations of life-size, freehand-drawn vignettes of his opiate past—and then critically ponders if the whole of his preceding, unpleasant, and wretched discourse, and their subsequent, sudden banishment back unto their flat ashen prison wall, with its black lines and lifeless shadows naturally embracing their grotesque netherworld, is but merely a figment of his drug-decrepit loss of half a mind and his feverishly unstrung and sleep-deprived imagination run wantonly rampant.

~~~~~~~

INCIDENTAL ENCOUNTER

Some see a handout as
    an opportunity to take more without effort,
    perceiving "giving" as a weakness to be preyed upon,
    and "taking" as simply the natural order
    of a wild animal-predator culling the herd.

Others see the gift of a helping hand as a
    self-imposed burden borne upon the days
    until repayment in kind assistance is made
    to others momentarily less fortunate,
    and that be the elevated human divine.

~~~

Motionless, Silver stands on the empty street corner with nothing to do, nowhere to go, and all day to do it. His dark upturned face absorbs the comforting, warm rays of a late-morning sun that slowly presses back the blight of another evening's cold and noisy misery that oppresses a soul alone in the dark. Back slightly arched, eyes closed, the man in the suit with hands dug deep in his coat pockets is apparently as idle as the street is vacant and as lazy as the single bright-white sunlit cloud floating across an otherwise empty blue sky. Indulgently he savors this moment to enjoy the stillness of this quiet location and the simple animal pleasure of the sun's warmth radiating to his cold extremities with a tingling sensation. The heat upon his skin slowly pulses to his core and begins to loosen stiff joints with a weight of ages falling off his old bones. What an invigorating feeling in the simple act of quietly sunning after having spent another troglodytic night in his darkened den under the always-noisy and uncomfortably cold concrete overpass. Alive, human, civilized once again as a man, he contemplates his next steps of the day . . . or not.

A smile stretches at the corners of his thick lips as with an ironic humor that is not lost to him, he reflects how his economically constrained life of idle leisure is not so dissimilar to that idyllic lifestyle of an elite, pampered few with nothing more to do than to lounge on a private beach while tanning under the same wide-open, blue sky and warming yellow sun as he, but—ha—is also a dream that a multitude seeks to obtain: the same fanciful notion of luxurious idleness.

His eyes open with acceptance to the reality of his world, which is not a sandy beach. As is his morning ritual—one step at a time—he begins to inspect the gray twill suit that is old and well worn, but spotless. With the flat of his hands, he casually brushes away a dusting layer of underpass grit while straightening the fabric of his jacket and pants. He cinches higher but does not fully tighten the knotted tie that loosely hangs at the open collar of his wrinkled white dress shirt. Next, he pulls the black belt a notch tighter against the hunger in his belly, licking his lips in anticipation of some future satisfying drink flowing down his throat. Lastly, balancing on one foot, he first shines one shoe against the back of his pant leg and then the other. After inspecting the high gloss of his leather shoes, and satisfied with the results of his personal appearance, he turns his attention to survey his corner fiefdom as he rubs his prickly two-day stubble.

Kyle sits behind Silver on a bench, idly tapping his foot as he blankly stares at the sidewalk. With his chin cradled in his palms and with elbows resting on his legs, Kyle's whole body pulsates in unison with his foot. His hoodie is pulled over his head, hiding his face from view. Matted strands of surfer-blond dreadlocks swing loosely from under the hood. The worn sweatshirt's head cloth offers a modicum of protection from the sun's constantly burning rays, although Kyle's face has long since absorbed the rich tan and leathery-hard skin of the permanent street living. Kyle is young and intimidatingly big, with a slow disposition that will complaisantly follow a pack leader's directions . . . as long as the instructions are kept to a simple two-step.

Patiently leaning against an adolescent tree that is the center of their street-corner domain, is Jake, an apparently middle-aged gentleman, wiry and thin from an addictive life of all sorts. His sunken eyes are mysteriously penetrating, not only with a seeming awareness of, but also an understanding of whatever they focus upon. Despite his bantam size, Jake emanates the impression that he should be the last one in a crowded room of conspirators against whom you should turn your back if a questionable deal were suddenly to turn bad. Jake is lucky enough to be sucking on a found cigarette butt and is enjoying every satisfying lungful of smoke.

Their enclave is a quiet street corner paved with kiln-fired bricks artistically laid in a herringbone pattern. Encompassed within the calming circle of salmon-hued brickwork reside three park benches, which in turn surround the still maturing Chinese elm tree. The triad of wet clay-brown concrete benches are positioned at ninety-degree angles to each other with the fourth section open to the street corner where now casually stands the man in the tweed business suit. Within the center of this artistic corner composition, the fast-growing Chinese elm shoots straight up towards the sky, arching its skinny limbs overhead in a leafy green umbrella that provides shade on at least one of the park benches throughout the day. An observant pedestrian would notice the tree shedding a fascinating mix of tricolors and textures from the camouflaged puzzle pieces of the thigh-thick trunk: the cinnamon-tan bark flakes in rough, bite-size strips of ashen chips, themselves speckled with red chicken-pox colonies of ferruginous lichen, to finally expose a baby-bottom-smooth, meaty flesh of white, before the cycle begins anew.

Despite the aesthetically pleasing picture that this corner beauty spot of relaxation provides, it is evident that this tranquil, sculptured scene has been shoehorned into the otherwise stark pavement as a long-awaited afterthought in consideration of human inhabitability. For rising high above the half-grown Chinese elm and dominating the entire length down both sides of the city streets stands the utility company's postwar, multistory, gray-slab building. The top corner edges of the windowless, concrete façade have ornamental appendages, clearly slapped on as an afterthought in some imitation of faux-Spanish Colonial design. In mocking vulgarity, swirling art-deco lines of apparently cheap plaster of paris protrude to interrupt the poured-concrete structure's flat wall midway down the street to scale from sidewalk to skyline rooftop and encircle the tinted-glass double doors through which customers enter and thereupon present their tribute—else excommunication with the utility turned off and a return to the dark times of the Middle Ages!—unto some monopolistic, baroque church of the Spanish Inquisition.

Across the street, a long row of low-rise shops quaintly opposes the looming gray utilitarian building. There is a warm feeling of individuality, a sense of physically pleasing texture, from the proprietary shops that have an eclectic assortment of building materials and colors. Flat-roofed desert-sand stucco structures stand next to wood-paneled A-frame buildings. Soft pinks and bold peaches abut a wine red that in turn resides next to light sand. The narrow post-dust-bowl-migration-era street speaks of a once-slower time of pedestrian-friendly hustle and bustle. Twisted wrought-iron-encased sidewalk patios provide a homey atmosphere within which coffee shop and local bar patrons can pleasantly chill after sunset. Situated haphazardly along the street curb, an occasional archaic equestrian hitching post is the local chamber of commerce's eccentric acknowledgement of the agricultural roots from whence the city arose but which now, sadly, appear to be in full decline. The faded hand-painted storefront signs intermingled with occasional bright neon lights of old are testaments to a bygone era. These mom-and-pop stores are in a losing struggle to compete with the far-reaching national franchises. The family-owned drive-through dairy can no longer compete with the discount-priced mega-box grocery store any more than the individual barista-owned coffee shop that also serves beer on tap can compete with a Seattle-based bean-grinding corporation.

It is a well-told twentieth-century Americana fable of the modern interstate highway bypassing a small town, and thus circumvented, the once-vibrant community economically languishes to decay slowly until there is only a single unmanned gas station paired with a drive-through fast-food franchise restaurant at the end of the exit ramp to service rushing travelers. Many an exit across the old Route 66 has the caved-in wooden shell of a once-vibrant café and full-service filling station. Conversely, the momentarily idle man in the worn business suit stands at the stagnant epicenter of a rich town that has prospered to city status. He is surrounded by fertile lands—blessed as a lush Garden of Eden and the envy of the world—with vast dairy farms and meat-processing plants all interspersed with revenue-generating oil wells. In good seasons, the rich fields produce more quality cotton than Texas, more almonds than Iran, and more rice than Japan, and all the while, deep underneath the bountiful valley resides the nation's military and emergency reserves of oil. Within an easy ten-minute stroll for the man of leisure sunning on the street corner sits a five-intersection roundabout—how quaint is that?—which speaks of that earlier era when the city center formed the hub of the thoroughfares for the major north-south intrastate and the western interstate terminus of those on their passage escaping the dust bowl to more prosperous points, all of which converged through the growing metropolis. The eventual, progressive, federally funded superhighway bypass did little economically to stunt the growing metropolis at the center of such robust lands. Rather, gentrification has isolated the city core. Additional connecting freeways have been built over and around the city streets to facilitate the bypassing of an aging downtown district. No need for stylish, trend-following shoppers to suffer the inconvenience of passing through slow, cramped side streets with unique, privately owned boutiques when these consumers can venture instead to obtain name-brand labels at discount prices from the big-box conglomerates that require vast and cheap tracts of land.

After dropping their kids at the middle-class schools on one side of suburbia, consumers rush at high speeds without a need to slow or to stop at red lights to the yuppie Nordstrom department store on the other side of town. Of the city's dozen Seattle corporate-owned coffee bars, not one is located within several square miles of the downtown section. Their coffee conveniently awaits shoppers at the bottom of each suburban connecting freeway exit ramp—the latest an accommodating drive-through. Many a child has never seen the aged city center and is therefore unaware of daily bypassing a heritage from which they arose. Only the grandchildren of age who are on society's fringes rebel from being uniformly designer labeled and escape in the evening from life in suburbia to cruise along downtown's narrow streets. They drop into one or more of the many dive bars that cater to their rowdy nature and their requirement for cheap drinks. After a long weekend night and early morning of carousing the streets while listening to the local bands with drinks in hand, most have attained their pre-stated goal of becoming intoxicated. Their revelry continues as drunken friends under peer pressure are led down darkened narrow alleys to the tattoo parlors that cater to just this occasion. The ass of the night is thus greeted with the day's hangover and the permanence of colored ink on one's buttocks, henceforth proclaiming one's uniqueness and independence to all.

From his vantage point on the edge of the red-brick curb, the idle man looks north along the tabletop-flat street into the near distance and sees the specks of automobiles busily traversing the raised freeway that connects symmetrically laid out tract homes with air-conditioned shopping malls. As it is physically above and thus disconnected from this five-corner roundabout, none shall venture his way. Only an occasional car on the way to somewhere else slowly cruises through their intersection. Glancing in the opposite direction, the man can see sporadic pedestrian traffic in the near distance enter the local espresso shop, the only daytime bohemian preserve in an otherwise dull and quiet vortex of an agricultural-based downtown. Behind him, he is aware of the regional bus hub that is the domestic reserve of a common community living in leisurely repose. The chronically dispossessed lounge idly all day upon benches under the terminal's awning shade, curiously watching buses come and buses go. Not one enters or exits the buses as they arrive and depart the connecting hub; the buses only pass on to somewhere else, for someone else. These watchers idly snooze while reclining on all their worldly possessions, which they use as comforting pillows under their heads.

Simple pleasures . . . in simple times . . . for simple people. The nattily tailored man takes satisfaction in having all that he requires within walking distance under free and open skies as his concrete-cold blood now pumps warm from his short time in the sun. His predatory instincts alertly catch movement approaching from behind him at a distance down the street. "Huh, now don't that beat all?" the man reflexively says aloud to himself as he turns and eyes a single male pedestrian walking towards him from midway down the street on the doorless side of the utility building. "Ain't that an odd duck outta water, yep?" he adds to himself after another moment of inspecting the isolated stroller. "Hep! Boys, ya wanna have some wake-up fun?"

"Huh? Yeah, sure, whatever you want," Kyle says, drawing his eyes from the red brick to look at the patient man on the corner's edge who still gazes down the sidewalk. "Why, what's up, Silver?" Having used all of his energy to come up momentarily from his still-hungover daze, Kyle places his chin back into his waiting hands supported by elbows resting on knees, to stare at the ground with open eyes not seeing.

Jake, as expected, says nothing. He takes a last puff on his cigarette stub and then flicks the butt in a high arc into the street gutter before following suit to look down the sidewalk.

"Don't know as o' yet, but maybe we gettin' us selves somethin' and maybe not. Can't tells as yet," Silver replies as he sizes up the lean, stylishly dressed gentleman walking towards him. "Now that ain't right," he curiously questions himself, focusing on the black satchel over the refined fellow's shoulder. The notebook-size bag hangs to the man's waist, with his thumb and fingers hooked around the forward strap to support his right arm. Instinctively, Silver feels the heat of being stared at from behind the dark, reflective sunglasses of the approaching man. Shrewdly, the experienced predator surveys his surrounding environment, taking in angles, lines, numbers, innate power, and, most importantly, exits. Feeling safe within his marked territory and within the presence of his back-covering companions, Silver steps into the middle of the sidewalk and hails the approaching stroller in his friendly drawl: "Say Capt'n, what's up?"

"Why the sky, the moon, and the stars above, my good sir," he answers, with only the slightest cock of his head in Silver's direction to acknowledge his interrogator's existence and no pause in his pace as he continues to close in on Silver.

Feeling a curious sensation of being self-conscious within one's own home, Silver remains silent and continues to stand immobile as the stranger intently inspects him from head to toe, finishing with a hard, lingering stare at Silver's feet before sidling past him in long, casual strides. The feeling of being the street freak on public display having passed in a moment, Silver quickly regains a semblance of composure to ask himself, *Now what's that about?* The stranger is stopped with his back to Silver, waiting for the light to change to a green walk signal. "Ain't no one who's waitin' for those lights round these parts," Silver helpfully offers.

"What's that?" asks the interloper as he turns to look over his shoulder at Silver.

"I'm sayin', ain't no one who's awaitin' for green walkin' lights round these here parts. You can looky see that there ain't a car coming from nowheres, see?" Silver turns his head in an exaggerated gesture for the daft, looking down each of the four empty streets.

The man sheepishly laughs. "Uh, yeah."

"You lost or somethin', mistuh? Anything I can hep ya ta find?"

"No thanks, just knocking about."

"Ya sures? I knows these parts real good an' everyone knows Silver. That's what theys call me, Silver, short for Quick Silver. An' I can get ya where ya going, quick ya know, or gets ya what ya need, or maybes more importantly, keep ya outta where ya ain't should be."

The stranger turns to take a step forward and square up with Silver, "Oh? And where ain't I supposed to be . . . Silver?"

"I don't mean nothin' by it," Silver offers defensively. "Ya just seeming like a you's new ta these parts, what with wandering on a strange side a town is all. An' I can help keep ya outta a jam 'cause I know everyone, or get ya outta a jam 'cause everyone knows me, if ya knows what I means?"

"I've seen worse . . . and I've been in worse."

"Well, sometimes what ya see ain't what it is, ya know what I'm saying? And I got friends around, and I got ways and things ta keep a man outta troubles," Silver says as he bends at his waist to reach down his left leg just above the ankle.

"You may reach what you're going for, but you're not going to get up with it."

Silver freezes with an instinctive caution at the change in tone of the stranger's voice. Bent over at the waist and grasping his left pants leg at the ankle with his right hand, he looks to see the stranger now standing with feet spread in a balanced stance, left leg forward, at a distance of just one and a half paces away. Silver immediately takes measure of the distance, of the man, and his own physical position to realize he has misjudged twice: once in taking his eye off his prey while reaching low to his ankle, and secondly thinking that the wanderer would be easily intimidated. Silver further notices that the hanging black bag is now off the man's shoulder and held firmly with two hands. The thin, cheap vinyl fabric bulges to reveal the sharp edges of an object within as hard and as pointed as the corner of a brick. Silver cautiously remains bent over, opening his palms submissively. He gauges the stranger's distance as one full, swinging step away from bringing down with full momentum the man-bag upon his own head should he rise with anything clutched in his hands. "Not ta be rude, suh, but my two boys gots my back covered, ya know?"

"Ha! Silver, a man's gots ta be well aware of his situational environment, and methinks you've misjudged your friends."

Silver turns his head to look past his leg on one side, and then the other way. It takes him no time to become fully aware of his predicament. "Well, I'll be damned if . . . now don't that beat all?" Silver is overcome by the most unpleasant novelty of finding his ace up the sleeve being trumped by this handbag-carrying outlander.

"I think you have friends that stick with you through thick an' thin, and when it gets too thick, they thin out," said the well-dressed man with an amused laugh and a wry grin.

Empty palms passively facing out, Silver slowly rises. Most of us have a tell that in a crisis exposes our character within and lets a perceptive observer know who we truly are. Silver's tell is the infectious smile that spreads across his weathered and fractured face. His affect is not that of a larcenous soul but rather that of a playful character full of a self-deprecating mirth. Silver now beams that sparkling, inviting grin that can quickly draw another like-minded person to him. "Say Capt'n, I knows what you be wanting."

Cautiously the stranger looks at Silver with the question of *What's that?* across his face.

"My shoes. You be wanting ta know where I gots my shoes shined! That's why's you was staring at me like that with your spooky look an' all."

The casual stroller reciprocates Silver's broad smile without saying anything.

"I didn't mean nothing a'tall ya know? I was just trying ta entertain da boys ya know, an' trying ta impress ya a little an' all, an' just showing ya I takes care of my peoples an' all. Why, my bads it is, fer sure."

"No problem. I didn't see any malice in your eyes, but you just had me in a corner with nowhere else to go. You know what I'm saying?"

"Yes, suh, I can see that now, yep. My bad fer sure. You ain't gonna be bustin' me or anything are ya? We be good now, right?"

"Well, technically, I haven't seen anything anyhow. So you could say there's hardly reasonable suspicion, never mind probable cause, and if we keep it that way, we be cool."

"Fancy words for a fancy man in fancy pants, now don't that beat all? So, seeing as we now be square, an' seeing as we be chatting it up an' all, who you wit', anyhow?" Silver questions. "Being on this side a town an' all, you be with a department for sure. But you be too skinny for sheriff. Not grunge enough wit da evil stink eye ta be DEA. Ya could be FBI, what with that clean-cut look, tie an'all, but theys don't usually goes travelin' 'bout by themselves, now do they? Lawyer fer sure. District attorney, what wit' those fancy tassels on your shoes an' all, but they never actually leave their office an' go out in the field an' do any investigation on their own. So, you must be public defender, but gone private I suspect. Yep, that be it. What you be walking the street all by's yourself with all them fancy duds an' all, huh?"

"Huh. I think it best if you don't know what I do. You just keep thinking that I have a badge, and that I'm maybe packing with it as well."

Silver cocks his head slightly, intent on peering either through or around the dark sunglasses in which he can see his own reflection.

"Now what's all the fuss here 'bout? Just bein' a little curious about a man's occupation an' all. Sure makes one wonder what'cha may be hiding or what'cha be 'shamed of, one would think, no? But I ain't saying, yep, nope, that fer sure. And best fer who, huh?"

"Yeah, I can see your honest point there so we'll just call it a favor until we get to know each other a little better. How's that?"

"'Kay, seems fair." Silver's face relaxes as he continues, "Well seeing as we gettin' on ta knows each other then, and you knows my name, what I gonna be callin' ya anyhow?"

"Hmm, well if you don't mind, seeing as you seem to be calling everyone Capt'n, why not change it up and you can be calling me Skid. How is that?"

"Skid, huh!?" Silvers starts in a low tone of menace that finishes in a high, sharp pitch of attention. His face pulls askew as his back straightens. He bristles with indignation, a warning of protecting his last vestige of collateral street currency, which has just been sorely wounded . . . his pride. "What? A stranger like you just walking around the streets an' bustin' in and implying something about us? Ya thinkin' a joining our here corner club an' all, an' being like the head honcho, what wit' your fancy threads and all? Or you thinking ya just throw some sorta smarty-pants slur ta the momentarily financially set back that yous don't think we have 'nough inter-lects ta catch on ta ya backhanded slap, huh? That be it . . . frat boy?"

A look of confused bafflement contorts Skid's face. Questioning, he looks deeply into Silver's seriously aggrieved mien. Slowly, with the light of awareness, a smile crosses Skid's face and then his own mirthful laugh bursts forth. "Uh, no, not really, and I can see why you may think that. I wasn't really thinking about skid row that way at all. But it does remind me that a man certainly needs to watch the words he uses depending on his social setting." Skid's face beams with happy pleasure as he elucidates. "I was thinking more along the lines of those black tire marks of rubber that one lays on the track just before one's race car skids into the wall; that's what I was thinking."

Silver's tightened facial features slowly relax. "Oh well, that be way cool then." Without missing a beat, his affable demeanor reappears with a smile to match Skid's. "Yep, I likes that. I'll calls ya Skid, spooky

Skid," he says with a laugh. "It was my bad before, just ta let ya knows," Silver continues, "bendin' over and reaching down an' spooking you like that. Ya can say we gots started on the wrong foot then, huh?" Silver laughs again as he picks up a foot and turns his dangling ankle to reflect sunlight off his highly polished, soft leather shoes.

Skid's smile broadens with Silver's laugh. "No problem, and you are correct about your shoes. You did catch me staring at them. The shine is awesome. How'd you get it? You do it yourself?"

"Why thanks ya," he replies, keeping his foot in the air, admiring the shine that makes a pair of old worn shoes look new again. "But no, no, I don't do it. My cousin's gotta shoe-shine shack over there on Chestnut an' Twenty-First across from the Burger Rack. Ain't no one better in these parts, that's fer sure. Looky that shine. Mmmm-hmm. There was a day, too, when he gives ya a real rich soul song, what with that manly voice of his an' all. Singing an' shining, an' snapping the cloth in time an' all. That was really somethin', his voice kickin' it, the shine cloth snappin', *crack* it was. An' sometimes a little drinkin' on the side. Good times an' all, yep, that's fer sure. The funny thing is no matters how much he done drunk, he never done stain the pants nor socks with the polish. Damn. Don't know how he ever kept it togethers like that, huh? But he's gettin' on now and ya can't quite getta song outta him anymore except a chorus in with the choir at church. And, drinkin'? Why hep, forget it. He been dry way too long for his own good I say. The dryness makes his edges sharp ta cut others, it does, an' he don't be loosening his tongue ta sing like he usta. Damn shame he done give them both up, too, I say. He's just tired now, I guess. He's gettin' old, old an' ratchety, I says. Heck, all of us gettin' old I guess, yep, that be fer sure. Anyways, he's just a few blocks down yonder an' over thataways." He points, but the light of understanding does not sweep across Skid's face. "You know, cut through Nineteenth down where's they done close down the street with the green hitchin' posts?"

"Well, yeah, for sure I've seen the posts, but I'm kind of confused. There are a couple ends of the streets with posts, aren't there?"

"Well, yeah, man, if you's closin' off one end of the street, ya knows ya gotta close off the other? You following me? Anyhows, you know, to get there ya cuts through the posts an' follow it out to behind the cell tower mounted behind da old mission. An' then ya turn left two blocks. Ya can't miss the little shack with window wrapping alls around, sittin' right there on the corner, on the edge of that big'n vacant lot used for parking. Simple isn't it?"

"Tell you what, Silver. I do like to keep things simple, that's for sure," replies Skid. "Seeing as how you're a man of business, I've got a proposition that's good for both of us. I'd really like to get my shoes shined. Here's a fiver now"—Skid opens his hand to reveal a greenback—"if you just take me over to the shack. There's another five waiting for you if my shine turns out as good as yours. Deal?"

"Well, I've got some mighty pressin' matters to be taken care of, ya know?" Silver replies with a thumb and pointer finger stroking his unshaven chin. "But, I think I can spend a few minutes with ya ta get you on your ways, yep."

"Tell you what Silver, let's make this interesting. I've got some time to kill before my next appointment, so why don't I take you on for a short time as, let's say, an independent consultant? You take me on a circuitous route to the shoe shack, and if you show me some interesting places, and you tell me some more of your interesting stories, I'll give you another fiver for your consulting time. How's that deal?"

"'Sir-cute'?"

"Circuitous . . . the long way round, Silver. And while we're at it, how about unique and interesting as well, if you can?"

"Well, like I said, I's gots some pressin' issues, yep, don't knows if they can wait."

Skid laughs. "We'll make it an extra ten at the end then. I have a lunch meeting a bit later and newly shined shoes will keep me dressed to impress."

"Well, I am a little financially distressed at the moment, how scenic you want it? I's got plenties ta show ya and plenties I can tells ya, yep."

"Yeah, I bet you do. How about we start by walking in the opposite direction of your compadres? Just in case they're not quite as bright and cool as you are, okay?"

"You picked up on that mighty quick, huh? You got some quick eyes behind them there dark shades of yours. Huh, yeah, I bet. Okay, this a'way we go. Now what's that fiver doin' comin' straight outta your hand, anyhow? I didn't see that comin' outta your wallet. So, where's your wallet?"

"Ha."

"No biggie. Jus' curious is all. Makin' small-talk conversations. Man's gotta have some of his own little secrets, I knows. Sometimes for protection from the man, sometimes from those on the streets, like me an' mi compadres, I knows. And sometimes, worst of all, protection from someone close. Yeps, I knows 'bout all of dat. So what's this appointment you have later, anyhows? Must be important, that's fer sure? Is that what you be carrying that bag for? Where's it gonna be ats? Not this part o' town, I take it?"

A smirk. "Silver, important is relative. To me. To them. I'm here, so it is to me, but we shall see."

"See if they show? But who be they, huh? Business? Personal? If they be payin' ya, they gonna show fer sure, else how ya gonna pay for your shine, an' my 'consulting time'?"

"Ha."

~~~

And so they venture forth together in that direction opposite of Jake and Kyle's exit with one as a native guide eager to impress the other with his intimate knowledge of the city's uniquely tangled streets and social intricacies, and the other as a curious tourist interested in learning of and peering into those unlit corners of an urban hive that the casual stranger may not find and to which he may not be welcomed. Silver's almost imperceptible limp does not go unnoticed by Skid.

"This here corner we're coming up to is like party central on weekend nights when all the young'uns come on out ta party after they's been paid fer da week an' all. Ya know, young'uns, they thinkin' they's rich an' all what wit' all that cash in they's pockets. Out ta have some fun an' get drunk an' impress them friends, an' tryin' ta hook up with all them cute girls, yep. They be spending all they's money. They ain't thinkin' they may need some for tomorrow, nope. And the more theys get in 'em, the less they's thinkin', yep. They gets all crazy and start tearing up the street. They's a bar on each corner and a few down each way ta helps them on their ways. Ain't nobody there now. Don't sees many respectable people comin' out this way. You be complainin' 'cause you think ya gots some bad things on your side a town and then another parts of town comes ta yours and ya come ta find out there's a whole 'nother pile a dirt on the other end, yep. Even the goods people is rowdy here, that's fer sure. Drunk don't change who you are, just brings out what you really are. Afta's a hot summer's night of drinkin' an' partying an' carousing, this place can smell mighty ripe, like Bourbon Street afta' Mardi Gras. You ever been ta Mardi Gras or N'awlins? I gotta son down there with family an' all. Ain't seen 'em in a while . . . damn shame . . . but you know what with business not doin' well now an' I've had a cash crunch lately . . ." Silver's voice wistfully trails off in self-conscious silence as they continue to walk.

"Now come on here thisaway," Silver offers up, turning down a narrow alley that is all shade and shadows of no direct sunlight. "This here's an interesting an' different place that I thinks yous might like, like ya asks."

As a long-lived adventurer exploring out of his natural habitat, Skid does well to cautiously pause at the sidewalk's edge before he enters a common path down to the communal watering hole shared by both fleet prey and powerful predators. He peers down the constricted alleyway noting concealing shadows and sniffing animal scent in the air. The passage is formed by a long row of blank, two-story brick façades alternating with truck-wide, corrugated-metal door entrances that are all shuttered. A slow trickle of discolored wastewater continually flows along the concrete gutter that traverses the center of the alley's badly pitted and cracked asphalt.

Silver holds his animated demeanor in check, patiently waiting without saying a word. When Skid steps forward, Silver follows suit.

"Now man, that 'twas mighty quick, you turnin' down this here alley with me being a stranger an' all." Silver resumes his chatter. "Ya got me curious as all get out now. What'cha packin'? Or what you thinkin', coming down this alley wit me? You ain't nevers been down here before, have yas? Come on, gives me somethin'. We gettin' along okay an' all and we be business partners now right?"

"Yeah, we're getting along okay, and no, I have never been down these parts before. So, since we seem to be getting along as partners now, I'll share with you. First of all, there is nobody coming or going in the alley. Second, there really isn't any place for a man to hide as I can see down to the far end, and therefore I can't be expecting anyone to surprise us. Third, it's still pretty early in the day for the types that one generally should be worried about, or for that matter, for them to be coming out at all. They're still sleeping it off. And even if they are up, they're still going to have too much in their system to be reacting very quickly as we come up on them. You can always see in their eyes how quickly they're thinking and how quickly they can move. Besides, I have you with me to keep me out of trouble, not get me into it, or at least to be used as a human shield should I need you for my getaway," Skid says with a grin as he artfully stutter-steps to end up walking behind Silver.

"Huh, some partner you be, using me as a back-covering shield ta take the first shot. An' you seein' all that in a one peek down da road? You be one trustin' fella, or man, you one scary spook, yep."

"Maybe I haven't been around these here parts, but I have been around more than a few blocks in more than a few different places."

"Yeah, I bets. Well, anyhows, I was thinkin' 'bout our contract. Maybe we could trade one of those fivers for a pint o' brew or two along the way instead? You know, kinda loosen up my tongue an' all ta give ya some more a dem int'restin' stories ya paying me for? A workin' man can get mighty tired an' need a bit of a refresher to cool down."

"Why do I have a feeling you've been setting me up for this?"

"Well, anyhows, this here's one o' those int'restin' places you been askin' 'bout." Silver stops midway down the alley in front of a previously unseen, recessed doorway covered with two rainbow tie-dyed flags that part down the middle as one enters. The brightly colored curtains, pushed by the high pressure of the air-conditioning within, flutter outwardly with an inviting, light gaiety. "This here's place kinda new in town. Don't really have much like it round these parts nor anywheres else, ya know."

"Interesting, Silver. Yeah, and I like the way you're thinking, my man." Skid laughs. "But methinks we are both asking for trouble we don't want if we walk in there. You know what I'm saying?"

Silver eyes him curiously. "You sures? I was jus' thinkin' maybe this 'twas kinda like da place where ya might like'ta hang afta' hours? You know, after work, what with your friends an' all? You knows, I was just observin' ya man-purse an' all, an' the custom-tailored slacks. Yep, I knows about fine clothes from back in da day."

"Well, Silver, my man, I'm paying you to keep me out of trouble, and not to get me into it. And well, I don't think that the two of us entering this here place together is going to be all that inconspicuous and could just attract unwanted attention, you know? Anyway, let's just keep a low profile and stay under the radar and keep walking and, if there's time, maybe we'll get that pint after the shine. How's that?"

"Well, yous can see how a guy might get the wrong impression an' all, what wit' you's man-bag and strolling up on the wrong side a town with dem shoe tassels swishing back an' forth," Silver says, wagging his finger in the air like a windshield wiper. "Not a sight a seen very often round these parts, ya know? I don't mean no disrespect . . ."

"No disrespect given, none taken Silver. I can see your point. Some parts where I come from and some parts I visit, these threads can actually be taken as rather boring and staid. They definitely can be easily misconstrued in different parts, that's for sure."

"Okay, jus' checkin' ya out. Ya got my curious up, an' all. Man's a curious animal by 'is nature. Why I've sailed round the world twice. Been in many a port o' call, why yes I have. There's some strange peoples out there that yous can't even imagine unless you've seen it yourself. They's ya average, normal workin' people wherevers ya go, yep that's fer sure, and that's most people. But ya get inta some of da' back alleys and ya nevers knows what yer gonna see, an' sometimes ya nevers knows if ya coming out, ya know what I'm saying?"

"You sure don't look like no swabby man to me, Silver."

"Yep, tanker man, back in the day. Tankers more dangerous than a carrier. Just one big vaporous bomb ready ta go off, ya know? And it don't take much, just one little spark. There ya are sailing along at thirty knots sometimes not ten yards from a carrier, what with a rolling ocean of rough seas. Scary close enough a man thinks he can jump from da bigger ship to the other. During the fueling there's gots ta be a man standing on each end of the feeder line with a large ax. You know what he doing standing there with an ax fueling a carrier? Do ya?"

"Wait, there're no carriers pulling up to the gas station. They don't need gas! Even back in the day all carriers were nuclear, dude. Who's trying to pull whose leg now? Ha."

"And what'cha think all those fighter jets flying off the deck are using?"

"Oh . . . yeah . . . gotcha dude."

"Mista' smarty-pants an' all. Just 'cause ya goes ta college an' all don't mean ya have any common sense. Sometimes practical street 'sperience is more importants than inter-lect from a schoolbook, ya knows?"

Skid remains silent, allowing Silver to continue speaking as they walk along.

"So's anyhows, as I was saying, in case you's following along"—Skid smirks at the jab—"case we get in trouble out there saddled up next ta a carrier, an' gotta cut an' run, a man's standing on each end of the hose with an ax. No time for disconnecting the line an' hauling it in. Nope. Just pull the 'mergency disconnect an' run. An' if for some reason the 'mergency disconnect ain't workin', an' that hose don't drop off inta the ocean like it supposed to, they's a sailor standin' at each end with his ax ta just cut it. Takes one strong sailor to do that, let me tell ya. And then ya got fuels blowing all over both ships an' yourself an' ya just hope ain't no one shooting at ya or any sparks flying from the ax. One brave man, too, let me tell ya, taking the order ta run a metal blade through a gas line, yep."

Silver cuts catty-corner across a quiet intersection of two one-way streets as he ignores the traffic lights while still being mindful of any stray cars, should they unexpectedly appear from a nearby driveway or around a distant corner. "This here's the Greyhound terminal, in case ya have a need ta leave town in a hurry for some other parts. Mighty handy, too, what with Greyhound buses here and the local hub bus terminal just down the block from the ways we come. A man can conveniently gets around town, or get outta town if he needs ta, ya know what I'm saying?" Silver asks as he looks upwardly askew to Skid.

Skid just perceptively nods his head in acknowledgement to Silver but says nothing as his face remains a blank slate.

~~~~~

Behind the bus terminal's ceiling-high window, which runs the length of the block, can be seen a populated hive of patient inactivity. Two young soldiers in transit back to base—not identifiable by well-pressed uniforms but rather from their squared-away appearance of shaved heads and teenage-skinny yet well-defined and physically fit bodies, shiny new blue jeans, tight-fitting, logoed T-shirts, and their bulging, military-issued green duffel bags at their feet—stand side by side and stare vacantly into the offerings of a vending machine. Soldier-erect and unmoving, they review several rows of plastic-wrapped sandwiches, potato chips, and cookies. Not yet of legal age, they are nevertheless nursing raging hangovers from one last night of leave after completing boot camp and months of training prior to their first deployment. From time to time one of the ramrod-straight pair will sway slightly as though a vertical pillar were being guided down a center shaft. Within a week, these two young grunts will be half a world away, humping over eighty pounds on their thin but strong teenage backs, either in the sandy desert heat between two rivers of a fertile crescent or high up in the cold, thin air along a bare, rocky military crest at the terminus of the world's tallest mountain range. A few brave ones depart to place themselves in harm's way and live violently so the many may remain behind and continue to live in peaceful ignorance. A slight, playful elbow nudge from one sends the other to falter a step before regaining his balance and . . . let the games begin.

Most of the travelers waiting in the crowded bus depot sit uncomfortably in stadium seats that run back-to-back in several rows along the length of the terminal. They stare with hope either at all the closed departure doors or, from an opposite facing row, out the windows to the street and a line of early model, mismatched taxis—Lincoln Town Cars, a Ford Crown Vic, previously family-owned minivans, with a sprinkling of subcompacts and a few new hybrid vehicles—that, in turn, have the multiethnic cabmen staring back in. The drivers, with their coffee or a soda or a cigarette in hand, cluster in several small groups. They lean against their cabs, hopeful that they will be needed to shuttle the few who require further transport on the next arriving bus. Within the terminal, a few waiting journeyers quietly doze in the hard plastic seats, only to startle themselves awake each time their unsupported heads drop and the weightlessness of free-falling jolts them back to reality. The cycle repeats as their heavy eyelids once again droop and their heads slowly nod . . .

At the single open ticket window at the end of the long terminal wall, an animated passenger speaks to an agent while pointing with one hand at the paper on the counter and circling in the air with the other like a directional compass. The bored ticket clerk looks at the client but does not see him, listens but does not hear. The inconvenienced worker is simply waiting for the customer to run out of air before replying with the negative answer that he had already formulated once the paper had been placed in front of him on the counter. Those few in line behind the upset patron feign disinterest by looking at everything but the ticket window while intently directing their ears to overhear the conversation and silently hoping that they will have something to say that will be of more interest to the agent.

Two short but thick lines queue up with their luggage behind two of the thirteen numbered glass departure doors along the back wall. All the doors remain shut. From time to time, those standing in line shift their weight from one foot to the other while deliberately avoiding any awkward eye contact with one another. Should one remotely review the waiting queues, there perchance resides a common cosmopolitan misconception of a single stratum of lower class with buses being the last bastion of egalitarian transportation for the poor masses.

True, all seats on the bus are purchased at the same relatively low price with no distinction as to class of service. Nor are there any optional amenity upgrades available, such as premier customer lounges or priority boarding to stratify by economic or social status. And yet, even among the economically handicapped passengers waiting within the bus depot, there remains their own subtle, distinguishable layers of social status and the uneven burden of economic inequality. Observable at the top of their hierarchical order are the few economically advantaged riders with rolling carry-on bags, which they can easily wheel along. The bags' high-telescoping handles allow them to support their arms casually while they stand idly in their faux designer jeans. One step down the ease-of-convenience ladder are the old hard-sided suitcases with wheels that allow passengers to push the heavy weight along with their foot without bending. Next are the big duffel bags of military quality and durability with both handles and a shoulder strap to assist in physically lifting and carrying their heavy load. At the bottom, with never a word said, are those who carry large black plastic garbage bags with brightly colored drawstrings that may not complete the journey intact and which always seem to come part-nered with owners wearing pants that have rips in them that are not necessarily designer statements.

Many waiting riders easily slip back and forth in their conversation from English to Spanish. More than a few can apparently converse only in Spanish. Accents identifiable within the spoken Spanish itself signify levels of an unspoken social-caste system. Inherently understood, the language caste is stratified geographically from the south to the north. It begins with an airy Castilian accent from Argentina that rolls off the speaker's tongue as lightly and gaily as spoken Italian over a morning cappuccino on a quiet sidewalk café, not often heard in a bus terminal. As the speaker's origin of birth rolls northward through the Canal Zone and El Salvador, speech flows faster and in a thicker tongue, eventually becoming harsh and guttural in a *muy rápido* cadence of unmistakable Mexican dialect, difficult for stateside Spanish-class students to follow and comprehend.

And then there are the perennial outcasts. Nervously hiding in the corner, a disheveled, young orphaned woman sits on the floor with both skinny legs tucked comfortably underneath her as she rests her sun-shy face against the cool tile wall. Her elegant neck is hidden behind a lacy, Victorian, high-collared, silky, purple blouse bought the previous day for only a dollar at the estate auction of a now-deceased eighty-nine-year-old heiress. Her soiled black jeans, bought long ago for just a few dollars more at the Army-Navy surplus store, have never been washed. Lying beside her is a backpack, which contains all her worldly possessions. Peering from under her motley, ink-black hair and from within a circle of heavy Goth-black mascara, her dark-as-night eyes occasionally flick away from the tiled wall to quickly scrutinize the busy terminal—for what?—with a glaring challenge of false bravado—to whom?—only to hide once again, her pale cheek pressed against the cold wall. Hiding, really? . . . and why is that? Unable to pay a misdemeanor fine and unwilling to do the time away from her daily drug-sustaining high, she is about to blow off her assigned court-appearance date and enter the subterfuge world of a fugitive on the lam. The cheap ticket fare of a one-way bus ride delusively offers her a convenient escape out of town and away from the local law's reach to a distant place and a new life, without the arresting, incarcerating inconvenience of providing authorized, government-issued papers as proof of her declared personal identity. The lumpy knot of a magic eight ball tucked deep within her boot is her only consoling comfort. Silently, compliantly, she waits, as do the others.

Annoyingly lacking in the busy bus depot is the sound-cancelling white noise of piped-in background music to dampen the intermittent spasms of social dissonance. The fits and cries of humanity are amplified and resonate from one end of the block-long terminal to the other as the sounds echo off the polished linoleum floor, the cheap plastic seats, and the hard, unadorned walls. Common are the impatient outbursts of marital discord with oft-repeated, stress-relieving—only for the one venting—verbal cries of emotional pain and frustration at perceived slights of previous discourtesies and indiscretions. Twice-admonished children have slowed their play in the seats and their runs around the rows to a slow-motion pantomime that taunts at the edge of adult supervision. Siblings subtly poke and prod, pester, and tease each other in a game of chicken to see who will break first in a cry of frustration that thus brings down the wrath of a parent with a slap and an admonishment of "Quiet!" Infrequently, there is the heart-stopping shriek of an infant simply announcing his or her momentary pleasure—or displeasure—for whom other than the parents can discern the difference as they both sound the same? Beleaguered adults, exhausted and weary from long hours of parenting without a break, lack either the energy or the imagination to cope effectively and sometimes overreact in frustration with a child-silencing discharge of their own. Announcements of arrivals and departures blare over-head, harshly quashing all conversations in midsentence. Young and old, black and white, seasonal laborers and permanently unemployed, all have the idle calm of the patiently waiting poor and dispossessed, wishing they were somewhere else—at the end of the line, or at least at the end of their journey—while pretending they don't care.

~~~~~

Absorbed in their search for a light of illumination within the shadows of their own thoughts while observing the eclectic mass of humanity on the verge of soon being somewhere far from here, Silver and Skid remain silent as they stroll a city street together along the length of the glass-viewed bus depot. Once past the terminal they reach a broad four-lane street with a grassy median dividing opposing traffic. The street is lined in both directions with mixed use three- and four-story buildings composed in a jumble of glass and steel and faux brick and concrete.

Waiting for the pedestrian light to change so that they may cross, Silver speaks up to explain. "This here's Main Street. Busier than most round these parts o' town. The stores are not like the fancy shops in the malls, nope, but a man can find what he needs here, yep." Silver and Skid cross with the green light. "My friend Moe has this here cor-ner pawnshop. Good location on the only busy street within town. He gives me a special deal sometimes, without askin' too many ques-tions, ya know what I'm saying? But I don't s'pose a gentleman like you knows much 'bout or have much need for a pawnshop? Nope, s'pose not. Anyhows, Moe an' I goes way back togethers, yep, that's fer sure. I remember when we was kids, I was hangin' with Teddy and him down behind his old place on the ranch. Just hangin' on the fence an' all, like kids do what with nothin' ta do. And then here comes my cuz Billy from the other side walking across the field in this bright orange shirt an' all. Well Moe's uncle had just gotten a young bull an' puts him in the field. Well, we's all forgots about the bull until we sees dust from him stomping the ground like a bull done do when theys get all lathered up and all. Well, we done hollers out 'Billy, the bull! The bull, Billy! Run,

run! Don't look back, just run!' Well, it was a near thing what with Billy having a head start an' all, and the young bull being all lathered up and faster, ya know? Why Moe's uncle comes out later in the day with an ax an' just cleaves that young bull betweens them there horns of his, yep. He done cleave that bull right through the skull in one swing of the ax, yep. Young bull chasing you an' all may be fun, but if yous ever gets a ton of bull chasing ya, ya ain't getting away, an' ya probably ain't nevers gettin' up, no siree."

"Silver! Is that Silver I sees?"

Silver and Skid slow their walk to look behind and identify the source of the high-pitched voice. Exiting the pawnshop, a middle-aged woman with a flustered air and dressed in many clashing colors quickly walks towards them. Her once brightly colored red blouse has washed out several shades to the edge of pink. Red-orange hair flames from her head and a heavy layer of red lipstick frames two straight rows of big, bright white teeth. "Why I declare! It is Silver. Thought it was you disappearing round the corner here. So, what's going on? What'cha doing round these parts here? Last I heard you be locked up an' put away in County for a while. Then just yesterday I hears there's a detective looking for ya. This him?" she questions with an unabashed look over of Skid.

"Well, that may have been the last word ya heard, an' I'm all choked up about your concern for me, but I ain't locked up now as you can right well observe."

"Well, mighty glad ta see it, you being a proper gentleman an' all. But sorry ta say, I also heard some nasty rumors going through the grapevine about you havin' a big ol' misunderstandin' what with ya sista' and your pension and whatnot."

"I don't knows who's doing all the talking about nothing they don't know anything 'bout, but there ain't no misunderstanding about it at all. But I 'spect ya be here in front of Social for gettin' a little somethin' for yourself, an' you spotted me an' thinkin' a gettin' a little something more from someone else?"

"Now Silver! I declare! They's something wrong now'days with a neighborly woman being social an' all? No harm in having a little friendly conversation on the street with someone ya knows from the neighborhood and all, now is there? Ain't seen ya in a whiles an' all an' thought we'd catch up, is all."

"You's just a social butterfly, all right, waiting to pick off unsuspecting people so as ya can pick up on the latest dirt an' converse with other peoples like you's miss knows-it-all 'bout others people's business when you don't know any more than anyone else, and what with you havin' more problems than most anyhow. That's simply all there be about that, uh-huh."

"Likes I say, ain't no's harm in a Christian lady havin' a little friendly conversation with a fine fella of the congregation, is all. Ain't like I'm the one been outta circulation for a while, while they's been all locked up in County an' all."

"Well, here's your door ta Social, and if I had a dime, I'd ask ya ta stay outta mine . . . business. So get what ya needs ta get everything straightened out so's you don't need be comin' down this street every day an' spotting unsuspecting people an' askin' for money."

"I ain't asking, I'm just saying . . ."

"Yeah, you just ain't nevers gettin' round ta askin' for it yet. Now pardon, but we got business ta be takin' care of ourselves an' we is gonna be on our ways, if ya don't mind," replies Silver as he picks up his pace to quickly walk away.

~~~

Silver and Skid soon leave the humming business district to cross another quiet street in silence. Traversing a clean but dusty sidewalk, they pass a long row of storefronts that have noticeably aged in architectural design. Window displays are of sun-bleached wares awkwardly out of date—or nostalgic reminders of a time past—and desperately in need of a feather dusting. More than a few fronts are shuttered with black wrought-iron grates lowered and old, sun-faded newspapers taped to the windows inside.

Along their route, Silver starts a quiet, stress-relieving one-way conversation with himself. "She knows mo' people down the street, she'll be all right. Yep, she's always taken care a herself." After a while he turns to Skid. "Normally, ya mess up ya gotta pay, ya know? Some people, though, they's always looking out for everybody else ta bail them outta their own mess, ya know? Like now it's your problem ta get 'em out of their own self-made mess. These people see a handout as an opportunity to take from ya without any effort. And they's the ones that see giving as weakness in another and then prey on them for some more. That be the natural order of the wild-animal predator culling the weak out o' the domestic herd. Then ya have the ones that see the gift of a handout as an obligation, a responsibility for repayment, a burden you carry forward to help the less fortunate. That be a human divine, that what that be." Silver drops his head to look at the sidewalk while stepping over the cracks. "Yep, we all being tested in strange ways in strange times. Times is so hard now, the peoples usta be the ones givin' a couple cases of food to the church, why heck, they's now the ones down there in line looking for the food handout. Heck, even the good peoples are thrown out on the street, what with all the foreclosure going on now an' all. And even they's being tested, what caught 'tween doing the right thing: either emptying the pools before ya leaves an' someone falling in an' crackin' themselves up, or leaving it full a' water and a nuisance for the neighborhood kids ta be swimming in an' the mosquitoes ta be growing in. Ya knows time's bad all round when they's checkin' for West Nile virus in pools of the abandoned homes that peoples done left behind 'cause the bank's done closin' on 'em. Damn shame it is. Life sure can get complicated sometimes. Anyhows, that's one sorry woman lookin' for one sorry man, ya know what I'm saying? They's some woman so crazy they's takin' their kid's money and gives it to their man, heck, that ain't right."

"No, that wouldn't be right," Skid quietly offers.

"What with the pressures of life an' all, peoples hooked up together, rely on each other, and take care of each others. That's just the normal natural order of things, that is."

"Yep, that is," Skid concurs.

Silver and Skid walk through a row of waist-high green hitching posts that block vehicular traffic to the street. They pass a busy diner with efficient, friendly waitresses who always have a good word to say and appear to have been working there since opening day decades ago. Next door is a long-ago-closed movie theater now renovated and reopened as an equity playhouse of musicals and comedy. The theater's art deco façade and colorful wall mural depict a bygone Depression era of strong men shaping metal and erecting tall buildings in an industrial-strength time.

"Silver, I'm just a bit curious and all and you don't have to tell me anything if you don't want to, but you seem like a pretty stand-up guy. So . . . what bank did you have to rob to get time in County for?"

"Huh, time in County wasn't nuttin' for nuttin'!"

"Come on, Silver, you don't spend time in jail for nothing. There's gotta be something behind it?"

"Yeah, that's what I usta think as well. I didn't know this shit happened, and then this shit happened ta me! They's be some crazy people out there that's just wants ta sabotage your life an' run ya outta town. You never know what's happenin', and then *boom!* they's gotcha. Ain't no one believes me, but it's true."

"So what were the actual charges filed?"

"Huh, there ain't nothing I'm tellin' ya. Here—" Silver reaches inside his breast pocket to pull out a white envelope with a colored stamp of a government seal and hands it to Skid. Skid carefully pulls a letter from the envelope and unfolds the paper to begin reading as they continue walking along.

"Jesus, Silver," Skid exclaims, "I've never, ever heard of this before: '. . . there is no factual basis for the charges and all files are to be closed and destroyed . . .' signed by both the chief deputy sheriff and the presiding county judge. Holy shit, Silver! What the hell? That's some mighty bad karma going round to get you in a mess like that." Skid replaces the letter and returns the envelope to Silver, who then carefully reinserts it back into his coat pocket.

"Like I says, you never know what's happenin', you'd be surprised. Someone uses false charges on ya when you ain't lookin' and then your whole life is all turned round and upside down and just like that . . . *boom!*"

"Well, that is definitely true sometimes, all right. Sometimes what you think you're seeing isn't really what it appears to be. Don't we all know a little about that?"

"Now why don't we cross the street here ta the other side for a little bit?" Silver changes the subject. "There're some mighty sorry lookin' fellas coming up on us that you may not wants ta be introduced to or associates with. They's all right an' all, they's just all jacked up an' havin' a bad time now is all."

Down the block they see a gathering of men interspersed with a few women milling about the sidewalk. Some lean against the long one-story office building that is cut every few yards with a home-style front door—wood-framed with dissected panel glass and a faux brass doorknob—for an entrance. Most pace, or rather it is more of a shuffle, in a slow-motion holding pattern from one end of the block and then back to the other. All are in need of a haircut, a bath, a cigarette, and a massive dose of Visine to get the red out. Only a few waiting pacers ever occasionally lift their gaze from the sidewalk spot that they occupy at that moment. Their self-delusional tripping is still better than their nightmare reality of cravings and pain.

"That's one odd clientele I've not ever seen in front of a medical clinic," Skid observes.

"Huh, you got the eye, you have, an' you be half right with what you observing, that's fer sure," Silver comes back. "That's the Janus medical clinic. I calls it the Greek god of hell, the delusional devil of pain and misery, with false promises and forlorn hope, it is." Scorn is thick in his throat. "That's the methadone clinic trying ta get all those all hooked up on H clean. But, man, it ain't workin', an' it ain't worth it, let me tell ya. The cure is worse than the disease. A man would rather kill hisself than have ta lives on that methadone shit—" finished with a spit into the gutter.

Skid gives a long questioning look to Silver.

"Well, I's might as well tell ya. Afta' the Navy tanker, what with my years of 'sperience working oil an' all, I got hooked up in town as a roustabout, moving from one rig ta 'nother as jobs opened up on the local sites an' all. You know, a grease monkey working on the oil-drilling platforms. Hard, dirty work, man's work, it is. Dangerous, too," Silver adds with the pride of a man grinding through the filth of a difficult job until completed. "I liked it and I was good at it and worked my way up ta roughneck and did all the jobs. Afta' a longs while I eventually become a tool pusher in charge of a rig. Being the boss and all, I just parked a trailer out there and lived at the site 'til I got a day off. Might simple life, yep, ands I likes it, too. Sometimes, though, luck just done run out, an' I was just run over."

Silver goes silent for a few moments before he starts up again. "Anyhows, sometime back, we was a man short that day so I was up on the rig covering when I got distracted. There I was yellin' over the edge with my back turned to get the delivery driver ta angle the new pipe where's we could get at it nice an' easy when the worm let the chain slip. Well now for an old hand like me that ain't no big deal 'cause you can see it coming and prevents it, or at least get outta the way once it happens, simple. But there I was leanin' over the rig, doing two jobs at once with my back turned ta the new guy for just a second, my dumb-ass rookie mistake, and I didn't see the loose chain come whipping around and take my feet out from under me and damned if it didn't send me flying off the rig. Damned might busted up an all afta's I hit an' all. You may notice my slight limp when I walk?" Silver pauses again, this time rubbing his hand up and down his left hip. "Anyhows, there I was hurting and not working and feeling all sorrys for myself and one thing led to another and associated with the wrongs types an' all and next thing ya know I'm shootin' heroin. What the hell, huh? Damn, a man nevers know where he's gonna end up, that's fer sure. So some-how I got a social worker that set me up at the Janus clinic ta get clean an' all. Man, ya thinks ya hooked on the drug, but that ain't nothing compared ta the cure. That methadone shit had a grip on me tighter than bark on a tree, an' made me squrrelier than a squirrel without nuts; I was all that an' more, fer sure. Anyhows, don't knows how I did it, but just one day I went cold turkey, yep, and just did it. So that be why I calls it Janus, god of hell and prevailer of pain and suffering, been nothing but that for me." Silver finishes in a monotone voice as a dry statement of facts, with no hint of an appeal for sympathy.

"New beginnings. Janus, the Roman god of new beginnings."

"Say what?"

"Janus is the Roman god of new beginnings or a doorway to a new life."

"Now don't that beat all, Spooky? How you know that?"

"A few years ago in Silicon Valley, where everyone was shooting a different kind of drug to be the new kind of corporate god, so they start by naming their start-up company after one."

"Man, you sure get around, Spooky. What gets you ta this side a our town?"

"And, 'a man never knows where he's gonna end up,' that's for sure. So, I'm hoping you know the guy following us and he's cool, right?" Skid says casually without missing a step and appearing to stare aimlessly down the street in the direction they are headed.

Silver turns his head for a quick look and continues walking as he says, "Herbie, yeah, he's way cool. Must've spotted us from the clinic an' started following us. It's best we stop an' chat now, 'cause we're not gonna shake him, and he's just going ta keep following us to wherevers." Silver halts and turns, and Skid follows suit to face and address Herbie, who continues his approach down the sidewalk.

"Is Herbie like an old rock star or something that's just done way too many drugs?" Skid asks.

"Uh-huh, oh yeah, Herbie's a superstar all right . . . in his own mind. Huh!"

~~~

They give Herbie an inquisitive look over as he continues to approach them with his uniquely odd shuffle commingled with some indefinable and endearing flair of a perpetual showman. Herbie looks as though he would walk best assisted by a cane, but he uses none as he ambles along with his body turned semi-sideways, his left arm swinging loosely in no detectable cadence to his double-quick limp that is still slower than a normal pace. Wearing a tweed smoking jacket with soft, brown leather elbow patches and a royal-blue silk shirt opened in a wide V down his chest, Herbie cuts a stylish swath against the chalky sidewalk and bland storefronts. Head cocked, his dirty blond locks, once flowing and light-reflective, are now stringently woven in twirling, dull clumps that hide a good portion of his face. Viewed through his womanly veil of hair, a prematurely aged face still shows the underlying structure of a once devilishly charming appearance that women would look at and say to themselves, "Oh, he's trouble . . . maybe with me?" The long-ago lead guitarist that ambles along the quiet sidewalk is a shell of a performer that is wrung out and spent, having stood under hot stage lights, and is now suffering through the artist's pain of double withdrawals—from an attentive, screaming audience and intoxicating, drug-induced highs.

Herbie does not slow his pace until he steps directly in front of Silver's face, violating Silver's personal space. The frail lead guitarist maneuvers the much taller and broader Silver until his back is up against the wall. "Dude, you got me all jammed up." He looks away from Silver to Skid. "That phone's not working and I can't do any business, ya know what I'm saying?" Back to Silver: "I want my old phone back—I can't get connected with this," he says as he holds up a cell. Accusingly to Skid: "Where's it at? I want it back." To Silver: "Ya got it?"

Herbie's odd speaking cadence coupled with twitchy, shifting eyes may be excused by some in recently introduced friendly circles as a nervous tick or possibly an awkward behavioral disorder; however, those who have lived through or with someone going through withdrawal can easily recognize and understand the addict's confused subconsciousness firing long-unused neurons for clarity of thought while trying to coordinate vocal cords with tongue and lip muscles for clear, rational speech.

"Is he cool?" Herbie asks Silver in a loud stage whisper that can be heard by all as his eyes continue to flick back and forth between Silver and Skid.

"Yeah, he be cool."

"Not a narc or a snitch or anything like that is he?" Herbie asks while leaning away from Skid, the diseased leper.

"No, man, I said he be cool."

"So, dude"—turning the full attention of his confused eyes back to Silver—"reputation is everything, ya know what I'm saying here?" Herbie continues while waving a cell phone in the air: "You told me this phone would be working and it's not. I'm not connected, I can't do business. I'm losing street cred, ya know what I'm saying? Reputation is everything and I'm losing mine because no one can get a hold of me and I can't hook 'em up. And then they just get all ornery on me and start spreading nasty things. So if I can't do business, then I'm gonna put a bad word on the street about you and then your reputation is shit and then you're outta business, and ya know I can do that." Herbie gives a hard look into Silver's face. "This phone doesn't work and I want my old phone back. Where is it? You have it on you?"

"No, no, I don'ts have it with me."

"Don't mess with me now."

"It ain't no longer in my possession—ya know what I'm saying?"

"Don't jack me, man. Come on Silver where is it?"

"I don't have it."

"Then where is it? Who has it? Don't tell me you gone and start messin' with the GPS in the phone? The new phones aren't like the old phones. They makes 'em now that ya mess with the SIM or the GPS and they knows ya messin' with 'em and they knows where you at and they're gonna start tracking ya ta get'cha. I'm tellin' ya fer sure, ya turn the phone on and they're gonna know where you're at and they're gonna get'cha!"

"My guy's just cleaning it, ya know what I'm saying? But tell ya what, I'll give ya my phone now and I'll make it all good to ya by the end of the day. You can make outgoing calls; just whatevers ya do, don't answer the phone unless ya knows who's it is, square?"

"I'm not being a dick, Silver. Ya know I gotta have a working phone or I'm outta business." Herbie exchanges phones with Silver. "So we'll hook up later and we'll trade again, but it's gotta be working or no switch."

"Yeah, sure, no problem, I'll catch ya later."

"Hey, Silver, no hard feelings, just business, 'kay? Oh, almost forgot, when I was with my PO this morning I saw that detective ya working with on your sister an' all. Well, he said if I was ta see ya, I was to tell ya to call him or go see him. Okay?"

"Yeah, thanks."

"Okay then, we'll hook up later and switch phones then."

Silver and Skid follow Herbie with their eyes as he shuffles away, already dialing on his new cell phone and putting it up to his ear in conversation.

Silver places the switched phone in his pocket. "Sorry ya had ta hear all that and be in the middle o' all that."

"No problem, just a little street business you have to take care of, sure. But what's all this stuff with a detective and your sister? It's never any good when you have a detective involved in family matters. What's the deal?"

"Damn. Well seeing as we gettin' along okay an' I thinks I can trust ya, it's like I says, ya never knows where it's coming or who ya need ta protects yourself from, and I nevers seen it coming. I was hit with personality theft doing my time while incarcerated."

"Identity theft?"

"Yeah, identify theft." Silver starts along the street again. "My sista' got hold of my pension account an' emptied it outta almost thirty grand," he says as his feelings of a misplaced shame lead him to slowly bow his head until his chin almost touches his chest. "Thirty years a workin' gone in six months, an' it ain't even for me." Looking down at the sidewalk, Silver notices the sunlight reflecting off his highly polished shoes and hesitates a moment to enjoy the manly satisfaction of a quality shine before continuing. "A man don't need much really, nope sure don't. I gots more than I need gettin' around town here an' my business an' all, yep that be true. Just can't takes care o' my family like I wants to, ya know." Silver looks at Skid. "I got grandkids, I told ya, that I like ta visits from time ta time, takin' the bus ta N'awlins and spoilin' 'em. An' I also have a daughter here that I haven't told ya about, with younger kids that needs taken care of, too. And my daughter's shacked up with my sista' and they's just one bad pair togethers they are. All theirs money goes ta their mans, or to their pipes. That ain't right. They ain't right in the head, takin' care of their man and pipe befores they takin' care a' them kids, ya know what I'm saying? Smoking too much crap just messin' up their brain, and they just ain't thinkin' right. And those kids, they be good kids, too. Ya don't needs ta do much ta get a smile outta them or a belly laugh, yep, they be real good kids." Silver goes quiet as he looks back down and begins his ritual of stepping over the stress-relieving cracks in the sidewalk.

"And what about the detective Herbie was talking about? Can he help you?"

"Huh, the detective, yep. Why that detective he done already told me the money's all gone an' ain't nothing he can do and ain't no way I is gettin' it back. My money's all smoked up, it is, an' my sista' ain't got nothin' more than her monthly social and I knows she taken the welfare with my daughter from the kids. One messed up situation, fer sure." Silver pauses for effect to let the painful reality of a loved one's deception and betrayal lie over Skid. "She done got me all jammed up, I'm telling ya. That's one thing ya don't do is go messin' with a man's kids or grandkids. The detective say all they gonna do is put her in jail. Why hep, I think I'm just gonna puts her somewhere else myself, that what I be doin' for sure. She may not be paying me my moneys at the moment but she sure gonna be payin' one ways or anothers, yep, there ain't no telling what just might happen." Silver turns away to signal the discussion's termination. Each momentarily escapes to his own dubious shadows of thought for fanciful and grandiose solutions to the reckless human condition and an unrequited desire of returning the world to their imagined, idealistic state of childhood innocence—or at least the innocence of childhood ignorance.

~~~

Having sometime back passed through and out of the city's business center, Silver and Skid are once again strolling the sidewalk by themselves along quiet streets. The downtown multistory mixed-use buildings have slowly transitioned to low-rise, single-story soft-sandstone-faced retail outlets. Windows running the length of the store frontage display their wares for sale or signs that list the services offered. A crisscross weave of heavy black metal security grills rolled down across a few storefronts indicate that those stores will neither open that day nor any day under the current storefront signage. Periodically, they pass an empty dirt lot where no building has ever risen. This outside edge of the city appears to have been built more upon future expectations of continued commercial growth that in fact never happened than on the then-present economic reality. Therefore, with its wide, empty streets and the intermittent vacant dirt lots, this section of town appears left behind and isolated, hanging floppy and loose as worn, oversized clothing passed down to a younger, smaller sibling for the second time.

Stepping past a print shop, Silver and Skid glance in to observe copy paper stacked six feet high along each wall and the customer desk disarranged with a deep pile of papers waiting to be handled in one fashion or another. At the forefront of the following Goodwill window display, they see racks of hanging shirts in an assortment of colors and sizes. The secondhand store contains a few senior citizens unhurriedly searching for quality clothing at bargain prices. Later in the day, cliques of fashion-conscious young women will descend upon the shop to walk up and then back each of the store's aisles in search of previously owned garments. And, in an art of the female species unknown to a common man, the women will quickly flip through and judge each and every article hanging on the racks in their continuous search to outfit themselves economically for that special parta, or in their own unique style of dress with a little different flair.

As the block ends, Silver and Skid sweep a turn at the corner liquor mart that sits along a wide and empty intersection. The store display windows are brightly postered with thin and full-chested women in colorful bikinis, each smiling with pearly white teeth, teasingly advertising the latest light beer while posing on some exotic beach—interestingly, the teenage-thin models do not appear to be of legal drinking age. Popular logos prominently stuck on the glass-door entrance indicate that the store accepts EBT and cash payments for recharging either cell phone minutes or debit cards, which are extensively used by the neighborhood's financially handicapped, who are unable to obtain revolving, monthly credit accounts.

Passing the mini-mart, Silver awakens to stir out of his contemplation. "There be my cousin's shoe shack across the street at the other end of this here block," Silver says as they cross the street towards a decorated storefront with a blaring neon sign declaring "OPEN." "Interestingly enough, this here tat shop was back in the day the place where I cut my teeth as a young roustabout outta the Navy." Large display windows are colorfully hand-painted in an esoteric juxtaposition of half men and half machines, bleeding red hearts spiked with pointed daggers, winged fire-breathing dragons, and other artful delights of man's wild imagination and frightening nightmares. Peering through the graffiti-stained windows with all of the parlor lights turned out, the two can dimly observe a center row of tattoo stations that run the store's length to a back wall located in the midsection of the building.

"What with my military 'sperience an' all, Old Canino hired me ta work outta this here shop. Old Canino was a wildcat servicing the oil companies in town when oil 'twas better'n gold. Made a ton of money, he did, and built this here shop for his office and a garage in the back for all his trucks an' tooling an' stuff. Yep, good old days, what with five national oil companies having regional headquarters here an' all trying ta get enough guys ta service and do the rigs. Then da price a crude done drop, who would'a thunk that back then, huh? An' all the regional headquarters all gets sold to just one, and the real estate market drops an' the next thing ya know the good times are over an' Canino closes this here shop of his, and we're all scrambling for work and when we gets it we ain't gettin' paid half a what we usta. Funny how ya don't knows ya right in the middle of the good old days 'til the good ol' days just done pass, huh? So now, long ago, the shops been passed down the family an' finally converted ta this here tat shop, mostly for the older kids and all. Canino was a good man to work for, damn shame he done pass on so early, sad thing. So anyhows, I saw his son grow up an' he's way cool. The kid, he lets me sweep an' clean out the tat shop every now an' then when I needs some pocket change, and he pays me in all the barrels of recyclables I can haul away. Make a pretty penny, too, what with all their partying they be doing and price o' aluminum an' glass nowadays, yep, a pretty penny," Silver says with a tightening of his lips into a smile as he reaches into his pants pocket to finger a handful of comforting coin.

~~~

Ambling past the tattoo shop and the sandstone-stucco building's end, they reach a weedy dirt lot that gives them an unobstructed view of their intended destination—the corner shoe shack. Isolated at the intersection's corner, it appears to be nothing more than an interesting little aluminum camper shell carelessly perched on cinder blocks. The rectangular thing sits lengthwise with the empty dirt field on one end and an asphalt-paved parking lot to its rear. "Shack" is the term that anyone actually noticing the structure would use to describe it as it in no way would ever be confused with a building risen from a planned construction project. Rather, it gives the odd impression of having once been a camper trailer towed along at high speeds that suddenly became unhitched and lost its wheels. One can imagine the wheel-less shell sliding and bumping along the street to finally bounce over the curb and come to rest in its present location. Banged and dinged and resting slightly askew after its crash landing, the cheap aluminum shell was lifted and then leveled with blocks placed under each corner. Except for the trailer-hitch end, which has only a single hole cut high in the side that's filled with a wall-mounted air-conditioning unit, long, narrow windows wrap entirely around the shack, allowing for an easy view both in and out. Protruding alone as an eyesore in a vacant lot as it is, it is nevertheless an invisible structure to the mind's eye and wouldn't be given a second glance unless one was specifically looking for it.

Silver opens the flimsy aluminum-framed glass door and steps up the two-stair entrance with his greeting: "Hey Cuz Billlyyy. What'cha doing, old man? Just sittin' round reading the paper in your lazy ways or are yous open for business today?"

From high upon his soft leather throne, Billy slowly tilts the newspaper, exposing his old weathered face. Glancing over the top edge of the paper, he silently inspects the newly arrived pair. "I's always open for business, when I gots paying business ta be done." He eases back into his comfortable tan lounge chair without taking his eyes off either Silver or Skid.

"Well I got a payin' customer for ya, right here, old man. My new business partner, Skid."

Billy curiously continues to inspect Skid. "I seen yas coming, all right. I ain't blind yet, ya know? I just figures you bringing me trouble that I don't want no part of, no siree." Finished looking Skid over: "Well, in that case, cuz." Billy sets his paper aside and pushes heavily with both hands upon the padded armrests to lift himself out of his seat. With an audible huff he stiffly descends the one large step. "I 'preciates ya thinking about me." Billy and Silver perform a quick, five-move handshake of the socially familiar and ritually connected, not too unlike the secret gesture of the fraternal Masonic order.

"Yeah, you doing all right, old man," Silver chuckles.

"Yep, better'n most, an' not as well as others." Turning to Skid, "Well, step on up, young man, an' let's see what we gots ta work wit' here."

As Skid climbs up and takes a seat, Billy slides open a large drawer from the base, which is a step up to the two spacious leather chairs. He lifts out two metal stirrups and places them in their base slots. He next grabs Skid by his ankles, which are hanging in the air, and firmly places his feet on the posts. Skid feels for the heel stops and pushes himself back to relax comfortably in his new throne. Working quickly with efficient hands, Billy lines up the tools of his trade, all of which he pulls from the drawer, and places them upon the step. His meticulous precision and organized placement of his brushes, cloths, creams, and polish that all lie within easy reach display a professional pride that he takes in his craft. Satisfied, Billy takes a cigarette from behind his ear and slips it between his lips.

"Man, ya knows ya too old to be smoking? It's gonna stunt your growth an' then it's gonna kills ya at a young age, yep!" Silver quips.

"Huh, it ain't lit up; it's my pacifier. I just uses it all day long, which isn't all day long, but all day when I'm here," says Billy while using a wet bristle brush to firmly scrub Skid's shoes clean. Without comment, the three men look up to watch an ambulance pass, its piercing siren wailing. Billy next takes a dry cloth and, with two embracing hands, wraps and then firmly wipes down each shoe. As he returns the damp drying cloth back to its drawer, his cell phone, which has also been placed on the workbench, begins to ring. Glancing at the caller ID, Billy says aloud to himself, "Huh, now ain't that most peculiar? Yello!" He answers his common greeting into the phone.

"What's that? . . . Whaddya want? . . . Uh-huh . . . Oh, I don't know, I'm jus' trippin' on this here strange phone call, yep, that's what I be doing. . . . Well, who dis is? . . . You be calling me. Now who you be calling?"

"Huh?" Billy questions his phone as he places it back in line. "That was one strange call. That lady had an attitude like a tear up the ground, like she afta' ya a mile a minute, an' I don't even knows who it be. Kinda peculiar, don't ya think? That someone be calling me to find out who I am?" Billy dips a finger of cloth into the colored shoe paste. "I might say a word or two but I ain't saying nothing much, what with all this identity theft going on nowadays." Silver and Skid cast a knowing glance. With two fingers, Billy rubs the paste in a circular motion into a shoe. "If theys don't say nothing that I knows them, then I hang up. I have ta know 'em before I tells them anythin'. Huh, I'm gonna get me another. It's time for a change, ya know? When things start messing up on your phone and too many people call ya that ya don't know, it's time for a change, yep. Silver, can ya hook me up and give me some time on it? I'd use my phone lady but I thinks she's the one gone an' screwed it all up, ya know what I'm saying."

"Sure cuz, I gotcha covered, you know that."

"Yeah, just checkin' on ya," he replies as he starts on the other shoe.

A lone, dusty gray figure trundles along the back alley. "Huh, sometimes ya think you have it bad, and then ya sees old Gandhi still hanging around," observes Silver looking out across the parking lot to the long alleyway. "And sometimes with all the things ya thinks a-going on and changing, things just don't change that much, do they?"—a rhetorical question they collectively let hang unanswered. Silently, allowing each a moment of introspection "and by the grace of God . . ."—they watch.

Gandhi shuffles along, leaning against a fully loaded grocery-store shopping cart: dancing partners moving together in slow-motion fits and starts. Black, crusty, rope-thick dreadlocks loosely swing from under Gandhi's crooked baseball cap, draping over his eyes and down his shoulders. His faded, oversized sweatshirt is way too hot for this day and his physical exertion. Worn sneakers are untied and flop with every step. Many colors of cloth—not necessarily identifiable as clothes per se—and paper, plastic bags, and other odds and ends are piled head high over the metal-wire frame of the overburdened cart. Like an overworked locomotive hauling a massive tonnage of freight, Gandhi leans forward and presses into the cart with the maximum momentum of all his weight to go faster and faster. Each burst is a succession of a half-dozen quicker steps before he tires, slows, and comes to a complete stop, resting while leaning against the cart. After a moment of respite, he slowly shuffles around the metal cage on wheels. He stops at seemingly random points along the way, gathering, rearranging, and organizing the accessible surface items in the bulging overflow as if the key to escape his station in life is his possessions' balance and weight distribution combined with the wind resistance of the cart's aerodynamics at high speeds. With droopy lids, his eyes lag behind the movement of both his head and his hands. One is left with the unshakable feeling that Gandhi will never truly awaken from the dreamscape of his alcohol-induced, half-comatose state and will be forever collecting and rearranging little odds and ends on this, his endlessly growing pile.

Billy places a tin lid back over the colored paste and picks up a stain cloth to begin the first polish. With two hands firmly grasping each end, he slides the cloth back and forth in a blur. As each section of shoe is completed, there is a single finishing snap of cloth. As he begins to work on the second shoe, an automobile with a young couple pulls along the gutter to park in front of the shack's glass-door entrance. Billy curiously glances over his shoulder only to straighten up with a "Huh. Now don't that beat all?" as a tall young man with curly dark hair exits the passenger seat onto the sidewalk.

"What choo gettin' on about, old man? Snoopin' on a boy an' a girl. You becoming a lecherous old coot now?" Silver asks.

"Huh, I ain't becoming nothin' of the sort. I jus' minding my own business on my own front porch is all I'm doing. A man's gotta right ta know the comings and goings on his own front porch don't he? Ya parks in front of a man's house, why he's gonna looky out the winda' an' see who it may be. And it may just only be an uninvited guest. But thataways he at least have a moment ta think about why he ain't inviting them in, ya know. Showing up an all without an invite or the courtesy a calling first before showings up unannounced an' all, ya know what I'm saying?"

"Man, you is getting ta be an old man, that's fer sure. Who you got wantin' to comes around and visit you at your place anyhows?"

"Now that's not the point, now is it? I'm just saying I'm mindin' my own business on my own front porch, hep, that all that be."

"Yer jus' jealous he got himself a young hottie. Ya gettin' ta be an old geezer, you are."

"Why I tell ya I ain't nothing a the sort. I just wondering why they parking way out here, at the other end of the block is all and nots in front o' the tat shop where they's from. Kinda suspicious ta me."

"Ha. Just a private fella not wanting everyone in his business, seeing his new squeeze and then makin' fun o' him like a fella's friends are ought ta do, I betcha. Ain't no harm in that. Kinda natural, it is."

"Huh! He ain't no shy guy and he ain't no preacher's son. He's dancing on several cards simultaneously, that's what he be doing, ya know what I'm saying? This is the third time this week, and theys all be different. Why this one here is dark haired, an' the one 'twas here yesterday is blonde, an' befores that, why hep, that one be someone different all together. Yep, ya heard that right, ya did."

"Well I'll be," Silver pipes up with a pinch of aroused curiosity in his voice as he stands to get a better view of the street.

Wearing faded jeans hanging low to expose boxer briefs underneath and a T-shirt with a cowgirl silk screen, the young man stands on the sidewalk as he leans into the parked car through the passenger door. A colorful tattoo sleeve on his left arm is exposed as it rests on the car roof while his right arm supports his weight on the open door. The girl sits motionless with both hands on the steering wheel while he speaks. Her head tilted towards her lap, she hides her face from view behind her long black hair. As the man pushes himself from the car and straightens, and before the car door is fully shut, the old family sedan speeds away from the curb.

Three inquisitive spectators follow the lanky young man with their eyes as he walks closely around their shack to the rear parking lot, climbs up into a lifted four-by-four truck, and then drives away.

"Now don't that beat all," Silver eventually comments to break the silence as the truck disappears down the street. Silver eases back into his chair as Billy picks up a brush to begin the final polish. Silver turns his attention to Billy. "Hey, old man, I kinda got me a hankering ta hear one of your sweet old soul songs, ya know what I'm askin'? Ya got a song in ya ta share with my new friend and me, do yas?"

"You should know better than most ta be askin' me for that." Having already anticipated a negative response, Silver has closed his eyes to concentrate on the remembered mellifluous sweetness of Billy's once-beautiful singing voice. Tenor notes from long ago that had once floated through Silver's ears, wafting around his aural senses with unashamed, manly sensuality, like a full-bodied red wine first swirled, then breathed in before being slowly passed over one's tongue to give up the pleasurable secrets of its vineyard and casting to the connoisseur's tongue. Elusively folded within the throaty rasp of Billy's aged vocal cords are glorious notes that once rang true and hung pure in the air. Silver can still fainly capture the distinct timber of song that one could viscerally taste as from any intoxicating fine, fine red wine—or was that his own wistful state of remembrance? Silver runs the tip of his tongue between his lips as a wish. He is surprised at the melancholy echoing through him and realizes it is not from never again hearing the beauty of what once was, and wanting more, but rather the souring of his once carefree companion and friend into this crotchety old man whom he barely recognizes, he with his sharp, impatient retorts, and the fearful trepidation that he himself may not be far behind! *Let it go for now.*

Silver pulls a wry smile across his face. "I hears ya in church sometimes, my old friend, when I'm standing behind ya and the choir's spirit is up with all they's rabble-rousing and such and you all thinking nobody's noticing. Ha, gotcha. I'm just saying, it's been a long while since ya kicking it here with just your friends in your own place. Give us a little taste, old man. I ain't askin' for a drink, I'm just saying I'm missing a few sweet tunes from ya. Why heck"—and his voice slows and falls in a dry tone of melodic sorrow—"you shoulds know we all be missing it."

"Well, one sure thing is that at my old age I don't let no one rush me no more, and I don't let no one push me no more, and that fer sure, so don't chu be doing either."

"They says ya only as old as ya feel," eyes still closed, prodding and cajoling, listening and wishing with a thirst more than a hunger.

"Well then, I sure is feeling it, huh."

"It sure is one sorry thing . . ." Silver trails off with a sorrowful hint of nostalgia in his voice at the lost art. Feeling a longing for what can't ever come back again—*Damn shame,* thinks Silver—he lightens up for his friend and with a smile in his words: "and I thinks ya owes me a big ol' tip anyhows for bringing ya this here new client."

"Ha, I gots plenty a tips fer ya, so how 'bout we just a start with lookin' both ways befores ya cross the street. How ya like that tip from this old man, huh? I gots plenty more tips for ya. Huh, and as for sorry, lots of sorry old things there are. Like I'm sorry I done miss my breakfast this morning, too. My old lady come rushing in ta the kitchen this morning and interrupted mine, saying she's got something more importants for me ta be doing now. Ya know what I mean when a lady interrupts ya and it always has ta be now, and on your dime? Always harping on ya until ya gets it done now and their way. I'd like ta tells her, 'I ain't going anywhere wit' you, I's going by myself, 'cause I gots ta gets off ta work afta' my breakfast on the table.' But, anyhows, she tells me the cat's up on the roof meowing and wanting ta gets down, and now that's my problem. Why? Anyhow I says, 'If it got up there it can get down,' right? I mean if it wants down, then why don't it just get down? It got up, didn't it? So anyhow, I get up from my breakfast table an' we went out on the porch an' sure 'nough it's sittin' on the roof gutter meowing. So I sent my old lady in fer a can a cat food or tuna to entice the beast down, ya know what I'm saying, being smarter than the cat an' all. Now don't be tellin' anyone this but as soon as she steps inta the house, I jus' grab the broom on the porch and puts it up there for the cats ta climb on or sometin', not really sure what, and it just sat there pawing at it. So I decides ta just sweep that cat right off the roof. Surprised the shit outta the cat, I did. Me too, I think. Anyhow, the cat lands on the grass and is off the roof and not hurt, and the old lady's happy, and I is more than happy not hearing the cat meowing or my old lady yammering in my ear, ya know what I mean? Anyhows, I had ta come in early 'cause some of the prison guards coming in ta pick up their boots befores their shift an' all, but what with all that I done, I done miss my breakfast I already been fixin' ta sit down ta eat. How 'bout that good deed now, huh? Anyhow cuz, I don't like missing my breakfast, ya know, what with my low blood sugar an' all, so I'm gonna step on out ta the burger shack across the corner as I'm almost done here and if ya can, just watch the place for a minute until I get it an' bring it on back? Okay?"

"You got it, cuz. I'll chill here fer ya, and longers if ya wants ta eat it there."

"No"—with a weariness in his voice—"I got boots lined up all day I gotta be workin' on. I'll bring the burger back afta' it's all fried up." Billy snaps the polishing cloth twice over the last shoe with a showman's flair to signal the completion of his work.

"Thank you very much, Billy," Skid says as he twists his ankles in the air to admire the shine, which brings a smile to his face. "They're looking better than new, Billy. I appreciate your work and now that I know you're here, I'll be back every time I'm in town." He pulls a bill out of his pocket and hands it to Billy. "Here, no change back, thanks."

"Why, you're welcome. Another happy customer with happy feets walking the streets. You just tell 'em when they ask ya, and they will be askin' ya, Billy's done the shine, they'll know." While chatting, Billy removes the stirrups and places them along with each of the assorted brushes, polish, and cloth into their proper spot within the storage drawer. "I'll be back right quick, Silver. Anyone comes while I'm gone you just tell 'em I's gettin' a soda cross the street, yeah?"

"Sure, cuz. I gotcha covered."

Silver and Skid watch as Billy tacks catty-corner across the inter-section to the burger stand. As Billy enters the fast-food diner, Skid speaks up, "Silver, it's later than I thought and I don't have a lot of time and 'I don't want to be late for a very important date.' So, I have another business proposition for you that I think you'll like." Silver remains silent with a tinge of narrow-eyed curiosity as Skid continues address-ing him. "I think all your burdens are silently bearing down on you and turning to a boiling anger within. That's natural, what with all that's going on with your sister and your lost pension. But, if at some point you don't let that anger go and move on with your life, it's going to make you mean. When the meanness finally consumes you, you're no longer going to care about anything or anyone, and then you'll do something rash to hurt someone and no good will come from it. So"—Skid pauses to study Silver's facial features, which have gone uncharacteristically blank and display no emotions or threads of thought—"what I'm pro-posing to you is that for all your informative consulting work with me today, for which I am most indebted to you, and"—Skid casually points towards Silver's leg—"for that metal piece strapped to your left ankle, which weighs so heavy on your heart, I'm offering you five hundred dollars." Skid opens his palm to display a tight roll of green currency. Silver shifts his eyes and observes that the first greenback is a hundred-dollar bill. "I think it's a fair offer for your time today, and I think it'll help you along to keep you out of trouble for a while."

Silver and Skid exchange a look over the money. Silver notices Skid is not thrusting the money at him so that it is within his easy reach, and so Silver remains reclined himself.

"Man, you sure are a spooky one, Skid. Ya keeps coming up wit' the cash, and I ain't nevers even seen ya put your's hand on your wallet yet." Silver smiles, but neither man moves. "What makes ya think I can't just take it all now anyhow? Ain't nothing nor nobody that could stop me, ya know?" The smile recedes from his face as he scratches below his knee.

"Heck Silver, you know it doesn't take a gun to take a man's money." Skid does not move as his arm continues to rest on his leg, supporting his open hand containing the cash. "I've had men armed only with pens take a hell of a lot more than five hundred from me. Huh, and now that I think about it, a few women as well, but I don't need to tell you about that either, now do I?" Skid does not allow a response from Silver before quickly continuing. "But, second, I don't think you have larceny in your heart. A wise man once told me, 'some see a gift from another as an opportunity to take or swindle more, whereas others receive a momentary handout while in need and consider it a burden of responsibility to be repaid or passed on in kind to another.' I can see you don't like being beholden to anyone. You are your own man—that I can tell about you. You display a pride in the way you dress and carry yourself, and we are not unlike each other in that way, Silver." Skid smiles slightly and cocks his head, defying a rebuttal. "You do wear your heart on your sleeve—huh, and I play too much chess and so have practice hiding my thoughts—and being the good fella that you are, you can be taken advantage of sometimes. So, what I'm telling you is that I'm not worried about losing what I have in my pocket. That's nothing, and worth nothing. This is all about who you are and maybe a chance to give you a little pause for time to change a few things for the better, you know what I'm saying?" This time Skid pauses, waiting for Silver's response, which is a few moments in formulating.

Embarrassed, Silver averts their staring standoff by admiring the shine on his shoes. "Billy's a good man, and does a mighty fine shine, huh? Yep, best in these parts, no doubt." Silver pulls his eyes off the highly polished shoes to meet Skid's questioning look. "Tell ya what, friend. As ya know I happen ta be a little strapped for cash flow right now. So"—his eyes flash with a tint of boldness—"let's say I'll do it for six." He pauses to let the effect of the number settle. "And we'll just call the extra hundred gratuity for your personal guided tour. I think that's a good deal all around, yep." The challenge in his eyes is tempered by the white, toothy smile across his face.

Skid gives a hearty laugh and Silver joins in with him. "Well played, my friend. You drive a hard bargain, Silver, and you're leaning on valuable time I no longer have. So six hundred it is."

Skid pulls a bill from his pants pocket and combines it with the fold in his hand. From high in his leather lounge chair, Skid leans down towards Silver, who extends his hand to accept the cash. Silver pockets the money without looking at it or counting it. Then he bends over to pull up his left pant leg by the cuff, exposing an ankle holster embracing a shiny revolver. There is an audible rip as the Velcro is unfastened. Silver pulls the revolver from the holster and, with his hand on the pistol grip and his finger on the trigger guard, he passes the gun, barrel first, to Skid.

Skid tenses and quickly rises from his chair, his right arm fully extended to meet the pointing barrel at the center of his open palm. His palm connects with the business end of the gun to thrust the revolver back, up, and away. His fingers firmly wrap around the barrel and, in a twisting motion, he pulls the gun from Silver's grasp. Obtaining control of the handgun, Skid eases back into his chair as his thumb instinctively flip checks the safety while his pointer finger rests on the trigger guard. "Very nice," he comments as he lightly slides his left hand over the metal and feels that cold, smooth quality of machine-tooled precision. "Really nicely crafted and well balanced. Definitely not a Saturday night special you can pick up off of the streets for a hundie. This is a classic, possibly an antique. How'd you acquire it?" They exchange looks before Skid offers up, "But a man's gotta have some of his own secrets, right?" Holding the breached revolver down and away with one eye closed, Skid barks out a laugh before asking, "Tell me, Silver, what did you plan on doing with this here piece, anyhow?"

"Whatever it takes ta gets my business squared away, that what I be doing wit' it."

"Come on, Silver, what kind of business like that you got going on?"

"Huh, well I'm not presently disposed ta go on about all my personal and business dealings, ya know what I'm saying?"

"Well then, I guess that you really don't have that much business now do you, Silver?"

"What'cha gettin' all on about? I said I got plenty of business ta be taking care of. Some in the streets and some not. Why hep, that's what I got going on, I'll have you know."

"Dude! There's only one bullet in the chamber!" Skid holds a single bullet up in the air between his thumb and forefinger for display. The revolver is angled away from Silver and directly down his line of sight so he can peer through and out the other end of the barrel and six empty chambers.

"Why I'll be a . . . ?" Silver looks back and forth between the single bullet and the breached and vacant chambers.

"Silver, dude! It's been my experience that a man with this type of business"—thrusting the single bullet towards Silver—"has lost something important that he believes he can't live without and may not be caring one way or the other about his future. Do you get the drift of what I'm saying?"

"I don't know what you are going on about!? 'T'ain't like that at all, I'm telling ya. It just makes an impression of protection sometimes in a mean street of business arrangements. That all that I be doing wit' it."

"Seriously, man? Come on, tell me what's up? You haven't got anything going on that you need that type of protection, nor will any good ever come from this," Skid espouses while rotating the gun in a circular motion.

"Man! What a you keep going on about?" Silver barks back in frustration at being misunderstood and the perceived slight regarding his intentions. "You're getting ta be like a woman, you are. Trolling around for something that don't exist, or repeating yourself 'til you hear whats you wants ta hear, that what I'm thinkin' you be rantin' on 'bout."

Skid's eyes narrow. "What am I supposed to think? A man beaten down and abused by those close to him and walks around with just a single bullet in his gun? This is not the first time you've been hit hard. I've seen and heard you talking all day about your trials and tribulations. You've already passed through the crucible of losing something that's important to you and dealing with it in the way it has to be. And, you're a better man for it. Now why on earth do you have to go on and test yourself again when you already know who you are?"

"Man, you don't know nothin' 'bout me, or what I've done or haven't done."

"No, but you're still here after you've been dealt a bad hand a few times, and I know life, and I know what different men live for. And you're a man walking around with one bullet in his gun and that's just plain scary."

"And you, sirs, appear to be a coddled, well-manicured trust-fund baby raised with a silver spoon in his mouth that thinks a single test forging a man's mettle is a life experience not to be lived again. It ain't like that. It ain't like that at all. A man's gonna get beat down again and again and he's just gotta get up, dust himself off, and keep going. You, smarty-pants, with all your inter-lect an' all, thinkin' the few years of sleepless tough times you had in law school is the worst there is, an' you only has ta do it once. Well that ain't the way life comes at you for the rest of us at all, no sir. Life continually grinds ya down, it does. We gets beat down by the man 'cause we don't know, or we gets beat 'cause we don't have the money, or we gets beat 'cause we just unlucky an' fall an' we ain't connected like you ta the experts that can put us back togethers like we was before the fall. A man ain't tested and forged once, that's important yes, but man, let me tell ya, life continually grinds ya down, it does. It really wears on ya, it does. The third or fourth time ya hauls your ass up afta' a beating and stands up straight again. You tell me you ain't lost a loved one, or had a limb crippled, or just been plain puts down three times an' more an' thinks ya lost everything, and then ya still gets your ass up off the ground and stands back up like a man, what with mud an' shit still clinging to your ass. But you tell me you nevers been hurtin' so bad an' just wanted to hurt anothers? Or once or twice ya just don't care one ways or the others about yourself an' ya just wanna take a gun and clean the whole mess out? Afta' you's been there, done that a few times, then you can tells me about what a man can lose, and what a man should do, and what a better man is."

"Well, I'll have you know that . . ." Skid's tongue fumbles to wrap around a befuddling slew of dammed-up words behind incomplete thoughts—". . . of course . . ."—his small mouth twists and screws—". . . that's not quite . . ." Wrestling with a storm of conflicting thoughts and emotions, he trails off. His face relaxes into a blank, unreadable palette. With a tenor of apologetic sincerity in his voice, he softly offers up: ". . . No offense meant, Silver."

Those pinched lines of anger that pull deep creases across Silver's forehead noticeably relax to then melt away. "'T'ain't nothing. No offense given, none taken."

An introspective silence of understanding descends upon these two closely confined men. After a morning's sojourn together wandering in a circuitous route upon city streets, peering into the social intricacies of an interactive hive that an outsider's casual stroll would not commonly shed light upon, they take new measure of the other. Each contemplates the widely contrasting social and economic weave of cloth from which they have been cut—one tightly constrained and limited by financial and social resources, the other free to explore and walk unopposed through life's offered opportunities, and, more importantly, with an economic safety net that comfortably allows for failure. Each perceptively comes to understand that, despite their having traversed widely contrasting trials and tribulations in life, those unique crucibles that have tested their mettle have nevertheless forged each with a common tensile strength of manly temper and rectitude. And it is that self-reliant fabric of character woven into their souls that threads a more binding bond between these men stronger than any perceived difference in their social or economic status, or the gulf of their ages, or the contrasting color of their skin. The wry humor is not lost upon them, that despite the disparate vicissitudes of life each has traveled, ironically their separate paths have nevertheless curiously wound and twisted to have then randomly crossed as they incidentally encountered each other as strangers on an empty, nondescript street corner. Their lingering, contemplative silence of mutual respect within the aluminum shack's stillness is broken only by the steady whirring drone of the window air conditioner and the occasionally *whish* of a car passing down the quiet street.

Silver breaks the silence. "Let me asks ya something, if I may." There is a barely perceptible nod of agreement from Skid, as he knows there would be no stopping Silver. "You a Christian fella?"

"Oh my god. I'm not quite sure how we got here," he says with an embarrassed look followed by a sardonic smile of awareness. "Well Silver, I'm not exactly taking your meaning of the term, but somehow I don't think I would fit your connotation of 'a Christian man.'" He turns his head away from Silver, the blackness of his sunglasses now directed in an idle look out the window and his face momentarily vacant in expression. Almost imperceptibly, deep fissures of emotion tremor a lower lip, and wrinkles fan out along the corners of his eyes as if some emotional pain reaches up from within to pinch facial muscles. Before continuing he chews a corner of lower lip. "So"—the words come with measured deliberateness—"let's just say"—and with a distinctness of enunciation—"I'm just your ordinary run-of-the-mill sinning man muddling my way through a life of my own self-binding bargains with the devil, for as you know, the devil walks one step behind us all." Skid's head turns back for Silver to once again see his own reflection in the insect-eye blackness. "You know what I'm saying?"

Silver studies the once-more composed face before replying in a preacher's voice of conviction, "For it is the man that righteously believes he is unreachable sittin' high upon his white horse of virtue that is the most easily swayed, for he knows not that Satan has well observed his immoral predilections so as to offer those innocuous offerings that bend and sway him so that he will voluntarily dismount to unknowingly walk with the devil along a sinner's wicked path. It is the man who questions those loose bonds of self-constraint that keeps in check his own moral turpitude and thus the surfacing of those vices that spurn the devil's false promise of innocent gratification. And which man is the better man that spurns the devil I ask you, the one that does it for moral right? Fear of eternal damnation? For family? Or just plain old ornery spite? And which is the man that you prefer to have at your side facin' down the devil in that time of temptation, I would ask you?" He pauses before continuing just above a whisper, "'Nough said, and 't'ain't nothing more asked, nor nothing more needed."

A friendly smile parts Skid's lips. "I hoped it was, 'cause you were really scaring me there for a minute. My goodness, Silver, you are so eloquent in your speech. Is that scripture?"

"I goes to church and I listens to the sermons."

"Well, you're a good man, Silver, and I'm glad I know you."

"Huh, 't'ain't nothin', and I thank you for everythin' ya done for me."

"Hey, Silver," Skid continues with nothing more to be done and very little left to be said, "I gotta take off now as otherwise I'm going to be late for my very important social date. So, I just want to wish you the best of luck. Now, you be good, and you be safe on those streets. And as my grandmother would say, 'Get yourself some ice cream and soda, and don't spend it all in one place,' you hear?" He laughs as he steps off the high leather lounge chair with a clenched fist thrust forward.

Silver reciprocates to bump Skid's fist with the knuckles of his own closed hand. "I been round this long and I don't wanna go like no rag mop, no siree, so I'll just be takin' care of myself, and I most certainly 'preciates your help." Silver flashes his full set of large, white, straight teeth that shine bright against his dark face. "Now you look me up next time you be here in town an yous can give me a tour of the places you been to and your turn to tell the stories, 'cause I 'spect you a man a many secrets you ain't lettin' on about, and that I can tell 'bout you."

"Just an open book that many aren't interested in turning the pages for reading, that's all. But for sure I'll be looking for you when I'm back. Later, dude."

Silver gets up to hold the door open for Skid and watches as he crosses to the shady side of the street. Stepping from the doorway, Silver thrusts his hands deep into his coat pocket, closes his eyes, and raises his face to feel the heat of a noonday sun. When he opens his eyes again, Skid has disappeared.

~~~

A familiar and cantankerous mechanical rumbling reaches Silver's ears. He looks down the street to see a large American sedan with a tricolor patch of faded and mismatched paint driving towards him. The early-model automobile, in a whine of tired energy and a shriek of metal on metal brakes, pulls against the street curb to park in front of him. A mature woman on the edge of retirement, wearing faded blue hospital scrubs, steps out of the driver's seat and drapes both arms over the car's roof. Silver takes her in with a glance. Over the noise of a leaky exhaust and without preamble she starts, "Hey, I been tryin' ta call ya all morning and no one's answering."

"Damn, been busy an' just lent my phone out ta a friend earlier, that's all."

"Anyhow, I was hoping I may find ya hanging around here. Ain't seen ya around in a whiles."

"Yeah, I been getting that a lot lately."

"Well anyhow, I just comes ta tell ya I saw the man come an' take your daughter away down at the corner mart."

"Damn woman, now what that be all about?" he asks as weathered lines of concern cross his face.

"Don't really know as I just seen it from afar an' I ain't no CNN reporter."

Silver's mind begins to focus on damage control. "The children. You know where the kids be?"

"No, I didn't see no kids, so I don't know the whereabouts o' any kids, an' I ain't no child services."

"Can ya run by the house real quick and check on 'em? Make sure they's there?"

"I just come by ta let ya know, not ta get involved. I'm sure they's with ya sista' inside the house anyhow."

"Damn," Silver says under his breath, looking away down the street as he copes with a rush of vivid memories. "Ya know, just seeing that pair just lights my fuse an' sets me off, it does. It's as if I don't even knows them as family any more. She's done got me all jammed up. Why I can't get my thirty grand back, an' all the detectives thinks that they gonna do is put her in jail. Why I think I'm just gonna puts her somewhere else myself." Bringing his attention and focus back to the woman: "Can ya give me a ride back to the house?"

"No, I'm late for work, and anyhow, I ain't no taxi driver, neither."

"Damn. Can ya hang around an' watch the shop for a minute 'til your brother comes back and gives him that message that I had ta run off? He only runs himself across the corner ta gets himself a burger."

"No. I ain't no Western Union handing out messages and I done already told ya I'm late for work, anyhow. All I knows is that I saw the man come an' take your daughter away and I don't know any more than that. I was just dropping by hoping ta see you at one a your old haunts and pass on the news, ya know?"

At that moment, Silver observes Billy exiting the burger shack door. "Hey, Gloria," he says with his half-distracted smile, "I really 'preciates ya stopping by and passing me the news. Thanks."

"No problems, Silver, we all do whats we can. Gotta run," she finishes while ducking back into the driver's seat. In a pale cloud of smoke and with sounds of banging muffler pipes, the car rattles away from the curb to disappear down the street.

Billy, with his brown lunch bag in hand, angles directly across the corner to Silver. "Now what's that old lady doing coming up an' then just driving away when I gets here?" Billy asks Silver. "That woman just got a mind of her own, she does."

"Oh, ain't nothin' for you," Silver defensively offers. "She just be nice enough ta come lookin' for me and lettin' me know the man done come and take my daughter away. That's all I be knowing, that's all I can be saying, and now I gots ta book and see what up about them kids, ya know?"

"Oh, yeah, sorry man." A look of concern comes into Billy's face. "Ya know they be okay but you go check on 'em now." Silver hears Billy but is lost in thought as he walks in a rush, with no noticeable limp, down the sidewalk along the edge of the curb. He does not hear the compact automobile racing up behind him until it startles him as it brushes close by with two wheels in the gutter. It pulls to a quick stop in front of the corner liquor mart. The two-door import is covered by layers of dirt that make the car's original, dark color unidentifiable. Out of the car pops a skinny young woman cloaked in a surfer's hoodie pulled over her head, hiding her face from view. Wisps of blonde hair peek from the hoodie's edges, and a white lollipop stick visibly protrudes beyond the fabric's folds.

"Well now, don't that beat all," Silver says aloud to himself as he is brought back to street consciousness.

With long, exaggerated strides, the young woman walks around the car's hood and steps onto the curb riding high on cork-wedge platform-heel sandals. Her knobby knees fully extend in that gliding gate of hers. Her skinny, satin-soft legs are a luxurious fawn tan. Girly surfer shorts allow a pleasantly pleasing peek of her tight butt-cheek pleats.

"Damn, now that ain't right," he says under his breath.

The girl disappears into the liquor mart as Silver dives into a curb-side trash can. He soon finds what he is looking for, walks into the street, and circles behind the driver's side of the compact car. He fully unfolds a newspaper before rolling it back up into a crinkled, soft ball and then begins to wipe the car's rear window. Within a few moments, he hears the loud noise of metal banging on plate glass. He looks up to see the girl rapidly tapping on the storefront window with a key pinched between thumb and forefinger. Having Silver's attention, the blonde, her eyes hidden behind large insect-eye sunglasses, begins to shake her head *no* and vigorously wags a finger at him. Silver ignores her and continues to erase the penis and testicle pictograph along with the words "LOVES DICK" that was recently traced with a finger into the heavy film of spotted dirt on the car's rear window. A change of tone in the banging sound piques Silver's curiosity. He looks up from his work to see the girl slapping the glass with the flat of her hand. Behind the checkout counter, his friend Syed looks at him with an appealing face of conciliation. Silver's answer is to reach across to the far side of the car's rear window and continue to purposefully rub away the hieroglyphics. He soon hears the tinkle of the ubiquitous attention-getting bells of the neighborhood convenience store as the door opens.

"Hey! You!" The skinny blonde stands defiantly posed in the open doorway. "Hey man, I'm telling you don't be touching my car now. Understand?"

"I'm just lending a neighborly hand, is all. It ain't proper for a lady like yourself ta be driving round town with something like that on their car, now is it?"

"Who are you?" The intonation of her voice rings with the impatient petulance of the young. "You ain't my neighbor, so don't be touching my car. And you sure ain't my pappy, so don't you be lecturing me about what's right and what's not . . . boy."

Huh, now don't that be a curious linguistic mistake of the highbred, Silver thinks as he pauses to look over the defiantly posed woman. *Just a mistaken faux pas of a young'un, or some darker implication?* Silver ponders the possibilities before addressing her. "'Scuse me, but it ain't all 'bout Missy Paris Hilton, now is it? Ain't right, is all I'm saying. Downright disrespectful ta women it is. Why hep, evens if yous don't care 'bout yourself, there be children an' all that are gonna be seein' this. This ain't just about you now, is it . . . girlie?"

"Ya know, like I don't really care. It's lika you sure ain't one ta be telling anyone how ta be proper an' respectful, that's fer sure. Why just looky you . . . you . . ." Her uncompleted sentence concludes with her twisted face of scorn that mocks.

"Well now don't that get out an' all." Silver straightens up to his full height while pulling his coat at the lapels. "Where does a young whippersnapper like yourself get off addressing a distinguished, helping, Christian gentleman such as I like that? Ain't you been properly taught ta respect your elders, an' not ta looks a gift horse in the mouth?"

"Boy!" There is an awkward attempt to stamp her three-inch sandals into the ground. "It's lika I don't really give a fuck. And I said don't you be touching my car and washing my windows. I ain't paying ya, and 'sides, the thing is like you people ain't wanted round these parts anyhow, ya hear? Boy?"

Silver pauses to ponder something darker and more insidious implied than to him as an individual. He looks over to Syed still standing behind the counter. Under a white turban, with a thick black beard, Syed's dark face appears, filled with a sad disappointment, sadder than Silver can ever remember over the many years that they have known each other. With a pleading in his eyes and the back of both his hands flicking at the wrist, Syed is shooing Silver away as a stray cat. Silver

turns his attention back to the woman propped with her tear-up attitude in the half-opened door. "Why, missy, I is so sorry"—his eyes
averted downward as his body rocks left and right on shifting feet, his
voice laced in submissive acquiescence—"why I just got all choked up
an' all, I did, seeing that drawing on your back window and thinkin'
'bout what it be doing ta all them poor little childrens seeing it and
all, ya know? I just don'ts know whys ya can't gets one a your pretty-
girl-lookin' boyfriends ta wash your car fer ya, huh? But I do have a
mind"—his voice falling back to its naturally rich and manly tone, his
eyes brought back up to lock on hers—"ta take ya over my knee myself
and spank ya like your daddy should'a ta teach ya your manners and
talk proper to ya Christian brothers. Why that's what you done be
needed, hep!" Silver leans over the car and begins to rub once again.

"Yeah, well provoke me more and I'm gonna be getting my grandpa's coon gun! I know where it is and I swears I know how ta use it.
Now you be getting your skanky boo ass moving along and be leaving
my car alone before I be getting that gun."

Seeing a wicked ugliness indeed in one so young . . . so beautiful . . .
so full of potential . . . and with so much future . . . spew such spiteful
words with the intent of denigrating another, momentarily less fortunate, and setting them off in a rage, Silver feels a deep sadness. With a
calm belying the fuse already lit to set him off, Silver calmly finishes the
rear window and then tosses the newspaper rag into the driver's open
window. With a gleam in his eyes and his teeth flashing pearly white
against his ebony skin: "So tell me . . . girlie . . . what cracker barrel
you and your family worm themselves outta? 'Cause I betcha it ain't
my family that migrated over as poor, wandering sharecroppers in the
Grapes of White Trash. Now you be going an' tellin' your grandpappy
what we done and what we said here today, and if he don't go and use
some soap ta wash the dirt outta your mouth, why then I just 'magine
afta' seeing ya here car and hearing you speak, that he and yous just
plain use' ta livin' a pig-wallowing life in da mud and dirt, huh?" Silver
turns to walk across the street.

With boiling young blood, the woman leaves the doorway to charge
the back of Silver. "Cocksucker!"

Silver slows his stride for a look over his shoulder and then stops. "Cocksucker? Why hemp!" In a masculine voice of seduction and a charming smile on his face: "Why I sure is sorry my little miss whitey princess, why yes I sure am, but you also be sure and be telling your grandpappy and boyfriends, 'cause I sure am, that I been hearing around these parts that you prefers ta suck black and spits white, 'cause that sure the manure I'm gonna be spreading round these parts, yep." Silver punctuates it with an exclamation point of hocking up a thick loogie and spitting it across the street, followed by a hearty, chesty laugh— *boom!* Before turning his back, Silver feels a self-satisfying glow as he sees his words score deeply in her brightly burning face. He does not look back nor noticeably react when he hears her piercing shriek.

Silver sets himself to thinking as he usually does in his solitary walks. As intelligent life on Earth walks a razor-thin comfort zone for a sustainable existence of just plus or minus a degree of temperature; one degree of tilting axis; one degree of distance from a nuclear, radioactive sun; and just one degree of bodily mass creating a gravitational field to hold a breathable atmosphere in place while loose enough to allow man to walk upright, the rational, human conscience of the desperately anxious and tightly wound is itself just a single, illogical, twisted thought, a personal witnessing of an unreciprocal vile act upon another innocent, away from falling momentarily off that slippery knife-edge of the rationally sane that most assuredly acts in selfless service of others. Once stressed and conflicted minds sour and then curdle rational thought as such, they can soon sink into a destructive, self-loathing bent to strike out and wreak the same havoc and experienced misery upon others—*push.*

"Life just ain't fair sometimes, no siree it ain't, either," Silver says in a mumbling whisper as he looks down at the sidewalk while stepping over the cracks on his well-worn path. "Some people, they just gonna do whatevers they wanna do, no matter the consequences or how it hurts others," he continues. "Why hep, they's just in it fer themselves, they is. They's just gonna take and take whatevers they can, theirs or not, whenevers they can, right or wrong, yes siree. Why they even be takin' candy from the mouth of babes when they can, fer sure. Ya can converse with them 'til the cows come home an' you's blue in the face, and they's gonna take even mores when they can and then smoke it up in Satan's cloud. Ain't no logically stoppin' 'em, no siree, 'cause they gots the Devil in them, yes siree. They only gonna change if someone just goes and stops 'em, ain't no other way, no siree. Sometimes ya just needs ta go an' cleans the whole mess out. Why hep, that just what done be needed." Silver pulls his vision up from the sidewalk as he reaches into his coat pocket to feel the reassuring crispness of six newly printed hundred-dollar bills between thumb and fingers.

~~~~~

With only a single foot landed over the threshold, an overpowering stench stops Silver in his tracks. All other sensory clues are blotted out as if that nefarious odor were a wet, rotting blanket pulled from an algae-overgrown swamp and then tossed to lie heavily over him. Feeling a lightheaded dizziness that will soon have him swoon, he pauses to maintain his sense of balance and lean against the doorjamb of the darkened den he is about to enter. For the moment, his eyes cannot adjust to see within the cloistered house. His ears do not register the street traffic noise passing out front. As his momentarily dazed and free-floating mind loses all bodily senses grounding him to Earth's gravitational laws, and his imagination bolts to a possible scare, Silver shivers with fear, asking himself: *Is this the stench of human death!? Yes? NOT!* The suffocating nausea of human cadaver rises to a singularly shrill smell, painful to the senses of those alive. This, he realizes with relief, is the continuous pungent layer upon layer of the still living. Ripe, sweaty bodies of the long unbathed—to be sure. An accumulation of trash piled high—a norm not so uncommon, no? All dishes in the house dirty and overflowing the sink onto the counter—how novel! Rotting food, and yet lucky enough of there once having been an abundance of food not consumed—of which there is no doubt. Rodent carcasses in various stages of decomposing flesh and guts—a very distinct probability. Bodily excrement—oh gross. Sex—*au natural*. Sulfur fumes of a chemical burning—oh my. Smoky, odoriferous wisps of volatile, designer-enhanced pharmaceutical drugs—oh yes! A most satanic salutation indeed! One disgusting, rotting smell layered upon another oppressively foul odor—ad nauseam.

Blackout curtains have been tightly drawn across the windows, allowing no hint of sunlight to sneak through and press back the shadows of an artificial night. Silver slowly sucks the heavy air in through straining teeth. His eyes squint as they peer into the dark void, searching. Four saucer-wide eyes stare back. Silver feels some calming comfort as he reaches for the newly acquired cold steel in his coat pocket. His eyes slowly adjust from the sunny outside to a room illuminated with a dull, blue hue from the coffee-table-seated LCD television within. Two small faces glow from the cold-light-emitting flat screen. Silver flashes that broad signature smile of his.

"Oupa!" The eight-year-old girl is off the couch running to Silver.

"Oufa! Oufa! Oufa!" The three-year-old mimics his older sister as he rolls onto his belly before he slides off the couch and runs to Silver with that happy baby-fat cherub waddle of the toddler on chubby, stumpy legs. They each grab a leg as they yell in an excited mixed chorus of "Oupa!" "Oufa!" "Oupa!" "Oufa!" Each tries outdoing the other for Silver's undivided attention. Tyler buries his face in Silver's pants, wiping his wet nose back and forth. In his high-pitched, wee voice, he yells "Oufa!" between each swipe. Silver laughs. He reaches down to stroke and caress his granddaughter's hair as she looks up at him with a big old smile on her face. Silver's heart wells. He sees the light of God appear in the smile of an innocent child and he feels the divine glory overwhelm him. In that instant he knows that within the blind, unlimited capacity of a child's love, there is a God. And then, with great reluctance and effort, he steels his heart.

"Hey, Rhonda. How's my favorite granddaughter doing?"

"Good, Oupa. Just hungry. Can ya take us to get a Happy Meal? Huh? Can ya?" she asks shyly with expectation.

"Hap' meal, hap' meal!" Tyler choruses in with an exuberance, showing no shyness.

"Yeah, hep! I can getcha somethin', fer sure," he replies with a smile. Not unaware of the answer he asks, "Hey, ya know where your momma's at? Or is Grand Auntie arounds?"

"No, Momma went out this mornin' for breakfast cereal and stuff, and nappies for Tyler, and ain't been back since. And"—Rhonda cautiously looks down the darkened back hallway—"Grand Auntie's in her's room with one o' her special man friends and ya know we ain't 'posed ta 'sturb fer nuthin'. She get mad, ya know?" Silver feels her grip tighten around his leg.

"Yeah, 'kay." Then addressing the issue of Tyler covered only in a long shirt with no pants: "Hey, they happen ta be just one nappie left around fer Tyler?"

"No, no, we all out. Momma left this mornin' fer some an' ain't been back since."

"'Kay, tells ya what. Ya find me some pants or a nappie for Tyler and we getcha that cheeseburger fer sure, how's that?" Rhonda says nothing as she excitedly scurries off. She returns shortly with a diaper and a pair of diminutive jeans.

Silver wrestles with the toddler to pull pants over the baby fat. "This here is what we's gonna do, Rhonda. You be a big girl now, ain't'cha?" With all the cuteness of an eight-year-old's serious face, Rhonda nods her head without saying anything. Silver suppresses his laugh. "So, I'm gonna give ya some moneys, and we's gonna puts Tyler in the stroller. Then I'm gonna cross the street wit' ya, and you guys go on ta McDonald's and getcha some cheeseburgers. Afta'wards, you two play as long as ya wants in the game balls. How's that, my big girl?" he asks Rhonda as he rests his hand upon her head while looking into her excited face. Rhonda nods her head vigorously up and down. Silver smiles with heartbreak. "Now I 'spect when ya comes back the policeman, he be here, but that's okay. Ya just tell 'em ya ain't seen ya momma in a whiles and your Oupa gaves ya some moneys for burgers, 'kay? The man prob'ly gonna wants ta give you and Tyler a ride, but that's okay now, you just go with them. They's gonna take ya ta a nice place an' feeds ya plenty. You'll be okay, now ya hear?" Rhonda nods her head with a question on her face. "Now I's told ya a lot but alls ya have ta remember is that Oupa always loves ya, girl, an' always wants the best fer ya, and that's all you have to remember." With suppressed emotions, he looks deeply into her dark eyes as he pulls Tyler off the couch. On the front porch, Rhonda shows Silver how to strap Tyler in the stroller. Silver guides it down the two rickety porch steps.

"Okay, girl, ya have the money in your pocket," Silver confirms with Rhonda as he squats in front of her with two hands on her small shoulders. "Now get Tyler and yourself some a them cheeseburgers and then play in them balls for as long as ya likes, and remember the most important thing is that Oupa loves ya forever." Silver kisses her forehead and, with two guiding hands on her thin shoulders, gently twists his precious around to shove her gently on the way. For a minute, Silver watches Rhonda walk down the sidewalk pushing the stroller in an erect stance of a young one acting the role of a watchful, mature adult. He ignores the solid weight of his petrified heart.

Back at the bottom of the porch steps, Silver pulls a small handgun from his coat pocket. He registers a little disappointment with the unkempt look and greasy feel of the gun, but thinks to himself, *Why hep, ain't nothin' that can't still do the job.* He swings out the revolver's cylinder. Satisfied after counting six full chambers, he tucks the pistol under his coat and walks tentatively up the steps and into the awaiting gloom of the oppressively smelly and eerily quiet house . . . that was not a home . . . simply a rotting burrow . . . in need of a cleaning . . . and now, with a new odor of anxious animal fear . . . most assuredly . . .

~~~~~~~~

. . . TWO FEET IN

Evermore may your eyes
    sparkle with joy
Under the bright
    stage lights of success
That shine upon
    your beautiful face.

~~~

Rochelle freezes at the thunder of power from the beast that has caught her standing isolated and exposed upon a lonely stretch of tabletop-flat tarmac. The pouncing black beauty fixates her worldly vision as would any huge cat of prey that suddenly leaps forth without warning from concealing brush. From the near distance, this panther-black machine streaks unfettered towards her. Under a full-sun sky it glistens alive, as with the muscular ripple of a hunting predator upon an open scrub-brush plain as it rapidly chases down its intended prey. Suppressing that primal impulse to run for one's life, the maturing adolescent nervously crosses one ankle over the other, shifting the entire weight of her well-defined athletic frame—whose elegant lines of female form are cloaked beneath a man's ill-fitting jumpsuit—onto one leg.

Proclaiming its unadulterated power over all it surveys, this highly sprung prince of the track lets out another threatening roar! as the throttle-pedal is momentarily blipped with well-practiced precision. With nowhere to run and no cover to hide behind, and with a well-practiced throw of *her* head, Rochelle swings her mane of alluring auburn hair over one shoulder to cascade in a luxurious drape down the length of her back. Her temper is quick to rise and match that of her fiery mane at being the intended target so teasingly toyed and played with.

And then another menacing roar, and an explosive spit of yellow-orange tail fire lashes out from the beast's twin tailpipes! Rochelle is aware that it is with perfect timing that the manual stick shift has been smoothly slipped into a lower gear. This has caused the engine's crank-shaft to instantly rev up as it matches speeds with the wildly spinning flywheel as it thus sends superheated gases that pass through unre-stricted header pipes and then exit as colorful flames of ignited exhaust.

Fighting her impulse for flight, Rochelle responds to the charging mechanical beast with an insolent fist of teenage challenge placed hard upon her hip. Her other arm swings freely with the pendulum weight of her protective helmet that with a sweaty palm she anxiously grasps through its chin guard. No lines of expression crease the unblemished skin of her youthful face, blessed from the womb to be born beautiful, to betray Rochelle's mounting excitement as she attempts to maintain her composure under the charging predator's unblinking gaze. It is into the glare of those captivating, hollow-white, cat-vixen eyes, set wide apart and low to the ground and intently focused upon its prey, that Rochelle returns the challenge with her own fiercely narrowed stare of emerald-green eyes. Under the depthless, open blue sky of a late afternoon sun, both sets of eyes sparkle alive with excited animal antic-ipation in their daring, staring glare of chicken to see which one will blink first—*Fuck you. No, fu...*—as the closing distance of their imma-ture racing duel continues to rapidly diminish. Playing a role with all the prima-donna assurance of a star upon a brightly lit stage, Rochelle flexes a well-defined calf muscle to then perch the entire weight of her youthfully trim body solely upon the ball of her right foot, and in an act signaling her surrender to the onrushing mechanical menace, her right arm slowly articulates out to her side ... with her hand displaying a fully extended middle finger!

The powerfully built, aerodynamically sleek race car, with haunches set wide and strong to accommodate fat, track-gripping racing slicks, flinches first, swerving from its uncomplaining victim to pull up in a high-speed, scary-close stop just under three feet away from its pretty—a mile for those drivers with the practiced skill to kiss, and thus swap paint with, a retaining wall at over a hundred miles an hour as it negotiates the last turn of a racetrack prior to entering the front straightaway.

Her excitement mixed with a breathless nervousness, Rochelle nevertheless remains unmoving in her defiant stance of grace and strength. Dark patches of sweat stain her undergarments, which are visible in the V-line of a jumpsuit zipped low to expose her belly button. The fire breath of the resting beast adds to her discomfort as combustion-engine heat penetrates the multilayered fire suit to her skin.

Under its shiny, smooth-as-glass bonnet, the low-slung, prancing, black race car settles to a soothing, rumbling growl. A high-performance engine's low droning idle that resonates deep bass notes within one's chest cavity becomes as comforting to an experienced person with racetrack-attuned ears as the lap-animal purr of relaxed contentment to the soul of a feline owner. However, as a cautionary tale, one will give everything it has and more before it self-destructs in failure, and the other—one day—may simply turn her back in betrayal and then . . . silently walk away.

Under a depthless afternoon sky, upon a barren expanse of heat-radiating black asphalt—the blacker the asphalt, the smoother the surface—confined within those vast retaining hills of the Central Valley, ghostly waves of light-bending curls lazily waft from the watery mirage of sunbaked tarmac to obscure this disparate couple from distant observers behind a shimmering veil of ethereal vapors. These two exquisite figures that appear to protrude upon the tar-black tarmac, as if from the strong hands of a sculptor's imaginative free form, irresistibly catch and then draw the human eye to follow and, with a knowingly guilty pleasure, slowly linger over their alluring lines. One born from rare earth elements and a coke-infused furnace fire, the other from the passionate heat of physical love and a woman's nurturing womb, each is a concealed wellspring of innate energy that when called upon can instantly leap forth in a dramatic demonstration of their physical prowess. One idly pants in that low, rumbling baritone felt as a sublime warning of aggressive power deep in the chest of others standing nearby. This black beast squats low to the ground with flat and narrow lines in the front that flare wide to its rear haunches of powerfully built hips that give it the intrinsic look of a restrained predator prepared to pounce—for which it was purposely built. The other stands reed-tall in a simple pose delicately balancing on one foot, which accentuates her dancer's frame of perfect posture. Hers is not the wispy-lithe body, short and lean, of the princess-light ballerina that launches from the stage floor to effortlessly float through the air with pointed toes like a Tinker Bell or a mystical fairy; no, this is the muscularly curvaceous physique of the solidly built jazz performer. Powerfully defined muscles are strong and coordinated, allowing her to enjoy momentarily brief airborne flights, yet most of her art is performed with feet planted fast on terra firma, or more preferably, on a semi-sprung wooden stage. The strong lines of calves and thighs flow to unmistakably feminine hips, with that adolescent-thin waist supporting broad shoulders, her back sensually arched in show, and an elegant neck of classic antiquity—are all of the aesthetic female form.

~~~

A helmeted man in the submissively waiting race car motions with gloved fingers, beckoning for Rochelle to climb into the passenger seat.

As is her deeply seated playful and mischievous nature, Rochelle silently laughs to herself as she pretends to ignore the driver, whose recognizable image she can vaguely discern behind his light-reflecting face guard. Slowly, in a show of strength and artistic control, Rochelle contorts her body, all the while still balancing on one foot, to display a not-so-subtle, insolent pose of her momentarily pissed-off teenage attitude.

The waiting driver shakes his helmeted head at her, and, with two fingers, taps at his wrist where a watch has never been worn to indicate that time is running out. Rochelle allows her head to comically flop to one side as her wide-open, expressive eyes mockingly stare into the empty space above the car's low roofline. Holding one finger up, the driver then slowly raises a second finger and, before he can finish with a third and final count, Rochelle pops off her foot to scramble into the passenger seat. The car's throaty notes trumpet once more as it swiftly drives off. Rochelle fastens her five-point safety harness. She leans her head forward to shake those long strands of thick hair over her face. With a quick flip, she swings her mane back again and then finger combs those silky threads back tightly.

The driver turns to her and, in a voice raised to be heard from behind his protective mask and above the engine noise, asks without preamble, "How'd your training class go today?"

Grasping the chinstraps, Rochelle pulls wide her helmet before answering with a clip tic, "fine." She squishes and wiggles and maneuvers her head into the tight-fitting helmet. While fastening the chinstrap through the double buckle she adds, "We did skid control through the water sprinklers today." A grimace of sharp irritation creases her face as she wedges loose strands of hair back between her scalp and padded helmet.

"Way cool! That was my favorite," he says. "And, 'when in a spin' . . . ?"

". . . 'two feet in,'" she automatically responds as she finishes with her hair and helmet.

"That's my girl."

Rochelle is silent for the moment as she concentrates on safely preparing herself for the always possible high-speed incident, tugging in turn on each side of the padded shoulder straps that snugly pull her in to become one with the hard, bare shell of the carbon-fiber bucket seat. Not sure how to bring up a self-congratulatory pat on the back in a nonconceited way, she finally, while staring ahead, just throws down, "Ah, you know what they told me?"

"Hmm, no, what?"

"Ah, they said I have like really soft hands." This she intones shyly so as not to brag.

"No way! Like 'soft hands'? Or like 'really soft hands'?"

"No, they said I have 'touch.'"

"Wow, really! Lucky you. You can't ask for anything better than that. Anyone can drive fast, but you can't teach soft hands. With soft hands, speed will come. Congratulations."

"Thanks. So what are we doing now?"

"Timing trials, pole qualifying."

"Yaw . . . really? . . . badass," she says with obvious, excited anticipation of the ride to come. Tentatively, she continues, "So, am I allowed in the car for that?"

"Well, that's a good question. I don't specifically know of anything that says you can't and if I run into any problems with the track master, I'll just tell him my penance was hauling the weight of your fat ass around. That should work. You'll probably put me in the last grid spot."

"Ha, thanks. Will I really?"

"You'll cost me a second at least, maybe even two, which will definitely put me last in class, but, 'we'll give it one red-hot crack.'" He effortlessly slots the car through the narrow open space between two concrete barriers, pulls a hard ninety-degree right turn, and comes to a stop at the end of pit out while waiting for a wave on from the pitman.

Their conversation is interrupted by the deafening roar of racing cars that tear the very fabric of air asunder with the power and speed at which they accelerate down the front straightaway just on the other side of the hip-high concrete wall. Communication with the outside track worker is achieved in a pantomime of exaggerated hand gestures and waving colored flags. The pitman points a rolled-up yellow flag directly at Rochelle while his other arm is square out to the side of his body, like a turn signal, and then he pulls it quickly back to his chest. Rochelle takes her hand off the car roof and pulls her arm inside, placing it on her lap. Continuing to point the flag at Rochelle, his free hand claws down his face. Rochelle's blank face clearly indicates she does not comprehend what the man is trying to convey. The pitman waves a flat hand up and down in front of his face. Rochelle smiles to him and with a silent *duh* to herself, pulls down her face guard. A smile of approval sweeps across the pitman's face. With his palm held up for them to stop, the pitman leans back over the pit wall with a look down the track. A few moments later he turns his attention back to the idling car and, with a serious look on his face, waves the rolled-up yellow flag back and forth signaling for them to "go, go, go!" Both driver and Rochelle reciprocate with a thumbs-up: *Ding hao! AVG into the wild blue!*

A gut-clenching excitement that begins in the pit of her stomach radiates as an electric tingle across the entire surface of her skin when the car roars in its attempt to quickly accelerate down the pit lane and gain as much speed as possible prior to safely merging onto the race-track, for which it fails miserably—attaining the matching speed, not the merging. Where only moments before the utilitarian carbon-fiber seat had felt like a hard bench to be endured, she now takes comfort sitting deep within its human form-factor mold that partially wraps around her hips and shoulders with its solid rigidity. She tugs at each shoulder strap for one last tight cinching of the harness. Still, she presses deeper into the seat as the race car attempts, and fails, to reach triple digits before the braking zone of the first turn. Rochelle struggles to suppress her nervous tension with the understanding that their first lap will only be driven at ninety percent of the car's capability—to warm up the tires to their ideal, track-sticking temperature before the optimum second timing lap.

As they complete their first lap of the meandering road course with its artificially constructed rises and contours nestled among the flat badlands of the Central Valley, the car steers into the last turn to touch with the inside wheels a small portion of the raised, red-and-white-striped chicane—thump! thump!—at the apex of the corner. Rochelle can feel a growing sense of excitement as they race towards the finish line and trip the computer timing clock. With a confidence in man and machine instilled from a successfully raced lap, the initial apprehension of flying out of control off the track at high speeds has slowly melted from Rochelle's tension-clenched muscles. She feels a rush of the ride as the organs of mechanical power open to full throttle to accelerate and hurl her and the driver down the half-mile-long front straightaway. The flat track is laid out before them in a ruler-straight black line that seemingly disappears over a ledge and into that valley scrub-brush land beyond.

Rochelle takes in the two-story wooden observation tower, its unfurled green flag limply hanging, located midway down the straight at the painted black-and-white-checkered start-finish line. Atop the second-floor tower, with its unobstructed view of the entire three-mile racecourse, the Starter has observed their car as it comes around turn thirteen and then looks away to once again survey the entire track before bringing his eyes back to spot the next car following. He continually repeats this process. On the other side of the second protective pit wall, observers casually lean against the waist-high concrete barrier, watching the continuous parade of colorful cars. Those among the crowd with keen eyes, attuned ears, and years of experience critique among themselves the mechanical performance of each passing car along with the technical skills of the driver seated behind the steering wheel. Beyond the observing spectators are scores of parked race cars, some in various stages of tuning: hoods open, or up on jacks, or tires off, or computer screens actively displaying the car's ECU readout for the technically inclined. Farther back still is a picket of parked motor homes for those with the economic wherewithal to travel in luxurious first class from track to track.

On an adolescent impulse, Rochelle whimsically sticks a thumbs-up fist out the window, carefully angling directly into the hurricane force wind so as not to dislocate her arm at the shoulder socket, to which the sharp-eyed Starter, leaning over on the open wooden window-sill, reciprocates, adding an appreciative smile of his own. Leaping down the straightaway, Rochelle is filled with excited anticipation of the physical thrill soon to come of being tossed and turned, thumped and bumped, by progressively stronger g-forces within the confines of her carefully constructed restraining swaddle. As a child, Rochelle had always enjoyed the amusement park roller coaster rides with their stomach-churning drops and violent changes of direction. She is now about to experience those sensations again—with the added apprehension and very real possibility of being suddenly thrown off those guiding rails.

~~~

Rochelle turns her attention inside the car to observe the movements of the driver's hands in coordination with his feet as he dances in closed frame with his partner. The car's interior has been stripped down to its bare aluminum unishell construction, thereby maximizing weight reduction for increased acceleration and top-end speed while eliminating any combustive material in the unlikely event of fire, thus offering Rochelle an unobstructed view of the driver from his gloved hands down to his fire-retardant red racing booties, which have been custom-molded to his feet for comfort, safety, and pedal feel. His left hand does not move from its light grip upon the steering wheel as his right hand quickly alternates back and forth between wheel and stick shift, and both hands move in synchronization with his two feet that swiftly manipulate the three peddles deep in the floorboard well. Rochelle watches as the driver quickly backs his right foot off the gas pedal while simultaneously pressing the clutch pedal into the floor with his left foot; then, with just a thumb and two fingers eagle-perched atop the shift knob, he firmly pulls the stick back into fourth gear and releases the clutch as the gas pedal is mashed back into the floor.

The speedometer soon passes triple digits. The end of the front straightaway and the ninety-degree, right-hand bend of turn one rushes upon them with the empty field beyond patiently awaiting any mistakes . . . and still the car continues to accelerate! Wait . . . with foot still heavy on the gas pedal . . . patiently measuring rapidly diminishing distance against their velocity and car mass, and the acute angle of the approaching corner . . . and wait . . . throttle still wide open. Rochelle outwardly plays it cool, her thumbs hooked into the shoulder belts; her stomach tightens as the car races to its braking point. Wait . . . wait . . . and . . . now! Straight-line brake! . . . brake! . . . brake! Rochelle feels the broad harness straps dig into her shoulders as she is thrown bodily forward with g-force deceleration.

With the all-artful intricacy of a danseur noble directed by the cadence of some unseen maestro's wand, the athletic driver now deftly coordinates the simultaneous manipulation of three pedals with two feet, both of which move in synchronization with his left hand, which grasps the steering wheel at nine o'clock, and his right hand, which is lightly placed on the stick-shift knob—all to manage and maintain control over the internally explosive, mechanical power of their prancing black beast. With his left foot fully pressing in the clutch, and only the upper ball of his right foot delicately modulating the brake pedal, his right heel flicks the gas pedal to full throttle—*ROAR!* Downshift with the butt of a gloved palm and clutch out. Continue straight line brake . . . brake!

Once again a full-throttle flick in another heel-toe downshift and, *ROAR!* Under heavy braking, the race car's front-end suspension has been preloaded to allow for the beginning of the car's turn in with a slight backing off of the brake pedal. The driver continues to ease off the brake pedal as the turn tightens until, with a thump! thump!, the inside wheels hit the black-rubber-scarred chicane apex, and now, fully off the brake, he calmly places pressure back on the gas pedal while slowly unwinding the steering wheel . . . more gas . . . unwind . . . now straight and gas, gas, gas! Upshift! Full throttle! . . . *Simple,* thinks Rochelle as she feels her heart pounding to escape her chest.

In the swaying motion of her compliant body, and from the directional change of balance in her inner ear, and in the shifting shoulder pressure of the restraining safety belts, Rochelle can feel the continuous interplay of driver with car and has come to understand that they are an elegant couple performing a beautiful dance together along a thin ribbon of racetrack. As any leading man with a woman upon a dance floor, the driver is partnered with his race car in closed frame: fingers of his left hand lie as lightly upon the steering wheel as a dancing partner's palms gracefully clasp in air—*nice*—his right hand firmly grips the shift knob like a flat hand that lies comfortably upon the smooth skin of his partner's bare shoulder—*yes!*—buckled in with a five-point harness, they are intimately connected at the hips—*mmmmh*—and his two feet swiftly manipulate three peddles in sync with the racetrack's serpentine beat as quick feet that move in time with the orchestra's fox-trot horns—*faster, faster!*

Driver and race car, leading man and dance partner, both are competitive teams in constant tension, never breaking their connection. This strapped-in driver can awaken at will throaty notes of power that growl with an attention-grabbing clamor as they leap together upon straight lines. Experienced crewmen have carefully four-wheel balanced this race car with this specific driver in mind so that his right hip will be the center point at which their combined, weighted mass

will rotate in their intricate dance together. With fluid control he seamlessly flaunts the race car as he guides it through the twists and turns
and undulations, along the slenderest cadence of smooth-as-dance-
floor racetrack. There is no off-balance jerking of the steering wheel,
no lost momentum with smoky curls of burning rubber tires, no false
falsetto of energy excesses lost in wasted noises. With one, and a driver's measured touch, he awakens tempest powers that sing in a guttural
song of approval from shiny steel pipes; and with the other, a man leads
his partner that follows skin to skin even should his hand accidently
slip to follow her sensuous contours as they peer into each other's eyes
with preferably a bond that is more than the dance, and she confidently
moves as one with his every step.

From the many years of her preparing prior to live stage performances, Rochelle understands that for a race-car driver to perform
effectively there is no actual thinking, no conscious thought, no adrenaline rush of excitement, no mind-freezing fear, only an absence of all
emotions that clears the mind for the driver to instinctively react. All
the anxious tension one heaps upon oneself in expectation of a flawless performance builds and is then dissipated by each in his or her
own uniquely individual routine—Rochelle has never mentioned her
ritual, preshow vomiting, to anyone—before one steps under the hot
stage lights or prior to entering the high-speed race circuit. For it is
his unconscious senses alone that are acutely attuned to the sounds
he hears, and the tactile feel of his steering wheel inputs, and the
vertigo-inducing change of direction in the seat of his pants, to which
he must instantly react to save the car and thus himself should it devi-
ate from any path other than that anticipated. Countless practice laps
have impressed upon him a mental image of the track and conditioned
his muscle memory to respond accordingly with innate timing, as in
the rhythm and beat of music from which the ballroom dancer anticipates his next steps. This experienced driver sitting beside Rochelle
knows each arc of every decreasing radius turn, has felt pass through
his body the unique and intricate thump and bump of every bulging
corner chicane at its apex, has observed the race car leaning away
from his steering wheel inputs along each section of off-camber track,
as his practiced eyes have memorized each key indicator for every

heart-stopping braking point prior to his turning in, so he may skill-fully convey their movements as he promenades the race car unerr-ingly around the racetrack. This thin ribbon of track is the orchestral song setting the pace for the driver to lead the car, just as laid-down sheet music dictates the steps of every dancer, so they flawlessly fol-low the twists and turns together, their spirited intensity displayed in the loud, brass horns of engine throttle, the twin exhaust pipes leaping with fire, and the speed at which they rush towards and then through every corner.

Sweeping around a soft, high-speed bend of the winding three-mile road course, Rochelle can feel the car respond to the driver's inputs as he feathers gas and brake pedals in response to his steer-ing wheel inputs. Rochelle understands that he is a patient partner, always pressing but never forcing, always politely asking in a whisper, never loudly demanding, for you cannot ask the car to over-perform and make up for your mistakes. Only with the lightest of touches does he ask what the car, his partner, is capable of performing as they dance together along a knife's delicate edge. Through each turn the driver expertly pushes his car to the very edge of the soft rubber tires' adhe-sion to the textured surface, but not beyond where they will cut loose from their mechanical grip. The brake pedal is firmly pressed to the edge of locking up the slotted, vented rotors, but not beyond where the tires will skid and, in unstoppable momentum, they are carried off the track . . . or into the wall. The engine is throttled up to maximum revolutions, but not beyond where high-speed mechanical parts warp and then detonate in a self-destructive mini-explosion. Smooth hands with "touch" upon the steering wheel give gentle input to guide the race car, knowing that to overcontrol the wheel will instantly make the car overreact and become a very scary, violent bitch indeed, sending them all spinning wildly out of control.

Rochelle relaxes, breathing normally, her spirit filled with unbounded, youthful joy as she is tossed around in her tightly cocooned, protective swaddle, confident of this skillful driver as he artistically fol-lows along the repetitive cadence of technically challenging twists and turns, and the stomach-churning rise and fall of man-made undula-tions, racing along this thin ribbon of asphalt black. The driver steps the car in rhythm with that phonographic groove of the racecourse that plays out its unheard soundtrack as the three of them, together in closed frame, dance to fill their souls with a merry thrill of delight.

~~~

Mmmmh, a profound pleasure resonates from deep between her thighs and out to the very ends of her excited, tingly body. Three high-speed passes of the car in succession over deeply grooved rumble strips, as the driver has skillfully stolen as much of these red-and-white-painted chicanes and roll-out pads as possible to maintain straight-line speed through the tightly wound S-curves, have sent this anticipated shudder from the deeply carved concrete through rubber tires and tuned suspension to resonate within the carbon fiber seats upon which the buttocks of both driver and Rochelle rest. Rochelle is fully aware that stealing too much of these rumble strips will drop a wheel over the edge into that tire-grabbing dirt rut on the other side that will . . . well, Rochelle actually does not know what but assumes it would be horribly violent, with wreckage and bodies spewed across a wide field. And somehow the knowledge of this proximate peril with a possibly bloody ending heightens the sensation of her physical pleasure.

Once again they round turn thirteen onto the long straightaway as the right tires, with what would be quite a forceful and unwelcomed nudge upon surface streets, tap the apex of the raised chicane. The steering wheel is slowly unwound as the car arcs around the curve and the throttle is gingerly opened. Rochelle measures the distance down the front straight to the Starter's tower and the finish line in expectation of a good qualifying time. The green flag remains unfurled and limp as the Starter, casually leaning on his arms on the observation deck's wooden windowsill, continues to observe the racetrack. As they pass over the grooved exit rumble strip, the driver continues to roll on the accelerator while unwinding the steering wheel. Rochelle does not detect the initial moment when the race car's rear end steps out, yet intuitively her heart skips a beat as out of the corner of her eye she observes the driver's precisely smooth hands abruptly flick left! then right! and then the car is suddenly lost . . . and in an out-of-control spin! She heaves a silent gasp behind her helmet's clear plastic face mask as she instinctively draws legs in and wraps her arms in an X across her body, assuming what she has been taught, the "oh, fuck, and tuck" position.

Gripped by the sudden, unexpected loss of control, Rochelle's senses are overwhelmed with a flood of loud noises, flashing images, and caustic smells. An ear-piercing shriek of protest bursts forth from overheated tires that have lost their mechanical grip in their clockwise skid and that then start to melt, laying down into the tarmac long streaks of burnt rubber. Her vision through the windshield momentarily fills with a picture of the hip-high concrete pit wall that suddenly looms very large and very-scary close. The pungent odor of burning petroleum wafts deep into her sinus cavities. Her mouth dries with a bitter, metallic aftertaste, leaving her thirsty and wishing for water. From the corner of her eye, she observes the driver's gloved hands gently counter-steering the wheel. A reverse view of turn thirteen, which they have obviously failed to complete, sweeps past her vision. Another quick flick of the steering wheel and the driver has finally caught the car's spin, only, as Rochelle realizes with a fatalistic inevitability, for them to once again be hurling towards the pit wall . . . ass backwards!

Whereas just moments before her thoughts were crowded out by confused animal fear, there is now a quiet, detached surrealism as she, like a third-party spectator, observes a great event that transpires around them. With the empty, recently plowed center field rapidly receding from their windshield view, and from their speed and position on the track, Rochelle coolly extrapolates that they will impact the wall at a forty-five degree angle . . . in just under three seconds! She is oddly amused that her senses so quickly become aware of the barely audible whisper of wind passing her open window and the refreshingly cool feel of air rushing through her helmet air vents and onto her face that feels so nice. A curious thought comes to her mind, wondering if antilock brakes actually function when traveling in reverse? As time continues to slow, Rochelle considers another odd factoid: for the wall rushing towards them at a high rate of speed to actually reach either of them, it will first have to penetrate the race car's buffer zones of a protruding rear end, the reinforced three-inch roll-cage tubing, a bulletproof Kevlar bucket seat, and their three-layered helmets. Why is that so odd? Huh, but this is still gonna hurt. Rochelle notices the driver's additional steering wheel inputs and comes to the conclusion his corrections are to reduce their angle of attack prior to crashing into the wall and thus lessen the force of the impact. Huh, brilliant, Rochelle postulates as she instinctively shies away from the driver's side, which will now bear the brunt of the collision.

POP! At the edge of her peripheral vision, Rochelle catches a glimpse of—and passively watches, for it happens quicker than the eye can blink—a shiny black shooting projectile that comes through the driver's window to grow softball large in her vision before striking eye level into her protective face guard—*crack!*—snapping her head back before continuing out the passenger side window. The cabin fills with swirling clouds of smoke and dust. The pit wall passing by the driver's window in reverse slows and then stops. The engine soothingly purrs in exhausted submission. Car, and driver, and Rochelle sit motionless, fully intact. For a quiet moment longer, both driver and Rochelle sit staring blankly out the windshield into the whirlwind of man-made fog that limits their vision to the end of the hood and the solid concrete wall that is within arm's reach of the driver's-side window.

"Holy shit, Dad!" Rochelle cries out, lifting her visor, "that was fucking awesome!"

Silent for the moment, he then, with a tired exhaustion, thumbs his face guard up to reply in a flat voice: "Huh, yeah, great, huh. You liked that?"

"Oh my god!" Rochelle giggles in nervous response.

With the jolt of a deep breath, life comes back to move his body, and he abruptly turns to Rochelle. "Hey, you all right?" he asks, leaning over to closely inspect her face.

"Yeah, good. What the fuck!?"

"I think the side mirror got pinched between the wall and car and then ricocheted into your helmet."

"No, I mean coming out of that last turn, what happened?" Rochelle asks.

"Huh, oh that?" He laughs. "If anyone asks," he continues in that tone of self-deprecating humor, "I'm just gonna say that the unexpected ballast of your fat ass riding shotgun upset the balance of my car and caused me to over-rotate." A teasing smile of sarcasm twists across his helmet-pinched face as he continues to inspect her. "And that's my story, and I'm sticking to it."

With eyes that all of a sudden beam bright and alive, and with a cool expression of detachment upon Father's now-relaxed face that only very rarely had she observed prior, he conveys to her with an intended calming effect: *Hey, that may have seemed really scary-fucking close, but I had everything under control the whole time, ha!*

"Yeah! And you're also going to tell them that you forgot to compensate for that extra weight that was sitting in the passenger seat for a full two previous laps as well, right? That'll go over well, huh!" Rochelle blurts out, as the effect of surviving a very near and devastating thing shoots an adrenaline rush coursing through her veins. She is profoundly surprised at herself as a surreal calmness had descended on her being after the initial shock and spatial confusion of their entering an uncontrollable spin, and what in that moment seemed like their inevitable, violent crash into the solid, unmoving wall. Once she had overcome her initial fright and confusion, and cognitively understood they were in a spin, time seemed to have slowed and she was amazed at her heightened state of awareness. Her unexpected ability to focus her mind into rational thought with no fear allowed her to observe the unfolding events as a third-person spectator. The windshield had become a large projection screen, providing her a sweeping two-hundred-and-fifty-degree panoramic view of the racetrack. The gallery of spectators and drivers awaiting their turn standing beyond the second pit wall or sitting in the bleachers all seemed frozen in time as lifeless, posed mannequins dressed in a multitude of colorful jumpers. The sound of the wind passing by her window and the draft of cool air upon her face—all these and more were things she would always remember. And now her body was electrified with an excited exhilaration more intoxicating than any thrill of applause after an encore performance.

Beyond the veil of slowly dissipating fog kicked up by tires traveling at high speed and through the debris-littered alley along the wall where other cars never purposely race, Rochelle's attention is now drawn to the vigorously waving yellow flag used by the corner worker as a cautionary warning of danger for those following to slow and not to pass one another. It is only when she turns her attention back inside the car to inspect for damage that Rochelle notices both of Father's legs—his left foot firmly pressing the shiny aluminum clutch pedal deep into the floorboard, his right depressing the similarly machined brake pedal—shaking in an involuntary, spastic jig.

As the enshrouding fog begins to thin, Rochelle asks, "Can we go now?"

"No, not quite. The flagman will wave us out when it's safe to go."

"We going around again for another qualifying lap?"

"No. We're already probably going to be late for your mother and we have many miles to go, so we're just going to bring the car in and kick it over to the crewmen for inspection and tomorrow's race."

"So, does that mean you'll be starting last for the race tomorrow?"

"Well, technically yes, I'll be last, but with a little schmoozing with the timekeeper, I should be able to sweet-talk my way up to at least back of my class."

"You going to see the timekeeper now?"

"Well, I think we're going to cut and run and not risk running into the track master and taking a scolding today that I can put off 'til tomorrow. He's probably going to be on the warpath and mighty pissed off you're in the car, and all the other drivers are going to also dump heavy on him for having to go around again with the yellow caution flag waving because of us on the sidelines. It'll be more hell tomorrow for cutting out today, but we've already got to face your mother's mounting wrath."

With the pointing of the yellow flag directly towards them, the corner flagman catches their attention and then motions for them to proceed by eagerly waving the flag back and forth. Father gasses the still-idling engine while engaging the clutch to pull away from the wall and, with a blip of the accelerator pedal and a flick of the steering wheel, whips the car's tail around to point them correctly down the racetrack.

~~~~~

"Khmmm, ahmmm." Rochelle hears Mother clear her throat, as is her usual prelude signaling everyone's attention to be placed upon her for some forthcoming, self-evident pronouncement of fact that she will make, which will in fact be an opinion, to be shortly followed either with a piercing rhetorical question or a callous critique. As was its intended effect, Rochelle, idly scrolling through her cell phone, lifts her eyes in anticipation. Seated behind and to the side of her father, Rochelle has a quarter-profile view of his face splashed with color from red tail and brake lights, and blinking yellow turn signals ahead, and the white headlights trailing behind that reflect from three separate mirrors precisely angled towards his eyes alone. Through the posts of her mother's headrest, Rochelle observes her flick that long, Hollywood-blonde hair of hers over a pale, bare shoulder. Rochelle swipes her phone to extinguish the pale-blue cast light and begins to scratch at the surface of her recent memory for some mother-daughter conversation that they have had—or have not—some constructive criticism Rochelle has not implemented, some compliment that hasn't been promptly forthcoming, or some other seemingly random event that will give some indication as to whom Mother's pointed barb will be directed. Rochelle relaxes onto her seat—and with good reason— assuming it will be Father's tardiness that Mother will start upon.

"So," Mother casually begins, letting the single-syllable word hang isolated in the air for a moment of affect, again as a declarative statement that commands everyone's attention to be on her before continuing while, with great theatrical nonchalance, she idly runs an emery board back and forth across her nails; a Surfrider beach towel, ocean blue and foamy white, lazily drapes over her lap protecting her little black dress. "You were late." Everyone remains silent with the *swish, swish, swish* of the sliding emery board across nails the only noise emanating from within their confining automobile cabin.

Father casually guides the car one lane over to the left to allow an entering vehicle to safely merge onto the freeway; once clear, he steps back into the slow lane, all the while passing cars driven in the four faster lanes, with no indication that there is an impending response to Mother's query.

"Do you mind telling me"—*swish, swish, swish* . . . wait . . . the emery board momentarily stops as she inspects her nails—"why you were so late getting home when I specifically told you how important it was for Rochelle to be there on time?" *Swish, swish, swish.* After another moment of silence. "Well?" she asks with the cool voice of reason.

"Yeah, well, sorry about that. We just got hung up a little longer at the track than anticipated. That's all."

Rochelle fiddles with her shoulder belt while looking out her side window into the night sky and at the bright lights of houses that ascend the coastal mountain range they will soon traverse.

"What exactly do you mean, 'hung up,' huh?" A single sharp nail flicks out.

"Well, what with all the cars and all, we got a late start on the pole position runs, and there were a few more yellow caution flags than usual, and then one thing just delayed the other. Just couldn't be helped."

"'Just couldn't be helped,' huh? Don't you remember me telling you how important it was for you two to be home on time? That we needed to leave on time and get there early so that it would be ideal for Rochelle to run into the director and admissions staff prior to the senior showcase?"

"Yesss."

"So, do you mind explaining to me why you are so late after I explicitly told you how important it is for Rochelle to be there on time to meet these people?" Another sharpened nail exposed.

"Asked and answered."

Rochelle tensed and caught herself looking for a way out of the inescapable backseat.

"Typical. Why do you always have to be so selfish all the time?"

Rochelle cannot see, but she is well aware from experience that her mother's facial features are slowly morphing to reflect her agitated tone of voice and will soon take on a menacing scowl, her jaw set hard and pressed forward. "Why can't you ever take responsibility and ever think about anyone else? She's your daughter for god's sake."

Father gives no acknowledgement to Mother. There is just a barely perceptible nod of his head to each of the three mirrors before returning his gaze back out the windshield.

"Well?" The emery board stops to hang in the air, midstroke. "Why is it always about you? Tell me why you couldn't have left the track an hour earlier? Huh? One good reason?" With just half a beat repose for a not-expected response: "That's what I thought. You're just a selfish bastard."

"I already answered you. What do you want?"

"I want you to feel as badly as I do now, knowing how important this evening is, and after I've put so much hard work into her applications and arranging her auditions, and you don't even have the consideration to get here on time."

"Sorry about that, we really tried but stuff happens sometimes."

"You haven't even asked me what I've done, and how hard I've worked researching all the schools, how much time and effort I've put in filling out all the applications, and how much trouble I've gone through putting her portfolios together, have you? Do you know? Do you even care? You're too lazy to even ask, aren't you? Can you just answer that one question, can you?" After a moment of silence indicating no response is forthcoming: "I bet you just stuck around to get drunk with your brothers, is that it? Why? Just so you can become a worthless alcoholic like your brother who works for the post office?"

"Mom! It wasn't Dad's fault! The track master was waiting for us and jumped us right as we pulled into the pits and he totally went off on Dad for us spinning out on the track and almost smashing into the wall, and the trail of parts and glass we left on the track, and then they went into his office together, and they were in there for like a really long time. So, it wasn't really Dad's fault, he didn't have a choice."

"What? What are you talking about waiting for 'us' and 'we' almost hit the wall? What's this about, tell me now!"

Fuck, Rochelle thought, *what the fuck did I just say?* She looked to Father for some sign of the effect of her declarative statement only to see him casually scratch his cheek . . . with a single index finger.

"Oh," Father starts up, "it wasn't really that close. Missed by a mile."

"Liar."

Memory is a tricky sensation not discerningly controlled. Fickle indeed is our memory that relegates once-past physiological and physical pain to the ash-covered bins of our mind. And yet, emotional and consummate pleasures of heart and flesh, now long lost, can unexpectedly flash as a visceral vision coinciding with a pang of loss. Fickle indeed, for how does the mind choose which memory to draw from that vast well of our yesterdays? As their family car travels along at freeway speeds and Rochelle's body lightly sways with the motion of the compliant suspension, and she feels the belt tight across her lap and the shoulder strap that firmly tugs her into the soft leather bucket seat molded along the lines of human curves, the vivid image of that afternoon's wildly exhilarating moment flashes back in her mind, with an adrenaline rush once more coursing through her veins and filling Rochelle with an invulnerable sense of being alive. And in that empowering moment of reliving the thrill of that afternoon's racetrack event, while now tightly confined within the backseat—with nowhere to run and no cover to hide behind—and Mother's constantly insistent, in your face, "tell me now," until you actually tell her now, Rochelle effusively bursts forth in that quick-talking, giggly voice of teenage excitement, rushing the words of the entire story together in one long, continuous run-on sentence. "Oh my god Mother, close!—it was so awesome, Dad invited me to ride along with him on his pole-position timing lap, and oh, you won't believe this, but on the very last corner we went into this wild, crazy-ass spin that got me so twisted and discombobulated around that I didn't know which way we were going, and next thing you know there we are all spun around backwards, actually in reverse, and it's so fucking gnarly we're heading into the pit wall at over a hundred miles an hour, and there's Dad just coolly sitting there steering the car ass backwards!; and oh my god, I found out that antilock brakes actually work in reverse, and who would've thought that, huh?, and next thing ya know we just miss this pit wall so close that we actually clip the side mirror and it comes shooting into the car and smacks me in the face so hard my head snapped back, and *ohhh sooo luuucky* that the pitman told me to put my face guard down before we even went out on the track, and oh my god, we came to a stop actually touching the pit wall and pointing in the wrong direction down the straightaway, OMG!, and I still can't believe it!"

Only a moment of stunned silence to confirm the story's conclusion passes before Father interjects with, "Well, a hundred miles an hour is quite an exaggeration. And even if we had hit the wall we wouldn't have been hurt that bad. Just kinda shook up a bit."

"What!?" Mother shakes her head to . . . bring herself back to reality? "Rochelle was in the car with you? Are you fucking crazy, or what!? What do you mean she wouldn't have been hurt much? Liar. Do you not realize that if she even sprains an ankle she won't be going to school next year, no program will accept her? Don't you even care about your daughter? And for that matter no more surfing either. The last thing she needs while auditioning is another bald spot in her head with stitches. Do you hear me!?" Mother slashes the emery board in the air as an officer's baton of authority.

"Yesss. You're sitting right next to me while yelling in my ear. How can I possibly not hear you?"

"And if you want to be your stupid, crazy-ass self trying to kill yourself, that's fine with me, but I'm not allowing you to risk that with my daughter. I'm serious. Do you hear me!? Well do you?"

"Yesss, again."

"I thought you were really smart and then you go off and do something like that. And why do you race anyhow? Just because you're having a midlife crisis doesn't mean that you have to go and kill yourself along with your daughter, does it?"

"Wait, so riddle me this, Batgirl, why is doing the things that I've done all my life, and define who I am, all of a sudden a midlife crisis? At exactly what date in time does that event transpire, may I ask?"

"And how do you think I would feel if you had a crash that killed you and made me a widow, huh?"

"Well, I know I wouldn't be feeling anything, because I'd be dead! But I'm supposed to feel sorry for you because I'm dead, is that it?"

"You just don't get it do you? You're so obtuse. You're making me a nervous wreck, do you know that? I can't stand you anymore."

Rochelle watches as her father smoothly drops the stick shift into a lower gear and then accelerates before sliding over one lane and slipping between two cars to pass another very slow-moving car that is actually using the slow lane. She is aware of the lightness of his touch, deftly maneuvering the car as there is no sensation of shifting gears and only a slight, lateral motion from changing lanes, and a mild thumping vibration transmitted through the car's frame from tires passing over Botts' dots as they move back and forth across lanes through the checkerboard-patterned traffic. Sometimes they glide along in a low gear for quick spurts of acceleration and then, with just a slight lift of his gas-pedal foot, he allows engine compression to slow the car, weaving through the randomly spaced vehicles, never touching the brake pedal.

"So, do you like my new little black dress?" Mother pipes up without taking her eyes off the emery board working back and forth across her nails. "Pretty cute, don't you think? I got it at Kathleen's Boutique today. Took it right off the mannequin display as it was the only size two. So, what do think about having a wife who can still fit into a size two? How does that make you feel?"

"Agh . . . good . . . ?"

"Why can't you just be happy? That would be the normal response."

"Okay, yeah, happy for your new little black dress. Looks great on you, for sure."

"Why a compliment for once, why thank you. Pretty cool, huh? Have you ever told your friends that I'm still just a size two? They jealous?"

"Agh, I don't really discuss women's clothing size with my friends."

"Why would you not bring it up? You know how lucky you are, don't you?"

"Uh, yeah?"

"Do you like the color? I know you prefer red but everyone else was saying that black makes my eyes bluer—what do you think? Look it. Tell me what you think. Tell me that you love it."

"Mmm, ahh, black, I love it."

"It was a little pricey because it's Parisian Couture, but it's the only thing that fits me perfectly and I needed something new, and I'm worth it, don't you think?"

"And so sayeth thee."

"What does that mean?"

"Nothing."

"What?" After a moment of continued silence: "God, you're intolerable. You just can't say anything nice about anyone else can you?

Just have a decent, normal conversation for once, would you?" Mother turns her head in Rochelle's direction, and without being able to see her daughter seated directly behind begins, "So, I met Kari's mom, Andrea, while in the shop today. She's a sweet lady, don't you think? Been through so much lately though."

Without knowing how or why a casual shop conversation can do so, Rochelle feels an uneasiness in the pit of her stomach as she anticipates being subtly probed deep within those nooks and crannies of adolescent secrets that are shared among friends. "Uh-huh," she she mumbles under her breath as disinterestedly as possible.

"She was saying that Kari is applying to community college. Good for her, huh?"

"Uh-huh."

"Community college will be a good transition for her from high school and then she can transfer to a four-year school. I think she'll do well there, don't you?"

Another desultory, "Uh-huh," attempting to signal her wish to discontinue the repetitive parental probing and her withdrawal back unto that quiet, secluded valley of thought within herself.

"Nice girl, Kari, she has a really sweet disposition as well. Have you spoken to her lately?"

An innocent enough question of casual family conversation that swiftly raises Rochelle from her idle contemplation to instill a disquieting anxiousness, for Mother rarely asks a question for which she does not have some semblance of an answer. "Noooah." Wishing to end this conversation or, more dangerously, move it along to its inevitable, needling point of her stupidity and Mother's intellectual superiority: "And where is this going, Mother?" *For I know you too well,* she thinks, but leaves unsaid.

"Why didn't you tell me Kari was a cutter?"

"What!?" Rochelle effusively bursts at the impropriety of her mother's intrusion into that elusively proprietary teenage life. "What are you talking about!?"

"Well I saw Kari's text messages to you, and don't you think that as your mother I have a right to know if your friend is a cutter?"

"What the fuck!? You're spying on my text messages now!?" Unseen within the dark backseat, emotional lines of deep, ugly anger contort the smooth surface of that beautiful face.

"What's that hostile tone in your voice? Where does it come from? I've done nothing wrong," Mother challenges with parental authority. "I wasn't spying," she modulates her voice into that sugary-sweet tone of mollification that is so annoyingly condescending to Rochelle's ear. "I was merely bringing you your cell phone when I heard it ringing on the kitchen table and I couldn't find you, dear. The screen just naturally fell back to Kari's last text message that was just sitting right there. I didn't do anything and I wasn't spying, I just want to help, poor dear. How long has she been a cutter? Do you know why she does it?"

"I'm not telling you anything my friends have told me in confidence. Why would I tell you that? And I'd appreciate it if you would stop reading my text messages!"

"Shell dear, I was only trying to be helpful, bringing you your ringing phone, that's all. Don't you want to answer your friends when they're calling you?"

Rochelle feels emotionally pulled and confused, for when challenged, Mother always has a bewildering way of obfuscating her innocence with her voice modulated to emulate a sweet child. *How does she turn this into doing me a favor and making it my fault that's she's reading my text messages?* Rochelle wants to scream, but quickly passes this frustrating thought as she has no time to follow that train of misgiving, and for now must contend with a more pressing issue: "Did you say anything to her, Mother? You better not have!"

"No, of course not, dear. Why would I do that? You should have told me, you know, I'm your mother. What if, god forbid, something happened and—"

"I'm not betraying my friend's personal problems that they've told me in confidence! Don't you get it? And I don't want to hear your opinion on what you think of all my psychologically sick friends. Nor do I want to hear how smart you are for knowing everything."

"Honey, you're a beautiful girl, you wouldn't cut yourself, would you? You'd tell me if you were, right?"

"Stop it, just stop it right now. And stop reading my computer screen every time you walk into my room while I'm doing homework."

"What? What are you talking about?"

"You walk in like you have something important to say and then you pretend to have an extraneous conversation off the top of your head with me but your eyes are not even looking at me. You're looking over my shoulder at my chats for incriminating evidence as to my friends' lack of intelligence or fecklessness so as you can insult them." Rochelle wondered where her mother obtained such self-righteousness to questioningly peer into every nook and cranny of her life and then have the unmitigated gall, in her sanctimonious tone, to tell her what to think and how to feel for every emotional occasion.

"What? Why that's the most ridiculous thing I've ever heard. I do no such thing, how dare you."

"Ha, you know it's true. You don't even like any of my friends and criticize all their little spelling mistakes like that's some indication as to their lack of character. Not everyone has perfect spelling or a photographic memory like you, and it's just chatting for god's sake; spelling doesn't mean anything."

"Well that's patently untrue. I like most of your friends. Why I even told Andrea how sweet Kari is and how well she'll do in school if she learns to focus, that's all. And I suggest, young lady, that we discontinue this conversation until you can speak to your mother, of all people, in a more civil tone."

Rochelle silently fumes while she twists and squirms in a tightened seat belt that holds her down as her mind attempts to escape an array of colliding thoughts and conflicting emotions that leave her lost and confused and in a world of frustratingly unanswered questions. How is it that under the guise of parental concern, Mother's constant probing always makes her feel like an idiot? A manipulative way of questioning that leaves her feeling trapped in a corner with no chance of escape and thus results in her own, and regrettable, vociferous volley? Rochelle had long ago learned that there is never any compromise, only one's supplication to Mother's will, as appeasement only reveals a weakness for more to be taken as she continually tramples over one's own self-esteem. With its increasing frequency—or is it that Rochelle is more cognitively aware of such—she has recently come to realize that it is within her mother's pernicious character to continually trespass beyond those normally accepted lines of social commentary to nonchalantly incite a well-directed personal affront upon another, and then innocently sit back with such an annoying air of non-affect as if to say, 'whatever is wrong with you?' as the target of her barb then overreacts in an emotionally animated conniption of their own. This constant confrontational drama has Rochelle afraid to bring friends home, or even to invite Mother within an intimate huddle of friends at social gatherings, afraid of her discomforting commentary. It was only at her last, end-of-school-year pool party that her mother had quietly stood among Rochelle's small circle of girl-chattering dance teammates when something all of a sudden prompted Mother to ask, "So, has everyone already gotten their Brazilian wax for the summer? It's so perfect for the bikini lines and so much cooler, don't you think? And so smooth, your BF will love it for sure, I know." Rochelle had been mortified beyond words, her only wish was to have never existed, or at least to have instantly died on the spot and save herself further humiliation. Her friends had all stood there stunned, looking at their bare feet, their drinks, the pool, anything but Rochelle and her mother. And whatever was in the meaning of Mother's allusion to a boyfriend? What boyfriend? Their boyfriends? Her boyfriend? What the . . . !? "Honey, I'm just kidding," she had offered up with that little-girl laugh of apology that she performed so often, "you know that." Draping an arm around Rochelle and hugging her tight, Mother asked, "So tell me, what's everyone doing for the rest of summer now?"

~~~

"Queen or Coldplay?" Rochelle's introspective assault on her maternal authority figure is interrupted because Father has thumb-punched on the car stereo. Again he asks, "Queen or Coldplay?"

"Fuck Coldplay," Rochelle hisses. She clamps down hard on her lower lip and pulls it into her mouth.

After another count of silence from the passenger seat. "Okay then, Incubus it is." From six hidden speakers, alternative rock music fills the cabin with its instrumental and vocal harmonies. Rochelle allows her mind to drift, and her body relaxes following the amplified lyrics of "Black Heart Inertia," which are so familiar to her ears, for it is part of her inheritance to have the temperament that could momentarily escape and take solace in the music of a catchy guitar riff or those haughty tones of a surreal vocalist.

She leans into the shoulder belt tensioned to catch her weight as the car enters a cloverleaf freeway interchange. Before the car completes the decreasing-radius turn, the gas pedal is gently modulated to accelerate their speed and maintain momentum prior to climbing the steep grade out of the valley. Rochelle can appreciate the same skill set, and has the same sense of pride as her father has in moving the family car along public roadways at a high rate of speed without any excessive feel of motion within the cabin, except for the bumpy and uneven surface upon which they travel, as well as in finding the limits of a highly sprung race car along a twisty and undulating racecourse. As they begin to accelerate up the coastal divide, Rochelle's eyes lazily follow the meandering red line of taillights up the grade until they disappear over the crest, where she then follows the oncoming, white headlights heading towards them until they in turn wink out behind the center guardrail.

A bright flash of light suddenly illuminates their small cabin interior as a result of their headlights that reflect back from a shiny stainless-steel tanker-trailer—the only other vehicle actually using the slow lane—that they have caught up with, lumbering up the coastal-divide mountain. Their car smoothly steps over one lane to pass this heavily loaded big rig. Rochelle experiences the same pleasurable sensation rolling over the braille guide marks of lane-dividing Botts' dots as they pass the gasoline tanker as she did passing over the burring, thumpety-thump of the racetrack rumble strips. Her mind hides her from her sense of the persecuted young—as they are wont to believe and want to do—within the stereo concert of familiar musical notes accompanied by the flashing red-and-white-and-yellow light show, and her body gently sways with rhythmic bass tones passed from the uneven surface they travel upon.

Passing—memory is a fickle thing—comes to Rochelle's mind: wisdom passed down from father to daughter during one of their many trackside chats observing other race cars circumventing the street course. "There is no 'trying to pass.' When you go in, you complete it. No sticking your nose in past the tail of another car for a looky-loo and asking yourself, 'Can I make it?' and then getting your nose cut off. You have to know, and have the confidence, that when you see that opening, you can make it. Remember, passing is the easy part; it's that braking after you make the pass to complete the turn without running off the track . . . now that's the hard part."

"Could you turn that music down a bit please, dear?" Mother politely asks. "You gave me such a stress headache this evening worrying about when you and Shell would arrive home, like you wouldn't believe."

"Sure, no problem."

Rochelle watches her father turn down the stereo volume a single digitally displayed number.

"Please," Mother insists, "it's too loud for my headache. I need to calmly rest after you upset me so."

"Of course. Just for you." Father again turns down the dial a single digit.

An uneasiness heightens Rochelle's awareness as she astutely perceives, disguised in his apparently compliant tone yet exposed within his indolent actions to Mother's simple request, that Father is playing, as he is wont to do, at the boundaries of Mother's already highly strung nature. This is a familiar dance to Rochelle: Father pressing Mother's buttons while teasing her to her emotional limits, only to pull back before she violently spins out of control. Father would not directly draw her out with an overt verbal inquisition, rather, he subtly probes and retreats, then returns to play at the margins of Mother's fragile emotional state to cajole and thus expose the blemished shrew that lies just within the shadowed edges of her character—just as he eases his highly sprung race car to the very outside edge of each cornering rumble strip—to find out at what point either will slip off and over that razor's edge on which each is delicately balanced, and for which each would result in a very scary and violent event indeed. Although there would be no indication in the lines of his face, nor altered inflection in the tone of his voice, Rochelle understands that Father could enjoy in some smug way his taunting to wedge wide his wife's fissures of insecurity, inevitably exposing the irascible child within. And, once having drawn out Mother's always-on-edge attitude—*Now! Because that's what I want*—to expose that apparently reactionary child within, Father then, in his patronizing way, simply sits back as an innocent third party to enjoy the torrid throes of a real drama queen that he has set in motion, condescending in his silently haughty and imperial airs. Once edged over into a violent outburst with real tears streaming, there is nothing Rochelle, or anyone, can say or do, not a hundred bolts of silky family compliments laced with compulsory flattery that can mollify the apparently physical and emotional hurt of a mortally wounded child who shrilly decries the turn of connived, domestic matricide upon her oh-so-loving and fragile psyche.

Rochelle hated that about her father, who knew better than to set free Mother's enfant terrible, and felt he only belittled himself when he treated Mother as an object to be teased and toyed with rather than as his dancing partner to be gently and happily led in unison towards marital bliss just as he, with precision, manipulated his race car around the slenderest of racetracks. Rochelle knew well enough to understand that such treatment of her mother was in fact disingenuous of her father's long-ago vows of marital felicity and quite contrary to his inherent, conciliatory nature.

"Turn down the music now . . . or you'll be sorry."

"Huh, sorry was oh so very long ago; I'm way past that now."

"Dad!?"

Mother calmly reaches over to pull from the stereo console a protruding, dull-red glowing memory stick and, with a flick of fingers, tosses it out the window she has just toggled open; it is instantly swept away in the rushing wind. "I told you! Why do you have to be so stubborn? You just like to make everyone else in your life as miserable as you, don't you? What, are you just choosing to make me angry?"

"Uh, the stereo is playing from a CD," Father comments as the music continues to stream without interruption.

"Oh, well in that case," Mother says, pressing the eject button to expose a shiny CD, which she grabs without interference and lets fly, following the thumb drive, out the window. She hits the eject button, and once again is rewarded with a CD, and with a "Fuck Coldplay," into the air it also flies. With the next CD, Mother comments "Queen," only to insert it back into the stereo. "Ha, Nirvana MTV, your fave. Goodbye once more, Kurt Cobain." Fling.

Silver CDs continue to silently fly and then spin wildly out of control prior to crashing upon the littered freeway shoulder until Father comments, "Wasn't that a signed XB-3? Weren't they one of your clinical patients and they gave you a signed copy of their new release as thanks? They're one of the hottest bands out right now."

"Yep, never really liked their music anyhow," Mother states nonchalantly. "There," she continues as she closes the window, "nice and quiet now. That should show you I told you so."

"Whatever," said with a shrug of his shoulders. "So, what? I'm supposed to cry you a river for twenty dollars' worth of music?"

"I don't know what's happened to you lately. All my friends' husbands treat their wives with respect. Why can't you be like them?"

"And I'm also so tired of hearing how the whole world treats you like a royal princess, except for the two people in this car. And I'm especially tired of how the parents of your ex–high school boyfriend, now married and with three kids of his own, treat you as some long-lost deity. What the hell is that about anyhow?"

"Well it's true. His family all *adore* me, unlike your family." Rochelle hears the well-worn reproachful scorn of playing everyone and everything that does not measure up to her unreachable standards against Father, which will forevermore now be his burden to bear. "And how can you have such an attitude after all I've done for your children?" Her indignant hurt is undisguised. "You should be proud of your wife for steering our children to the best universities. And speaking of which"—Rochelle is amazed at the transition of Mother's roles for her tone is now unmistakably one of maternal authority—"don't you have any plans on leaving the cast party early tonight after the show. I know how you'll want to cut out for your race tomorrow so I am letting you know right now that will not be happening. I don't want you making a scene by trying to leave early. What time did you plan on leaving tomorrow morning, anyhow?"

"Five thirty."

"Well, I don't care. We are still not leaving early as you know how important this evening is for our daughter."

"That you don't care, this I know about you; that's why I'm just letting you know."

"Come on honey, why on earth would you be leaving so early? Doesn't your first race not start until like ten or eleven?"

"Yep, ten. Over an hour and a half to get there, and while it's nice and quiet I like to check out the condition of the track, like the moisture if there's morning fog, and give the car a look over—fluids, kick the tires to work out air pressure to air temperature for the race—and the earlier I get there, the more time I have to do things like that. And then there's the mandatory racers' meeting at eight thirty."

"Why then don't you just hire someone that actually knows what they're doing to do all that for you?" she asks, returning her attention back to the nail file sweeping across her fingers.

Rochelle is constantly amazed that one who is so perceptively attentive to reading others in order to subtly stroke their egos and thus bend them to her will so often off-handedly dismisses her husband. Or, as the married woman, does she already have everything that could be controlled and possessed of her husband, and perhaps the return on her platitudes of vanity is simply not worth the marginal return on her investment?

"Ha." Father turns his face away and then back to look out the windshield. "I've told you before, I do have a good mechanic that works on the car and we do consult on how the car is set up and tuned, but in the end, I'm the driver and everything is my responsibility."

"Well, can't you at least call them to start the race an hour later so you can get a little more sleep and you don't wake me up so early? I'll never get back to sleep and I'll be a wreck the rest of the day. Don't you care about me? Could you at least try for me, please?"

There is no response.

"Well, why can't you? What's so hard about asking? Why can't you just do that one little thing and try?" Poking his arm with the emery board: "So what, you're not talking to me now? What, you're punishing me, is that it?"

"No, we've had this conversation before and you just keep asking me the same question over and over again. You have this irascible logic all its own that I just can't seem to follow and it's just exhausting."

"Well, I only keep asking you because sometimes you change your mind and I just want to make sure. So, you're sure you can't get the race time changed?"

Only the burring noise of inflated rubber rolling over pocked asphalt at high speeds and the barely perceptible swishing of wind flowing over, under, and around the car can be heard within the cabin. Rochelle observes no movement from Father, other than his slight, continuous steering wheel input as he remains silent, looking straight ahead out the windshield.

"Okay Mr. Silent, I swear, you're just like a little boy"—Mother affectionately taps at his arm—"worse than having another child. Okay, just so you're clear, we're not leaving early tonight?"

"Clear."

"Okay sweetie, just because"—her voice morphs once again into that soft teenage tone of affection that is puppy-dog suffocating to Rochelle's ears—"I want everything to be perfect for this evening, and knowing how you tend to forget people's names, and god, I don't know what you would have done without me hanging on your arm at the fraternity house alumni parties when you were president and I would whisper in your ear the names of the graduated brothers and their dates' names before they came up to chat with you, you remember that? Honestly, honey, it was your house. Anyhow, I want my handsome husband by my side." She throws a lip-smacking air kiss of false flattery, playing as the guileful mistress. "These are the important names of the admissions and theater people that we will probably run into this evening for Rochelle . . ." Mother meticulously names in order of perceived rank and authority each of the expected attending deans and professors along with their position in relation to the university's two-step academic and performing-arts admissions process. Her authoritative tone is with that phlegmatic precision of the adjutant-general issuing the order of battle to a loosely gathered huddle of commanding officers within sounding of an enemy combatant. Mother next coolly lays out her intricate social weave for the upcoming evening, a pattern Rochelle is quite familiar with from their many previous East Coast campus tours.

Idly staring out into the night, Rochelle sighs and listens to the words without processing their meaning, for she has come to learn that Mother's enigmatic conversations filled with polysyllabic words of nebulous importance, when strung together and spun around, seem to have some crystal-clear logic understandable only unto herself. Anyhow, her instructions are superfluous to them, for as is the nature of Mother's strong, take-charge determination, she will lead from the front herself, with Father and Rochelle simply arm adornments adding colorful commentary upon cue. As Rochelle has seen so many times prior, entering the room of an expectant party with family props in arm could transform Mother's combative and skittish nature unlike anything else. After several days of highly anticipated preparation, and with Mother now meticulously groomed and dressed, her self-confident, choreographed walk into a crowded room of strangers is, over years of practice, a finely rehearsed entrance of nonchalance onto her stage of life. The three will enter together with a leisurely pose at the door, for the human eye is instinctively wired to catch female forms of exquisite lines. As anticipated, the gathered party will casually turn their gaze to take in the full measure of this striking blonde with that still innocently alluring body void of voluptuous curves—the better never to show signs of age—with long, teenage-skinny legs that disappear into the always-short dress that gracefully adorns her. With a quick flick of her coiffed hair splayed wide to expose its luxurious sheen, she will take a glance around the room with those wide-open—and nary a skillful surgeon's laser line upon smooth skin to be observed—starry blue eyes that are so quickly observant and youthfully alive. Mother will then hook an arm into Father's and lead the three of them in a casual stroll around the room, all the while taking in those admiring looks. Mother will glow with an infectious smile and a sophisticated charm that Rochelle knows so well to belie a scathingly sharp mind, so quick to judge and lash out, for there is no gray, only black and white; but this she saves only for close family members who have nowhere to run. The handsome couple cannot be resisted, and will be readily invited into conversations within an intimate circle of key influencers whose path Mother has specifically meandered across. Having set the stage with the visual introduction of a flashy character, Mother's elegant entrance allows her natural talents to play to the coterie's expectation of the consummate stage-mom floozy.

This West-Coast-born-and-raised woman gaily warms her audience with Southern charm, speaking with a barely noticeable drawl learned long ago from those new sorority sisters of hers while lounging to escape the afternoon humidity in the cool shade of the school's ancient weeping willows with iced sweet tea in hand. Her audience listens with pleasure to her lively and animated conversation laced with a warm voice of womanly overtones. Mother loves to play this role and wrap it around her like a soft mink over bare shoulders that she luxuriously rubs along its length with her soft cheeks. Rochelle has to admit to herself that she never loves her beautiful mother more than in those moments when proudly standing by her side as she regales her audience with intricately woven stories of their family's accomplishments that Rochelle herself, in her mother's retelling, finds astounding. What leaves Rochelle constantly confused and emotionally tormented is the duplicity of her mother's nature that has their own closed-frame dance in combative tension: instantly ready to fight with husband and daughter, and yet before strangers of perceived wealth or influence, this brilliant woman turns on lavish charms to curry favor.

As played out many a time before, unbeknownst to this small circle of quaintly bemused listeners who cast patronizing looks of intellectual snobbery at Mother's patina of Hollywood sparkle, her weak front of showy activity has been deftly offered up with all the subtle screening of Napoleonic misdirection as she attracts and holds their attention while their unprotected flanks are slowly being turned. This small group of academics will be regaled with casual observations from the family's previous countrywide tour of other university campuses. Innocuous comments on dorm living, cafeteria food, and the surrounding city life will be bantered about to lead them along. Purposely chatting with a sparkling champagne cocktail in hand, a prop that lasts all night and is never finished, Mother will appear to suffer the slightest slip of decorum with an inadvertent comment that carries unmistakable undertones disparaging all those universities that are not at the academic level and quality, nor the elevated social prestige, of Ivy League universities, present company unmistakably included within the slight! The bait is tantalizingly offered and, in spite of themselves, these kindly professors and mild-mannered administrators will surely bite in the spirit of educating this delightful waif who is way out of her league, for they will ask the obvious, pointed question: "Well, did you attend an Ivy League school?" With a flick of that long, Hollywood-blonde hair to cover a shoulder . . . wait . . . Mother's lovely, expressive eyes open wide with an innocent look of *Whatever could you mean, a dumb blonde like me?* . . . wait . . . and then a purposely shy riposte of "Well, not as an undergraduate" . . . wait . . . for them to ask the next logical question, "What, postgraduate?" . . . wait . . . a soft smile flashing straight white teeth before they even know they have been outmaneuvered, and "Well, my residency" . . . wait . . . giving them a moment to process this new information . . . "What, you're a medical doctor!?" A beaming smile of reward acknowledging their deductive reasoning will sweep across her delicately small face as they finally realize their flanks have unexpectedly been turned, and surrender to her charm is now their only honorable option—and to such an innocuously beguiling creature! "Oh, why yes, currently within the hematology clinical trials group for Johnston Pharmaceuticals" . . . wait for . . . "And Rochelle is your daughter? What, did you have her in high school?" . . . wait . . . with a nonunderstanding look of *Whatever do you mean?* and then with that innocence beaming that makes them feel years younger themselves, "Oh . . . why that's so very sweet of you to say," as she casually caresses their sleeves as a reward in acknowledgement of their now-shared intellectual acumen.

From a lifetime of observations, there was no doubt in Rochelle's mind that these unscripted performances are a flashback of an excited and adrenaline-fueled rush to that anterior life of Mother's performing upon a stage as the center of attention for an entire student body. And yet still, even having seen it herself many times, Rochelle could not resist being swept up and carried away along with these authority figures they had only moments before met with the same enthusiasm for this woman who regaled them with stories bent to impress, and that made Rochelle proud to be called her daughter.

With this small circle of judgmental listeners now captivated with her charm and personality, and Mother now placed on an equivalent, intellectual plateau, Rochelle can foresee that this evening, Mother will once again shift the sand beneath the feet of these experienced educators' perceived reality and will offer profuse apologies for Rochelle's and her own tardy arrival. This group will collectively demur as no apologies are required of a responsible peer. But Mother will insist with an embarrassed demeanor, and in that knowingly maternal tone that will be understood by those in charge of and responsible for other adults—legal adults who are neither mature nor responsible themselves, for the still-growing frontal lobes have not quite as of yet connected both sides of the brain, an elemental requirement to reach a higher plateau of rational, cognitive reasoning—will for sure begin to offer up her own version of today's father-and-daughter racing event. Casting a sideways look while speaking in a hushed tone of conspiracy inviting this intellectual circle to lean in closer, she will quietly begin, "Oh no, you wouldn't believe . . ." followed by what will forevermore be woven into the continuing fables of Father's foibles and that she will probably title for the academic audience, "Close Call of the Daring and Lucky," or no doubt later, Rochelle can imagine, when once again within the confines of the car's cabin, "My Asshole Husband, the Backwards Racer."

Rochelle well enough understands that any of Mother's narrations will ignore the reality of events for facts that are a hindrance to her stories, and she has no desire to know them; nor if she knew them would they interfere with her version of events because they are simply dismissed out of hand as she will embellish the racing action to keep enraptured with her cub this inquisitive group of gatekeepers that surrounds her. Mother will make them feel for themselves the high speed of Father's race car whipping around the racetrack's last corner, with just the appropriate pause in her narration for them all to collectively catch their breath at the impending danger of colliding with a concrete wall that unexpectedly looms large and very close in the windshield of the out-of-control race car with her most precious cargo on board. Smiles of relief will broach the concerned faces of the collective as Mother, with an excited breath of confidence, finishes her story with the race car narrowly grazing the wall before coming to a stop with all on board intact and safe. Regaling them with the morning's trackside drama will have its intended effect upon Mother's audience as they will now take new measure of this family, different from others, and, as was her intent, Rochelle herself will be considered in her university application with an interest and certitude of being escalated above those tied with her GPA or standardized test scores.

Even as the unwanted subject of these unscripted soliloquies of praise, Rochelle herself, while standing by Mother's side with guilty self-satisfaction, cannot help but be amazed in the retelling of these stories, and then despite herself, to be filled with a sense of pride that this petite-waisted woman, who could sell snow cones to an Eskimo, is in fact her mother. What continues to leave Rochelle ever confused and bewildered, and with an ache of maternal loss, is that from family members closest to her, there could apparently never be the correct measure of praise or sympathy for Mother's long-ago achievement of homecoming queen or sorority president, and, Rochelle had to admit to herself, that adulation was no longer forthcoming, for Mother's constant retelling of these stories had long ago worn thin and now fell upon deaf ears. Wistfully, Rochelle prays that in some measure those maternal attributes that can enrapture with a warm glow those she wishes to impress had been generously passed along to and heaped on her—mixed with an underlying apprehension that she will be unable to separate from herself the patina of personal character that is easily shattered to explode in outbursts of perceived persecution. And whether or not such separation is possible? Or if one is genetically, and emphatically, entwined with the other? And there lies Rochelle's real fear.

~~~

Overcome with a tiredness of adolescent confusion from yet-undefined maturing and conflicted emotions, Rochelle shuts her eyes—as the weary are wont to do—against an unfair world—as the young are wont to believe—and allows her head to listlessly bounce against the window that oscillates with the car's road-bound vibrations. Awakened from the subconscious edges of her childhood is a fond remembrance of those long-ago late-night rides home curled up in the backseat of the family station wagon. Familiar feelings of comfort to soothe her troubled soul wash over her as she recalls the swaying motion of that old automobile that would gently rock her to sleep as she laid her head upon an armrest. Slowly she would let float away all conscious thought as their creaky family car played an orchestral session that would flood her half-listening ears with a melodious arrangement of omnidirectional mechanical notes: the squeaking metal of springs and body frame became staccato, high-pitched, chirping flutes; rubber wheels bouncing over the irregular freeway surface, the thumping of muffled drumbeats; and from the variable engine throttle and exhaust notes, the continuous background drone of competing brass horns.

Unseen within the darkened confines of the backseat, Rochelle cautiously retreats within to momentarily enjoy this quiet, remembered bliss of her long-ago childhood, for it is with an anxious and persistent foreknowledge that she will inevitably be swept up and carried out to sea by that unseen emotional riptide that threatens to drown her as that time when she was very young and turned her back on the surging ocean, and was sucked under and then carried out to sea. A fonder memory of childhood washes over her as her body gently sways to and fro upon soft leather seats while her scalp, pressed against the pulsating window, is gently massaged. Too soon, she feels her stomach knot. Annoyed, she curls her long dancer's legs into her belly, relieving cramps. She smooshes her face harder against the cool glass, seeking a respite that will not come, for she cannot help but be swept up in that circling, fickle whirlpool that is her ubiquitous mother. For the umpteenth time she attempts to reconcile conflicting sentiments of a daughter's love for her mother's overt maternal displays of protective warmth and concern with the dichotomy of their frustratingly contentious relationship that with a bewildering quickness sucks her under in an emotional suffocation as Mother annoyingly attempts to control her every spoken word and every felt emotion.

Rochelle is confused with that adolescent insecurity of identity: whether within the entanglements of their mother-daughter relationship she actually has any free will at all, or whether Mother, in her self-knowing, manipulative way, has constantly foisted herself within Rochelle's head to throw her off balance and chip away at her self-esteem, thus sending her in a spiral of bewilderment and torment.

From a lifetime of emotional jousting, it seems as if the very foundation of their relationship, for which she can never seem to feel a firm grasp, is based upon a comforting walk together, hand in hand, along soft coastal sand that unexpectedly begins to shift in its supporting texture and fall away underfoot, as from the waters of some unseen, rising tide. Along their walk in ankle-lapping surf, Mother constantly whispers reinforcing dependence in her ear, "You should feel lucky having a mother who is concerned and cares enough about you to check up on all your unstable friends and protects you from their fecklessness. Now don't walk away from my protective reach; you'll be sorry." Any attempted independence of Rochelle to let go of Mother's grasp and wander off with an inquisitive curiosity of her own along their seaside walk causes the very emotional ground upon which she steps to surprisingly morph as she sinks thigh deep into an inescapable quagmire of motherly accusations that are utterly futile to attempt to escape. It is as if in that walking-away independence, however short the distance, Mother challenges her every move with an, "I dare you to distance yourself from me," and hopes to catch Rochelle in some miscue, however small, so she can look upon her daughter with that innocent look she has mastered, questioning, "Why did you let go of my hand?" Mother can then be the heroine who comes to her rescue, gloating in the self-satisfaction of Rochelle's misguided failure to follow her advice, which very nearly resulted in drowning. "Well aren't you glad your mother cares enough to be concerned about you, and is so smart to protect you?"—all said with that attitude of how intelligent she is and what a fucking idiot you are for not listening to her. *Aghhh*, Rochelle frustratedly screams within her head.

~~~~~

As Mother comes to the end of verbally mapping out her order of commanding directives for their social engagement, she reaches over in her attention-grabbing way—*I'm here, I'm right here in your face, look at me now*—to gently poke Father's arm with the flexible emery board. "You understand what I am saying, dear, and how important this evening is for Rochelle, don't you, dear?"

"Yes."

"Okay. So I know we are all on the same page, what are the names of the important people for Rochelle tonight?" With each of the half-dozen names with their titles that Father rattles off, Mother dotingly nods her head in agreement. "Very good babe, you are so intelligent," as she lightly caresses his sleeve. "Now, no drinking tonight, I don't want you going off on one of your funny, intellectual double-entendre jokes that nobody tends to get. You have a way of doing that when you have a drink or two and your tongue loosens up and you get all silly spewing your wry English humor, and you sometimes embarrass yourself."

"Yay!" Rochelle laughingly preempts any reply from Father. "You mean like he did at our end-of-summer cast party?"

"What do you mean, 'like he did at the cast party'?"

Rochelle's mind races as she searches her memory for the chain of historical events from that evening, and the paths that Mother's inquiry will surely follow, for Mother's tone has once again morphed from the supporting wife to that sharp cutting-edge tongue that Rochelle has so often seen slash through the unwittingly defenseless, only to leave them mentally shaken and unable to parry with a deflecting rejoinder of their own.

"Didn't I expressly forbid you from going to the cast party?" she says with a twisted iciness meant for Rochelle to spill the hidden contents of her teenage secrets to avoid what will surely be an endless verbal flaying until she does.

Damn it! Rochelle thinks. Then, calmly, "I'm sure we must have told you about the cast party after *Chorus Line*? Didn't we?"

"What do you mean, 'we' told you? Your father was involved in this as well? What a surprise. Don't lie to me, young lady. You know I expressly forbade you from going to the cast party as you're the only one in the whole ensemble that is not home-schooled and actually attends public classes. Do you know what that means? You were already back in school when the summer tour ended, and you have to be in school on time every day or get hauled in front of the vice principal after only three tardies or absences, and that goes on your permanent record that colleges review. Are you aware of that? Are you?"

"Oh, I was fine for school the next day," she replies. "I got four hours' sleep. And besides, the VP, Mr. Block, and I get along famously as he was a musical theater major in school. And by the way, it was Dad you should be worried about; he was the one that was totally hurting the next day."

"You knew about this?" Mother gives Father's arm a quick jab with the emery board. "And you were of course hiding it from me"—as she finishes with two more quick prods in succession.

"Agh . . ."

"So, tell me, what did your father do to embarrass you in front of all your friends? I know he did. So typical"—as she goes back to filing her nails.

Before answering, Rochelle casts a glance over to Father who lightly scratches his cheek . . . with two fingers. "Oh my god, how did you know? It was like so funny; Jarrod actually thought Dad was try-ing to hit on him! Can you believe that!?" Who among us can turn a deaf ear to that sweet, charming voice of the teenage female who flows an entire paragraph into one run-on sentence, infectious with its youthful exuberance and excitable platitudes? "I was like walking out of the karaoke room for a break from the party and there's Dad sitting at the sushi bar and he asks me, 'heh, what's your choreogra-pher's name again?' and I go like, 'Jarrod, why?' and just then Jarrod comes back from having gotten some air out front and Father goes, 'Hey Jarrod, I'm not hitting on you or anything; I'm Rochelle's dad, I just forgot your name and wanted to thank you for keeping Cruella away from Rochelle during the show,' and then Jarrod just stops and looks at Dad kinda funny and all, and then he sees me standing there next to Dad and Jarrod gets this big old smile on his face and goes, 'Oh my gosh, of course, you're Rochelle's dad, how are you? I'm so sorry, I get strange people hitting on me all the time and I just ignore them and keep walking, and you know, sorry about that,' and Dad says, 'What? I'm not your type or something, is that it?' and Jarrod screws up his face in this all-confused look and all, and Dad has a big ol' grin on his face and laughs, and I'm just standing there dying inside, ya know, and I'm thinking, 'oh my god . . . what is going on here?' and then Father says, 'Hey, that was brilliant letting Rochelle use the men's dressing room to hide her from Cruella; I really wanted to thank you for that, and also let you know I've never seen Rochelle perform better than when she's up on stage next to you; you really bring out another level of talent from her,' and now I'm just thinking, 'oh gross, Dad, please stop and don't embarrass me anymore,' but then Jarrod said some really nice things about me, professional compliments, ya know?, like way cool, huh? And then, oh my god, Dad has to keep going, you know him, and he asks Jarrod why Cruella was such a bitch to me and screaming at me all the time in the halls backstage and constantly pulling at my costume before entering so that I usually had to make my entrance from opposite the one choreographed, what a mess, and Jarrod explained that Cruella was a talented director with money to produce shows so that she had a good reputation in the business to get things done, and that I wasn't the only one she picked on, that for some reason she always had a whipping bitch for every show and I just happened to be the one for *Chorus Line*, so it kinda worked out okay, and Jarrod said some really nice things about me, he was really sweet, and he's *sooo* talented and now he's showcasing in London, so that's like really way cool and all, huh? And maybe I can go to London and showcase with him, huh?"

There is a moment of respectful silence to confirm the conclusion of Rochelle's narrative before, "Wait, what's this about you hiding in the boy's dressing room? You know if you had told me, I would have taken care of that problem. Your director would have been so sorry she ever crossed me, I can tell you that. And why in the world would you not tell me what was going on?"

Rochelle gazes out the side window into the night sky void of visible stars, pausing for the effect she has learned so well, before stating, "Mom," and then with a pace of mature calm, "that's why I didn't tell you. Don't worry about it; I'm old enough to take care of myself now." One by one in an accordion ripple of pieces slowly falling free, all those nailed-up, child-restraining, whitewashed posts of Mother's artificial control slowly fall away from her psychological picket fence of maternal constraint.

Mother's intuitive instincts pick up on Rochelle's subtle, maturing vocal notes of self-assured confidence that are for the moment, she realizes, unassailable, and so, as is her subtle nature that leaves most confused as to, "Wait, what were we talking about? Didn't you just say? Or did I imagine it?" she shifts her attack to her husband. "And so, what do you have to say for yourself? Taking your daughter out to Hollywood late at night after I expressly forbade it. What type of respect does that show your daughter if I say no and then she just uses you to reverse my decision behind my back? Can't you even tell that she's just using you? Huh, well? I'm waiting."

"Agh . . . well . . . I actually didn't know what was going on, anyhow. When she asked for a ride that night I just assumed we were going to Barnes and Noble and it wasn't until just before getting on the freeway that she said we were going the other way to the cast party, and I knew nothing about any cast party and so I knew nothing about you saying no to something that I didn't even know about anyways. And, I was thinking, ah . . . we would have been out 'til midnight at the bookstore anyhow, so, I told your daughter we could stay out until then and she said 'fine.' I mean midnight in Hollywood or midnight in the bookstore, so why not just a quick run over the hill for Rochelle to spend a little time with her friends before they all go their separate ways, ya know? And then, there we were, with me just sitting at the sushi bar reading while they're all having the karaoke party in the back, and I didn't want to, but she talked me into it, you know your daughter, and she asked if she could stay a little longer, and I'm like, 'sure, whatever, in for a penny . . . ' and the next thing ya know it's two a.m. closing time."

"So, you're telling me you're out drinking until two a.m.," Mother begins her inquisition, "and then you're driving your daughter home from Hollywood, is that what you're telling me? How smart is that?"

Rochelle hears the unmistakable contempt in Mother's tone as she obviously believes she has laid out the parameters of what is an inescapable trap of stupidity for Father, which he will willfully step into.

"Agh, well, like I said, I thought the plan was to be there only until midnight, and I was pacing myself with just two beers while reading a little Camus and I was fine until then. It wasn't until after midnight, when Shell asked to stay a little longer, that I started doing the sake bombers with the bartenders," all said with a calming tone of inept innocence, which Rochelle understands to be in fact subtle baiting of Mother.

"What!?" Mother punctuates her question with a hard stab at Father's arm. "Are you fucking kidding me?" Shifting in her seat, Mother leans close into Father. A complement of flowing blonde hair hides her face from Rochelle. "You're doing sake shooters all night long with some unemployable musical-theater bartenders and then you're driving your daughter home? Is that what you're telling me now!?" Behind that silky curtain of blonde hair so meticulously blown and brushed for their formal evening out together, Rochelle can imagine Mother's small face taking on a menacing scowl, her jaw pressed forward in that matriarchal sense of self-righteousness she so often displays with those ugly pinched lines of unconcealed scorn at Father's apparent utter failing of his paternal responsibilities. Rochelle has intuitively come to learn a familiar pattern to Mother's explosive outbursts, which Father would be quite aware of as well before playing Mother's discordant keys. Inevitably, one prerequisite is Mother maneuvering her intended subject into the confines of some seemingly inescapable space, such as some intimate social setting of one's peers from which one could not simply walk away, or in a moving car, within which they presently sat, and thus the delayed questioning of Father's tardiness from his arrival at home until now. For Father, in his self-serving way, and contrary to the unspoken contract of marital felicity, has subtly played Mother to shrewdly pull wide and expose her instinctively reactive nature to control and dominate every aspect of their lives, resulting in Mother's demonstrative intensity, which Father would have well anticipated.

"Ugh, no. I never said I drove us home."

"What? What are you talking about, 'I never drove us home'? How did you get home then?" Mother stabs Father with the flexible emery board.

"Well, if I didn't drive us home . . . 'why it's quite elementary,' my dear Miss Ivy League."

"Stop it!" Stab. "Another insulting remark!" Stab.

"Whatever."

What leaves Mother so annoyingly vexed is that the whirlwind of her performance has lost its effect, for the harsh indictment she's made in biting overtones does not have the intended effect of unsettling either Father or Rochelle, both of whom remain quiet, their impassive faces portraying a casual air of disinterest, insolent, in fact, in the face of Mother's emotional venting.

For rather than Mother's diatribe setting her uncomfortably on edge, Rochelle turns introspective, questioning her own sense of confused and clashing emotions for the role she is about to play. Waves of conflicting and misunderstood guilt from somewhere deep within take hold of her, leaving her feeling uncomfortable in her own skin. Then she cuts loose and plunges in. "Oh my god . . . Mother!" Her voice is laced with exasperation to the depths of her soul from constantly intervening between these two sparring partners who fence with sharp sticks until one eventually cries out. In that moment of silence that hangs heavy with expectation, Rochelle catches herself with a deep, fatalistic sigh of unsettling introspection at her own guilty duplicity. For whereas, just moments before, she had placed herself in a position to judge Father and found him lacking, and thus condemned him for displaying a paucity of spousal empathy in his constantly playing on the insecurities of Mother's shallow nature, Rochelle herself is now the one about to scratch at her Mother's volatile character and dig in. For unbeknownst to Mother, Father, in his feigned parental incompetence, has cleverly, or peevishly, for Rochelle is not certain, scripted this scene of baiting Mother with innocent wordplay to its climax of Rochelle's dramatic entrance.

Rochelle, with depressingly sad angst at her parents' continually contentious sniping, shuts her eyes to meld her own persona within an assumed character of fractured principles for this reversal of roles about to be played. "Mother," she once again begins with that formal address that only rarely does she use to catch and hold her parents' attention. "Father did not drive us home, Mother dear," said in accented tones of proper Queen's English elocution from seventeenth-century aristocratic society, her vowels drawn out long and slow, adding an arbitrary air of importance and snobbery to each spoken word. "Why no, of course not, Father would not, could not, because I did! . . . 'why quite elementary, wouldn't you say' . . . Mother dear?"

Unbalanced with the shift of facts from that train of thought she had presumed and followed all along, Mother asks, "What?" Placing a teenage-thin arm to rest upon Father's seat, Mother awkwardly shifts her weight around to turn and stare Rochelle full in the face. Her narrowed eyes of accusation search for a lie upon Rochelle's soft features. And yet in only a moment of her inquisitive stare there is then a confused and then deflated demeanor upon Mother, for when she reads the truth upon Rochelle's blank expression of non-affect, she must reluctantly let slip away those preformed barbs of rebuke that were ready set to let fly.

Behind her calm display of dispassionate composure, Rochelle feels her life song resonate with sour notes as she is filled with an empty sense of sadness for which she weeps at being continually locked in her beautiful Mother's closed-frame dance of constant tension; partnered in life with one out of step, who constantly looks to place the blame, even if there is nothing wrong; who accusingly searches for a point that has no significance; and knowing that Mother will always be right, even when they are in agreement. She frets that their life's dance together will always be softly tapping feet upon delicate eggshells, with Rochelle ever fearful that even the inflection of one's voice—too much or, god forbid, too little—will crack the fractured, wounded child of Mother's persona, allowing her the excuse to let fly the enfant terrible hidden within. That demonstrative creature, with no apparent urging or cajoling, will bring biting judgment as to your sincerity and felicity and will shame you in her persecution of your humanly flawed character until you submit to her will.

As Mother's constantly in motion, nimble mind allows her to do, she quickly recovers before Rochelle can complete this thought of sinking into a self-loathing abyss, and redirects her line of questioning made ready to trip up. "So let me get this straight"—as she twists back into her car seat—"you let our daughter with a learner's permit, who doesn't have a driver's license, correct? drive home at two o'clock in the morning, right? With all the crazies and drunks out on the road as well? That was your clever plan? And that's your story now?"

"Ah yeah, well knowing how I was, I let Rochelle drive us home. Smart, huh? She's underage and can't drink anyhow, a captured designated driver you might say, yaw! Anyhow, she's a good driver, and even if she got a speeding ticket—she was speeding by the way—better her at ninety-five than me with a DUI."

"Hey, Dad," Rochelle interjects, sensing that for the moment Mother has lost the initiative and will not object to the interruption. She is rewarded as Mother eases her thin frame back into the passenger seat and Rochelle once again hears the familiar *swish, swish* of her file sliding across nails. A thought—both fickle and beguiling can be the bitch memory—but what the hell: 'in for a penny . . .' comes to Rochelle before continuing. "What are the odds, Dad. We're actually passing the Cognewaugh underpass as we speak. I want to do that again sometime, Dad. Huh, can we? Huh?" Expectantly Rochelle stares into the rearview mirror and is soon rewarded, as with laughing eyes of sarcasm, Father casts her a quick glance. He shakes his head. Rochelle cannot help but squirm with delight, thinking, *Let's see what we can do with a hard-stomping Irish jig now, yay!* "OMG Mother, it was like so much fun! It was so totally awesome, just like rally-car racing with Dad sitting there as a copilot calmly calling out the street route and road obstacles."

"Wonderful dear, just wonderful." *Swish, swish, swish.*

~~~~~

From the point at which Cognewaugh apparently rises from the cool, sparkling sea, this boulevard is a most interesting asphalt ribbon, quietly beautiful and sensually alluring with an old soul of exquisite style and impeccable character. One will feel a pang of envy over expansive green lawns that beckon to refined old Spanish-style mansions, and then feign confused bemusement at the opulent and crass Greek-column homes with naked, painted statues, while when eventually traveled along to its inland, heat-intense genesis—where will be found its hidden mistress with a tramp stamp—one may wish to turn a blind eye and shy away from the modern intensity of the economically marginalized composed of smooth-talking shysters, and all-dressed-in-black meth-head Goths—creatures of the night—intermingled with those unbathed masses struggling for subsistence living while seeking temporarily permanent accommodations within seedy motels overbuilt upon littered gutters.

Built back in the day prior to ruler-straight, high-speed freeways, and before the never-ending, geometric grid of timed traffic signals, Cognewaugh, as one of the first asphalt streets in a burgeoning city, was a novelty when all the roads were composed of hard-packed dirt; it connected the birthing, bustling downtown metropolises with the then-faraway smooth, sandy beaches of respite that lay astride an invitingly cool blue Pacific Ocean. In a city falsely rumored not to have a public transit system, when, in fact, the second largest bus fleet in the Americas resides here, and where the streets are laid out in a high-speed grid sometimes six lanes wide with an additional four allowing for turning either left or right in an attempt to facilitate fast-moving cars along, Cognewaugh is an anomaly of old and slow. This two-lane-each-way road begins its run to the ocean in a semi-straight line from under the downtown four-level interchange, passing cash-providing pawnshops of semi-stolen goods, and cheap motels that offer decrepit housing for the newly arrived illegals so they may hide from Immigration before integrating into ethnically similar enclaves in other parts of the city, and cloud-high meth heads who stare idly into empty space planning all night for . . . nothing, as well as those women of ill-repute for whom it is such a dangerous challenge to make ends meet as they occasionally must walk the streets, a paradox in this, our wireless and fiber-optic-connected Internet age, for their own reward of a bittersweet cycle of drug-induced highs.

A few miles farther towards the setting sun, inroads of urban reclamation have recently been made by those fashionable, fedora-wearing hipsters—how young these skinny, middle-aged folks look!—with their just-way-too-cool wine bars and their morning-after coffee-sipping shops, before this street enters brassy Hollywood itself with its tourist-attracting hand-imprinted concrete sidewalks of the celluloid-made-famous at the intersection of Vine: "Buy your map of the stars here!"

Beyond this tourist-congested and business-intermingled section, with its hundred-yard-paced stop-and-go traffic signals, comes the laid-back iconic Hollywood restaurants where a gaggle of paparazzi lurk outside front, back, and side doors of the presently "in" club waiting for that pernicious celebrity shot—"Look Ma, no underwear!"— that sells for big bucks to the *National Enquirer*'s star-in-disgrace feature of the week. Commingled with the star-chez eateries—where being seen and with whom you are seen is more important than the cuisine—are the famously renowned rock 'n' roll venues of lore, where most of those fables are intricately woven with truthful cords, still intimate and quaint, where one is lucky to score tickets for their yet-to-be-discovered band with a small following of a few-hundred rabid fans: "I remember when Jim Morrison . . ."

The last outpost upon the commercial trail before this metropolitan street becomes a road that meanders through residential housing—without, for many miles, any further interruption from traffic signals, and from a point at which Rochelle will begin her narration—is a nondescript midrise that houses, at sidewalk level, a popular sushi bar that transforms itself into an even-more-popular after-hours karaoke club. Abruptly, beyond this forgettable gray building of glass and steel, albeit one possessing many memorable stories, are posh estates with rolling green manicured lawns that stretch to opulent homes where some of Hollywood's, and America's, and the world's, richest of the rich reside, or at least have ownership so they can say "Pickfair," "The Manor," "Casa Encantada," regardless of where they actually live. It is at this point that Cognewaugh begins to meander along a path loosely following the base of the Hollywood foothills, past these multimillion-dollar mansions of those million and billionaires.

For Cognewaugh, that beguiling street that more than any other boulevard seamlessly interlaces business with entertainment, unclean masses of reality with the celluloid of fantasy, and the homeless who, in impeccably accurate costumes, portray action heroes and movie stars for subsistence-living tips within walking distance of opulent exclusivity—can you say .1 percent?—has once again transformed as this road now begins to twist and turn, and wind and bend back on itself, then rise only to fall away, never to run flat or to lie in a straight line, evoking a driver's emotion of the classical Grand Prix racing course—Spa! Suzuka! Nürburgring!—with a delightful feel of actually traveling past points of interest and the expectation of going somewhere one wants to be. Along this circuitous, undulating route that captures, no demands, your attention, driveways blindly empty directly onto the curvy road, celebrity tour buses slowly cruise and claim that any number of a half-dozen celebrities live in the same house that is hidden behind lush green shields of eight-foot-tall hedges and sprinklers that overspray estate lawns to dangerously wet the old city street, which is severely cracked and potted and is desperately in need of repair—What!? In the richest city in the world!?

~~~~~

"When the valet brought the car up," Rochelle chatters on, "Dad just got in the passenger seat and told me to drive, and I'm like, 'no way, way cool,' and I was so excited just zipping along Cognewaugh, and you know how that road is past the university and towards the freeway. It just twists and turns like crazy, and Dad is sitting there as my rally-car-like racing copilot, and he tells me to not worry about shifting and to keep it in third gear, just work it really, really hard. And then he just casually starts calling out the road, 'cause you can't see around like any of the bends and curves, or over any of the hills, and he's just calmly sitting there calling out things like 'decreasing radius turn, pothole coming up on the left tire, off-camber slope, use the fire hydrant as the apex marker,' all this stuff you can't believe he knows."

"Are you sure your father was cognizant enough to give you safe instructions, dear?" Mother interrupts.

"What? Yeah, he was fine. Anyhow then we came up behind this Lambo like really quick, sitting there in the middle of the road straddling the white line, and it scared the heck out of me because we came at it so fast without seeing it from around a curve and it's so low and wide slowly going up the hill, not knowing if he's in the right or left lane, and Dad says, 'pass it quickly on the left, we have a short, clear straight here before the rise to see any oncoming cars,' so I just blip out to the other side of the road, and then back, and I don't think the Lamborghini even knew we were there, must've been lost and confused?, dazed and now amused, fer shura, and then we go screaming along, and it's so much fun, and as we drop down the hill coming up on the freeway entrance, we see this way cool Turbo Carrera all white with this badass black pinstriping, beautiful—and why do people with all this money keep buying these fast cars that they don't even know how to drive them anyhow? what a waste—so anyhow, he's going slow with his turn signal on for the freeway as well, and Dad says, 'He's gonna brake a mile away, so just take him on the outside of the turn, brake late, and as you come in wide it will straighten out the freeway entrance for you and you can use all your momentum for climbing up the hill,' and sure enough the Porsche starts braking like a hundred yards away from the entrance and we just pass him on the outside even before he enters the freeway turn lane, and we dive back in way clear of the Porsche. He never even saw us either, and I straighten out the S turn on up the ramp for the freeway like Dad said, and that gives us this great speed momentum as we start climbing up the valley pass and Dad asks, 'Is the Porsche pissed?' and sure enough, I look in the rearview mirror and once the Porsche straightens out onto the freeway, he just hammers the gas, I guess he was just afraid of the S turns, NASCAR driver, and those twin turbos must've kicked in 'cause he's like really hauling ass now, but I have like all this momentum and it's taking a long time for the Porsche to close on us and Dad says, 'You can go as fast as you like uphill, but you will be doing the speed limit before we crest the grade for any waiting CHP on the other side,' so, how cool is that?, and the freeway's almost deserted at that time of the morning anyhow, and oh my god, we just went flying up the hill and finally those twin turbos got us and he went screaming past us and oh what an awesome sound from that wide-open-throttle Porsche, I want one of those, can I, huh?" Rochelle finishes reliving the moment with a quickened heart.

Mother clears her throat. "How fast did you go, dear?"

Rochelle pauses in her answer, calculating all the permutations from which Mother's innocent probe can pry wide chinks and then dig deep with her nails.

"You don't want to know," Father quickly interjects.

"How fast?" Mother forcefully demands.

"You . . . don't . . . want . . . to . . . know." Father's staccato elocution closes the subject to any further discussion.

"That's nice, dear. After all that I've done for the both of you. I'm so glad that the two of you spend your time entertaining each other by conspiring to hide things from me, how charming." *Swish, swish, swish.* "And how do you think that makes me feel, as your wife and mother?" Her soft, lyrical voice carries that so-well-rehearsed undertone of the wounded child whose affronted soul aches from an intentional familial betrayal.

How did this turn into "poor me" again? *God, I will not feel guilty! I will not feel guilty,* Rochelle says to herself as that cold chill of confused uneasiness rises within with the thought that possibly she is that ungrateful offspring. *What did I do wrong? Telling her? Not telling her? My attitude? What!? Fuck! I am not a demonstrably self-centered bitch, I am not . . . am I?*

"So, once again . . ." Mother recovers her willful voice with an irritating quickness—*What? How does she do that?*—that leaves Rochelle confused as to whether to ever again be truthfully forthright in that heartfelt conversation with one's mother that she so longs for, or to continually hide and thus avoid weathering attacks as to her own continually feckless and ungrateful attitude. "You let our daughter, without a driver's license, drive on the freeway at that time of the morning, speeding, with all those drunks and crazies out there at the same time? Really, how responsible is that?"

"Well, you know she's a good driver, and she had driven on the track a few times, and she had had her learner's permit for a year already anyhow."

"Only six months"—Mother gloats in that casual inflection of dismissal that, due to an incidental error of fact, renders her husband's entire statement irrelevant—"because you've already forgotten how you were late taking her for her learner's permit and then how you wouldn't take your daughter to the DMV on her birthday for her test. How nice and responsible you are. How lucky she is to have you as her father."

"Oh yeah, you're right; it was a few months later, wasn't it. I didn't take her on her birthday did I? What was I doing? Must've been busy or something else."

"Busy or something, yes, always busy trying to kill yourself. And you, young lady, you were out 'til two a.m.? No wonder your grades are so horrible. My word, why can't you be like your brother and get straight As? Do you have any idea how much your poor grades are going to cost your dad and I in lost grants and scholarships? What sacrifices we have to make? Huh, do you?"

"Well I have an idea," Father steps in. "Why don't we just forget all about this whole college thing and get a nice red Ferrari for you instead?" Father glances at Rochelle through the rearview mirror. "It's about the same price, and you won't have to spend four years in an old dumpy and damp brick dorm and going to classes listening to all those boring lectures and spending all those late nights in the library studying and doing homework."

Rochelle looks away, smiling to herself, and then swiftly says, "Dad, that's so old-school, going to the library—really, we have wireless iPads now. I've never actually even been to our high school library in four years."

"I'm so glad that after all my hard work and hours of effort I've put into this that the both of you find it so amusing. Just because you went to a state school doesn't mean your children can't do better. And listen to me, young lady, the university you decide to attend has statistically been shown to impact what test results you can expect on your MCAT or LSAT. And how can you get into such a good university if you stay out 'til two a.m. not studying and getting poor grades? Only the top ten percent are accepted from college into grad school, and you're not even at that level in high school."

And there lay the rub laid out once again. Only for a moment does Rochelle hesitate before she plunges in. "Mother, I'm not going to grad school." Before her throat closes tight, as the fear of this moment wells up, she continues, "I'm going to take four years of dance, music, art, math, science, and business and get my degree, and then I'm going to be—no, I am—an artist, whatever that is. That's what I have to do, that's who I am. I'm sorry if that doesn't conform to your ideal of what an obedient child is, but that's just too bad." There, said.

"How can you say that!? How can you be so ungrateful for . . . ?" With a theatrical sigh Mother stops before plunging in herself. "Such a waste," her hard-edged tone is mollified with a thread of concern. Then with a confident, impartial voice of reasoning imparting with the advice of an experienced mentor: "You're brilliant. You're even smarter than your brother if you would put even a little effort into your schooling. You have the brains and the personality-plus to be a real successful professional—a doctor, a lawyer, that's where your talents lie. And an artist? Really? Honey, what type of an artist are you going to be now anyhow, honestly? Just because you have stage roles now means nothing in the professional world, dear. Ninety-nine percent of all actors and musicians are unemployed; you're smart enough to know that, aren't you? So you're going to be a waitress all of your life, is that what you're telling me? You had better be happy waiting tables because that's what you're going to be doing."

"I don't know, but I'm not going to be a lawyer in a high-rise office of glass and steel just because you want me to. That might be fine for Dad and you but I'm going to go out and do something. It's in me, it makes me happy, and it's what I have to do. I'm sorry if you don't understand, Mother." *Because I really don't understand myself.*

With this seemingly innocuous clarification of her lifelong intentions, which she has alluded to so many times and yet had shied away from specifically stating, there is an unburdened relief: yes. And still, she frets, twisting in her seat as the ache in her belly returns, for she knows that Mother's feigned acquiescence of a life waiting on tables is proof indeed that this discussion is far from over. For Mother, experience has foretold, will soon begin to constantly chip away at her commitment with innocuous statements of twisted truth intended to instill doubt and importunate questions in front of family and friends to shame Rochelle to her will. All of this and more to pollute her daughter's logic, giving her no rest as thoughts that constantly conflict bounce around with no reconciliation in her head with a weariness that leaves Rochelle to agree, if only to stop the mental drilling.

"Say something dear." Stab. "Or are you just going to sit back and do nothing as your daughter throws her life away? Well?"

"No, life is never a failure if you live with passion . . . if you are truly in love."

"God, you are truly useless. So typical. Well, just so you know, we have to follow your grandfather's trust fund, which specifically states . . ." And so it begins as Rochelle tunes out the refrain she has so often heard. Mesmerized by the myriad banner of red lights that snake along their path into the seeable distance, and the approaching white lights that flash in and out of traffic from the opposite direction, Rochelle, as she curls up in the backseat, allows her mother's voice to merge into the background drone of engine throttle and thumping rubber on the irregular asphalt. Easing her head to rest against the window, she once again takes solace in the familiar musical notes from the many working parts of the race-tuned sports car within their encapsulated, private space . . .

~~~~~

"What is the essence of your soul!?"—fickle, and yet powerful is the memory!—the theater department chairman asked Rochelle as they stood together at center stage. Under the emotional power of his words, Rochelle had palpably wilted. Not that he was going to physically harm her in any way, but it was the truth of his words that resonated deeply into her sensitive core. Innocently the chairman had disarmed her social defenses as they casually chatted about her forthcoming interview.

"Rochelle, I see this beautiful façade of a poised woman with eyes that are excitingly alive and whom I want to get to know," the director stated in a perfect pitch of concern, "but what I want to know is beneath this patina of finely applied cosmetics and poised stance of self-assurance that you so perfectly portray before me now and to the rest of the world: Who is the real Rochelle? And what are you afraid of? What is in your heart!? What!" he exclaimed with a deep basso of authority booming from his chest as his wide-open eyes stared into hers only inches away, and that had shocked and scared her. "What!"

he asked of Rochelle in his Shakespearian-trained voice, "is the essence of your soul!?"

Her face fell, and she had wanted to step back and run for the exits, but, with a momentary flinch of indecision, she stood her ground.

"That is the essence of Rochelle! That's the woman I want to know that will not run and resolutely stands in the face of fear to use that energy to perfect her craft! Can you handle that pressure until changing roles becomes as second nature as pulling on an old, familiar pair of sweats? You don't get there by accident. You have admirable traits of self-determination, confidence, looks, and education, all boring . . . boring I say. Our craft demands that to catch and hold the attention of an audience that we continually play at the very edges of highly stressed characters who then fiercely fracture, or the misfits of society with thinly disguised personality flaws. Can you delve deeply into your own humanly flawed soul, where you have never tread before, and you should be afraid to venture for some have never returned, to perform these unique roles?"

The experience had left Rochelle shaken and filled with an apprehensive dread for she did not yet know this of herself; for she feared that when she would be asked to cloak her own persona and reach within some unlit depth of herself to perform these well-known stage characters in front of an expectant audience and fellow thespians, that she would be found lacking in any range of emotional depth and artistic talent, and that is what she was truly afraid of.

"You have to suf-fer!"—the chairman had continued, dramatically raising an open hand in the air and then, in a display of vim and vigor, slowly pulling his arm down and squeezing his hand closed as if clutching her beating heart, just as a savage casting director chats and toys with one's feelings, feigning interest in previous roles and then laughing at your sarcastic character analysis until, swiftly, he strikes as a vampire, deep into an emotional vein that sucks the life force out of you—"to be a great . . . ACT!-TOR!"

~~~~~

". . . so, you understand all that, don't you dear?"

"Okay, so? None of that would really change any of my plans anyhow."

"Ah, well, anyhow, that trust is not necessarily so," Father interjects.

"What?"

"Well, without going into the details, all the money is in a trust until she turns eighteen, and then it's all hers, free and clear. I took Granddad's money, which may have paid for a semester back in the day, but wouldn't pay for a single class today, and merged it into an ITF account with money that has been added to over the years so that it will now almost pay for four years—and by the time college starts next year I should have put enough away to eliminate the shortfall. Anyhow, it was just easier to add and move money in an ITF rather than an educational trust fund, so that's what I did. And don't go and start grilling me about what I did, or when I did it, and why I did it that way, and why I didn't tell you. I don't remember seventeen years ago, and I'm not a trust fund lawyer, and it's all complicated stuff, and I just made it as easy for me as possible. But the reality is that the money is all hers, that in my name alone I control, until she turns eighteen. And I'm sorry I didn't tell you sooner, I just never really thought about it until now but the money's all there for Shell and that's the only important thing."

And check, Rochelle thinks to herself as she listens to the *swish, swish, swish* that continues without pause. It had been a long time since Rochelle had heard Mother so completely silenced. *Swish, swish, swish. Good Dad.*

"So Rochelle, you have an English paper due Monday that I'm presuming you haven't even begun as of yet?"

God, where does she get this shit from!? With that exasperating clairvoyant power of hers, Mother had once again reached in to intercept Rochelle's very thoughts and displace them with those of her own. *How the fuck does Mother get into my head every single time like that? Unbelievable! And even if I told anyone, nobody would fucking believe me. Shit!* "Yes."

"I hope you're not then planning on going to the race tomorrow with your father, are you?"

"Nooo."

"Have you even started your paper yet?"

"Noooah."

"Shell dear, why must you always be so recalcitrant to begin your school assignments and procrastinate to the very last minute? I just don't understand?"

"It's all in my head—well a good outline at least—and I do my best work under pressure anyhow."

"So you hear that, honey? Don't plan on absconding with our daughter tomorrow and dragging her off to the racetrack; she has an English paper due the next day, okay?"

"Sure, no problem, wasn't planning on it."

"Great, babe. Now let's put your racing skills to use and get us to the preshow reception on time. And remember, you promised no drinking tonight, can you do that for me?"

"What the hell? I have to be up at five thirty in the morning and you're still harping on me not to have one glass of wine?"

"Why can't you just do as I ask, just because I'm your wife?"

"Fine, tell ya what, I can do that as long as I don't have to hear any stories tonight about you being homecoming queen or class valedictorian. How's that?"

"Why? Does that threaten you somehow, or make you feel inadequate in some way?"

"Yeah, right, that's it. You get me every time."

"You're jealous, is that it?"

"Nooo."

"Why?"

"Nothing."

"What? You just can't stand it when the attention is taken off you, can you? Is that it?"

"No. It would just be interesting if for once . . ." His voice trails off.

"What?"

"Nothing."

"Tell me!"

"Nothing!"

"Listen to the venom in your voice, would you? How can you stand speaking to your wife that way? None of my friends' husbands speak to their wives like that. Rochelle, did you hear that? All I can hope is that you find a man who knows how to treat a lady and doesn't belittle your talents, unlike your father here."

"Perfect, just perfect."

"Can't you see what you've done to your daughter? You're a smart man. You must see that you have an anger management issue that needs to be addressed. It's nothing much, just an edge that a good psychologist can identify and address in a couple of sessions, I bet. Can you do that for us?" Mother entreats. "Please?" Her voice morphs into the innocent young voice of a pleading child—*please, sir.*

"Fine, just fine."

"Thank you, you're a good man. You know, I think your problems are rooted back in your childhood with your alcoholic father, don't you?" As she pulls at his sleeve, he instinctively lets that tugged hand drop off the steering wheel.

"There is always that possibility, for sure," Father replies, "and there may once actually have been life on Mars as well."

Rochelle observes Father stretch his neck as his facial muscles pull tight.

"So let me ask you something. I've always been curious to know—and you're such a smart man"—behind that veil of golden blonde hair, Rochelle could sense Mother's unsheathed claws about to scrape across a soft underbelly—"whatever did your rocket-scientist father see in your uneducated mother who just stepped off that refugee boat? I'm not saying she is unintelligent, just uneducated. Was he drunk back then, too, or did he just become an alcoholic after he had you?"

A suffocating shroud of sorrow falls oppressively over Rochelle's young heart. How sad are the complexities of life's song that seek only for the harmonious happiness that beats within our soul, a song that is seemingly so simple in its rhythm and melody, and so simple in its human wants and needs, and yet for which missteps continually abound, leading to the stepping on one's partner's toes. *Ouch,* she thinks. With her constant callous critiques, Mother is the only person, with what Rochelle fears is a pathological lack of empathy, who is capable of plucking at all of Father's discordant strings that can momentarily conjure up all the frightening, icky ugliness of a demonstrative beast demanding to be fed its bloody pound of flesh!

With a sudden look of serious consideration in Father's eyes: "As you often misconstrue—you do, my dear—let me once more inform you, for you are quite aware that Gran's schooling ended early as everyone's did so as they could all go work in the war factories. But let me ask you something, my dear, if you don't mind . . ." A queer sensation of being unattached and adrift now overcomes Rochelle, sitting encapsulated in the backseat of the car that oscillates with the road surface, hearing in Father's flat monotone precision of non-affect that is so chilling to her ears. ". . .'cause I've always been curious as well." Her young heart flutters as a smooth stone thrown skipping across the reflective surface of a tranquil lake. "So tell me something, back in the day, when you were dating fashion-model Bruce, was he really already gay? Or did poor used, abused, and confused Brucie just figure out it was better to be gay than to continue dating you? Because I certainly know how he feels. It's too bad though that he made that choice and died of AIDS. I only wish I had that option."

A sick horror! of spoken words that sets Rochelle in a bewildering fit of emotionally painful torment, wanting to openly weep for the lost essence of one's soul.

A delicate hand with slender fingers, bejeweled with colorful rings and an intricate, golden bracelet, sweeps out to smack the shoulder of the other. "Asshole."

"Bitch."

"Fu—"

"STOP IT!" Even before she has had time to realize it herself, Rochelle reflexively kicks the back of Mother's seat with all her strength, low in the back with her knees and high in the headrest with open palms, lurching Mother forward to silence her in midword. "Just stop it, the both of you! God, I can't stand it anymore. The both of you make me sick. You two are both worse than any three-year-olds. Just listen to yourselves, will you? For god's sake, if you can't say anything nice, just don't say anything at all!"

The cold, confined silence that follows is of no-man's land: eerily quiet only for the fear that no one dare tread into that empty, full-of-death space.

With a melancholy sadness of living with intractable frustrations, Rochelle wearily rests her forehead upon the distracting, vibrating, cool-to-the-touch, smooth glass. She looks up into the yellow pallor of the night sky and then back towards the receding hillside they have traversed. Homes upon the hill with porch lights that shine bright, and uncovered windows that proudly expose happy families inside for the curious passerby; for what resident would care for open windows if they carry dissonant voices of squabbling spouses, or undrawn drapes to expose a household of spatting discontent? Her eyes lazily follow the maze of meandering streetlights that snake in lines up and around the hillside leaving dark, voidless patches of black that seem woven with the same scary blind spots that arise from her morose imagination where she fears to delve. She takes in the queer sky, eerily cast in an otherworldly yellow glow from those long strings of low-pressure sodium-vapor streetlights, vainly searching the night heavens for any bright, twinkling stars and wondering if they still exist. With a deep breath she compartmentalizes her grievances to prioritize her next actions for the evening. *All right now, enough self-pity, let's get back to making everyone else happy.*

"See what your disrespectful selfishness has done to upset your daughter? Typical. You okay, baby? Just ignore your father. He means well."

A glance catches Father as he drops both hands off the steering wheel into his lap. He turns his head away. Fingers flex wide before delicately retaking hold of the wheel with just the thumb and forefinger of his left hand. He casually leans his body onto his elbow, resting on the center console. His right hand lightly massages his brow, hiding his face.

He pulls his hand away and turns to face Rochelle, and in that glow of the trailing headlights, gives her a chance to consider those fatherly eyes, which have discretely monitored her for as long as she can remember. Those watchful eyes that had once unexpectedly popped up directly in front of her face from deep under ocean water with only a casual, "Hey, what'cha doing way out here all by your lonesome?" Looking back with her preteen vision to see the distant shoreline she understood that, unknown to her, some fast-moving, unseen riptide had swept her far out to sea—as is its nature. Uncomplaining eyes, where she had never seen fear, or pain, and that had flashed with joy as she had walked into his hospital room as he lay in bed, paralyzed. Now she sees upon his strained face a fractured smile of apology that fails miserably—the smile, not the apology—for reflectively shining in the center of that dark stain of shame that mars his countenance are tear-filled eyes—"what is the essence of your soul?"—and in that revealing slick of emotional crude across his face, which he quickly lowers, averting her inquisitive gaze, and those shiny, welled-up eyes, Rochelle begins to understand Father's unmitigated contrition for allowing that stinky ink of ugly, that we all hide away from the light in the catacombs of our twisted psyche, to escape and percolate to the surface in his scathing words of spurn and scorn spewed simply to inflict as much spiteful hurt as possible towards his spouse. And that fills her with a sad sense of despair as well. And from the concealment of his agitated face, Rochelle subtly senses an enshrouding cloud of dark emotions hiding some other inner anguish that continually torments him so and impels him to lash out in those scathing words of derision . . . flash-back shocks of real physical pain from debilitating wounds past? . . . an irreconcilable emotional loss? . . . his unfiltered bitterness? . . . is he also sometimes lost and confused in frustrating doubt? . . . or do parents have symptoms of hopeless melancholy as well?

~~~

In that moment of her perceptive intuition, and with Father's eyes again looking up with that familiar, disarming smile of his, Rochelle's expression opens up with eyes full of wild surprise conveying her shock! and fear!, unable to say a word! Without pause or even changing the expression upon his face, and in that instant before turning away from her, Father's feet instinctively react without thought to reflexively transition fully onto the brake pedal.

Once again, Rochelle is thrown into her restraining seat belt as the tires claw for grip and stop before plowing into the white Escalade that looms large and near, for it has come to a complete stop in the bunged-up traffic and now stands unmoving and as solid as any pit wall. Instinctively searching for escape, Father casts a glance to his right and the concrete barrier set close to narrow traffic for the continually under-repair freeway; then he nods left to observe a line of waiting cars that have already come to a complete halt, leaving the only room for wiggle in the rapidly decreasing space to the rear end of the Cadillac that begins to tower high over them, unlike a pit wall. With the keen sense of experience from countless laps around the black asphalt ribbons of winding road-course tracks, Rochelle hears and feels the car shudder and places the commotion on antilock brakes pulsating the left front calipers to compensate for the loss of tire traction from some randomly loose street gravel. Her vision is drawn to the SUV's shiny silver bumper hitch, which they are surely going to hit. As Father drops his hands from the steering wheel, Rochelle crosses her arms over her chest. The chatter of brake-pulsation ceases, and the hood noticeably dips lower as the left front tire once again fully regains its rubber-adhering grip. Rochelle holds her breath in anticipation as their hood slowly passes under the protruding, bulbous hitch, and they stop inches from the impeding rear bumper. The front shocks decompress, slowly raising the blemish-free bonnet to rest with a barely audible metallic clap under the protruding trailer post.

"Looks like someone needs to go back to driving school and relearn the basics of keeping their eyes on the road," Mother casually intones without taking her eyes off her nails and the still-working emery board that she has never dropped.

~~~

It is in that vacant state of relief, the mind void of all thinking just having averted a very near disaster, that Mother's unexpected words draw forth in Rochelle an unfiltered, wicked thought that frightens her. An emotional consternation . . . a terrible truth!? For it is in Mother's steely-calm demeanor with that unaffected tone so unlike Mother's usual demonstrative nature in the face of near disaster, that a truth sweeps across Rochelle, an ugly chill that both deeply saddens her and makes her sick to the pit of her stomach, for as she peers beyond the edge of light into the darkened shadows of her soul, something ugly and scary that is of *her* character peeks its beastly head out. At first she pretends it's not there, but like any original thought of our own, it is not to be pushed back into the rotten burrow from which it continues to worm its way up to take the full form of a malignant being. Rochelle next unsuccessfully attempts to deny it is of her origin and instead projects the construction of its being upon some other, unknown third party. For she is in a high state of anguish, filled with a self-loathing as the selfish, ungrateful daughter that she may in fact be, all of which has been set in motion from her suspicion of Mother's unstated desire of them preferably having smashed into the back of that pit-wall-standing SUV. *This is not true. How could it be? This is not my thought. Where does it come from? Sick.* She languishes in her self-loathing.

And yet, like any spiral virus once biologically attached that cannot be attacked with antibiotics and must be patiently endured to fully run its feverish course, Rochelle follows this idea to the root of its suspicion. She dolefully adjudges that there is no denying that Mother's quick-to-find-fault temperament and her combative in-your-face nature of always being right and her desire of always having one more human foible to continually use as leverage over another is all thus, ostensibly, to retain some semblance of control and to get them to do her bidding or else face the lash of her castigating tongue.

Suddenly, Rochelle is interrupted from further exploring this musty cavern of thought for Father has fully turned to Mother with something terribly frightening in his manner! It is with alarm that Rochelle sees in the half-cast shadows of fractured lights what previously she had never before seen upon his demeanor: a scary, out-of-control look with glassy eyes wide open and bulging, his jaw set hard with pursed lips ready to once more spew forth with angry, vicious barbs . . . and, and physically tensed . . . for something more? . . . from the fouled crevices of his poked and prodded depths . . . and this intrinsically sets Rochelle delving deep into that wellspring of her noble heart to unconsciously whisper with her gentle touch, *"Dad."*

Fickle is the memory—as who can deny the self-awareness that recent torment from those closest to us can permeate our being as a very real corporeal pain. A tangible twinge that can inopportunely be conjured up from within the psyche and thus narrow one's vision, shroud cognitive thinking, and transpose itself upon the body as an acute ache that demands immediate relief. And when precariously standing, perched solo with toes over the ledge of our impassioned precipice, wanting to plunge in and thereby purge our wretched misery, one may wish to use the momentum of that magnified emotional and physical ache, which conjures up all previous trespasses upon our wounded pride, as the excuse of an irrevocable force of having actually been pushed over the edge by that other offending transgressor and thus the self-righteous justification to unmercifully lash out upon that proximate soul and thereby assuage our own hurt heart and appease the cravings of our pitiless demons. Looking into that long-brewing, emotional pit of pain and suffering, it is easy for the rational mind of adult human thought to let go to the instinctively reactive animal from which we have all come, and of which we are still mostly composed. When that moment, alone and trembling upon the threshold, overlooking our abyss, comes to us and all restraint to moral boundaries appears lost, there may be a momentary flicker of doubt, if we are lucky, from a subtle distraction that gives us a slice of reflective pause, one might say, and asks to be tacitly heard from behind that angry suffering—perhaps a gentle touch of a reassuring hand laid from a precious loved one, or simply, a single-syllable word said in a voice of endearment—For is it the word? The fetching tone? An inexplicable stirring from those long-familiar vocal cords?—and that simple act alone may possibly stay our vindictive, animalistic way. *"Dad."*

And so . . . pursed lips ready to spew . . . soften, as he holds his tongue . . . and clenched jaw ready to snap . . . slackens, so as not to bite . . . and glazed eyes blink long and hard so as to stay back? . . . then, with a snort of breath . . . and an implacable demeanor void of all spirit . . . he simply, silently, turns away . . . and never . . . to turn back again.

~~~

And in that expectant moment of holding her breath, Rochelle comes to reluctantly accept that both father and daughter are irrevocably caught, to be emotionally ripped and torn by the same dangerously controlling and unseeable undertow, as is the nature of its cover, which was just beneath the beautifully exciting surface of Mother's personality. Mother's disposition, as captivating as a million points of sparkling cut glass upon the ocean's surface, is invigoratingly alive with unbridled passions and with a quicker mind and sharper tongue than most, she presents a façade to the world that is her quintessential charm—naturally inviting and pleasurable to be around, and one that leaves all feeling the better of themselves for having done so. And there lies the familial frustration that is not easily defined. For only to those closest to her does Mother let loose with that fiery will of control that lies just below that patina of artificially agreeable charm. Any family disagreement, any struggle to assume an identity of one's independence from Mother, and without warning her personality turns malevolent with reproachful words to trample on one's humanity and self-esteem until one bends to her will. Mother does not seem to be aware that her constant needling to corral those closest to her with her psychologically construed picket fence of containment often sends those very loved ones stampeding off in an outburst of their own so they don't feel her fiery hot tongue lashing out about their feckless attention to her emotional distemper, for which the family itself is blamed as the root cause, assuredly resulting in her then being left deserted, and very much confused and afraid at her isolation.

Frighteningly exciting shore-pound surf—fickle is memory that leaps unbound to past visions of real physical danger as an escape from a present, emotionally binding consternation—that crashes like a thunderclap upon exposed sand, comes to her, tired mind. When she was a young girl, Father had taken hold of her as they ran headlong into the ocean, carefully timing their run to launch between shore-pound waves, diving into only thigh-high water and safely ducking under the oncoming breaker that towered three times over her head. With nervousness, Rochelle had felt the competing tug-of-war between Father's firm grip around her small arm pulling her deeper into the cold ocean, and the sucking wave lifting to take her body away, and from a great height and with driving power, thrash her upon the unforgiving-as-concrete sand. Once they were floating outside the breaking surf, it was Father who had taught Rochelle that when inevitably caught up in a fast-moving riptide, the best response is not to exhaust oneself in a futile attempt at swimming back to the beach but rather to relax and float laterally along the shoreline until you feel its controlling grip slacken before attempting escape by turning to land.

Rochelle will no longer fight. Her mind shifts once more to the many picture-perfect university visits and the disparate variety of those campuses: of red brick buildings thickly covered with climbing ivy, and those lush green expanses of grass, grass that she had never seen so green, so soft and thick, so luxurious, and at the other end of the country those whitewashed stucco buildings roofed with earthy, desert-red Spanish tiles, and so many bicyclists and skaters casually cruising along from class to class, and those claustrophobic dorm rooms, disheveled and messy and smelling like an old downtown bar, and overly spiced prepackaged food, and of bodies in continuous motion, all this soon to be her domicile to call home for a few short years.

Facing her eventual escape from an indefinable tyranny that she yearns for, to this soon-to-be new place of her residence and a new life as a college freshman, Rochelle reluctantly lets go of her rage at her mother, for which she cannot actually place any definitive act of torment and which makes it all the more frustrating. Escape, Rochelle sorrowfully realizes to the depth of her soul: sometimes the circumstances of our social obligations and binding responsibilities to our family, our friends, our lovers combine and conspire to create a captive environment that do not allow us to simply turn our backs and silently walk away. And that this knowingly, self-imposed internment continually immerses one in a caustic brine that inevitably will contaminate and foul even the most steadfast and gentlest of nature's souls. Tightly bound in an environment that subjects one to being constantly poked and prodded to expose one's flaws and insecurities, which are then unmercifully flayed and, at the most inopportune time, placed on display for public consumption, inexplicably contorts our very nature to act out into ugly things we don't want to do, and imperceptivity mutates our essence into unseemly people that we don't want to be.

Rochelle studies the impassive face of Father that glows an eerily devilish red from the brake lights of the stopped SUV ahead. Those vacant eyes that gaze out unseeing into space. Her own eyes, wired as a predator to catch the slightest of movements, are quickly drawn to Father's legs that bounce spastically in a tightly wound up and down involuntary jig, both feet still firmly planted onto the single brake pedal. As the line of bunged-up cars begins to move ahead and the blocking Cadillac pulls forward, Rochelle observes as Father lifts his left foot off the brake pedal to step fully on the clutch and, with a twist of the ignition key, restarts the stalled engine, *Ah ha!*

As their car begins to move forward with the flow of traffic, Rochelle pipes up, "Father," her voice heavily accented in proper Queen's English of seventeenth-century lore, "Father, I am truly disappointed . . ."

"What!?" said in a harsh tone that conveys his rattled and contentious demeanor. "We missed the Escalade and we still have plenty of time to get to school and the senior showcase. So . . . what!?"

"Father?"—reprising one of her favorite *Pride and Prejudice* characters as her voice falls deeper into that centuries-old, entitled-by-birth accent of the well-heeled English duchess, a role she adores to play and have fun with—"I am rather disappointed for in our panic stop you have forgotten to clutch in and stalled the car. Why, Father dear, whatever happened to 'two feet in'? Very disappointing indeed. What if we had actually been in a spin? You could have stripped out all the gears and actually detonated the engine. Very poor indeed. Why, I must say, if I dare, it looks like someone indeed does need to go back to racing school and relearn the basics of, 'when in a spin,' and why, yes, I rather do say, wouldn't you, Father?"

There was a disquieting moment when Rochelle was unsure of her timing and doubted her effect until a whisper of a smile noticeably relaxes Father's cheeks and she is then made to silently giggle with teenage glee as she witnesses him casually scratch his cheek . . . with his fully extended middle finger!

In that momentarily quiet solitude of relief from familial entanglements of melancholy worry there is that long-fermenting and wondrous maturation of this innocent adolescent with an awakening humanistic disposition intricately weaved with those sensitive threads of an artist's empathetic spirit that leads her to infer the essence of a soul upon Father's noticeably softened face. For Rochelle thoughtfully construes, with soft lips no longer pursed, and his gaze no longer vacantly staring out unseeing into space, a somber sadness of no regrets for all that easily could have, should have been, but never was; and in those tense shoulders that relax to slump forward, and fingers that stretch catlike to then wrap with pleasure around the softly compliant leather steering wheel that just fits his grip, a reluctant acceptance and resigned contentment of the way things are; and in his pensive, reassuring eyes with a thoughtful glint of expectation in a momentary glance over his shoulder to her that she reciprocates with a sparkle of merry delight shown shining in her own mischievous eyes, an excited trepidation for all their unknowns that will be.

~~~~~~~~

Baja Flowers

Sitting astride my cruising bike
  along a lonely stretch of ocean beach,
Just a-chillin' to the setting sun,
  lost in thought, alone and detached . . .
Not a pair in sight, hand in hand
  strolling up or down the sandy coast,
Not another soul having fun
  rolling atop the winding concrete path,
Not a one lying bare upon dry sand
  soaking in the last waning rays of sunlight.

Whence out of nowhere
  over the dunes you danced,
A skinny, creamy Black Irish lass,
  your spirit in arms wildly flapping in air,
    A hidden anger
      in pinned-up dark-forest hair,
A girlish abandon exposed in feet bare,
  kicking up sand to the edge
    of the ocean's fathomless lair.

A high-prancing filly in fluffy sea foam,
  surf wetting worn jeans

that stains with remains
   of a sea's salty poem.
Wading out, deeper still, turning around,
  returning to shore, looking about,
    Zip . . . off with your pants!
     . . . off with your underwear!
Innocently enough tossed anywhere,
  not a trace of tan lines observed
    along the curves
     of your sun-shy derrière.

Lying, then rolling in sand childlike,
  I thought I heard a shriek and a laugh!
    upon the sudden wet thrill and cold body-shock
of your meeting the awaiting surf with a splash.
Sitting up, reaching down, grabbing sand,
  throwing it in contempt
    into those ripples that attempt
     to nudge you back to land,
Your lower nakedness concealed from view
  beneath the sea's reflective surface obscure.

Then came head-high, set-wave white water
  washing away your submissively yielding body,
Rolling, floundering, laughing lightheartedly,
  borne upon a wave back from whence you came.
Now standing half-bare, with dripping wet hair
  all shiny black and smoothed flat back,
A sandy, skin-clinging veil
  thinly covering your female vale.

Freshly alight and safely out of the rip,
  leisurely . . . panties on . . . pants on . . . and zip.

An *elegant* transformation, invigorated,
  a sultry woman striding the beach,

A clingy, salty wetness glistening,
  every womanly shape on display,
    a sunlit, ripened peach.

You came to me,
  two inquisitive,
    black-pearl orbs
      taking in all of me.

My heart skipped a beat,
  palpitations sublime.
    "Hey," you said
      going by.

"Uh, hey," I shyly replied.

"Beautiful," your head flicked past me,
  back to the setting fireball,
    your face softly cast in warm glow,
      the sea sparkling a million points
        of rippling cut glass.

"Beautiful," I said to the fireball before me
  that tempers the soul taking out all woes,
As one passed me by slow,
  and the other slipped below sight . . .
One leaving me in afterglow,
  the other in twilight.

~~~

"Kick!"

　　Black lips curl back to display those perfect rows of sharp, white teeth of CoCo's before she bears down with a predator's force upon that neck covered in a long exo-layer of coarse hair and a thick undercoat of down-soft fur. A *yelp!* from the wounded barks out as the canine yanks away with a mouth full of hair and fur, albeit absent of flesh and blood. Without missing a step on her running chase, CoCo drops her head low to pull at the vulnerable hamstring of her fleeing faux prey when she is suddenly jerked away as her neckline is snapped taut. Using the energy of her youth and the quickness of her lighter frame, CoCo, in four quick strides, has come head-to-head with her target and once more pulls back her lips to strike a painful bite upon a thinly covered triangular ear. Another high-piercing squeal of animal pain as CoCo pulls away and furiously shakes her head with blood streaking from the corners of her mouth.

It is her own blood that she tastes and that stains her polar-bear-white fur for it is Kimba's teeth that have raked Coco's gums in defense, never clamping down, only bared as a shield to hold back her attack. While never losing stride in her pack-animal hunting pace, or allowing slack on her harness, she continues to swing her head from side to side as she licks the blood from around her mouth. With her head laid low in momentary submission, Kimba leans in with bared teeth to give a snarling, high-pitched bark of warning directly into Coco's ear. The braced couple continue to argue—yelping and nipping, occasionally dancing on hind legs in feigned attacks upon the other—as they assert their pack-animal status while leaning hard into the harness that they pull even as they play out that primal excitement that rules them.

Belying his anxiousness, Patrick calmly calls in a master's voice of authority, "Traillll . . . out!" He is aware that for the next few minutes the bickering dog and bitch will pay no mind to his commands as they continue to intimidate or wound each other in nature's natural selection of the fittest to become the alpha that will lead out at the head of their pack. Along their winding beach trail, anything or anyone will be run over in the unseeing, mindless gait of the instinctively wild until they expend their wolfish enthusiasm. Knowing that any dragging slack will quickly be caught up in the front wheel, snapping the dogs to a sudden halt as he is then unceremoniously somersaulted over the handlebars, Patrick cautiously modulates the bicycle brakes to keep constant tension on the harness line. Skating on a slippery sheet of smooth concrete, his observant eyes survey the path to pick the cleanest line upon which to roll the tires amid the shifting rivulets of fine sand that swirl and dance as fairy dust with the gentle sea breeze.

The crested sun is an unlocatable backlight that casts no shadows and throws no heat into their gray world enshrouded in an early morning fog. Shore-pound surf cracks intermittently, the small waves' shots amplified beyond their energy by the cool curtain of dense, moisture-laden air that veils the ocean just yards away. The few pedestrians along the path hear the fighting pack in advance and wisely clear a wide berth for their passage. The working team slowly settles their bickering as muscles leaning into their harnesses tire. Pink tongues soon peek out from the black-line-rimmed mouths of their smiling faces. Highly evolved ears independently twitch as nature's twin sonar, rotating in scanning mode until their sensitive hearing identifies the high frequency rustle of scurrying prey, and they lock on their target to chase and hunt it down. The rhythmic clapping of long, wolfish claws along the rapidly passing concrete reminds Patrick that their nails need trimming from the lack of continually tracking and chasing prey as free-ranging predators born into the wild . . . tap, tap, tap, tap . . .

Tongues soon hang long and whip loose with frothy spittle flying. Patrick is thankful for the early morning fog for it keeps the working dogs cool under their thick coats. He has come to learn that their speed and distance is directly related to the air temperature. High upon his soft, springy comfort seat, he is the first to observe a seagull idly squatting atop a hillock along their path and shouts out, "Moose! Moooosa!"

With a wolfen cry of excitement, the dogs leap in their harnesses. As they crest the hill and spot their "moose," one more high-pitched and spirited *yelp!* and then a mad dash with assistance from Patrick's peddling sends them sprinting towards their prey. The seagull gives the team a lazy look of insolence and turns away. A pause, then a step, gray wings spread wide, another step, and . . . liftoff.

The dog and bitch turn on each other with barks and nips: *"It's your fault."*

"No, it's your fault."

As the team surmounts the rise, it is now Patrick's reactionary, animal id that is alerted, for ascending the gentle grade towards them are the elegant lines of female form that are impossible to ignore. With two strong snaps on the line for attention and a single word of command, Patrick sharply calls out: "Slow!" And then, in a long drawl for setting a new pace, "Sloowwa!" The run-out dogs are happy to comply and settle into the working trot that their conditioned muscles can maintain for miles and miles.

Well, well, and what have we here, here my beauty? he asks himself, eyeing the woman who inline skates up the rise. *Wow! Must be the latest in designer bikinis that I haven't seen before.* With a wetness on her golden, sun-kissed skin, she glistens with feminine loveliness, every womanly shape on display as her silk suit clings like a second skin to those hard body lines of youthful vigor.

He takes in the sun-bleached hair that is pulled tightly back in deep, finger-combed furrows and that still drips with salty seawater. Closing the distance between them he comes to realize that it is not a bikini swimsuit that the skater wears but rather in fact panties and bra made sheer see-through from a dip in the ocean. Preformed upon his lips, the single-word greeting of "Hey," commonly used as a beachside salutation among casual strangers crossing close paths, is suddenly caught in his throat—for there on display for all to see, is the demeanor of a wounded soul, one that has suffered intractable loss, with a human heart that still beats but does not feel. Her unseeing eyes are empty, black pools devoid of life, reflecting a human hurt now inwardly focused on hunting a predator that bleeds white innocent hearts. For her predawn submersion in the still depths of a cold ocean has forged flesh and bone to match a heart chilled to the perfect, subemotional state for revenge and murder!

They pass within touching distance without acknowledgement: he with trepidation of intruding upon her private space, she pulled within to a grim resonance, and the dogs with hunting eyes only for nonhuman animals. Patrick turns his head back for a last, lingering look, following those lovely, shapely legs up to ladies' lacy . . .

~~~~~

What a wonderful feeling floating in the comforting swaddle of an overwhelming sleep that he wishes never to be aroused from. Tap,

tap, tap. *What is this intruding inconvenience upon my forehead? Just ignore it.* With an exhaustion he has never felt before, Patrick lets go of all mortal concerns to continue drifting sky-high in his dream clouds. *Agh.*

Tap, tap, tap. "Patrick, open your eyes, talk to me. Tell me your name."

Who is this constantly annoying bitch that keeps bringing me down to earth and won't let me drift?

"If you open your eyes and tell me your name, I'll let you go back to sleep."

With eyes still closed, he pronounces, "I am known by many names, given the company I keep and the place I am, although, 'maniacal, self-centered bastard' is the most common I hear, but long ago that lost the sting of its venom." *And who might be this bitch from hell?* With the hope of flying alone once again, he relents. "Patrick, as you seem to know so well."

"No, your full, given birth name?"

"You're kidding me?" With a noticeably reserved strain of vocal cords, "Patrick," then, nice and slow with a French pronunciation missing the *H*, "Henry," and then finishing quickly to leave behind the slow-witted, or others wondering as to the trueness of their listening ears, "François."

"I am quite well aware of who you are, trust me. But for now, Patrick, what day is it?"

"Well then, thank you for asking me what you already know, but Thursday it is then."

"No, what is the date?"

"Really, you have got to be kidding me? I don't even know what the date is on a good day. And I have a feeling that this is not a good day."

"If you tell me the date, I'll let you go back to sleep."

Oh, this bitch has my number. "Hmm, Thursday the fourteenth of May." *Aghh.*

"Look at me."

"My eyes hurt."

"Look at me!"

At the commanding voice, with its air of urgent importance not to be ignored, Patrick reluctantly opens his eyes in narrow slits against an overhead spotlight that penetrates through fully dilated, sleep-dark pupils to bear down with a great weight and discomfort somewhere in the center of his head.

"Where are you!?"

Not a good question anytime, anywhere, in anyone's life. "Hmm," with a shifting of his eyes for a look around through half-opened slits: "a long arm adjustable spotlight in a bare, white room with a stained tile ceiling, empty except for the bed in which I lie and one door. A lovely, haloed angel in faded blue pajamas with hair pulled constrictively back in a bun and a black stethoscope necklace. Shit, I'm in the fucking emergency room at Pacific Coast Hospital!"

"Good job. And you know this so quickly how?"

"I am quite acquainted with hospitals and emergency rooms, and PCH is the closest hospital from which I last remember being, so—quite elementary."

"Very good. And how are you feeling?"

"Just tired, sleepy."

"No, how do you feel?"

Patrick has been expectantly processing this question since awakening and, with practiced experience from many a fall within a wave and crashes into a wall, has itemized his prioritized checklist: mental processing good; vision and hearing clear; head and neck fine; a dull, inconvenient pain somewhere between the shoulder blades, *let that go for the moment*; lower back good, *lucky*; legs and feet good except for a dull burn down the right leg, *hmm?* "Good, except for a dull burning down my right side."

"Do you know what you have?"

"Well, there are no shooting pains and there are no limitations to my movement, but something's broken for sure, and I am restrained—or I can't move?"

"Well, generally I can't have this conversation with a patient as I am not the attending physician, but your wife was quite insistent that as soon as you awoke I was to inform you of the MRI results."

"Oh, if you've met my wife she would also have informed you of the arrogant bastard I am, so you do know me quite well then."

"That aside, true or not, radiology has done an MRI and you have what appears to be a burst T5 vertebra, which is right between your shoulder blades and means, in general, that the bone is shattered and cannot support itself. If that is so, a surgery will be required for inserting two titanium bars as a temporary brace, just like a cast, until the vertebra heals and eventually fuses together the T5 as one with your T4 and T6. Otherwise, without the surgery, the bone will collapse and begin to impinge on your spinal cord."

"And you slowly lose control of all your bodily functions until eventually you can't breathe anymore and you suffocate to death, *The Sorrow of War*. Lovely, just lovely."

"What's that?"

"Oh, nothing. Just something I read a long time ago. So, you're the ER nurse?"

"No, I'm the hospital charge nurse for night shift; your wife ran the first two nurses off. My night shift had been over for a while but I was reviewing some patient charts when apparently all hell broke loose when your wife came in and found you unboarded, with air in your IV line, and about a half-dozen other transgressions. She ran the first nurse off crying and after one look at the second nurse wouldn't even let her in the room. After a two-minute conversation with me, she said, 'Fine, you'll do.' She then proceeded to redo your IV, backboarded you, then cut off all your clothes and gowned you. Oh, you soiled yourself by the way, which isn't unusual for a head trauma. Your helmet was cracked through."

"Damn, I don't remember a thing. Last thing I remember is watching this skater come up the hill. How long was I unconscious for?"

"You were never unconscious. You were semiconscious the whole time, responding and talking to the paramedics, giving them all your contact information and numbers, and chatting with your wife."

"Wait, what did I say? I didn't say anything inappropriate to her, did I?" The concern is evident on his face. "She wasn't asking me any funny questions or anything?"

"No, what? You guys were fine. Hey, this is a no-stress time. The only thing important for you now, and for the next few months, is for you to relax and stay calm, to speed the healing process. That's it, nothing else. Probably take a week at least to get an open surgery room scheduled for the operation."

"Yeah, sure, everything is good. So, where's my wifee off to now?"

"She went off to see the chief of staff and get your surgery scheduled for later today. I told her good luck with that as all the rooms are scheduled out for the next month or so and you'll have to slip in with a cancellation, and besides, the surgeons have been here since six this morning and they're tired, so, good luck with that."

"Who's your staff surgeon?"

"Dr. King is the hospital's neurologist and he's *very* good."

"Yeah, well, call Dr. Walsh. He's my orthopedic and I've seen his group's specialists for wrist, elbow, knee, and hips. They're the best. I know he has a spinal specialist that I've never seen before, but if he's in Walsh's group, I know he's also the best; I don't even have to ask. Just tell Dr. Walsh that Patrick requested him, and if he's in town, he'll be here for my surgery, for sure, no questions asked. You know him?"

"Dr. Walsh? Of course, he comes into NICU all the time. But he's pediatrics. What's he doing seeing you?"

"Long story, but all in the family, as they say, and since all my kids are taken to him for their injuries, makes sense that he just sees me at the same time. Wait, where are my dogs?"

"Oh my word! That's right, those were your dogs. They are *sooo* beautiful!"

"Thanks. Where'd you see them?"

"Well, they aren't supposed to, but the paramedics loaded them up in the accompanying fire truck and brought them back to the station after bringing you here, until someone collects them. You don't mind do you?"

"No, of course not. How did they catch them? They like to run away."

"From what the paramedics told me, their leashes were still wrapped around your bike and they were just lying there licking your face."

"Ohhh, dog slime, yeck! I hope you disinfected me."

"Least of your worries, as I'm sure you are aware."

"Hmph, yeah, fer sure."

They are interrupted with a knock at the door and with the waving of a hand, the charge nurse is motioned out. With her return a few minutes later and a perplexed look upon her plain, clean face with no makeup, she says, "Huh, I'll be damned, your surgery is scheduled for two this afternoon with Carlson performing the surgery, and Walsh as second, and our chief of staff as anesthesiologist. Unbelievable."

"Ha!"

"Okay, now the million-dollar question: When was the last time you had something to eat?"

"Last night about ten. No time to eat this morning before running the dogs. They heard the clinking of their harnesses as I was lining them up in the garage and the other dogs just went berserk, barking and tearing each other apart, so I had to get them out of the house really quick."

"Perfect. We are a go then, yes? Any medications or drugs in the last week? Allergic to anything? Any medical conditions?"

"Nope, nope, and nope."

"Okay, we are going to do this real quick to get you prepped for surgery this afternoon. A full physical checkup, you're going to give me lots of blood, and if you have a little left and can give me a urine sample, that would be awesome."

"Hey, kinda weird I know, but will you do me a favor if you can? When they put me under with all that truth serum flowing through me, and I get all dopey and silly, uh, don't leave me alone with my wife, huh?"

"Rather odd, but sure I can do that. Any particular reason or anything I should look for or do?"

"No, no, and no, and you will know."

As she sticks him at the crook of his arm with the first of many needles, the color drains from his face, and his eyes lose all focus, and with an eternal exhaustion he once more begins to float soft and free.

~~~~~

The air is cool and fresh around his body. There is a quiet efficiency of muffled noises. A metronome-like *beep . . . beep . . . beep*—somehow highly important though he cannot seem to grasp its meaning for the moment—awakens him. He feels other bodies close, but where? Whispered voices of no emotion, clinical in their diagnosis: "Yeah, it's a full burst, if you look real close along here. And it appears we have about a fifty percent compression already and almost a full thirty-degree rotation. That intruding spur has me a little concerned, not much on the posterior to grab hold of to flush, and he's complaining of a little burning sensation down his right leg. We'll just have to open wide and see what options are available."

His eyes open to an antiseptic surgery room of adjustable over-head spotlights and surrounding white drapes. Two scrubbed doctors in full-length gowns and face masks review MRI film on the wall. A doctor turns to him and, seeing Patrick's open eyes, silently walks over. "Hey, how you doing?" he says. "How long have you been awake? You weren't listening to our conversation were you?"

He gives the doctor a look of confusion as his answer.

"Just two doctors with a little shoptalk before we roll you over to start, nothing to worry yourself about. I haven't seen you or the kids in a while. You guys playing it safe? Good for you. So, your wife wanted to scrub and attend the surgery but we have enough going on without any added distractions so we told her no. I hope that's okay with you?"

He nods his head in assent. He feels a comforting warmth begin to radiate throughout his body and once again he lets go of all earthly concerns to float in those billowy clouds of no gravity and no time that he yearns for.

~~~~~

He opens his eyes to a dimly lit hospital room with someone in a white lab coat standing next to him holding his wrist while looking at a watch. "Hey, Doc, what's going on?"

"Good morning and how are you feeling?"

"Fine, what time is it?"

"Five thirty a.m."

"Damn, what you doing up so early?"

"Nice and quiet, patients rested, and no one around to ask you questions and slow you down. Best time for rounds."

"So, 'Dr. Carlson I presume?' You're the spinal specialist from Walsh's orthopedic group?"

"'Yes, and I feel thankful that I am here to welcome you.'"

"Hey, and thank you so much for coming in on such short notice. I really appreciate it."

"No problem at all. How are you feeling?"

"Fine. Old and slow. Feel like I have a lead brick inlayed between my shoulder blades, heavy and restrictive, but no pain. So how did it look in there? We just miss everything by an inch?"

Surprisingly, the doctor's face turns serious. "An inch, an inch? An inch is a mile. You were a centimeter away from dead and a millimeter away—the thickness of a fingernail—from being paralyzed for life."

Patrick takes a moment to digest the cold, hard truth of the simply lucky surviving a very close thing indeed. "Okay then, so how did your work go in there?"

"Well, I really like my work." The understatement of a consummate professional of his art, confident that all that was possible was done.

Patrick comprehends an answer of no promises, rather a "let's wait and see." Hopefully, he says, "My legs feel good. No radiating warmth down my right side."

"That's certainly the welcome news we would want to hear. You are the poster child for spinal surgery. Thin and lean, all the anatomical markers on your back are easily identifiable, easy to slice into, and not a lot of layers to work around to get to your vertebrae. Solid, solid bones, not soft at all. Screws went in real nice and tight, perfect. We opened you up wide, however, as we did not know what to expect. You were scheduled for three to four hours, but we had a lot of work to do and you were on the table for almost seven hours."

"Damn, you must be exhausted from working all day yesterday and then another full day in the operating room working on me."

"That was two days ago, Patrick. Today is Saturday. You were in and out of semiconsciousness all day yesterday. Not too surprising, with all you've been through. And your head trauma was more than likely a slight concussion."

"Crazy. Another day I don't remember. So, everything feels good then and if it all went well I can be back surfing in six months?"

The doctor laughs. "You may do whatever you like but I'd be surprised if you'll even be able to suspend yourself by your arms from a bar in six months. Even now it's probably a week before you can get your hands up high enough to brush your teeth, and a month before you can reach up to wash your hair. I would prefer that you do no sports for at least a year—that's the minimum time required for the bone morphogenetic protein to fuse your T4 and T6 together with your T5. But that's your call. The two titanium rods are your 'cast' until your bones fuse together as one. Up that high you will barely notice the loss of flexibility. The rules of the road for you are simple—don't fall, get up as soon as you can to walk around, do not get your sutures wet, nobody touches your back for anything, no massages, no physical therapy until I say it's okay, and no sleeping on your stomach for a full year, and of course don't fall."

"Okay, sure, that's easy."

"And you will soon learn that you will not laugh, cough, or sneeze for the next six months."

"You're kidding, right? How will I not do any of those things for six months?"

"It will take your body about a week to shut down those reflexive actions, but you will soon learn. In addition to your shattered vertebra, we opened you up wide and stressed all the muscles along your back and around your chest. Without the Dilaudid IV drip, you would have great difficulty breathing right now, and even with Dilaudid, the first time you cough or sneeze, you will regret it and come to fear it. So, press the button for your Dilaudid as you need it for pain, but I want you using it at least once every four hours. No need for you to stress by attempting to push the pain. I have it from a good source you are not very compliant, so those are doctor's orders."

"'Kay, Doc, whatever you say. And thanks again. I'm just gonna rest my eyes for a bit here, if you don't mind?" Patrick hears the clinical beep from the IV button he has just pressed and soon a radiating warmth permeates his being, setting him gently adrift of his hospital bed.

~~~

There's a party going on and he's missing it. There are many familiar voices very close, speaking in hushed tones. There's the occasional clinking of glass and a wonderful smell in the air that reminds him of someplace that he just can't seem to grasp. He slowly opens his eyes to take in a room full of friends quietly chatting while eating slices of pizza, drinking from bottles of beer, and watching TV. "Hey, you guys, glad you all could make it. What's going on?"

"There he is," his brother Matt pipes up. "We got the pizza and beer you requested, and we've plugged into the TV to play last week's F1 race. How are you feeling?"

"Ugh, hammered. Old, slow, and like I'm top-heavy from gaining fifty pounds right between my shoulder blades. Why, hello, son, thanks for taking time out of your finals' studies to see me."

"No problemo, Dad, needed a study break anyhow. You're looking good considering. You feeling okay?"

"Been better, but it will all be good. Where's your sister at, what's she up to?"

"In deep shit. She's out on the island on the school retreat, remember? With everything going on, we forgot to inform the school for a day, and when we did, they went out to her camp only to find that she had, without telling anyone, switched places with a friend and was way on the other end of the island at another camp. It took another half a day to drive around the island and get out there and by then she missed the helicopter, so they stuck her on the boat, which will arrive later this afternoon."

"That's great to hear," he says with a laugh. "Where's Mom at?"

"She said she had to go get her hair done today and then she was going over to meet with the hospital administrator and to tell you that she would be over a bit later."

"Cool. Hey, I have to pee. Someone roll along my IV to the bathroom with me." His brother escorts him to the toilet and then exits, leaving the door open. Patrick stands before the bowl for a moment and then calls out, "Hey, hey, a little help in here." Matt returns. "It's so funny, but if I relax to pee, all my muscles are going to let go and I'm going to fall down. You have to hold me."

"You could sit like a girl."

"Nice, but I'm nowhere near strong enough to get up or even get down." Patrick relaxes his muscles and his legs buckle. Matt holds him up. When he gently rolls back onto the covers of his bed, he feels an exhaustion in every part of his body, as if from some great exertion without sleep for days on end. "Whew," is all he can manage.

"Hey, I almost forgot—I have a little present for you from Jim Speed," Matt announces as he fishes a logo-riddled shoebox from under his seat. "Speed said he's sorry for what happened to you and hopes you get better soon."

"This is really nice," Patrick says as he opens the box to eye a pair of Italian-crafted red racing booties. "I've always wanted a good pair of Sparcos. What's this for?"

"Speed was being nice since you can't make the race finals tomorrow, and as you're in second place in the series so far, he thought he'd just give you the second place award. What the heck, ya know?"

"Well, thank him for me. I was planning on winning both races tomorrow and taking first place, but that's totally cool. You're missing qualifying today, Bro, so you must be starting last tomorrow, huh?"

"No, P2. Speed said, since I qualified second last race, and as long as it was okay with the other drivers, I could start P2 again without qualifying."

"That's way cool. Ya know, you can beat Bill and take the series."

"You think?"

"For sure. As we're given that slight weight advantage for being the rookies, and if you don't bog like a Webbie Red Bull or a Fisi Ferrari, your lightness will launch you ahead at the standing start to take him at the apex of turn one. But Willow is a twisty track so with Bill's better technical skills through the turns he'll be right on your ass the whole race. He'll be smart and won't play pass and repass with you the whole race so he'll wait for two or three laps remaining, then watch for him to pass you underneath at the second entrance of those back-to-back one eighties. You'll think he's got too much speed and is going wide to miss the apex for you to do a reduck and under, but he's gonna brake really, really hard to block you. Such a badass pass. Anyhow, don't get all pissy on his blocking move and go and nudge him or you'll be black-flagged. As you come around the last turn prior to the straight he's going to pull an Alonso's slows like was done against Schumacher at San Marino, fast down the straights and overbraking into the turns so you lose all your momentum. You're gonna have to play it way cool and stay right up his ass without bumping and accelerate with him down the front straight. Stay in his draft and then slingshot underneath him into turn one. It'll be all about who brakes deeper and controls the trail braking through the turn. But you've done it often enough to me, so I know you can make it stick with Bill.

"Okay. And you know all this why?"

"Because our first time out at Willow that's exactly what he did to me. I was faster but every time I tried to set him up with my speed into the turn prior to the straight he countered by braking hard into the turn, so I lost all my momentum. I was all impatient and wasn't smooth on the wheel or gas and then on the one chance I had, I got overanxious and was way too hard on the brakes and locked up the tires to skid wide past the apex. Bill's brilliant, but let's take him now while we have the advantage, before next season when Speed kicks us up to the next class and adds weight on us to balance us all out. Hey, I'm hungry," Patrick says as he maneuvers the hand controls to raise his bed to a more upright sitting position. "That's better. Someone pass me a slice and a beer please."

"Dude, is that mixology going to work with your morphine?"

"Morphine is for babies. This is a Dilaudid drip, ten times stronger, and I have this little button here hooked up to the IV for whenever I want more, yeah! Someone grab my water straw and stick it in my beer, please. Oh, and do me the favor of cutting up my pizza and give me a fork, thanks."

"Jeez, I hope you're not wearing diapers, are you?"

With full mouths, the room becomes quiets as each enjoys their pizza and beer while watching the Formula 1 race.

"Hey, you haven't seen any pics from my Baja motocross ride last month. I have them on my laptop. You wanna see?" Matt asks.

"Yeah, for sure," Patrick says, finishing his beer and trading an empty bottle for the computer. "Wow, it's been such a long time since we've been surfing down there," Patrick wistfully mumbles, scrolling through the pictures. "I can't believe after all our Baja safaris I've actually never even been to the Sea of Cortez side. The desert is so beautiful in the springtime with the flowers in bloom. How long did it take you guys?"

"Well, it was a week total from the border, down and back. One day I took off with two other guys and we rode our bikes from the Sea of Cortez to the Pacific and back all in a day. Those pictures you are looking at are of that day. Luckily we made it back by dark, two flat tires from cactus and a thrown chain, lots of work. Gnarly cactus man, straight through the tires. Got back to the cabin an hour after the sun set with barely any light left."

"I forgot all about the cactus. Look at them—it's like a forest of stick figures all across the desert floor, thirty feet tall with arms sticking out in different directions with all those beautiful bright yellow and red flowers. How was the ride?"

"Fun, not too technical, mostly dirt roads and open desert with just a few tough climbs. Why don't you come with next year?"

"Yeah, well lying here laid low not being able to scratch my nose, thinking about taking two years to recover, and then chancing all that with surfing or motocross honestly scares the crap out of me, ya know? And once I'm mended, do I really want to chance it and end up here again? I don't know; I'll have to think about it. And I haven't ridden motocross in twenty years anyhow. Another header over the handlebars is the last thing I need."

"Well, we'll take it easy. Hey, you were a good rider until you went down that one time."

"Yeah, well I'm kinda gun-shy right now so one step at a time and pass me another beer, will ya please?"

Beep . . . beep . . . beep . . . beep . . . "What the hell is that noise?" Patrick asks no one in particular. With blank looks or questioning faces and no answer forthcoming, Patrick twists in his bed to once more hear the beep. "Damn, I'm lying on my Dilaudid feed and I've pressed the button a half-dozen times. I think I'm going to OD now. Uh-oh."

"Uh-huh, yes . . . Okay then, thanks." Patrick finishes talking and fumbles the phone to another waiting hand to be hung up. "Good news, there's a ten-minute minimum time-out between Dilaudid drips. But hey, with that extra shot, I'm feeling really great," he says with a lazy smile and lids that droop lower than on one fully conscious and aware.

"Hey, hey, look at this!" someone exclaims while looking at the TV, which is replaying an aerodynamically shaped race car, with more wings and curves than a supersonic fighter jet, that runs off the race-track across a field of loose gravel, and then disappears from view as it burrows itself nose first within a wall of rubber tires cabled together. Only the highly polished silver stabilizing wing protrudes from the multilayered, head-high tire barrier that has parted way to accept the high-speed intrusion.

"Ugh, that was at the end of the front straight at over two hundred miles an hour before braking, and then leaving the track," someone in the room comments without shifting eyes from the screen.

The room is silent as each man experiences a familiar sickness in the pit of his stomach while they watch track workers rush across the gravel pit to the stricken car. One worker, unable to stick his helmet into the bored tunnel, turns around to the world television feed and raises crossed arms overhead. The hive of workers in white helmets and orange jumpsuits struggles with the tail section and seems to be at a loss as to how to pull the race car out from under the pile of tires to reach the driver. As more workers arrive, they all lean in together and, with a single coordinated pull, extract the car. Anonymous track workers with faces hidden behind clear shields lean over the cockpit as a collective. A long minute later the driver stumbles out.

"Lucky."

"Lucky bastard."

"How come the crashes that should have killed you, you walk away from? And the crashes that you should have walked away from almost kill or cripple you? Remember that time when Michael went into turn four at Willow and tried to pass Bill? Speed had always told us never to pass in turn four and then Michael sees this inside hole and goes for it and gets two wheels over the chicane into the dirt rut and it just grabs the car and flips it into a barrel roll, over and over again. Fuck, that car was ripped apart. I thought for sure Michael was dead but he just walks out with sprained wrists because he forgot to drop his hands from the steering wheel soon enough."

"Yeah, and that time Alan goes airborne over the chicane and lands flat and straight, and nice and soft in the gravel pit, like it was no big deal, but he almost loses his leg when the driveshaft comes through the floorboard and spears him. Six inches over and it would easily have killed him. He still limps—and hurts."

They all watch as the F1 race driver is whisked away in the waiting medical car.

A nurse enters and the room quiets. A few disarming smiles are offered in deference to one who has autocratic rule of her domain. She eyes the crowded room with the extra chairs that have been brought in and a wastebasket full of empty beer bottles. "There's a central bin behind the nurses' station where you guys can drop the trash into." Reaching for her patient's arm, she asks, "And how are you feeling?"

"Oh, I'm not complaining, I'm just dealing in my own way." He holds up a half-empty beer bottle. "Thanks for asking. Grab some pizza, or whatever, if you like," he offers with a crooked smile.

"Thank you for the offer. Possibly in a bit." She glances at the TV screen. "You boys and your fast toys—you're going to end up in here with your friend."

"If we sit on the couch eating potato chips while drinking beer and watching TV we're eventually going to end up here anyhow. And our friend was riding a cruiser on the beach path and look at him. And why were you wearing a helmet anyhow, geek on the beach?"

"Don't know really, just been wearing one lately."

"Lucky."

"Lucky bastard."

"You know, the older you guys get, the less flexible and resilient you are. Bones break easier and it takes much longer to heal, if it ever does," the nurse chimes in.

"Well, we better play now, then, before we get too old and decrepit. Besides, we can't worry about the inevitability of growing old; we have to start worrying about living."

"Dumbness among us."

"If you haven't done anything dumb ass enough to be lucky to be alive, you haven't lived yet."

"Suit yourselves. I'm paid the big bucks to pick up the pieces."

"And speaking about dumb ass and pieces to put back together and almost dying—you guys remember that last time we paddled out at Big Rock under a full moon? Maybe a dozen guys out at midnight and it was perfect. Fun overhead with the offshore Santa Anas standing the waves up. The pack kept moving farther and farther behind the rock for position and I ended up about twenty yards behind it when this set came in. I had priority, and fortunately, even on my paddle in, I was angling right to clear the rock, and just before I stand up the moon goes behind a cloud for a total blackout, and I think I have this wave, and not until I smack the water and start tumbling do I realize I'm off my board and was free-falling the whole time, and now all I can think is, 'Fuck, did I clear the rock?' And I'm bracing for the impact and . . . nothing, I missed. So now I'm underwater, not knowing which way is up. I've never, ever gotten vertigo before, but free-falling in the dark I lost all sense of direction. So I just reach and kick around to see if I can feel the bottom or the surface and—nothing. Then I open my eyes and—more nothing, pitch black. Next I blow bubbles to see which way they go and—again nothing, too dark. Then I put my hands over my face and blow bubbles to *feel* which way they go but my hands are way too cold to feel anything. So now I'm getting a little nervous because if I start swimming I could be going horizontal and never hit the bottom or reach the surface. I figure my buoyancy will take at least a minute to reach the surface and I don't think I have enough air for that, and it's probably gonna take longer anyhow. Finally I realize I have my leash, so I reach down to my ankle, grab the leash, and pull myself to the surface. Lucky I didn't start swimming because I was actually inverted, head down at forty-five degrees and never even knew it."

"Why didn't you reach for your leash first?"

"Never thought of it. I've never used my leash to pull myself to the surface—that was the first time ever. Crazy, huh? Anyhow, I come up and my board's snapped in half and you guys are sitting there just off the shoulder waiting for waves, and I go, 'Hey, I'm going in. You guys take all the time you want, I'll just be sitting on the beach,' you guys remember?"

"Yeah, you came up as white as a ghost, I could see your face even in the dark—I'll never forget that. And you snapped that old pig board with the sixties love flowers and colors—that was a really fun floater."

"Yeah, and if I had hit that rock I would've been a floater and in a lot more pieces than that board."

"Really, that's not very smart, surfing in the dark at night. You boys are going to kill or maim yourselves someday—you're all crazy."

"Well, we've each actually maimed ourselves at some point or other doing something, but we've been surfing and training for this all our lives."

"And nothing worth doing comes easy, and safe is relative, anyhow. How long did it take you to get your nursing degree? RN-BSN to start, five years right? And then another couple years for your master's, with probably a semester in the county psyche ward? Not very safe with all those psychos around for a petite lady like yourself."

"Touché. And you would know this, why?"

"Says your degree right there on your name tag."

"That's right, forgot. Sharp eyes. Okay, you're looking good. I'll be back shortly to change your bedsheets."

"You need me out?"

"No, you're good. I'll have you roll left and right. I'm good at it; I've had lots of training and practice," she says with a smile.

"To the left, to the left . . . right, right, right."

"In the meantime, if you happen to get tired, kick these boys out, as you need your rest. And keep the noise down please," the nurse says as she gives one last look about before exiting.

"That was cool, huh?"

"Yeah, way cool."

"You see that look on her face when she walked in? She was none too pleased when she saw us, and I was scared she was going to kick us all out."

"Yeah, made me nervous, too. Have you guys ever psyched yourselves out and been afraid of nothing there?"

"What do you mean?"

"Paddled out by myself a few years ago, out past Boneyards, to Cloudbreak. You know, it has to be ten foot plus for Cloudbreak to even pitch. Got only two okay waves, but I was out there in the middle of the ocean all by myself waiting for a long time between sets and then I just got this scary shark feeling. Everything eerily quiet and still and you just get this crazy *Jaws* feeling that you just can't shake. I was totally fixated on: that's the spot where they think those two long-distance swimmers got it twenty years ago, and they found pieces of one way up north past the naval base and nothing of the other. Anyhow, just scared the crap outta me sitting there all alone in the middle of nowhere, and I was driving myself crazy and was ready to call it a day and paddle in when this set comes over the horizon and I realize I'm sitting too far in. That far out, all your land markers are gone and even the impact boil fills in and goes quiet. So now I'm scratching for the horizon, trying to make it over this set, and I realize—I'm not scared of sharks anymore, just please get me over these set waves."

Everyone in the room laughs with a shared experience.

"Yeah, sharks scare the crap out of me as well. That's why I only surf with someone else out."

More laughter. "No, seriously, I'm not scared of sharks surfing if I'm sitting with someone else. I figure it will get them first."

"I'm not going surfing with you again."

"Yeah, me neither."

"You guys ever see a shark?"

"No, I've never actually seen a shark. You?"

"No, never."

"From what I've heard, you never will see them and will never feel them 'cause their teeth are so sharp, like a surgeon's scalpel."

"Good to know when I look down to see a leg missing. So, are sharks real or imagined?"

"Real, of course. What kind of question is that?"

"So, you're afraid of sharks but you still go out in the water?"

"Yeah, everyone is afraid of sharks and we all still go surfing."

"So does it matter if they're real or imagined? You're still going in the water."

"Yeah, I guess. There's a hundred ways to freak yourself out and we've all done it one way or another. I almost didn't jump off the pier that one time when the breakers were too gnarly to paddle out 'cause I was freaked out about hitting a fishing line or snaring on a hook, and I was the last one jumping."

"I thought that was illegal?"

"You bet it is—be quick and disappear. Anyhow, I ask because I've freaked myself out many a time on an airplane ride as well, although a few Bloody Marys seem to help. Is sitting in your seat and looking out your window wondering if the wing is going to fall off real or imagined?"

"Imagined. Sharks are real. Wings don't fall off airplanes."

"And yet Aleutian Air fell out of the sky and crashed in the water not ten miles off the naval base just because a nut fell off of a stripped bolt and then the tail fell off. So why is looking out the window wondering if the wing is going to fall off any different from sitting in the middle of the ocean wondering if a shark is going to come up and eat you?"

"Well, one is a man-made error that's preventable and the other is just a random act of nature that's out of your control."

"If it's random for a shark to come up and take a bite, then it's just as random as to which flight you take. So, why is a wing falling off that different from surfing with sharks? When you go in the water you know you've entered the sharks' food chain, and that's your choice and just as preventable as well. I bet the odds of getting eaten by a shark are considerably less than a wing falling off your airplane, and both are simply random acts if they happen to you."

"Yeah true, but at least you reduce the odds of being munched by fifty percent if you surf with one other person," which drew another laugh from the room. "No, seriously," said in earnest.

The nurse returned with a roll of white bedsheets.

"So anyhow, how was Cloudbreak?"

"Big and shifty. Breaks in a right peel like Sunset but it's really hard to line up in the right spot. And the last wave I took just walled up and I was tired, and so when it sectioned off, I belly boarded in and the craziest stuff—you wouldn't believe. I see this three-foot-high seaweed wall that I'm charging into and I close my eyes because I'm thinking I'm seeing things and sure enough when I open my eyes again there's this three-foot wall jutting up in the middle of the ocean that I'm going to crash into and I grab my nose and pull it up as I close my eyes again waiting for the impact. Somehow I end up unscathed, standing on this rock post right in the middle of the ocean, and I'm like, 'What the fuck?'"

"No way, I'm calling BS. I've seen Cloudbreak from the bluff and there's no jutting rock."

"No, there is, for sure. Same thing happened to me once. You know that kelp bed a hundred yards off of Little's take-off spot? You see it boil sometimes? That's because it's a reef that will suck clear at low tide and in a large swell when the incoming waves draw the water out."

"That's way out there."

"Left, please."

Patrick gingerly rolls onto his left side.

"Anyhow, I'm standing there in the middle of the ocean on this kelp-rock post and the following ten-foot whitewash wall comes charging in, and I turn to jump off the back end and this kelp has me so tightly wrapped up to the thighs that I can't even move, and I'm thinking like, 'No fucking way.' I have a choice of being snapped like a twig with this incoming whitewash or ducking into the kelp bed and getting wrapped up to drown, and no way I'm drowning. So I toss my board to the side and just lie flat, facedown on the surface of this two-foot-deep kelp soup with this ten-foot wall coming in, and next thing you know I'm back out in the middle of the ocean. I don't remember feeling a thing—the wave, or being lifted, or tumbling, or anything. Crazy, huh?"

"Yep, same thing happened to me once. Scared the shit out of me. I thought I was seeing things. Pulled my nose up just like you did and ended up standing on the rock as well. Friggin' incredible, right in the middle of the ocean."

"So what, are you boys looking for something, or running from something, or not happy with something in your lives, or just plain adrenaline junkies?"

The room quiets, idly contemplating.

"Wow, that's a heavy trip of pseudopsychology to lay on us. Where'd that come from?"

"Someone here opened the door of my county ward experience and I thought I'd simply walk through and apply some of that training to you suicide boys, who seem to fit the psycho profile so well."

"Touché."

"Right, please." Patrick rolls to his other side. "So what is it?"

"I guess you could say, yes and no and maybe to all of the above. I guess it depends on who you are and where you are in your life. I've probably pushed myself at one time or another for each of those reasons."

"I've thought about it before and we'd all say first and foremost it's the thrill of surfing—the adrenaline rush of the weightless free fall when you drop in for sure, and the speed of the wave. But it has to be something else, something more, for on a good day you'll get maybe six waves in an hour and an average ride is only ten seconds or so. That means one minute of actual surfing time for about three hours of driving, paddling, and waiting."

"You guys are used to that then, hours of chasing and foreplay for one minute, and that's on a good day."

The room busts up. "Oh, snap! No, you didn't girl."

"And we hardly know you."

"That was a good one."

"Yeah, but from your psychoanalytical perspective, I would have to say that surfing is therapeutic, for whatever demons or malaise are in your head are cast aside as soon as you enter the water; there's no room for anything else. Only a few times have I paddled out and thought about work or the kids, or something else, and I just got slaughtered. You lose concentration, or turn your back on the ocean, and it comes up to bite you. It's a hundred percent or nothing."

"And around here, the water is so cold, after a few hours it just totally drains me. You remember that early spring day we took those two girls out in some small surf and we got back to the car, and before we even begin to peel off our wetsuits they just started shoveling bananas and nuts into their mouths with two hands and they look at us and go, 'What? We have the munchies, we're so famished and we don't know why,' and we just start laughing because we know why. The ocean just saps all your energy and you come in starving."

"Yeah, physically you may be drained, but you always come out stoked after a surf session. You just become more alive by the peril of being slapped around hard and held down deep on a big day, and nothing on dry land seems to scare you anymore."

"You guys remember crazy Chris—Spicoli incarnated? He had more stoke than all of us, he'd surf anything, no matter how big or small, stormy, blown or whatever, and then one day he just up and stops surfing, and then a year later he goes and offs himself. I always felt if he had kept surfing he would have worked out his demons, whatever they were. I can't help but think that . . . I should have pressed him more to go out with us . . . and for that I've always felt a bit guilty."

"Yeah, your problems seem to become really small and insignificant sitting out in water. And the ocean always offers up something to push you past your comfort zone, to find out what your limits are; that's really scary sometimes. It can become a test of who you are—all encompassing, mental, physical, emotional. The world disappears as you need to only focus on the ocean, the swell, the wind, the tide, and the other surfers around."

"Surfing even seems the simple part nowadays, anyhow, with all the crowds out. Not like in the old days when you could tuck into some off spot and surf by yourself. Now there's always somebody out everywhere, no matter how small or blown it is. There's a lot more social engineering now, what with the crowds and all. No one lets you take a wave, you have to earn it. First thing I do when I paddle out to a crowded peak is take the biggest, scariest jacking wall and let everyone know that if I turn on it, I got it, and I'm going no matter what. That way they back off on my next wave. Paddled out at El Porto once on a fun A-frame day with waves peeling left and right, and on my first wave I TOAD. I think I was looking down the line to thread my way through the crowd and my nose must've gone straight in. Man, I just paddled two hundred yards down the beach to another spot because I knew nobody was going to let me take off without shoulder hopping me. I know I wouldn't if someone else had pitched over on a set wave."

"Back in the old days, with an AM weather-band radio and Judd the Fish, you could sometimes catch a swell before the crowds hit. Now, with live webcams and phone apps, not a chance. And remember when we started surfing with those old logs that Steve Chang from next door gave us? We couldn't even get our arms around those fat logs so we'd carry two boards down to Rats with us sandwiched in the middle, one in front and the other in back, so as we could get our arms around the tapered nose and tail."

"And those beavertail wetsuits that we bought used at the dive shop, about three inches thick with the metal clasps that would go slap, slap, slap against our triple stringer boards with every step. And then we would pull the beavertail between our legs to clasp them in the front so that we would then lie on these half-inch metal buttons digging into us for about two hours of fun."

"Hey, you guyths hear the one 'bout the beaver an' the head nurth?"

"Ohhh!" in chorus.

"Okay then, what we have here is a patient who has reached his limit and needs his rest, so everyone please say your good-byes."

"'What we haveth here is a failure to communicath . . . No, no, ith really good, I thwear. This beaver walkth into a bar, and ah . . . no, no I got it . . .'"

"Who's the baby now that can't handle a little mixology of alcohol and Dilaudid?"

"Hand me your bottle please."

"Nooah, the party's juth tharting and I don't want everybody to leave."

"No, of course not. Finish your beer, plenty of time to party."

"You're not going to take my beer?"

"No. Are you going to give it to me?"

"Nooah." He cradles the bottle to his chest.

"Then take your time, finish up."

"Okay, then, juth one more thip an' I'll give yath the bottle."

"Thank you very much."

"Hey Matt, I wanna go with you guys to Baja nexth spring."

"You sure you'll be up for it?"

"Fucketh, I don't know shit. I'm just lying here betting on the come that they put me back together okay. And I can't do anything for a year or thwo, though if not next year, then the year after. But I wanna go. I'm not gonna thay I woulda, I shoulda, I coulda, ya know?"

"Sure, no problem, we can fit you with a bike and just a month or two of weekend training up at my buddy's ranch should be enough time for a Baja trail ride."

"Cool. And if any of your friends athk about my riding thtyle, tell them like a twelve-year-old girl, thlow and careful. I don't fall, but I get there, eventually."

"That'll work."

"And if anything happens to me along the way, throw me in the ocean and tell everybody it was a thurfing accident. I'm a thurfer. That'll be cool. I'm not a biker, ya know?"

"Sure, no problem, you'll be fine."

"Hey, hey, you guyth, thankth for coming. They want me in here for at leatht a week, but I planth on leavin' tomorrow. We shall thee, we shall thee. I'll mith my Dilaudidth drip, that'th for thure."

"And I'm turning off your drip until you wake up again, just to play it safe."

"No, noah, I want my Dilaudid. I'm fine, I can go all day 'n'all night, athk the guyth . . . just . . . my lidth are getting a little heavy . . . *and I'm just gonna . . . rest them for a minute . . . thanks for taking care of me . . . love you guys . . . hmm . . . nice and warm . . . that feels good . . .*"

~~~~~~~

Of Loves, Lovers, and Mistresses

A good mistress—
  and all ladies want to be good—
    keeps her lover whole, sane,
      connected . . . and a man.
A good man
  serves many a mistress,
    which keeps him true
      to his love, and a better man.

~~~

Oh, oh, my head, Tara softly intoned as she leaned over the sink and splashed cold water on her face. That brisk shock was a welcomed salve to hold at bay the hurt of her thumping head but did little to settle her stomach—which continued its backflips. She could not decide whether to stay and lean over the sink as she stared into the white basin of clear water, or prostrate herself in front of the porcelain god and empty the contents of her stomach down to the ends of her digestive track. *Maybe time for a change of scenery,* she thought as she threw herself onto the tile floor in front of the toilet and the first eruption from her stomach projectiled into the bowl. *And then there was a change of scenery, 'and it was good.'* Tara laughed and cried, not sure which she wanted to do more. And again . . . and again. And then once again she laughed and cried to herself as she took pleasure in the cool porcelain that she hugged and that felt so fresh and pleasant on her skin, *ugh, gross . . . hmm, sooo nice.* She spat with a thick, dry mouth . . . and again with a few tiny chunks, as she wrongly thought, *it can't get any worse.* Then with her face lying sideways upon the refreshing rim, she spotted the cockroaches that scurried along the baseboard, their personal highway behind the toilet. *Oh wah, please, my head, my stomach.* She questioned the tears rolling down her face and her dripping nose: *Am I crying? Is it the pain? Is my body liquefying?* She reached up for a towel to wipe away the tears, and snot, and bile from the corners of her mouth, *yuck,* and then she stopped. For it was then through the bathroom door that she spotted the leg that protruded from under the sheets and beyond the bed. *What!?*

She followed that pale leg that stuck out from under the covers and hung suspended in the air to unexpectedly stop and focus cloudy eyes on the intricately French-tip painted toenails. *What?* From behind that dreary fog of a long night, and much longer alcohol-laced morning, she attempted to reconstruct a body, a face, a name to go with that smooth, shapely, hairless leg. *What?* Her mind plodded along in spurts to recollect the fuzzy, puzzled pieces of her previous twenty-four hours that had so sumptuously begun with awakening with her *dalliance* by her side, and then he had so abruptly . . . *Hmm, should he stay or should he go?* She did not as of yet know.

~~~~~

In that semiconscious state, stirred from the depths of a most satisfying slumber of an expended body, Tara felt what she could not see and snuggled into the heat of his body. Arms wrapped around her to press them tightly together followed by a kiss placed upon her dark hair. Too soon he released her, and with a gentle nudge he slipped from her and from under the sheets to stand beside the bed. Tara lazily rolled into his warm spot and, with eyes still sealed, sleepily asked, "Sweetie"—her face wiggled deeper into his warm pillow—"what are you doing up this early, the sun isn't even up yet?"

"You have things to do to get ready for your San Francisco drive. You should leave early and I'd just be in your way." He efficiently finished slipping on his pants.

"No silly, we have time, come back to bed, at least until it's light." With that casual expectation of getting what she wants from a man, she flung the sheets off to expose her nude body that stretched and then shivered in the early morning cold.

"Almost nothing else I'd rather do, but I must run off to the cold embrace of a fickle mistress of mine before she disappears, for she's not a patient one and easily slips out of my reach and I know not when she shall reappear," he replied as he pulled the "No Fear" sweatshirt over his head.

"What? What are you jabbering on about?" He was always such a tease to her. Or a coy scoundrel? She did not know.

"Mia Bella. A good man has many a mistress and one true love, no?" he asked, while he leaned over so that she could feel his heat of wanting her kiss.

"No, that's not fine," she pouted. Too tired to fully protest, she showed her displeasure with the simple act of turning her back. He was quicker and lay across her to pin her to the bed. His face in hers, she turned away from his passionate advance. *"No."* He tracked her moves as she feigned disinterest and turned again. They struggled and she rejected him, but she knew he was nothing if not patient with her. She protested once more, and he countered with a hand that slid up to entangle fingers in her silky mane and add resistance to her head that slipped side to side from his. *"No."* She tired . . . and slowed . . . and then struggled no more: *"no."* He moved his lips to hers but did not plant the expected kiss. She exhaled; he breathed in. He exhaled; she pleasantly drew him in.

"My hair's thicker."

"My hair's longer."

"I'm smarter; I've already graduated college."

"You have a kid in college."

"Be nice to me, you have a fiancé-to-be."

"You have a wifey that does not know of me."

"You can be married without a wife, and you can have a wife without being married. And don't ask me to explain what I am talking about for even I don't understand my married relationship, such as it is, nor do I even know how to describe it. And even if I could possibly tell you what was going on, which I can't because I don't know, no one would believe me anyhow, so just let it be."

And for some reason, she believed him, and let it pass . . . for the moment, for her curiosity fixated on his interesting turn of phrase "no one would believe me anyhow." *Really?* Probing on a slightly different front: "And what happened to you anyways? There was a totally weird change that came over you towards the end of the semester. You were so funny and sarcastic bantering questions with the professor, and then all of a sudden you became so quiet and withdrawn."

"And speaking of changes, Mia Bella, why may I ask, with your FTB, did you agree to model for my final project?"

"I really liked your work in class. And why would you choose me anyhow—there are much prettier girls in class?"

"Mia Bella, there is something about you that, just in the way you have of walking, that exudes a woman. I don't know how to explain it."

"Really, you think?"

"And I'm also curious as to why you kept taking another layer of clothing off while I was shooting?"

"I don't know." And she didn't. "I just felt really safe and comfortable with you somehow."

"And do you feel safe and comfortable with me now?" he questioned, slowly grinding into her body.

"Hmm . . ." She moved in rhythm to her lover's music. "I'd like to get a shot of us now," she naughtily whispered.

"Well thank you so much. And there's no way I can't get an A on my final project now, thanks."

"But you wouldn't dare turn in my naked pics would you?"

"Mia Bella, trust me. You'll be nude but not naked. Absolutely beautiful." He felt her tire of his weight and slid off to let her roll away. With her back turned, he laid his warm hand on her shoulder to sensually appreciate her silky-cool skin as they spooned.

She grabbed his hand to guide it across her body and place it comfortably under her bosom and, in that childlike mind of awakening honesty: "You're too old for me."

"Don't be mean . . . I know you're trying to shock me but you're not telling me anything I don't already know, for 'You and me, are not meant to be, and yet that which will never be, conspires to unbind and set us free, free for thee to melt with me, with me forlorn and lost in thee.'"

"Hmm, that's really pretty. Who do you write your poems for? Is that for your mistress that you're leaving me to go and see?" she finished with a back heel into his leg. He reflexively pressed them tighter together.

Patiently in her ear: "I am the sum of all I've ever done, and the sentiments of our former lives I include as well."

"Do you love her?"

"Mia Bella, as I am sure you do, I love many things and many people, but do you for a moment think that if I were in love with another that I would be here with you? Is that the type of man you think I am?"

And then with unfiltered thinking from the deep subconscious on a problem long mulled about, it came. "That's it; you *were* in love with another; that's what happened to you before the winter break, isn't it? What happened?"

"Beauty and brains, you are one dangerous woman."

"I see a sadness in your eyes when you look at another type of woman in class. They remind you of her, don't they?"

"*It burns, it burns Master, please . . . no more.* Yes, you are correct, it makes me sad for what is no more, but I am here with you now; nothing else matters. Besides, I'm still processing, and guys are notoriously not good at sorting through those things so let's give it some time and maybe we'll talk about it later. But I will tell you that you will never know how important you've been in me keeping it together. Your smile and heart have made me man again."

She understood this to be an honest answer in that annoying riddle form of his, peppered with just enough clues to be followed for the truth to be found if patiently tracked to the trail's end. She knew his naïve honesty would allow her to fully explore her questions at another time, but not now. Not sure if she really wanted to know, she went on, "But you also have another mistress?"

"I have many a mistress, none of which takes away from you, but gives me more to love you, to love life."

"Cad." Kick!

"You think that my mistress takes away from you and that I love her more? But no, she opens my life so as to be unafraid to share with you."

"I don't understand. If you have another mistress, then what am I?"

"Why, my lover of course, yes, and there is no other, no? And I am your wanton dalliance, yes? For what else could I be, but simply a woman's affair of the heart, as you have a fiancé-to-be, no?"

Yes, what else could he be? "Then who is your mistress?"

"You would like her for she is ageless and fresh as a breeze with a beautiful surprise every morning. She's a fickle and cold-shouldered bitch, though, that more likely than not will give a hard slap in the face as a 'good morning,' for the sea is a harsh mistress, and I am off to go surfing this morning to catch a swell and share the energy as we share our bodies."

"You tease!" she squealed as she turned into him. "Why didn't you just tell me you're going surfing? Do you have to go now? It's still dark and so cold." She comforted herself as she slipped her hands under his sweatshirt and buried her face in his chest.

"Well, there's not much surf out there today as it's still a building north swell, but you have to go out early before the onshore winds come up to blow out the surf, and you have to stay in shape for you never know when the first big winter swell will roll in."

Her fingers pressed to curiously explore below the surface of those almost-imperceptible points of raised skin caused from the intricately laid steel rods now a part of his spine. "Aren't you scared you're going to get hurt?"

"Oh, you're going to get hurt at some point. For some reason, though, all your anxiety and fears evaporate as soon as you hit the water and start paddling. But when that fear does rise up again out in the water, you try to use that adrenaline rush for a quick burst of speed that can hopefully keep you out of trouble. Nothing like a ten-foot wall of moving water to motivate flagging arms."

"Aren't you too old to be surfing?"

"Oh, thanks, Mia Bella, just keep it coming. You got any more behind that? I may be too old for you but I'll never be too old for surfing, for I've been surfing for long before you, and I will be surfing long after we are no more, because that's all that's left for me is surfing. For once I, too, as you do now, lived in a bubble world of just school and work without any time for thoughts of complicated relationships. I was a boy, even older than you now, yet still full of ideas about circling the world on surfing safaris. And I can still do those things now and still be considered a man. The sad thing is: you won't be considered a full woman until your fanciful notions of love and romance are gone." He breathed long, and slow, and hot into her ear. She sensually arched her neck. He brushed his lips over her closed eyes with those long Spanish-dancer lashes and came to rest upon her pouty lips. She opened and succumbed to the carnal bliss of their heat joining. She luxuriantly stretched flat as he expectantly slid on top. She could feel his erotic heat through his clothes. They began to wrestle in that delightfully warm, touching style of their lovemaking as she feigned reluctance, twisting away with him grappling for control and position, grabbing her hand and pinning it to the top of her head before letting go, catch then release, pin then escape, resist then submit, all body parts continually in play. She looked forward with a thrill to what he would do with her body, partners in bed dancing together in primal rhythm, never a tool to be used and then tossed aside. Their fingers interlaced to tightly clutch before he stretched both her arms overhead, heightening her awareness of his demanding strength and her pleasurable vulnerability. Tara's body flushed and bloomed as he pressed hard and they breathed each other in. He lifted his body to slide his warm lips between her breasts whereupon she felt the cold air rush in from his absence and then the covers were gently laid over her as he quietly tucked her in with a kiss.

"Oh, stayyy . . ."

"The guys are waiting for me. You drive safe today and let me know when you get there. You'll be back by Tuesday for class?"

"Yes, of course." Tara rolled towards him with eyes still too tired to open. "Are we going to do a happy hour before class? We can review our notes and what questions we want to ask the professor about the final exam."

"No, Mia Bella, you do not want to go out with me. Where's your FTB at?"

"Still in New York."

"Call one of your boy toys then. Tell them you're wearing a Bebe short skirt—they will like that."

"Oh, and what would you like me to wear when I next see you . . . my dalliance?"

"Why only your priceless smile of delight, of course, that is all I ever need of you." And with that he was out the door.

Tara drew her legs in to hug them with her arms. Sleepily, she stretched, rolled onto her other side, and slowly lost all conscious thought as the deep folds of night once again wrapped her tight.

~~~~~

Tara gave an exasperated exhale with a glance at her dead cell phone once again. *What the hell,* she thought. And then, within the randomly maneuvering, bustling crowd, she spotted that unmistakable sashay of her ever-fashionable *tía* as she strolled in her brightly gay colors across the long, concrete expanse of Union Square. Such a striking figure, thought Tara, with her auntie's rich, black hair and that colorful silk scarf of haute couture fashionably flared around her neck and shoulders, offsetting her flawless caramel skin and those penetrating black-pearl orbs. And, as her *tía* was so talented in doing, she swept in from afar with that forceful personality of hers to displace one's own difficulties with her own urgent air of self-importance. "Oh, Tara *amor*"—giving her an air kiss of vanity on each cheek before sitting next to her at the outside coffee shop table for two. "*Dios mío,* I am so sorry about your timing, *este es muy horrible*," said Auntie. "And I was so worried about you—you never called or texted back, and I had to come all the way out here to make sure you were okay . . . so inconvenient."

"I don't understand? You're the one who told me to meet you here so I thought we could go shopping for a bit?"

"Yes dear, but that was before. We must have had a water leak all night somewhere between the walls or ceiling of the second floor and sometime after you and I hung up it all came crashing down in such an uproar you wouldn't believe so I thought we were having the *big one* and all the dogs started barking and running around and what a catastrophe. We have a water restoration crew in now and you can't believe the turmoil we're in. We're going to have to move out for a few days and all our plans must change and you simply can't stay with us. I have you in the Francis across the way. And didn't you get any of my messages? And I was so worried about you, you should have called back to let me know."

"No, I'm sorry, I didn't get any messages from you—my battery ran out. When you called you caught me along in Paso Robles and you told me to meet you here so we could go shopping, so that's why I'm here, and then I was talking with Chad until my cell phone died. I was busy last night and forgot to charge it, and then slept in this morning, and in my rush to drive up I didn't notice my car charger missing, and I just thought we were meeting here so we could do some shopping together?"

"Oh no dear, our plans must change as I have to rush back. I just came to make sure you were okay—I was so worried. And how is lovely Chad, such a wonderful boy, have you two set a date yet?"

"No, I've told you we're not technically engaged yet. And nothing's going to happen before I graduate at the end of next semester anyhow. I never should have told anyone that we talked to each other about marriage, I'm not even sure now if we were serious or not." While the conversation itself was true enough, Tara wasn't certain if they were just teasing one another while playing at grownup. *And should he stay, or should he go*—Tara did not really know her heart as of yet. "You guys just keep pestering me. I wish you'd stop until I tell you."

"Well, you're such a lovely couple, and you're such a beautiful girl, and you're not getting any younger you know. Why, when your mother and I were your age we already had three children."

"Yes, I've heard the refrain many times, but this is a different time and place, and with schooling and paying for it by working, things just take longer now."

"And let us do something about your hair while you are up here, dear. We have such talented people in the city and you have such thick, glorious hair from your grandfather that we simply must do something about it."

Wait, what, my hair? Self-conscious and off balance for a moment before quickly ready to play—"Oh *Auntie*"—shifting with the changing sands of Tía, and not to be outdone by her Auntie: "Thank you *sooo* much for inviting me up to shop in San Fran." Tara laughed to herself as Auntie's lips curled sour with Tara's dreaded abbreviation of San Francisco. "And all the *boys* love my hair like this. You *know* what *they* like to do," Tara coyly continued, and with a sly giggle and demure glance, she ran her fingers through her jet-black hair that lay the length of her back. Tara gave herself a congratulatory *you go girl* as she was sure that if Auntie had any milk in her stomach it was curdled by now.

"Yes, of course dear," replied Auntie dryly. "I was only thinking that your father and mother have worked so hard for you, and our family has come so far from the old country, to now be *basura blanca. Comprendes cuando yo hablo en español?*"

"Yes Tía, *yo comprendo Español.* I'm just not very fluent speaking in Spanish and it makes me tired and gives me a headache when I do it for too long."

"Such a shame your parents didn't speak Spanish in the house."

"And that was a different time and place. To speak Spanish was *cholo.* Times have changed now."

"Well, I hope with your children you'll make a concerted effort to bring them up bilingual. So important for the development of their young minds, you know?"

"Yes of course, Auntie, you know I will. Although, it's possible it could be Mandarin if Chad and I break up . . . and I marry a Chinese."

Auntie gives Tara a momentarily confused look before she takes a glance at her chirping cell phone, "*Dios mío,* the dogs have gotten out. I have to run. We have a reservation for you at the absolutely lovely Francis across the way. I'll call you later and we'll make plans for a brunch tomorrow with your uncle and then some shopping with the girls, if we can get this terrible mess of the house under control, *mi hermosa sabrina."* And with an air kiss across the small table, *Tía* is up and quickly walking away with the phone up to her ear, *"Habla con mi . . ."*

~~~~~

Punta pendejo! To no one in particular Tara cursed that bad word for which she did not know the actual definition. *The hotel should be here?* Clickety-clack, clickety-clack, the overnight bag spoke back to her as she pulled it along the sloping sidewalk. *Where the hell? Damn it.* Clickety-clack, clickety-clack. Tara wasn't sure to whom her anger was directed: her Auntie for not giving her a clear idea as to *which* Francis hotel reservations had been made for her, or the hotel clerk for presumably giving her bad directions, or just her plain inattentive, impatient self for only half listening to either? For apparently, as she was dryly educated by the natty front desk clerk, within walking distance of the Square were several hotels of the name she was looking for: Francis, Francis Drake, the St. Francis, and the Francisco, none of which—for the hotel clerk had been very helpful in calling the other hotels—had a reservation for her and all were beyond full with an important world-wide Java plus plus coffee convention. *What, double-shot espresso?* At the deflated, confused look on her face upon hearing there was no place to stay, the clerk had warmed up enough to make a call and reservation for her "around the corner" at the Pacific Plaza. The clerk had warned her that it was not in a bad part of town, but the Tenderloin was certainly not a good part of town, so she should pay attention and keep moving quickly along.

Clickety-clack, clickety-clack, in the gathering dark under a winter's stormy clouds with a heavy mist that lazily floated in the air, and was surely about to thicken to a drizzle, and a few yards down a quiet side street, Tara had to admit she was now all turned around and didn't know which way she was to go. Clickety-clack, clickety . . . and then she stopped. *Which way, up or down?* But she was now definitely pissed at something very definitive: *damn dead cell. And whose fault might that be?* She retorted with an exasperated sigh.

A well-lit, heavily foot-trafficked street was just a few seconds walk upwards, but she felt self-conscious about approaching a sidewalk stranger or entering a convenience store, for which English would presumably be the clerk's second language, and asking for directions all the while pulling along a carry-on bag. She could feel the presence of the old, gray buildings that reached high overhead and that quickly absorbed the last of the fading light and the now, as expected, light drizzle that gently fell to dampen hair and shoulders and gave an impending warning of a heavier rain to come. And then she spotted a disheveled, darkened mound of blankets, bags, and paper lying three steps up upon the landing of a sheltered doorway. Face to the wall and back to the wind, *a true San Fran bum, yes*, she gave an excited silent laugh that heightened her awareness of her situation and a challenge to herself: Would she dare? Such a curious response one might think for a young woman alone, in a strange part of an unknown neighborhood, past sunset. However, an image of her playful *dalliance*, who teased and toyed with her often, came to her, of his story when on Wall Street long ago, walking lost and confused long after the bars' closing time, searching for his hotel in a winter's blustery mess. And so Tara walked two steps up and gave the indigent a gentle toe poke and, naturally, as one adjusting to having prodded a strange creature in its natural environment, a silent squeal to herself and a half step back. Nothing. Next she put her heel in his back and gently pushed as she said, "Excuse me sir." Tara cringed and looked up and down the momentarily quiet street for a white knight in shining armor. None was forthcoming. With the next push, Tara leaned her body into her foot and rolled him into the door with a thump, "Ooooha, owwwa, sorry."

"Hey officer, I was just resting. I'm mov'n along," he slurred.

"Here's five dollars for waking you up and another five dollars for when you get me to the Pacific Plaza," Tara offered as he sat up and looked at her with dull eyes and pokey hair that reached out in a multitude of directions. Tara's stomach gave a flip as she got a whiff of something long dead wafting as he awkwardly arose to stir the air from under his many layers of never-washed blankets. Tara would never speak of this to Chad, for if he knew Tara had actually touched such a creature, she was sure they would never get naked together again. He was most fastidious about cleanliness and staying in chiseled shape and he looked it, *mmm*. She pushed that thought aside for the moment. "You do know where the Pacific Hotel is?"

"Yes ma'am, just down the street. To the Pacifico Hotel, right now ma'am." And with that the indigent gently reached out with his tattered woolen gloves missing a few fingers to the offered greenback. "Thank you ma'am, thank you much." He shed many layers cloaked about him to let them fall where they might and as he slowly stepped off that partially sheltered porch, leaning heavily upon the railing: "This way, this way, just a bit down. You want me pulling your bag? No problem, the gentlemanly thing to do."

"You're so kind, but no thank you, I have it handled."

"Kinda like a lady an' her purse, huh?"

Upon landing on the sidewalk, this incongruent pair, one a shifty and mysterious chameleon of the streets that shuffled along in short but quick stutter steps, the other stunningly beautiful, brightly gay, and stepping along with those long, confident strides of the agile, were off together in a falling mist along the wet streets of this now very exciting city indeed, clickety-clack, clickety-clack . . .

As she trailed along behind, Tara felt safe and had a confidence in this man of indeterminate age who she thought was surely much younger than his deeply weathered face appeared, for she saw the fabled truth of those fanciful stories in his glassy eyes that were slow to focus, and the words from lips that were difficult to purse, and a dry tongue that had a hard time rolling and articulating letters, and in his slow-motion movements that appeared weighted with the constant resistance of a great atmospheric pressure. Tara did not doubt the strength of his whisper-thin frame whose bulk came from the many articles of layered clothing worn, for he was a man and she still a woman, but rather her rationale was based on his mental acuity and physical speed, which were very much slowed from what Tara could only assume was a lifetime of substance abuse, and that left Tara with the ability to see through his thinking process and be faster to escape should any of those thoughts or his actions be untoward. And so she concluded this slow-witted, nonthreatening man with his childlike demeanor of forthright honesty and with unfiltered compassion and understanding was a perfectly secure companion upon these strange and darkened streets.

"Watch your step on that elevator plate, ma'am. The metal's slippery like ice when wet. Just down this way, not far. You're one pretty lady, a real woman, smells nice, too, you do, you don't see often in these parts. You here for the convention? We have lots of conventions here nowadays what with all the techie yuppies and whatnot. Some puttin' a lot of money this a-ways buying up places to be in town. You gonna be buying a place? I know some nice lofts just around the corner that would sell at not too bad a price if I say, and not too sketchy a neighborhood at all. Better 'an this, anyhow. How much ya thinkin' of spendin'?"

Tara couldn't help but laugh at this stranger who spoke as if they were the most fast of friends. "No, not buying anything. I'm up here for a few days visiting family and friends."

"That's nice. Family's the most important. Who you up here visiting, if you don't mind my askin'?"

"No problem. I was supposed to stay with my aunt and uncle just over in one of the painted ladies, but they had a water pipe burst and looks like everyone is out for a few days until they can fix the mess."

"Oh, *sweeeet*. I could tell from the first you was a classy lady from a nice family. Those Victorians are mighty nice an' grand. So your family is loaded?"

Tara laughed. "Well, my uncle has done well."

"Here we is." He stopped in front of a hip-high wall containing a small patio with a few empty restaurant tables and chairs of bare metal.

Tara was confused, for the entrance appeared to be for a disco with a gouache-painted exterior of an ocean blue that had badly faded and a wrought-iron grate crisscrossing what once was a storefront display, the glass now coated in a layer of blackout paint. "This looks like a bar. Is this the Pacific Plaza Hotel?"

"No ma'am. The door on the left is the bar and that door to the right is the Pacifico Hotel. The Pacific Plaza is a little farther down, if you like?"

"What?" Tara thought for a moment. "Okay, we're here, but is this place"—she hesitated—"safe?"

"Oh yes ma'am, very safe. I wouldn't take a classy lady like yourself any place that wasn't. Check it out. I'll wait here. I don't think they'd want anybody like me in their lobby. It's okay, go check it out, go, go."

Tara was pleasantly surprised walking off the gritty street into an aesthetically pleasing, postmodern lobby that was tastefully done in that minimalist, utilitarian fashion. In the air was the smell of the fresh and the new from recent construction, from the lacquer on the distressed wood floor that stretched from wall to wall, and that forthright, functional leather furniture of the 1950s, and the Picasso-esque wall paintings adding tasteful colors to the room. This city continually was full of surprises for Tara, for behind the desk was a person of . . . indeterminate sex. "Um, hey there, ah . . . would you have a room available for this evening."

"Yes, we have a few rooms available."

The nasal monotone voice offered Tara no clue. "'Kay 'kay, I'll be right back." Tara stepped out of the entrance. "Hey, here's your other five I promised. Thank you so much. Don't spend it all in one place, and be safe." Back inside, Tara eyed the slightly overweight clerk, wearing a plaid shirt cut with colorful suspenders, with a plump face and small breasts or man boobs, and with white, sun-shy skin that made darker the close-cropped, tightly wound, jet-black hair. "One for one night, please . . . Charlie." The name tag gave no help either. *Whichever, whatever?* "And is that clock on the wall correct? I'm supposed to be at Riley's in thirty minutes to meet a friend. Do you know it? Is it far?"

This person, man or woman, turned out to be another caring soul and offered to wait for Tara to unpack and freshen up and to then escort her in what would be a short walk over to Riley's. As promised, Charlie was waiting after her change of shift, and, as they stepped out the lobby door, grabbed Tara's arm to pull her in tight and keep the umbrella over her freshly brushed hair. Arriving at Riley's, Charlie had sent Tara in with the umbrella. "You need it more than me, honey. I don't have time for a pint; I have to get home to my cats. Tell the barkeep Charlie dropped you off; they all know me and will treat you right. Return the umbrella in the morning. Bye-bye now." And with that Charlie was off at a fast clip with collar pulled up and head bowed, uncovered in the falling rain.

~~~

"So, where are you from?" asked the woman on the stool next to her.

"What?" Tara replied self-consciously as she leaned over the bar to plug in her cell phone. "Why would you ask me that?" Tara feigned being busy as she continued to attend to her phone.

The barkeep had rhetorically questioned her: "Really, you're asking me for a cell phone charger? You're the first person who has ever requested a charger in this bar." He had then pulled out a small box with every available device. Tara had sorted through the box to pull out the one that fit her phone and passed it to the barkeep to be plugged into an outlet under the counter.

Ki—the woman sitting on the stool next to her—provided Tara a patient pause with a sip from her wineglass held by soft, feminine hands that flashed exquisitely manicured French-tip nails.

Tara turned her phone on and sat down, waiting for it to boot up.

"Why this is San Francisco, my dear," Ki said with a disarming smile of sweet seduction that caught Tara off guard. "Very subdued, natural makeup, just a tad too much for this city though, but not bright enough for LA. Those Wicked boots scream New York, but your ensemble is too unrestrained with color, not the all-in-black de rigueur. A Latina from the Northwest is so rare, and your warm layering is too light for the Midwest. Hmm, and not a trace of accent. You are an enigma for the moment. And really, a Malibu Pineapple?"

Huh, this is something different from LA, Tara had thought upon entering Riley's. Inside was what Tara expected, a quaint and intimate Irish pub with a long wooden bar intricately carved and comfortable, cushioned booths opposite, and a glowing, warm fireplace on the back wall with a few tables and chairs set around. But it was the crowd that altogether set itself apart from what she had supposed. Only a quarter full, the bar was a mix of young and old, mostly men but a sprinkling of women, some casually dressed in drab and plaid for blustery weather outside and some in snappy hipster attire accented with a beret or fedora. Not at all the homogenous bar scene one typically sees in Los Angeles: either dressed all in black, or slick-suited Hollywood agents, or pierced and tattooed Goths, or vest- and fedora-wearing hipsters, or any other number of the stratified crowds one anticipates in the typical LA bar or lounge. And now Tara was the one feeling that middle-school awkwardness of being picked out of the playground as the one not belonging.

"Here you go dear." The barkeep smiled as he placed the bright fruity drink with two red straws and a cherry on top. "Sorry, we don't have any pineapple slices but I could get you an orange or lime slice if you like?"

Tara could only offer an embarrassed half smile at her new bar mate, with whom pleasantries had been exchanged upon purposely sitting down next to another woman, not wanting to be single and alone in an unknown bar. "No thank you, I'm good, thanks." Tara made a subtle, surreptitious review of the woman several years older than herself with those rosy cherub cheeks of baby fat and a cute button nose. Ki had looked up from scrolling through her tablet, her pretty face framed with naturally wavy hair of golden-cornflake blonde with curly bangs that hung between brow and eye, and offered with a smile upon Tara's questioning intrusion: "Yes of course, please sit."

Ki's expectant wait was once again rudely interrupted with an insistent *ding-ding, beep-beep, chirp-chirp* announcing awaiting voice mails, text messages, and social media of all sorts.

"Oh my god, oh my god, so sorry," expressed Tara as she quickly reached for her phone. "I can't believe this is happening, so embarrassing." She looked to Ki and saw laughing eyes that brought a smile to Tara's face, reciprocated by Ki's own flash of white teeth and a giggle, which together grew to laughing. "I am so sorry." Tara put a hand upon her chest in an attempt to control herself. "So embarrassing."

Ki placed a reassuring hand on her shoulder. "Yes dear, you are the first person ever whose phone has unexpectedly gone off in a quiet bar."

Tara was glad she had chosen to sit next to this delightfully warm woman, who plainly took some fun in teasing her. "Give me a moment? I was supposed to meet a friend of mine here this evening but the cell has been dead all day, so this will take a minute." Tara began to ramble to her bar mate in that open and sharing nature of hers: "Oh oh, so Marsha's daughter, Arianna, is sick with a fever and can't make it out, poor baby. That's why she's not here. I'll just let her know I love the place she picked and I've met an interesting new friend"—as she glanced up to Ki. Tara was one of those lucky few who could type and talk at the same time: "Oh, and I'll let my auntie know I'm at the Pacifico Hotel and not have her worry with all the details of how I got there, and have her let me know about brunch tomorrow."

After some time typing, Ki noticed Tara's face turn concerned. "Everything okay, dear?"

"Yeah, fine, just my fiancé is all bent out of shape because he thinks I hung up on him today when my phone went dead and I haven't called him back and he's flying in tomorrow and wants me to pick him up at LAX for what he says is an important business dinner of his." Tara looked to Ki. "Oops, I wasn't going to tell you; I was going to make you work for it. Well, technically we're not engaged per se"—type, type, type—"not until the end of next semester when I graduate, and then he wants to move from New York to LA, but I'm pretty sure I have a few New York internships lined up with some fabulous designers that I want to do, so it's getting all complicated. And Chad has a trust fund so why can't he just stay in New York for another year anyhow?"

"Is Chad bi?"

"No, what? Chad is my fiancé; he's not gay."

"No silly, is he bicoastal," Ki explained with a teasing smile of an unstated meaning that had left Tara a tad confused.

"Oh." A light of awareness shone.

"So how did your soon-to-be fiancé, Chad, and you first meet?"

"Oh it was way cool and so natural," Tara started up. Type, type, type. "I was at this house party with a few friends and he just comes up to me so casual and naturally and goes like, 'How's your day going?' and all, not like you're so beautiful or you're so pretty, you know? I'm so down to casual guys like that, right?" Tap, tap, tap.

"Yeah, right, me too."

"Well, anyhow, my friends and I chatted with him and he was so cute, pretending he was talking to everyone but I knew he was interested in me and then he asked all of us if we would like to go waterskiing on his boat sometime out on the lake, with Jim, the guy's house we were at for the party, and we all said, 'for sure, that would be lovely,' and he used that as his excuse to get my number, so cute, huh? Anyhow, we talked on the phone for like an hour that night and he asked some really personal questions and I'm like laughing, telling him, 'we haven't gotten there yet.' And then we chat again the next morning and then later that night he like left a voice mail about one in the morning that I didn't get 'til later saying how well we get along an' all and how he likes me, you know being sweet and all? And I just somehow got the feeling he wasn't a partier and all, I could tell that about him. And he asked if it bothers me at all that he went out with Cindy, one of the groupies to Jim's house parties, you know? And I said like 'no way because I don't hang with her people and all,' and he goes, 'like way cool then.' How sweet is that, huh? And I'm like, hmmm, mmmmm. Anyhow, we just seem to fit really nice and naturally, and started going together. Then we started talking about him helping me get a New York internship after graduation with all his connections in the city . . . and we were laughing about it at the time. And now it seems he doesn't want me in New York and wants to come out to live in LA. Anyhow, complications among us." Type, type, type . . . send. "There, that should get him up-to-date and keep him happy for a while. Men are so funny, all masculine and macho-independent, and then they can just get so clingy and controlling sometimes, pretty crazy, huh?"

"Yeah, tell me about it. So here's to the men we can live without." Ki raised her glass to Tara's Malibu Pineapple sans pineapple slice for a toast.

Tara took a nice sip of her sweet drink before she turned back to her phone. "Okay, one more, I swear I'm done."

I know you are okay, but just be nice and let me know to put a smile upon my face, or otherwise, off to the prof go those naked shots! xo.

Tara giggled at her *dalliance's* text. Type, type. "There, done," she said as she placed the still-plugged-in phone in the relative safety of a dry napkin on the bar.

"That was a queer message?"

"Ha, that's a funny one in San Fran." Tara gave her an innocent sideways glance, knowing Ki could not possibly have read any of the details upon her display screen. "What, you're serious?"

"I do know that the shortest message is the only one that brought a smile to your face and is the only one you readily dismissed with a two-word response?"

"Oh, just a friend from photography class asking about our final exam next week."

"Sure, a one-liner from a photography classmate with no profile pic and no name, just a phone number, and then you deleted the entire thread? Just a friend? We all need more friends like that."

Tara flushed at the uncovered indiscretion.

Ki leaned in close with a lingering study of Tara's averted eyes before continuing. "Really, a mysteriously dark woman put together in a beautifully eclectic style I've never seen before comes walking into my bar and sits next to me and you don't think I'm not going to notice every little thing? But hey, we all have our own layers of personal secrets, I understand that. So, tell me, what were you and your friend you were meeting here this evening going to do later?"

In that first blush of excitement meeting someone of interest that you instantly trust and bond with, Ki and Tara each quickly warmed to the other's still-youthful energy and vibrant enthusiasm from romantic dreams as of yet unfulfilled. As they redily enjoyed the company of one another's open and sharing dialogue, their conversation bantered along from the common touchstone of fashion and family, and in the course of time, as women are wont to do and men but fear to tread, to delve around the edges of those complicated romantic relationships and obligations that women seem to enjoy playing with like any cherubic six-month-old is delighted in the splashing of their bathwater.

The evening whiled along in that quick-talking, animated cadence of still-young-at-heart women, and in a pause of their confidential girl chatting with a sip on the second round of those delicious drinks, Tara and Ki's conversation was interrupted by their bar-stool neighbor's introduction. "Hey there, my name's Ted. I was wondering if I could ask you ladies a personal relationship question. I wasn't eavesdropping or anything, but I heard you talking about boyfriends and I had a question."

Tara and Ki gave each other a curious, sideways glance and expectantly turned to him to ask, "Yes?"

"Well, I want you two to know I like women; I love women," Ted said.

The women turned to each other with wide-open eyes, and with Ki grabbing one of Tara's hands, they gave one another a squeeze and a questioning look of *Okay?*

"But I have this girlfriend you see that I really, really like, and I haven't called her in three weeks, and I was wondering if I was in trouble?" continued Ted.

Tara and Ki both started to giggle as they squeezed each other's hands tightly. Tara leaned in towards Ted with her soft doe eyes with those black-pearl orbs and said with a soothing voice, "Oh Ted, yes you are in trouble, but call her now, as any woman in San Francisco should be happy any time a real man gives her a call."

Tara and Ki started to giggle uncontrollably as they hugged one another. Ki grabbed the cell off the bar to place it in Tara's hand and pulled her off the bar stool. "Come with me, let's bounce."

"The tab," Tara said as she grabbed her purse.

"They know me."

Out the pub door they bolted; Ki latched on to Tara with a directional shove upon her waist. "Wait," Tara said, as she stopped short to snap open her borrowed umbrella. Ki pulled them in tight against the cold air as they briskly set off together, fast friends with arms about waists, down the wet street popping in bursts of raindrops. The blustery night was an unexpectedly welcome change from the warm pub and alcohol glow of Tara's Malibu Pineapple, a favorite of hers when lounging in a bar's shady patio along the beachside path. Her friends would always teasingly sit Tara upon a stool along the hip-high wall, squealing with delight at the crashing commotion of skaters and bikers lingering to look just a tad too long upon her naturally well-endowed figure that no bikini top could contain.

"Taxi," Ki called as her arm shot out.

~~~~~

Breathing the crisp, fresh air of a wet and wild evening had cleansed the cavities of Tara's nose and so she was suddenly awakened to the wonderful variety of unique aromas and smells emanating from a working kitchen in full bloom as they stepped off the sidewalk through the glass door of a small restaurant. *Garlic, garlic, garlic, yes,* thought Tara, *the heavy-handed stamp of an Italian kitchen.* But wait, and slowly she processed and discriminately distinguished through the many scents to separate and find the rosemary and the oregano mixed in with that patiently simmering tomato marinara, and a few other smells that she could not quite define and put a name to. *Hmmm, yummy.*

"Ki bella, so wonderful to see you again," said in an Italian accent.

"Giovanni."

"How are you, my dear?" He placed a hand on her thin waist to lean in with a kiss to one cheek and then the other. "And who is your lovely friend?"

"Tara, Giovanni. Giovanni, Tara."

"So wonderful to meet you, and thank you for coming. *Mi casa es tu casa.*"

"*Gracias por tenerme in su casa.*"

"*Mi niño encantador, tú iluminas nuestra casa, tú iluminas nuestras vidas.*"

"Why thank you so much, I'm sure, but sorry, *gracias* is the limit of my conversational Spanish. That and, *dos más cervezas por favor,* ha."

"Oh, and your accent is so Castilian distinct. Spain or Argentina?"

"Argentina, from way back in the day, as they say."

Giovanni leaned in to whisper in Ki's ear. "We are busy yes, so follow my lead." He stepped back to the podium and in a loud voice to be heard in the noisy atrium: "You are late and we should not have held your table this long, but you are lucky and the previous guests have just left, so follow me please." Giovanni took them through the full restaurant in a U-turn around a dividing wall to seat them next to the large viewing window overlooking the sidewalk. "A bottle of Pinot Noir, of course my dear?"

"No thank you, Giovanni. In fact, my new friend here has never had pizza *and* beer together, so that's what we are going to have, please. It seems I shall be her first. Your recommendation of course."

"Peroni Italian beer, it will be then. You'll find it much lighter than our fellow English or German beers so as not to overpower the flavors of the food. You will like it. And the pizza? Vegetarian for you and your friend?"

"No, not necessarily. Apparently my new friend here is both a breeder and a meat eater." The joke was lost upon Tara as she was temporarily distracted watching the pedestrian traffic passing by.

"What? No, I'm good with whatever," Tara responded, when she noticed both sets of eyes turned to her with a questioning look.

~~~

Freshly baked bread and basil, thought Tara, *of course, hmm,* as their hot pizza with that brick-oven perfection of a golden-crisp crust and ripe-red tomato slices with deep-green basil leaves over a background of melted mozzarella cheese was presented by their young waiter properly bending at the waist. With all the well-anticipated comic relief of watching one managing those multiple cheese strands that stretch and stretch until snapped and then dangle to swing in the air for a moment prior to being swiped up with the spatula, a slice upon a plate was served to both.

"Selfie," proclaimed Ki, as she came around and sat on Tara's lap. "Hold your beer up with the label out for the commercial . . . cheese! Firsties. I can't believe you've never had pizza and beer before?"

"I know, pretty crazy huh?"

"Crazy, crazy. Yummy, yummy, just like our waiter, huh? So tell me something, are you in love with Chad?" Ki casually intoned prior to taking a bite.

"What!? Yes, yes, of course, we're soon to be engaged. Why would you even ask such a question?"

She doth protest too loudly. "Oh I don't know, maybe because you still seem to have a wandering eye checking out all the guys. You can't deny you gave our waiter a look over?"

"Ah, well he was so cute, don't you think?"

"Yes, quite so of course, but somehow I get this feeling you just like the way trust-fund Chad hangs on your arm as the good-looking couple, that's all. When you were at that house party when you met Chad, how did he actually make you *feel* the first time you saw him?"

"Wow, that's so funny you should ask. I was just thinking about that party again drinking beer," responded Tara as she finished hers and motioned for *dos más por favor*. Tara remembered and explained to Ki how she had noticed Chad when he first walked into the room and he had given her a good, long, hard look up and down that made her feel all girly inside before approaching her group to chat, and how everyone said they were such a good-looking couple. Quickly catching herself: "Yeah but that's not it, we do love each other."

"So were you enthralled with that first look and smitten in love?"

"No no, you have to spend time with someone and then decide if you love them. You choose who you love."

"Oh, *mon bébé*. That may be the nice way it should happen but you can simply fall in love at first sight and then you're screwed because you can like someone and not love them, and you can love someone without being in love, but the absolute hell is to be in love with some-one that you don't even really like. You can't choose who you love, love chooses you."

"There's no way that's possible. You have to find out who they are to see if you like them, and then you can choose to love them, or just choose not to love them, simple."

"No, you cannot control what or how you feel for another per-son, no matter what they may or may not have done to you, you can only choose how you act out on those feelings—either as a conscious, caring human being, or if they've messed and whacked with you, as a wounded, vindictive animal."

"So I take it then you've fallen in love at first sight?"

"A few times actually, I hope to stop one day. Believe it or not, I once heard a laugh that clutched me and I turned to see a group of people with no one laughing anymore, and in that instant I could pick out the one person that had laughed, and that I had already fallen in love with."

"And?"

"We loved each other but sometimes it doesn't work out. I don't really actually know but somehow I think I incidentally screwed up and they were merciless and just disappeared, no conversation, no good-bye. So that has made me a lot more tolerant of others' mistakes now."

"So *saad*. What, you don't see him around anymore? You're not still friends?"

"Ha, no no, never friends. In or out, everything or nothing. For me it's always still love anyhow so just too much pain to keep seeing them. Well then, Tara"—Ki cast a mischievous glance—"with a fiancé soon to be, tell me truly how you felt the first time your photography classmate looked you over, and don't be coy with me."

Tara flushed as she returned Ki's questioning gaze, and then with a drink of courage, she slowly started to explain how curiously different was that first look when she had walked into class and had seen those sad puppy-dog blues simply gazing into hers, as if into her soul, never taking his eyes off her face, until finally she had to turn away. *Huh.* She explained to Ki, for she could not sort through her strange impression and whether he was aloof or just a self-absorbed asshole, or was he plumbing something of her that she herself could not as yet comprehend? "But anyhow, everyone had warmed up to each other in class because we have to critique each other's work and some of his battles with the professor defending others' style of shooting were quite comical, because a lot of what we do is so subjective, and oh my god, it was especially funny when he defended this one pic taken of some horses behind a fence that was shot from a moving car, the whole class was rolling, and then we started assisting each other, and anyhow I just happened be his final's portrait project. Pretty crazy, huh?" Tara finished with a weak smile to Ki and a tingly giggle of remembrance to herself at his veiled threat.

"I wish I were the one-line text that made you laugh when read," Ki uttered as a wistful whisper of desire.

"Lovely ladies, and how are we enjoying our pizza and beer?" Giovanni asked as he made the rounds as the attentive host. "I hope everything meets with your expectations, no?"

Tara and Ki pulled away from each other to effusively thank Giovanni for his hospitality and delicious food. Tara made special note of the fresh basil leaves, a distinctive flavor that will linger fondly in the swell of her memory.

As Giovanni moved along, and the women's attention turned to enjoying their pizza and beer in the hustle and bustle of the busy restaurant, theirs became a warm, comfortable silence of having someone close. And so in their warmhearted glow and in the confines of other amiable patrons, they eavesdropped on a nearby conversations or two and, with guilty pleasure, exchanged conspiratorial smiles and looks to one another. As the night lengthened and the falling rain lessened, they took note of the increasing foot traffic that passed by. Tara felt a satisfying glow.

"You good?"

"Yes, very much so. And you?"

"Yes, very much so."

"Let's bounce."

~~~

Arm in arm up a steep and narrow street of North Beach, with a closed umbrella, the rain having abated for the moment, they walked the busy sidewalk, occasionally catching a brief lick or two of music overflowing out the doors of several clubs they passed until Ki pulled Tara into a corner pub that beckoned to them with that wavy reverb of a jamming steel guitar in a surfer-rock band. Past the door bouncer, Tara once again took note of a mixed crowd of young and old, and of the animated instrumental foursome upon a slightly raised stage that was crowded around with couples and single women dancing in rhythm to amplified music. Tara caught the riff and could not help but move her body in step with the beat as she lip-synced along with the harmonious vocals that were so well known. As they slid up to an open slot at the bar, Ki took the umbrella and hung it on one of the hooks underneath. The ornately cut and crafted dark wooden bar reminded Tara of an old Western gunslinger movie with the chiseled stars wearing either white hats or black hats and those leather belts worn askew to place the holster at midthigh of the favored hand for quick reach of their pearl-handled and silver-barreled revolvers.

Ki leaned into Tara's ear. "Time for dessert. I'm going to order us a couple brandy separators . . . you'll like."

"Hmm, sounds delish . . ." Tara's head nodded on the full beat as her hand tapped into the air at the keyboard's quarter notes. She felt a wisp of something at her back and turned to see a younger woman, layered in what apparently, she was coming to understand, was the de rigueur bundle of natural cloth fibers in subdued colors and wearing comfortable shoes, delicately playing with her hair.

"Oh my gosh, I just love your hair. It's so hella long and beautiful, and I'm so jealous," said the lady with short and spiky jet-black hair—which was so easy to maintain out of the shower—as their eyes caught.

Tara was flattered that someone had actually commented on her hair, for no one ever did that back in LA, and so she responded with, "Why thank you, that is so nice of you to say. And your hair looks fabulous; your pink accent streaks are just darling."

"Yeah, but your hair is so long and thick and dark, and I am so jealous. Must take hours? And I don't know anyone that could grow-out like that anyhow, and all I have is this—" She tugged at her spikes. "You are so lucky. So, where are you from?"

Tara laughed to herself: *Really, is there nothing of me that is not that obvious, even my hair now?* She chatted with her new acquaintance to explain that she was up from Los Angeles visiting friends and family, with an introduction to Ki upon her return with their layered tan-and-cream drinks.

"Come on"—Ki pulled on Tara—"last song before the band's break, so let's dance." Onto the dance floor they went, slow rocking along with drinks overhead in that mellow rhythm of a cover song everyone has grown up with, the crowd loudly filling in the refrain as backup chorus.

"I could use another drink of whatever that was please." Tara handed Ki her empty glass as they headed back to the bar.

"Whoa girl, take it easy. It may be sweet but it's called a separator because it separates your mind from your body without you ever feeling a thing."

"Yes please, another."

"OMG girl, stay close."

"Hey, I'm Nagai," said the tall, chiseled Asian gentleman whom Tara had accidentally bumped and saddled up next to as they squeezed along the crowded bar. "That felt good for me, and for you?"

For some reason, Tara found it rather funny that there was absolutely no trace of an accent in Nagai's voice as he spoke, rather like a nationally broadcast news anchor, and in her open and friendly nature, fueled with an exotic elixir, she openly commented so.

"You don't know of any Asians that don't have accents?" he asked with a flash of his big, white smile.

"Oh my goodness, I have no idea why I said that, I am so sorry. No no, I go to school with some Asians and some have accents of course, but most don't. And I am so sorry, dumbness among us."

"Here you go, dear." A strikingly tall blonde with a baby bump returned from the bar to hand Nagai his cocktail.

"Thank you, love. This here is my wife, Ava, and Ava this is our new friend . . . ?"

"Tara." Tara checked herself, admiring this good-looking couple, who were such the inverse of her and Chad, as Ki's commentary resonated somewhere within. For whereas Tara was a chesty Latina with long, flowing charcoal hair, Ava had a very German St. Pauli Girl look, with boy-cut, short blonde hair that was pulled straight forward to frame her lovely face with high cheeks. She had a lanky runner's body, innocent of breasts, and was quite tall, for it was a rare occurrence indeed for Tara, while wearing full heels, to have to look up to another woman. And Nagai, with his dark features and jet-black hair, was so unlike Chad's Eastern European, light complexion.

"Tara, Tara that think me quite funny for not having an Asian accent, *chop chop.*"

"Oh my word, so embarrassing. You're not going to let that go, are you?"

"Are you kidding? A Latina commenting on an Asian's accent, that's as priceless as it comes and will last forever. To new friends, *kanpai!*" he says as he raises his glass for a toast. *"Kanpai!"* in chorus as Nagai is then left hanging in the air solo, for neither Tara nor Ava have a drink in hand. "Oh well, that's embarrassing," he adds with a laugh and a sip. "So Tara, where you from?"

"Really, is there a sign on me or something? Why does everybody keep asking me that?"

"Why I just assumed the class that you were speaking of was for acting or modeling and as such you have a professional stylist that puts together your outfits, so you must be up here from LA for some sort of gig?"

Ki returned with Tara's separator and, after introductions, Tara wove for the expectant audience the interesting story line of her unglamorous, wet, and lost arrival from Los Angeles into their fair city for a visit with family and friends. And as for the eclectic match of clothing that adorned her so gloriously, thank you, she explained it was of her own fashion sense, of which she actually owned only one article outright. For it was only those fabulously slender, knee-high, leather lace-up boots with spike heels that in fact she had purchased; the rest were borrowed or stolen or inherited. The skirt had surreptitiously escaped unbeknownst from her sister's closet; the blouse she wore was from the Melrose boutique she worked at while the puffy scarf elegantly wrapped around her neck to drape over one shoulder was on loan from her roommate; her shawl she inherited from her grandmother; and the belt with the intricately-laced silver flashing was of her own personal design and handmade by a friend and worn for the marketing of such.

"You're in the fashion industry then—that makes sense."

"Well, not per se, I hope to be soon. I work at my friend's boutique on Melrose that has a large wardrobe inventory in the back for studio rentals, which can get pretty crazy sometimes, and that's how I got to borrow this blouse, and I'm going to be there until I finish my bachelor's degree this summer. Then, who knows what, off to the Manhattan fashion scene hopefully?"

"My turn then," Nagai said with a Cheshire grin of mirth and folly to follow. "*Oh, so sorry,*" he comically intoned in a sing-song voice. "You seem a little old to still be in college?"

The twist of the joke was not lost upon Tara. "Yeah thanks, I think. I'm so brilliant it's taking me eight years to get a four-year college degree. I spent my first year studying fashion at FIDM and then got this fantastic internship for another year working in New York at Parisian Couture, for free of course, before I decided I wanted to get my BS marketing instead. So now that's two years wasted, and all my money is gone and now I have to work and go to school at the same time. And in doing all that, I screwed up and missed a required arts class that I'm taking at City now, and I have to finish with an Accounting Two class, which is only offered at State and only in the second semester and I start night class in two weeks."

"Tell you what, Tara"—Nagai looked to his wife, then back to Tara—"give me your number. I'm going to text you an address just across the Golden Gate in Sausalito. We're having a brunch tomorrow in a mock-up warehouse for some friends and business partners that I'd love for you to attend. In two months' time my wife and I and my designing partner are opening a clothing boutique with half our own line in a new place called Tender Alley. It's a new, built-out alley just behind the Francis Hotel in the Tenderloin, which you now seem to know. The alley has been torn out and repaved with cobblestone and the building faces all stripped and redone with large storefront windows, and there's a bunch of entrepreneurs going in with new restaurants and salons and no-name boutiques. We're taking a great chance that people will like what we have and make the walk around the corner to our upscale, pedestrian-only alley. It's really exciting and adventurous, and, I have no idea how, but I love your energy and what I see about you, and I think you would be a real asset to us and I'd love for you to be a part of what we're doing. So swing on by tomorrow and meet the group. From what I know of you, you'll love what you'll see and the people you'll meet, they're all high-end energy and simply amazingly talented. No promises."

"Wow, wow, I don't know what to say? It's such a crazy incredible offer . . . wow there's so much . . . but I don't really know if I can?"

"Tara, you have a talent for something and I don't know what that is but I am willing to gamble and pay you to find out. You rarely regret things that you do, even if you fail, but it is those missed opportunities, generally, that scare the crap out of you, that you turn down, that you regret for the rest of your life."

"Well thank you so much but as I've told you I've got to finish this one class for my degree, and I've spent eight years doing it, and I just have to finish, you understand, don't you?"

"Tara, I understand perfectly and we'll take care of it, but you have to realize we're all good—only those that recognize luck presented to them and run with it are the most successful. There are three state schools up here that any professor or dean would bend over backwards to get an eighth-year senior a seat in one class to graduate, no problem. So let me share with you a little story that I don't believe I've ever told anyone else before. After taking six years to graduate, myself, I went back to San Diego to party one last spring break with friends and pick up my diploma, as I finished in December without the pomp and circumstance, and before starting a position in Silicon Valley. Anyhow, at the window, the clerk informed me that I had never completely withdrawn from one psychology class my freshman year, that I thought I had dropped, and I could not graduate until I got either a passing grade or was signed off as dropped, and that only could be done by the professor, or the dean of the college, or the university president, and I had two hours, as noon was the cutoff or it would be six months before they would process diplomas again. So, the professor was on vacation, they could not find the dean, but the university president's secretary said he would see me. Now why a university president on a campus of thirty thousand students would see me was . . . maybe what? A matter of luck? Because I was on the school newspaper and had met him twice prior and maybe he remembered me, really? Anyhow, his secretary had me cool my heels for an hour waiting, and time was running out. Finally she tells me to go in, and I'm all ready to roar with my story and pleadings, and that my new job requires my diploma, and I walked into his office and just completely lost it. Around his conference table were the eight deans of colleges with all their eyes turned to me. Tara, to this day I don't even remember what happened or what was said; it's all just a blur. And why the university president signed off the withdrawal slip for some stammering, incoherent Japanese kid, I have no idea. But I knew I was lucky and I've run with that luck, and any others that have been presented to me that I don't really deserve. So, no promises, simply take the time tomorrow to see our fashion line and meet our fabulous people that you'll be immensely impressed with and will love."

"Okay Nagai, no promises, I'm already so overbooked as it is, and I don't think I'll have a fiancé anymore if I do. But I have to tell you I am totally nervous about walking into a roomful of professional people that already know each other and I'm the awkward odd duckling out, you know?"

"Tara, I would find it difficult to believe that you could walk into any roomful of strangers and not have two friends in five minutes—that's why I'm extending you this invitation."

"Okay Nagai, and thank you for the compliment, and we shall see . . . but seriously"—with teasing eyes sparkling and a flip of her scarf off one shoulder to the other—"I simply don't have a single thing of my own to wear."

After their exchange of phone numbers, Ki pushed Tara to take their leave of the happy couple as the band started anew, and they returned to the crowded dance floor to once more sway and play in rhythm and beat to the cover band's musical treats. The night happily rolled on with the mass of bodies moving in motion as Tara's thoughts slowly slipped from the consternation of innumerable options and possibilities that had recently presented themselves into her life. Her bewildering stresses of fiancé and *dalliance*, school and work, and finances and family obligations were forgotten for the moment.

Ki clasped Tara's right hand to slip her other arm around Tara's waist and began to move them in closed frame to the musical rhythm.

Tara bucked to escape with a stiff arm to Ki's shoulder. "Stand down, madam, I dance solo, or I lead the man."

Ki laughed and pushed into Tara with a forceful step. "That may be with other men"—pull, back step, left-side pass—"but not with me for I am not a man." Hands lifted high, right-side pass, spin, step, as an arm wrapped tight around the waist with a hard pull to squeeze them together and grind in tight. "But if you're nice to me, at the next club maybe I'll let you lead sometimes, for I also know how to follow. Ha!" Push, back step, hands high, twirl. "Hmm girl, I must say . . . you really do know how to use your hips."

Another drink and with the music tempo slowed in that couple's dance rhythm, Tara and Ki leaned on each other, enjoying the company and luck of having met the other. The evening played out to lengthen past the witching hour.

"Come on, I know a place. Let's bounce."

~~~

"We're off to see the Wizard, the Wonderful Wizard of Oz . . ." Tara and Ki sang as they skipped in step along the sidewalk, braced arm in arm to enjoy the warmth of each other against the early morning chill. *"Because because because because becaaause . . . because of the wonderful things he does . . ."*

"It's not too far, but I didn't want to get a cabbie all pissed off at us for such a short drive and we can use the air anyhow."

"Ole, o-ee-yaw. Ole, oh-e-hah . . ."

"No no, it's *we are . . . the old ones, we are . . . the old ones.*"

"No no, listen to me, there are no words, it's just *Ole, o-ee-yaw. Ole, oh-e-hah.*"

"No no . . ." And so their playful banter went on, a lively spirit of jabbering lyrics, girlish giggles, and skipping heels on concrete rising to fill the still silence in a low-rise, mixed-use neighborhood with the first-floor businesses now shuttered.

"Shhh, shhh."

"No, youuu *shhh.*"

"Here here, this way." Ki tugged on Tara to pull her along the main boulevard lit up in flashing colored lights from the long row of electric storefront signs and displays that pressed back the dark of night into those nooks and crannies of irregularly matched buildings and intersecting alleyways. Tara leaned into Ki as she blindly followed along in silence and as they tired competing against the discordant noises of engines revving, and thumping rubber wheels, and suspension bouncing on the cracked and potholed surface from rapidly passing cars that continually interrupted their harmonies. The singularly blank wall they passed had given Tara no particular indication that they had reached a destination until . . .

"Hey hey."

"Hey. IDs please," asked the solidly built bouncer dressed all in black and hidden within the shadow of a recessed doorway, half-seated upon his stool with one foot on the ground. His flashlight flicked to each for a moment. "Thank you." He stood and opened the door to a delightfully unexpected world within this city that excitedly awoke

Tara's senses from her listless following—the music and rhythms of a live salsa band were drifting to her ears. She identified a trombone that was laying down its distinctive low-tone notes for its turn at a solo as the other horns, bongo drums, and clave sticks stepped aside in subdued support. As they entered the club, Tara took note of the young and well-dressed heavily Latina crowd out for a social and dancing evening.

"Come on, shots." Ki pulled on Tara's hand to weave them through the crowded club to the back bar. "Okay, you get us two beers here and I have to step over there for the tequila."

The construction of the bar Tara stood in front of reminded her more of a street vendor pulled up in a long wooden cart for his daily clients, with the wheels taken off and just left planted. The tequila bar alongside was different indeed: a real-life Peanuts cartoon of Lucy's hip-high wooden box with an overhead cardboard banner edged with frilly brown grass—albeit missing the words, "Psychiatric Help, Five Cents"—with rows of empty plastic shot glasses and a small tin bucket half-filled with lime slices, and the clear liter bottles of tequila the barkeep pours from. *Too funny.*

"*Hola. Cuál te gustaría?*"

"*Dos* Pacifico, *por favor.*"

With the *cervezas* served and Ki's return: "Okay okay, here's what we do." She grabbed Tara's hand, bringing the corner of thumb and index finger into Tara's mouth whereupon she licked with a hot press of her tongue. After doing the same to herself, Ki then applied two shakes of salt on each. Ki took Tara's salted hand, offered her own hand to Tara, and together they licked. They raised the shot glasses with "*Salud!*" Tara felt a fiery kick down her throat and a warm glow that began to radiate out from her core. Ki placed a lime wedge upon Tara's lips, and Tara bit down and closed her eyes against the sour and bitter shock.

What had caught Tara short was when she felt Ki's lips press against hers and she relaxed to linger and enjoy the others' softness and hot breath with that delightful taste of tequila infused with salt and lime. Ki pulled back. "Okay"—as she reached for the beer bottles and handed one to Tara—"chug." Tara finished almost half the golden brew while Ki drank just over a quarter of hers. "Come on." Ki once again took Tara's hand. "I have a feeling you'll be leading most of the time, but I'll have you know I'm pretty good for a white girl."

Hand in hand, Ki slid them through the crowded dance floor to a momentarily vacant spot. She then turned on Tara to press them in closed frame, placing Tara's right hand under her own shoulder blade and putting her left hand atop Tara's right shoulder. Ki set the pace with a pull of Tara's high left hand to indicate the follower was in fact leading. Tara quickly flowed in rhythm with Ki's gentle push and pull, taking only a moment to wrap her brain around the reverse steps of a girl that were now required of her. They danced and danced, Ki gently leading Tara into easy and familiar steps, Tara losing conscious thought, having adjusted to being led in what to her were backwards steps. Tara then surprised Ki with a flash of a wicked smile, and a hard squeeze of their clasped hands and a shoulder-blade pull, indicating she was now leading. And so they danced, and they danced.

"Whew, air, time-out, drinks." And so once again they retreated to the pressboard bar and a repeat of tequila shots and *cervezas* that they teasingly challenged one another to finish with happy smiles.

"I wish I knew you, and we were friends when your hair was long and flowing down your back. That blonde, curly hair is so beautiful and natural as a golden bowl of cornflakes." Tara enticingly ran her fingers through Ki's silky goldilocks.

"No you don't; I was a skinny, shy little girl. You wouldn't have given me a second glance."

"Ah, *pobrecita*. Sucks to be you."

"Be nice to me or maybe I'll crop your hair a little butch and then tie your hands up with silky ribbons for some light S and M play."

Tara was much slowed indeed, and was confused, and wondered why "be nice" resonated so? *And what was that other? M and Ms . . . what?*

"Come on, let's dance."

They laughed and giggled as their playful wrestling match continued once more to romp and frolic on the dance floor, each in turn to lead, and then to follow. Tara became warm and light-headed and dizzy in the frenzied commotion of bodies throwing heat, and their epic tension of the salsa dance, and tracking the count, and flashing colored lights, and loud *música* of horns and bells and drums. On the twirls she noticed a cool breeze riding up her skirt past her knee-high Wicked boots onto her bare thighs, which felt so good. Tara mis-stepped and was about to be spun off and lost when Ki's fingers tangled in her bra strap to catch her momentum and snap her back. "Oh wow, that was so lucky."

"Really? And how about this?" Ki's fingers slid down the strap to find and quickly unlatch Tara's bra.

Tara threw her head back with a deep, alluring laugh of abandon and returned to pull Ki in tight with an unexpected kiss. "I'll meet you at the bar. I'm gonna relatch in the ladies' room."

Tara found Ki back at the bar with a ready Cheshire grin about to slide off her tired face and the requisite tequila shots and beers lined up and good to go.

"Are you thur you're ready for this?"

"No. Leth do it." And they repeated their ritual, leaning on each other with a cough of fire breath and a laugh. "Oh, *mamma mia.*" Giggle.

"Have you noticed that everyone'th looking at me?"

"What? No girl you justh drunk, that's all."

"No no, I thwears I'm like the only white girl with blonde hair in the whole place."

"No thilly girl, you're so cute when you're drunk, that's your little Than Fran white, elitist attitude, you're justh being paranoid." With lazy eyes, Tara scanned the crowd. "Oh my goodness, you're right," she said as she leaned in to hug Ki and instinctively shield her.

"We must plan a thrategic retreat, yesth we must. Is anyone look-ing at us now? No! Don't look!"

"Mithter Wizard, Mithter Wizard, time for these two losts souls to come home. Quick quick, click your heels three timeth."

"Okay okay, thlowly and grathefully now, so as not to draw any attention to ourselves, let's make it to the door." Ki knocked a half-empty bottle of beer over that got away from them. They stared in shock and disbelief as they watched it roll and roll away in that exasperating slowww and just-out-of-reach motion with a rattling commotion, and foamy liquid flowing to leave a trail along a good length of the bar before it fell over the edge to land with a clunk upon the rubber floor mat. And indeed, with no paranoia, all eyes were upon them.

"I have a plan. I have cash in my pursth." Tara raised an arm to catch the attention of the inside bouncer who then approached. "Please Mr. Bounther sir, if you could be so kind, as you can see my friend here haths had too much to drink and can't handle her liquor, no thiree, oh did you hear the one about how French women hold their liquor? Oh my, where'd that come from? My apologies, dear sir. A taxi, Mithter Kind Gentleman, if you please. Twenty dollarth here if you escort my friend and I to the front door of this most amazing club of very, very good people and plathe us into a taxi back to my hotel, that would be soooo kind of you, why yesth thank you."

The bouncer slipped an arm around each waist as he escorted them towards the exit, and Tara could remember the rush of cool air as the door opened . . . and the bright streetlights . . . and then . . . fade to gray . . . and . . . nothing . . .

~~~~~

Leaning against the toilet that felt so nice and cool to the touch, Tara caught herself staring vacantly above and beyond the bed onto the far wall where hung a rather unremarkable picture in lithograph abstract of what Tara for some reason assumed was a mother and child walking hand in hand down a Parisian alley. And yet, *crazy how just several lines with no detail definition can evoke the emotion of mother and child casually strolling?* The bedsheets stirred, a body rolled, and a head with an untamed blonde mane appeared, to then bury half a face in the pillow with emerald eyes that looked out at her.

"Hey."

"Morning."

"How you feeling?"

"Huh, I have cotton mouth, my head's abuzz from a hangover that I feel in pain everywhere in my body, and my stomach is still queasy from puking, so okay I guess. How about you?"

Ki moaned. "Yeah, the same. So, hey thanks for last night, that was really fun."

"Yeah, like crazy fun, huh?"

"So my friends an' I are having a little get-together in a bit for brunch. Why don't you come along? I'd like to introduce you to my friends, they're all a real hoot and you'd really love them. We can make ourselves a Bloody Mary hair of the dog and Karen cooks this most amazing soufflé that's totally off the hook that you wouldn't believe."

"Ah yeah, well thanks, ah, I'm not exactly sure or remember what happened last night but as you know I have a fiancé, so we can be friends, that would be nice, I would like that."

"No . . . I won't be a friend," quietly said from a deep resonance of something sad, something once slipped away, as she blankly stared at an empty wall. "I'll be your best friend and your lover . . . or you can just lose my number . . . and we can pretend we are strangers, if perchance we ever once again see one another."

Not exactly the response Tara had been anticipating. And was it only just yesterday morning that an offer of herself had been so soundly rejected by her *dalliance* so he could go off and traipse with his mistress? "We're both big girls now, and I'm sorry, but I just thought . . ."

"No, don't start!" Ki sat up with a drape of sheets pressed to her bare chest. A disheveled mass of hair shook loose as unfocused, wild eyes came back to look at Tara, but she was not sure if Ki was actually seeing her. Ki shook her head in the negative—*No*—with that loose hair wildly whipping about. Ignoring those strands that draped down her face as a veil over her eyes, she intently peered with that morning-after alcohol-laced anger of twitchy, short-circuiting nerves. "No, no, don't placate me with placebo words of empty promises and forlorn hope." Her thick, hoarse voice of unrestrained passion demanded immediate attention in her declarative: "This is where you think you're actually doing something by saying sorry for everything but never actually sorry enough to do anything or change your actions or do anything for the other person. And then when you do it again, you just say sorry. Fuck you, don't say another word; just actually do something for once. But you can't because you're not really sorry and you're just gonna do the same thing again." Ki paused with eyes that welled up, and she let fall her sheets as arms swept open to flail at the empty air. "We did nothing . . . and it's all for nothing." She put a closed fist to her chest—"and continue to live your life where everything you do means nothing." She brought her hands together before her. Her attention turned to blankly stare at empty, cupped hands as she began to weep. "Nothing . . . nothing!"

Tara's bosom heaved heavily at her bewildered loss of something special—or at the pain of an accusation that so eviscerated the essence of her soul? In that initial confusion and disorientation of an anguish that left her a shell of herself that only time could alleviate, and yet there she still remained, Tara fell into that forthright, meandering habit of muddling through in the mundane, rote routines of her daily life—for nothing she could do would bring back that which was lost, never to be recovered—by the silent gathering up of her few things to be packed into her carry-on bag, unsure of her feelings, of what to say.

"Continue to live your life under the shallow light of false flattery from those pretty, pretty little club boys that comment on your beauty and that you so enjoy listening to, to stroke your ego, for it's a rare, self-assured woman indeed that would not be taken in so. I want to earn it; I want to deserve the love I receive for who I am. I don't want to just exist. I want to be the best person I can be before I share myself with another. I want that constant tension with my lover, to push and pull each other, to grow together."

Tara wanted to cry, but was dry. She had things to do, and her head hurt, and she was confused in a fog of inattention: an expectant auntie, a Sausalito showroom, a fiancé in the air who would soon be waiting at the airport, and finals to prepare for. *What to do? Which way to go?* She zipped her bag closed. "Okay." Silence from the bed. "I have people waiting for me. You know I have things to do." Silence from the bed. "Okay, thanks for everything." As she reached for the door, Tara could feel the heat of eyes that bored into her back.

"If you expect unconditional love for doing nothing, and feeling nothing . . . get yourself a cocker spaniel!"

~~~~~

Under the expanse of a great awning bridge of a warm orange hue that threw no shadow from an overcast sky of swirling gray that earlier had wrung dry its tears, Tara sat momentarily lost and confused within her idling car, having unexpectedly arrived at the dead end of a quietly active parking lot. She could observe behind the partial shield of open car doors and upon their laid-out towels several teenage boys and a man in various stages of undress and re-dress as they stripped off their clothes prior to slipping themselves into those protective, shiny black suits, gloves, and booties that covered them from the tops of their heads to the tips of their fingers and to the ends of their toes, with only a small portion of face visible under a short duckbill, from upper brow to lower lip. Sitting comfortably in her car all bundled up with the heater blowing, Tara could not possibly imagine stepping outside into that wintery-chill air to strip nude and then pull on a cold, rubbery wetsuit for the purpose of jumping into even colder water. Her thoughts went back to work upon the errors made, and the route taken in her driving to inadvertently arrive at this particular location, while half a mind formulated a way to extricate herself from this dead end that spilled over into the ocean. Or into the bay? *Huh, is there an actual demarcation line for that?* Idly pondering the permutations of an egress, she gazed above to that long expanse of a high-overhead, intricately woven, steel-rope-suspended highway crossing fast-flowing tidal waters. *Well, not exactly lost, am I?* For she knew precisely where she was, just not how to get where she was going. And there lay the rub she postulated: *Where am I going?* She preferred the avoidance of making a decision at this moment, knowing that to do so would require her to delve into the angst of those emotional undercurrents that undulated and swelled within, and thus she misconstrued, she did, placing blame on an exhausted mind that floated and bounced, unable to focus on a particular subject, from the aftereffects of an alcohol-laced all-out evening without much sleep. *Oh my brain hurts.* Misconstrue the head with the heart, she did.

She watched as a few of the young surfers grabbed their surfboards to jog away down the seaside path towards the pre–Civil War fort of red masonry under the bridge at the water's edge. *They have a plan.* Her exit plan would not come, for Tara knew not which way it was for her to go. *What are my unfiltered thoughts?* At Land's End, a spray of whitewash shot high overhead, reaching for the unattainable bridge, before falling back to earth in a heavy rain of salt water with a lingering mist that remained gently floating in the air. *With whom do I wish to melt?* She looked at her cell phone flashing with lights that insistently declared she had awaiting voice and text messages. *How can I be a better person to deserve their love?* Her heavy heart heaved in despair from having unintentionally wounded an innocent so deeply . . . and at the possibility of deeply hurting another she may have to intentionally walk away from. She began to silently weep in that way of a contorted face of no tears. *Stop it!*

A giant swell lumbered in from the depths of open ocean, and in that ponderous, unstoppable roll, rose up in a dark mass to blot out the far shoreline. The swell became a wave as shallow shoals pushed it skyward and its peak, traveling faster than its base riding upon land's resistance, thinned and tapered. Tara watched in fascination as the awesome wave pitched over in a cascading avalanche that exploded in ocean phosphorescence upon impact and began to wrap around the point from sea into bay.

A curious, fluorescent trail that flashed along in a thin line within the dark, yawning cavern of that heaving swell of water caught her attention. Her heart leaped with the realization that upon that sheer, vertical face of a moving black wall was the tiny speck of a surfer that raced to some indefinable point of escape. Tara reached out to will that surfer to stay ahead of the avalanche of water that attempted to gather him up as some incongruent flotsam and indiscriminately toss him upon the rocky shore to which the wave rushed with great speed and was now very close. *Go, go, go . . . please don't fall . . .*

She silently wondered to herself what he was thinking, standing so small under that thick canopy of pitching water upon his fragile surfboard of thin glass that streaked along within the eye of a calm vortex with violent power moving all around. *Is he afraid?* And in that moment of questioning another who had purposely, and with great effort, exposed himself to the apparently indiscriminate whims of nature's tempest throes, came a clarity of self-awareness that she had not previously understood. *Huh, who would have thought?* With this realization came a focus of mind and a strength of self-willed deter-mination. The vague outlines of a plan began to take form and fill her with an excited trepidation. *I wonder what they'll say?* As the surfer launched himself high into the air in his escape out the back of the almost-spent wave, Tara smiled for the first time that morning. *We did it.*

In that energy of her renewed spirit of idealistic, youthful enthusi-asm, she gave a big arm wave out the window and a "Hey hey, you guys have fun! Be safe!" to the few surfers passing by, which they recipro-cated with bemused smiles to this woman with long, dark hair flowing out from the car and a sharing warmth radiant upon her face. *This can't possibly work out the way I think it will, but what the heck . . .* Tara eased her car into gear to step on the gas pedal, flipped her turn signal, and accelerated away with the excited anticipation of the young at heart with many wildly romantic ideas and possibilities imagined . . .

~ fin ~

ACKNOWLEDGMENTS

Some were a spark of inspiration, some helped me keep it together, some early on in this manuscript said a simple word of encouragement: "beautiful."

Some thrashed me through an emotional range that I did not know possible, and many more—who remain unnamed—were incidental encounters which indelibly remain a celluloid vision impressed upon my mind's eye: Mallorie Pashilk, Theresa Francos, Ron Gurse, Allyn McNamara, Marlow Jones and his cuz, my witch Shannon Lee Santos, Brian Silver, "Sexy Ki," "Sticky Niki," Michelle Tancraitor, Angelo Canino, and of course my daughter, Ashley.

~~~

Thank you to the many professionals; some who flailed me to the core of my apparently 8th grade grammatical competence, some who changed but a single word, some who kept me alive—all made this work significantly better: Bill Andrew, Elaine Partnow, Ben Marcus, Michael Bednarsky, Todd Larson, Jim Hall, Robin Quinn, Dr. Mark Wellisch, Dr. Elliot Carlisle, and of course Girl Friday Productions: Ryan Boudinot, Scot Calamar, Rachel Christenson, Connie Gabbert, Paul Barrett, Courtney Calon, and Meghan Harvey.

~~~

Thanks to those who—in following each other out and about into the wilds—often left me wondering how we ever made it there and back. To those who silently helped simply because they were there:
Randall, Craig, and Brent,
Brittany, Bryce, and Ashley.

ABOUT THE AUTHOR

Roger J. Couture was born and raised in Southern California and has always lived close to the beach, except for two high school years spent on the East Coast. After graduating from California State University, Long Beach, he worked for a few Silicon Valley start-ups. For many decades now, he's resided in the Conejo Valley of Ventura, California, where he writes, hikes, bikes, and surfs.